YOLANDA FAYE DANIEL

Starfall

Telluric ~ The Queen's Children

First published by The Write Dream 2022

First edition

ISBN: 978-1-957231-01-3

Advisor: Xavier~Olijujuan~Cassius~Zaria
Editing by Grace Wynter
Cover art by Robynne/Damonza.com

This book was professionally typeset on Reedsy.
Find out more at reedsy.com

Contents

Acknowledgement	v
Chapter 1	1
Chapter 2	13
Chapter 3	27
Chapter 4	39
Chapter 5	52
Chapter 6	60
Chapter 7	69
Chapter 8	84
Chapter 9	96
Chapter 10	106
Chapter 11	120
Chapter 12	126
Chapter 13	135
Chapter 14	141
Chapter 15	149
Chapter 16	156
Chapter 17	162
Chapter 18	170
Chapter 19	178
Chapter 20	191
Chapter 21	201
Chapter 22	213
Chapter 23	223
Chapter 24	231

Chapter 25 242

Chapter 26 253

Chapter 27 264

Chapter 28 279

Chapter 29 293

Chapter 30 303

Chapter 31 316

Chapter 32 325

Chapter 33 334

Chapter 34 347

Chapter 35 357

Chapter 36 369

Chapter 37 376

Chapter 38 384

Chapter 39 392

Chapter 40 401

Chapter 41 410

Chapter 42 419

Chapter 43 430

Chapter 44 437

Epilogue 447

About The Author 452

Acknowledgement

To the absolute best mother in the whole wide world, I love you Carrie B. And to Zay, Juan, Cas and Zari, I couldn't ask for better collaborators. My babies!

Chapter 1

"Star up high, oh so grand

open the sky, and implant the land

Blazing to ground seeds Soonahyin..."

The rhyme, a sweet rhyme sang in youth at a father's knee, wheezed in the ears now. Croaks didn't harmonize too well with a babe's melody. Tierney or Tierahna (well Tierney to anyone with the good sense to call her what she preferred) was having a crap of a time catching her breath as her feet sank and crunched snow deep enough that her knees broke the powder too. The crunching added beats. Rhythm to her song. Her most favored. *At least I have that,* she quirked and kept croaki...singing. She was determined about it, after all. The distraction welcome like you wouldn't believe in the mission she'd gotten herself into. This march in a near blizzard with nary an idea on whether what was trying to be gained was even plausible.

There was punishment for such audacity as there always was for such things; snow loosening into the tops of one's boots...and collecting there, of course. *It would never just warm and melt away. That would mean some good fortune was actually coming my way.* Chuckles had her breaths rasping her throat for her efforts, and she ended up strangling on the next gulps of air.

Essentially, snow covered everything here, everywhere one thought to look here. Common in every corner of the land, it perpetuated cold as what will be. Uniquely, the snow had a sheen to it. As it fell and so only retained a defined amount of contact with the land, melting over time, it had a peculiarity as simply to glow. The snow held fast to the sun's light and repeated it back. Then off a ways, the flakes of ice looked to be lit like a heat source and could guide a body in the moonlight. "I am grateful for all things favorable!" she shouted to the extent her lungs would let her, as exposed as she was to the elements this night in Telluric's cycle. Any sign of efflorescence: greenery blooming in the prairies, meadows flowering with plants, the trees springing their foliage was celebrated in the acknowledgment of subsistence. With the season of new life came the dance of belief in renewal after the cold hadn't ended them.

Given another chance—which wasn't likely, what other chance was there with everyone else wielding power over her?—Tierney would endure every bit of this season's usual state of being again. This slog through the snow, and pretty much everything that led up to it was worth it to be right here in this moment. To get here and take up this mission to activate her life was the whole point in the first place, right?

"Bak'rah!" As ever a devoted companion as could be, prowled as usual at her flank, panting, *the poor fellow.* "Having a hard time catching your breath too, huh? You can calm it a bit now. We're here." He had to be happy at the sight of their refuge. Finally appearing behind snow-draped hills, Outliers' domed wings sprawled in a flat a ways beyond them. The lodge announced itself as a beacon of sanctuary amidst the barrens of snow. "Hmm..." A little of the fight went out of her with the scene of light proudly brandished around like a babe just born, and the boast of the crowd to contend with too. After nearly more than two days alone? And the impetus that pushed so hard to make this trip not the urge it'd felt like when they'd started? *Yeah, I think it'd be best that we pass on the social.*

"This is it, by the way. My break for any possibility of a life I would want." *If I can't get it started, who knows how long it is before Mother commits me to that frozen tundra sanctum against my will. I must move fast too. So that I can counteract her before she knows what I'm doing.*

"I am not unstable!" she shouted to the winds again as if they should have heard what waited right below her breast. The refrain that hummed in the gut and chipped away at any so-called self-assurance that had been the other catalyst to kick-start this journey. The winds *did* answer in return, rushing flecks of ice over her face. Except, the act of talking to the winds itself highlighted something of a contradiction in the words. A whisper on the air, "*Hold up there on claiming sanity. None of us are owners of it all the time.*"

She bore on. Coldness escaped down her legs, a freezing trail of muck. Regardless of the slush freezing her toes, slackening her pace, emptying her wolvien-animal-fur boots of nastiness would set her back. So what, if the muck threatened the shukka-warming mechanism inside the boots. A person who'd lived as she did forfeited the luxury of entertaining the cold. For what had gotten her here anyway?

Biding her time. Tierney's truest way of being. Her whole youth had been worn away within her spans of the planet, Telluric's laps around the sun.

Their land Soonayah rested atop the world wiling the time in an existence beyond the lands who had more heat and more fair days than they. All twenty-four spans of her life, she'd spent in deference to the queen in the frozen Soonayah. *"Yes of course, I'll do it. Anything you say"*—a going refrain everyday of her life. And at high time, forced to the point that she thought she had no choice, now she verged on breaching the queen's rules that had bound her forever. Or losing herself to her domination.

Either option would end with a person choosing the catalyst that would determine the rest of their life. *Her choosing, mind you.* It'd still be her who gave away her autonomy. Whether she'd come here or did nothing she'd have made a decision. Action or implicitly going along with someone deciding for her. *In that case, I had no choice but to go with breaching the queen's rules.*

Frozen fingers and sopping fur are of little account. Mother would say, "It's a matter of what you want, isn't it?" A bolt across the whole Soonahyin land. Her mother…(the queen), none the wiser. Alone. A good start on rebellion toward living a life in some land far away from Soonayah. She would see a different place other than their frozen oasis even if it killed her.

"All in-kind—plant, animal and man." She kept forcing her lungs to squeeze the rhyme out as a comfort to herself as she marched. *Alright. Just need to get through this one step at a time.* Twisting backward to Bak'rah enabled her to run eyes over how the snow soaked his coat through. A bit of it had gotten into his nostrils and made him sneeze, so she asked him to distract him a bit from his discomfort, "Outliers has a full house this night, do you see? Needs must, I hope they have room for us too."

The lodge sprawled with its lights fanned out over the domed structures and the surrounding area. Each annex attached stretched farther than the next while shapes of people, *society unfortunately*, danced in and out of sight of its windows. A signal to strangers who traveled through the night that emblazoned, "*Welcome.*"

Honestly, the people who had sought refuge here couldn't be blamed for crowding the place. They weren't betting their lives on this venture like she was. The paralyzing blizzard must have driven them to seek warmth. Even the locals would be inside. *I'm the only one foolish enough to volunteer for this drudgery.* No one would have prepared for conditions this harsh this far west either. Near the boundary lines of Soonayah snow rarely fell heavy. Self-directed road clearers wouldn't have deployed to this sect yet.

Tension eased from Tierney's thighs as she struggled mightily to calm the contrary reaction—her body's default to the weather—hacks wheezing her throat posing as breaths. Forever grateful that at least the height of the blizzard's destruction had passed before she'd needed to trudge on foot. *Okay, you did it. Breathe. Everything is right in front of you now.*

Must've been Outliers' attendants who'd dug out its court-yard to the thoroughfare running perpendicular. Crude, yet effective. Skies loomed—heavy, dank, clear, no transport traveling in any direction. Those were a few of the only things to be grateful for in the moment. The main one being these same conditions she'd met since she'd had to leave her snowcraft covered in sparse woods off the side of the road seventeen or so parses back. For all the good it'd served, at least the blizzard had calmed. "Who could have guessed the snowcraft was a useless mechanical bust?"

Meant just for one, the transport had been a tight fit, but it'd suited the circumstances fine. The only care was that it had speed and mobility to cut across great distances as fast as it could. She and Bak'rah had been warm and dry. Then the stupid thing had quit on her. Her toes screamed at her abuse now. Having ice-blocks for feet was a joke to someone like Tierney. *Pampering accustoms the princess of the land.* She snickered at the predicament she'd pretty much brought on herself. Singing had been the support to keep going. Bobbing to the cadence, then trudging, bobbing—she'd rest for a few moments—then trudging, bobbing and trudg...

"Ugh!" *White Moon's setting in the sky wanes five finger-spans before the horizon.* "I'm stupid late!" So late, her contact at Outliers border lodge might not await her arrival. *I can't afford to miss him with Mother's silent threat of committing me waiting for me when I get back home. He must be here.*

A few more paces tromping ice and the urge to her heart threatened to burst. Flurries showered from the wolvien pelt covering her head when she glanced back at Bak'rah. Who took the position since the cliff—through whose bank she trekked snow up to her knees—gave cover on one side. He traveled, his scrutiny sweeping the land back and forth, on the other. No matter the snow and the cold, she'd miss her homeland once she discovered a way out of it. It's nurturing from the soil enhanced a body to carry on in this blizzard. Soonayah's inclusive culture conditioned its people for this very subsistence. Rituals and history were passed down from one homestead to another, rondavel to rondavel, from each ancestral clan to its descendants, to survival in this moment. Ultimately, to her ploughing onward with her precious song. "Star so rich empowers everything," she managed one last line before a sigh escaped, stinging her chest and frosting the air. "Bak'rah!" The wolf, his white fur was easily lost at times during their lumbering with wind swooping flakes into their eyes. He clipped forward to come even with her.

Anyone who glanced in their direction would see her as a shadow alongside the cliff. Bak'rah couldn't be differentiated from the snow. They could study the building at leisure.

Tierney crouched and pushed her hand brusquely through Bak'rah's fur out of habit. Why the urge for a connection to his soul-energy? She didn't know, but laid her fingers as close to his heart as she could get. Not that she had to slouch far. Her precious wolf's torso brushed her waist when she stood tall. He was a big one, even for one of his kind—as the whole Soonahyin land shaped its inhabitants and every little thing it touched, breaking down their make-ups to a level of transmutation in their cells. Enhancements that remodeled the building blocks of a being like Bak'rah. It endowed birds with feathers plumped with hot air to withstand the snowy weather too. Rendered steeds with hooves of such force they were known to crack the heads of snowcats like nuts.

People were not excluded from these adaptations either. The people's evolution enhanced them with what was known as gifts. Abilities in Soonayah's populace more pronounced than all the other lands, which garnered covetous yearnings from said lands on occasion.

Tierney extended her other arm to encompass the yawn of snow leading from Outliers. "Bak'rah, see!" she commanded Bak'rah's use of one of his enhancements right then. Through the insulation in her mink glove, the wolf's soul-energy kicked up. He loped a couple of paces away. "It's okay, my boy. I understand." His kinship with her was such that, she waited with baited breath for him to answer her back one day. *It could happen.* She believed it so. Point of fact, he sniffed around, then scanned the horizon in perfect line of sight of Outliers, right then.

Bak'rah's coat flashed as bright as the sun. *Blinding!* Cringing and squinting, Tierney braced herself. She couldn't see his eyes, but the orbs should now flame a golden incandescence. He was using his oculusion to see beyond what the normal eye could. She could see what he saw if she touched him, but he'd moved away.

"It's fine, Bak'rah. I know better than to siphon off the soul-energy you reserved through our long trek." He'd need his soul-energy, the life-sustaining power within every being, and would use it to stay on guard. They were approaching an unknown situation. When Bak'rah stopped scanning, he didn't growl a warning, but looked at her, then proceeded to walk the flat toward Outliers.

No approaching threats. Perfect. Most appreciations.

She breathed and followed. *My dutiful boy. You're always conforming yourself to just what I need.* Stomping snow from her boots once on the lodge's stoop was a guise as she skimmed the perimeter. "What should we expect upon entering Outliers I wonder, my boy?" In her sub-conscious, her precious rhyme still dragged on and on. *Come on, no putting it off any longer. You can do this. Just get it started. This is what you've always wanted, remember?*

Although, being exposed to the cold for so long racked a body down to the sinews, numbing the bones—the true tremors came in the form of panic from within. Wasn't that the reason the decision to begin this was made in the first place? How long was a person to wait before they developed some gumption? Forever, if she hadn't known about her mother's threat. So in a way, she had her mother to blame for this journey. *Though Mother would be clueless that she was the cause.*

"Wonder who is inside on this brutal night, huh?" A question to a pup who if looked upon—by anyone other than family and those who knew of their inseparability—would not be mistakened as anyone's idea of a wolf in pup stage.

His flinging excess snow off was in accordance with her own intentions. She gave no thought to going in without him. Anywhere she chose he went as well and would shepherd her closely when they entered. Their connection wasn't symbiotic, but his heart beat in tune to hers and its peculiarities. This night his vigilance would be *sharp.* If this meeting went as planned, this could set into motion leaving home forever. Bak'rah had every right to be on edge, because goodness knew she was too. "We did it, my boy. We made it here. A first real venture totally independent."

"Come now, its up to us to set its path." There was only one direction for them now. Forward. She scoured the courtyard. *Snowcrafts overfill this place.* Smaller crafts were the closest at the entrance. However, it was those on the outer edges that gave her pause. Luxury varieties with sleeping quarters for large parties. Some had similar symbolage on their sides, indicating they were a part of caravans, although, none bore the discreet but recognizable emblem like the one she'd hidden in the woods. *Good. No one from the royal house holds up in Outliers.* There would be time enough to tell what she was doing out here without someone from the royal house doing the telling for her.

"Bak'rah!" Tierney snatched at the wolf's coat and missed him. With his jaws snapping, he'd ripped around her. "Bak'rah! Come back! What do you see, you...wolf?" The last thing she had time for was to be lead further from her mission by a frippery that could pull a dog's attention astray. She sprinted to catch up to him. "What is that?" A shadow—something sinister-looking shifted and spooked her a once steady progress.

And weaved in and out of the trees, though it only added to the clouds eclipsing the sky and the gloom that already hung on that side of Outliers' property. Woods abutted the boundary on a slope. And rolling dips and rises angled the treeline like monuments alongside each other at the woods' divide. They competed as they blocked out the sky.

There was nothing for it. Lumbering a few more steps, she forged on after Bak'rah all the way to the edge of the courtyard. If there was anything dire he could see better than she, he might need her help. And he'd get it. Already tired, her breathing hitching and...

"Oh." There she froze. *I see. Not a dog's frippery at all.* Every bit of wind inside her lungs whooshed out.

Bak'rah's growls were echoing a menace he'd spotted. A shag of matted hair and filth and viciousness in wolf form couldn't disguise a frame as emaciated as it was. Even still, the trees had hidden the scourge in a black well enough. No wonder Bak'rah's oculusion hadn't detected him sooner. The ferber trees' effect on the mind was suspected to be just as much of a menace as a *rabid wolf.*

Tierney searched over her shoulder for...anybody, anything, a vagrant's presence would do if he could help them. "We are *way* too far out here."

Nobody was coming to their rescue. Several figures cresting the rise, trailing the exact path from where they'd just come were too far away, even though they'd started to run toward her, some of them speeding. She frowned because she hadn't noticed that people traveled the path right behind them. In any case, that was neither here nor there given the terror in front of them now.

A shift got the frothing wolf back in her sights. "This freak of an animal may well get to us before we get inside." Those people would never make it to them in time.

The black wolf was stalking them. Slathering. Snapping. Tierney edged back and latched onto Bak'rah, who was in a frenzy in response. "Come on, sweet pup. Shh." Could she initiate a move fast enough to speed them back to the stoop? Her soul-energy triggered and heat ignited in her gut. "Come on." Again she eased back, only to hit a loose tread and stagger, a tuft of uneven ground rolling under her foot.

And oh indeed, the wolf attacked!

Bak'rah reared to clash with the snarling blur of black, but Tierney lurched in front of him. "No Bak'rah! He may be rabid!" Before the beasts collided, she snatched the strange wolf by his throat. For a body of bone such as he was, he was as tall as Bak'rah. Subduing him was like trying to hold back his snapping jaws within a hurricane. *This wolf could kill me and no one may ever know why I was here. So much for planning, Tierney.* Her contact would never reveal her reasons if she hadn't had the chance to tell him to. Bak'rah, fervid in his efforts to protect her, savaged the beast's thrashing leg. *I have no choice, if he kills me he will have a clear path to Bak'rah. I must...*

A flare of her soul-energy pulsed right from her hand. A tug from deep inside the heart of her pulled the energy up in a teal plume with alabaster tendrils...and exhaustion, really. An eve of snow-walking and a day and half of traveling would do that to a body. Enough energy was barely there to fight the wolf and catch him in his neck as they struggled. The menace...the *terror* in black shrieked in pain. Fur where she'd struck the pulse into him withered to a sickening grey.

His howl were so haunting, she shivered even though she was the one to cause them in him. They reached them from the woods that had enveloped him as he scrambled away. "Wretched dog. I had no choice."

Chapter 2

She tripped over herself getting inside Outliers. *Okay. Okay. Inside. A safe place. We can replenish in here.* Blinking wildly, her eyesight adjusted to a flood of light instead of the pitiful excuses she had in comparison, torchlights worn attached to her shoulders and the snood of her cloak, her armset too.

Brightness was the order of the lodge—off the tiger and teak Soonahyin columns, the hardwood floors, the balustrades, everything. Its glimpsing blinded her momentarily after that furor in the dark and the snow. But better blinded and finally inside the place rather than frozen to death or mauled by an animal mad with rabies. *And as fortune would have a raging blizzard thrown in just for me.* For the life of her, she couldn't remember why she'd chosen this lodge when it was clear on the other side of Soonayah. *Because you are always up for an extra challenge, right Tierney?* She snorted.

The smell of the ferber wood beams that comprised the walls permeated the structure. Why dead wood kept its fragrance was a wonder, but it happened on occasion. This was Soonayah after all. The redolence of it drifted like peat and redvine mixed with a bit of sarsaparilla to cloud a person's nostrils, blending wood scent with aromas of food and the scent of people mixed with the loamy smell of furs the people and the lodge wore. And all this carried along with the sight of wood grain, banisters, and paneling. Disarming. Hugged in warmth after escaping the freeze of night. Rugs scattering color about the hallowed refuge were the pelts of all walks of Soonahyin animals. Tierney stopped just short of prostrating herself in the furs and kissing what had to be the worst things imaginable walked upon on the underside of the common boot.

"You might want to get a feel of the place before you make it your inert lover," she grumbled. She'd had enough of beds that provided no one's comfort but her own in her life. She would pass on a whole lodge full of them.

Leaving her cloak cinched, a desirable spot needed to be decided on to get noticed by her contact. One secure enough for their conversation before she called attention to herself. *If* he was here still. The buzz in the room had already muted some the moment she'd trampled in with a wolf frothing at the mouth. Pinpricks of eyes followed their progress across the reception. He may have wanted to avoid detection, skulking around Outliers on his own for so long, and had left.

Just her luck the perfect spot was the corner the farthest away. Several more steps and it was practically a given she'd have to jerk her cloak back and ready it for an ease of mobility so that she could snatch the collar of someone touching her.

Oh, oh great! The woman's face bulged. For goodness sakes, her cheeks even trembled. Sheesh. She was overreacting. *Only you could do this to yourself.* Mandatory security drills, trudging through all that snow, and of course, a raving, attacking wolf had her too uncouth to keep the company of polite society. Just what she'd feared being in the snow with nothing but her fantasies of out-maneuvering her mother to keep her warm.

Letting go of the woman's tunic, mortified at the fright she'd put in her, her eyes slinked away from meeting the woman's pinched face. "Why do you approach me so?"

The poor woman squirmed and scoured about for her friends nearby.

Each of them like stutter-steps stood crowded around a fireplace. In their similar furs the color of heated honey worn from the Ukihne region, they hunched their shoulders and lifted their eyebrows. Their faces wore varying degrees of wonder at her ever having approached Tierney in the first place. And why had she? Their drinks and food were complimentary enough to the hum of fellowship found at the lodge's bastion of shelter. Why leave that to approach a stranger? "I...your wolf. He's a beautiful creature. I thought to touch him...

Tierney skirted on ahead of the woman, glad she'd decided to slink past them and go about her business, pretty sure her behavior had convinced the woman that gaining her and Bak'rah's regard just wasn't worth it. *My pup is in about as bad a shape as me.* The fur between a Soonahyin wolf's brows normally calmed him when touched, save growls vibrated the hand she'd placed on *Bak'rah's* temple. They both were too on edge for socializing. They'd probably scare the most hearty of people away. *Geez! You have to get it together or you won't be fit to do what you need to do here.*

"It's okay, my boy." Glancing around, her heel's tapping ceased with a clinch of sheer willpower. Of course, it would be okay. She had no choice but to will it so. They were here now. Nerves riding that edge ebbed at the scene the lodge offered. This setting portrayed the essence of all Soonayah. Gravitating to fifteen or so fireplaces in convenient spots amidst an open-schemed floor plan, people did what any Soonahyin would expect them to do. To witness the familiarity was a balm to a harassed soul.

They sought, as all Soonahyins must do regularly, heat energy—life for them. The wonder for many in their land was how people from other lands raised their soul-energy.

Soonahyin custom was to take stance. Standing helped their energies stay innervated in their frozen haven. The spark in the solar-plexus activated by the compulsion to survive. Life willed out. Their constitutions had carved out an existence for them a millennia ago in this...arctic, somehow. The soul-energy was a quintessence found as an ember in a being. It flamed higher or lower according to its carrier. For some reason, a Soonahyin's could be tapped into and activated at their will. Different from all the other peoples of Telluric.

Tierney smirked. A contest of her will against thigh-high snow and a fight with a rabid animal left her too exhausted for tradition, Soohanyin resilience or...anything expected of her. *They will have to forgive me for not taking stance this time.* Her backside plopped into a seat. She put her back to the wall and sidled closer to a fireplace she must've garnered *some* luck *somewhere* to have to herself.

The sopping boots came off first, then a center of their leg-holes toward the fire. Removal of her cloak quieted the lodge's buzz completely and prodded *her* into raising an eyebrow with a pleat creasing her features. She went ahead and pulled the cloak well free of herself and her hair, and so caused gasps to murmur across the room. And took it all in.

The fur cloak like all furs in Soonayah wasn't bulky but tailored to fit rightly to the body. The tunic too. Both contoured so their shukka warming mechanism hit at the pulse points, ensuring no hypothermia even in blizzard conditions. When on, the garments outlined her silhouette like a signal fire to all those who would recognize her. Her presence here couldn't be hidden, so she would use it. Anyone curious enough would show themselves eventually.

Soonahyins were known for their radiant, deep-ebony skin. Tierney's shone as if a fire burned beneath it, as a mark of who she was. Everyone was going to know she was here, anyway. Hair rolling down her back in thick puffs, and reaching her buttocks, was what differentiated her more than anything else. The one most obvious legacy she remembered left to her by her late father, the King.

If only these people would give me a few moments to gather myself!

Goodness! Another woman approached from tending a drinks station. This one wore her hair in an easy twist that fell between broad shoulders with a smock draping her figure. "You grace us here at Outliers to serve you this eve."

At face value, Tierney took the woman to mean strictly what she said. Having unease was nothing new. Whenever she was on her own, she became a super-vigilante of her own security. What fool would approach with ulterior motives in mind with Bak'rah at her feet? The woman eyed Bak'rah and scooted around him. From the trews that shaped the woman's legs, worn to the wear and tear of faded seams down the side and near the crotch, to the earnest look about her eyes, hard work was born of the woman's pores.

Although she'd never visited here, Tierney'd heard of Outliers lodge when she sojourned to the borderlands. Anyone with the savvy to understand the need for a lodge in such a precarious location and who could make a success of it without deluges of incidents from both sides of the border would do well not to be taken as anyone's fool. "It's a great rest spot out of the abominable snow. Are you the owner?"

"Yes. I'm Peetah Pearl Ticana Ahn'Creet, the proprietor. Most call me Peetah Pearl. Can I make you more welcome with food for you and your companion?"

"None for me. But bone broth for Bak'rah would be most appreciated. And be sure you leave extra fat on the bone along with the meat. Bak'rah has a liking for the fat." Peetah Pearl dipped her head and left, and with her should've taken this need of Tierney's to feel like she had to be on at all times.

Sure, that would happen. She loosened a packet of umbereen from inside her cloak and sprinkled a small amount of the crystal-like sand into her boots before turning them back to the fire. Then kneeled and shoved her hands into Bak'rah's coat where he settled before the fire. His position, supine on the floor was a complete deception. Energy from his torso burgeoned against her hands like she was touching the fire itself. "Build your soul-energy, sweet pup," she crooned to him close to his ear. Though there was a level of comfort here, it wouldn't do to let her guard down too much. Unfortunately, she'd been taught since the cradle, that to be suspicious was to have the most comfort she'd need as a royal.

Like now.

Movement...more a bit of a shuffle really in spatial awareness caught the eye in the opposite corner of the reception's expanse. Across hardwood floors, past several groupings of people at fireplaces and patrons standing drinking at drinks stations, why is the occupant there hiding behind a balustrade separating his booth from everybody else? For a moment she could have sworn she glimpsed a flash of green. Now, all that could be seen was the occupant's arm. He was Kalameshee. From here, his flesh showed bright of a hint of sun in its tone as was common for those from the land of Kalamesh. And that was an odd curiosity.

A Kalameshee? This far from the border? The boundary between Soonayah and Kalamesh yielded some Kalameshee who chanced a venture into the depths of Soonayah's climate. The teeny percentage from those that could actually get in, that is. The farther traveled the colder it got. Rarely were their constitutions bold enough to make it to the western borderlands.

"Bak'rah. The Kalameshee behind the balustrade," she rubbed him while she whispered to him. Instantly, the predator in him shifted as canny as his brethren, the fox. Now that Bakrah's instinct for the hunt was roused toward the one loafer in the room, Tierney chuckled. *With fox-wolf on watch, maybe I can try to be more relaxed.*

If just to rest her head and take into account the surroundings for a moment. Heat innervating a person's soul-energy was as Soonahyin to any Soonahyin as dancing. A stretch of the hand to the fire and a lean back had heat permeate down to the smallest corpuscle inside. The tiniest molecule of the tension deep-rooted like was accustomed—which smelted that permanent edge to the bones—frittered away in the ether, the flames doing their job well. Lowering her eyelids to slits, she didn't fall to slumber but studied the lodge and its occupants. *They can think my eyes are closed. Anyone fool enough to believe I would sleep in public can encroach upon me if they want...*

Laughter bubbled underneath her breath. This was why taking sojourns on her own to explore other dominions was a must. Outliers screamed succor. "*Relax!*" it said. Its rich walls, offerings of food, and rest professed a presence of understated luxury. If you paid attention. A perfect getaway. Benign as ever. *Yet, I sit here searching for threats.*

At least at home, she could relax. That is before she was forced away to make this journey. Her ultimate goal was to find that same composure anywhere she traveled by herself. Outside her homeland too, if she chose. *I should be able to be at ease somewhere and my training not take over who I am.*

Which was the whole purpose of this, wasn't it? If ever a person wanted to lead a life of their own, they had to learn to be okay wherever they went *or some modicum of okay. Not this hyper vigilance, forever on edge.*

Outliers had a good air about it. Indeed, it should be kept in mind for future travels. It was as good a place as any to develop some new self-possession.

Steam rising from the skin on top of a tureen wove its way through the crowd, carried by Peetah Pearl. Tierney stopped her before she could slurp at the bone broth to show how she tested it for them. Why was it tolerable for an upright Soonahyin like Peetah Pearl to fall to food poisoning? The royals should be no more important than anyone else. Such imperial obligations were asinine. Bak'rah looked to her.

She nodded. Only then did he eat with lusty chomps at the fat.

"I trust he likes it well. I buttered the fat extra for him."

"Much appreciations. It was kind of you to bring us food. There wasn't a smorgasbord spread for banquet when we came," Tierney said to her and swiped the armset console strapped to her bicep. The gadget shrilled. A virtual image of silver mints popped above it. The blipping indicated they were ready to be traded off.

Peetah Pearl shooed it away like payment was an afterthought. "It's an honor to serve you. And you *wouldn't* have found any food waiting on banquet. The crowds sacked every crumb we had prepared earlier. The roasting jets were refired for you and your friend here." She gestured toward the cookery located on the far wall where the roasting jets blazed. Their fires started to taper down as an attendant finished off its cleansing to close it for the night.

It was good to know Peetah Pearl had served the food out of courtesy and wasn't some zealot-type obsessed with getting close to a royal. "I see you know who I am." Royals tended to come across at least one every other time they went on excursion. The patronage could exhaust a person at the end of the day when you just needed a state of anonymity to wind down the eve.

But she returned Tierney's appraisal eye-to-eye, her arm swooped crosswise from her chest, palm up to about waist height in a salute fit for a First Princess. And as appropriate, a bent head in acceptance was the only response to give, even if you person were trying to be low-key here. "Yes, from the moment you entered. There is rumor you always travel with a wolf. Never knew it could be, until you walked in with one as big as any man. And of course, once you removed your cloak there wasn't a doubt."

Legend of her looks preceded her even to territories to which she'd never traveled before. As was her habit when a bit too much attention came her way, she scrunched her nose and flicked at the puffed hair laying over her chest. "My hair betrays me."

"Yes, but your looks too. And your skin." Peetah Pearl's stare raked over the frizz of hair and frankly noted the wolvien boots, still fluffed and unmarked announcing they were only newly acquired, and the unworn look to her tunic, with unabashed curiosity. "You look like no other."

A blush warmed and spread beneath the skin Peetah Pearl lauded so. Wishing the heat from her face, Tierney fiddled with the arm of her seat until a change of shadows in a corner of the lodge flitted in her periphery. Another bend of light on the darkness, where she'd seen no person settled when she'd checked out the lodge, had her whipping her head around. *And oh!* She spied her uncle Haarth's emergence from the dark space. Sneering and focusing only on that spot, allowed her time to shed some of the awkwardness from Peetah Pearl's scrutiny. Geez *Uncle. No subtlety at all.*

His whipping his cloak back announced, "*Here is a man of distinction.*" And it created an effect like he'd materialized from swirling shadows as he walked up on Peetah Pearl from behind. Blanching, she then looked to him, then to Tierney once...twice. With a wrinkle to her brow that spoke to all kinds of questions she must've asked in her head about the two royals, she drifted away.

It shouldn't take this long for family to see one another in person. When she rose, Tierney and her uncle beamed at each other. Their Soonahyin greeting was automatic: skin-to-skin, opposite hands to forearms. The sleeves on all Soonahyin tunics had sensors so that they opened when bent and touched to another's, then sealed automatically when released based on the wearer's movements. Along the seam of their arms tingled innervation between them like Tierney held hers out to the fire again.

He hadn't aged much over the spans since the last time they were together. No lines marred brown skin. His body looked as sound as any a man of her own age. Her uncle's grin declared him acknowledging the moment as well. They wrapped their other arms around each other still, sharing each other's heat for some time within the hot connection.

Exhaustion from her blizzard march had leached into her bones by now though. Her knees collapsed of their own accord, back onto the seat. She gestured to her uncle to take the seat opposite. He shook his head and Tierney said, "I insist, Uncle. I know it's not done. You can't take stance on me now. My knees won't keep me standing after the drudgery I have just gotten through. I beg you not to make me strain my neck looking up at you as well."

"Haarth Kyuumbuck Soonayah Ahn'Trunkh." *Every one* of his names in *first respect.* He was still a *prince* of Soonayah after all. But that didn't stop her waving her hand toward the darkness from which his arrogance had given him leave to appear. "I see you treat our meeting as a casual thing, while I tempt Mother's wrath beyond legion." Haarth, who hadn't come through a door brought attention to an uncle who wasn't supposed to be here, meeting her. He didn't need to know she was in similar circumstances to his. Soon to be exiled, committed to that sanctum, an outcast from the royal house just like him.

"You save the seat of most vulnerability for me. I take it," he chuckled, "because I trust your abilities of vigilance. But you don't believe in my capabilities of surveillance?" He shrugged and tilted his head to Tierney. "The time I awaited your arrival wasn't spent idle, Tierahna. Each person within this lodge has been accounted for."

She shrugged too. *I won't ask for forgiveness for a late arrival because of a malfunctioning transport.* She'd tried in good faith to communicate her circumstances to him. The blizzard wasn't her doing. "I just thought it odd you would enter so. But since we gauge each other's strengths. Why has the Kalameshee in the far corner not shown his face once in the time I've been here?"

Haarth's expression remained as bland as unmarred snow. "Because he's a Kalameshee scout sent here to spy on our meeting."

Tierney shot up. Her attention flew to the corner for confrontation with the foreigner. Bak'rah stood too, growls gunning from the bottom of his belly.

"Be calm, Tierahna. We mustn't alert him we're aware of who he is. Then we will have cordoned off his first move." The touch to her arm appeared casual, Haarth's grasp though was actually vice-like and held her and the wolf at bay. "Allow him to reveal himself to us, and we'll counter as needed. You must admit his observing our first reunion must mean it's of consequence to varying interests. Besides, if his intent was harm, wouldn't your beast have warned you by now?"

Even as her mind raced with the implications, her frame halted as stiff as a piece of petrified wood. She looked into her uncle's face. Really looked this time. Comprehension dawned with what the Kalameshee's presence here along with Haarth's must mean. "What's he doing here, Uncle.

Telling body language for a Soonahyin royal the likes of which had never been associated with Haarth before; his glance slunk away into the fire. "I have no idea truly why a Kalameshee scout would be here, Tierahna."

No one close to her, besides her mother, ever called her Tierahna. "It's Tierney to my family...*Uncle*. Now how could a Kalameshee scout *know* to be here to spy this meeting?"

"I didn't bring him, *Tierney*."

"But he followed you?"

"No. He was here before I." He hesitated and clenched a fist and rubbed a hand over his face. "But, I'm sure Larza fed information of our meeting to the Kalameshee Royal House. There could be no other way."

Word of their meeting had reached across the Kalamesh border by way of Haarth's flighty-loosed-tongue consort, Larza? To keep the disrespectful words on her teeth from slicing into him, she shrank back. Apparently, Larza had an agenda of her own.

And there she went again, tapping her foot against the floorboards, soothing herself with rhythm, like sing-songing her way through a blizzard.

And boy, do I need soothing right now!

Haarth was known for his dalliances with amenable women. Evident from his confession, even Kalameshee royals were not excluded from his eclectic tastes.

Tierney had worked up an excuse to tell the queen on her way here about this meeting. So, Haarth had been exiled to the southeastern borderlands. They weren't supposed to communicate, but he was a master negotiator. Her mother would forgive her for violating his exile in that case, wouldn't she? She sucked her teeth. *That was doubtful.* She would just have to express her urgency for Haarth's expertise. Maybe saying personal ambitions pushed her, would do it. The queen was big on her offspring's growth. She'd better include lots of tact too. So sneaking off and making formal plans with Haarth to begin talks to open all the borders surrounding Soonayah more wouldn't seem an outright betrayal. The queen was steadfast in opposition on the issue.

A lot of hoohing and haahing will probably go along with it too in whatever speech I come up with. Her mother could suss out just about everything about her. She needed to keep quiet that she was pushing this so hard because she knew she was on the verge of being committed. The urge to get the borders open for all of Soonayah was meant to cover the private urge to leave Soonayah too.

By the time the queen decided on putting her away in that sanctum, the borders would be open more, and she could slip away into some other land and get the crap away from here.

"Maybe I was wrong to think I could have a different outlook than Mother. You can't stay from your consort's bed long enough to keep your head before your tongue. Now our first meeting may as well have been held in-Keep at Mother's feet."

"Maybe it should have been. Ahead of our first objective perhaps is the start."

"You say that Uncle because news of this meeting is now out." Haarth's position wasn't surprising. He'd stressed to her she was old enough to speak her piece to her mother from the beginning. In his arrogance, he must have thought it beneath him to meet his own niece behind the queen's back. Not being a girl anymore, the queen's tight hold had stunted her into acting and feeling like she still was sometimes. It was now that time was pressing, she'd decided to test her mother's restrictions.

"No. Think on it, Tierahna. Kalameshee interest is what we seek." Haarth leaned forward, his gaze piercing hers.

Off in the corner, hidden behind that balustrade, the Kalameshee hadn't stirred from the original place she'd spotted him. "Whether it is or isn't, I think it's best we take this meeting to an enclosed space. We have roused enough interest. Everyone here will begin to speculate, not only the Kalameshee."

Peetah Pearl stood attentive at a drinks station with some of her patrons. She came to them in brisk form the instance she and Tierney's eyes met, as though she awaited a summons from them.

Tierney donned her boots now wafting the umbereen's fragrance. She always kept some ground in its crystal-like sand formula for instances just such as this. To use its properties of freshening while effecting a quick-drying process. The compound found in abundance in Soonayah had many uses. Hers? Saving her snow-sodden wolvien-shukka boots. She flexed one calf then the other, flattening her feet, filling the boots, and beamed. *Dry. Even to the toes.* Then looked up at Peetah Pearl.

"We seek accommodations for the night, Peetah Pearl. I know you must be close to capacity in this weather, but if arrangements can be made, they would be most appreciated. We won't forget it."

"The uppermost rooms can be made available to you. They're our largest and promise the most comfort and security."

Tierney paused brows raised at Peetah Pearl making exclusive accommodations available for them on such short notice. "How long before they're ready?"

Peetah Pearl gave a matter-of-fact nod. "They're already prepared."

Evidently, when Peetah Pearl witnessed the entrance of the Soon-ahyin princess and the long-lost brother of the king—who some said had been exiled, having a clandestine meeting in her establishment—she figured they might just need private rooms for whatever they could need to talk about.

Chapter 3

She wasn't so inclined, but if she were, Tierney could have walked straight into her suite's fireplace. The thing was huge. Golden-orange flames reflected off eyes that didn't really *see* anything.

The tasks she and Haarth had set for themselves preoccupied them, rolling around in the fire and subsequently reflecting off said eyes until the muddle knotted her belly up with more curls than a labyrinth.

This was what you wanted? What you snuck off like you had some pressing mission for, was it not?

She cackled at herself because she hadn't thought about the aftermath of telling her mother. Braving the flames seemed a better idea than confronting the queen. To innervate her soul-energy here, before Outliers' behemoth of a fireplace for the rest of her life, was starting to have a lot of appeal. The fireplace had character like the opulent ones around the Keep at home in Dameerh, the dominion of Soonayah's high seat.

Tierney sighed. *For someone who trumps up a reason for a sojourn whenever you can—it's a wonder homesickness plagues you in the middle of them.* Admiring the fireplace transported her to the Keep for a moment, away from the conflict miring her brain. The tailspin life had taken on at bay with the fire's wield of its bits of magic.

Funny though. Sometimes her connections kindled a curiosity like she communicated with the fire. One of those things where a person could spin a circumstance into just the escape they needed. Take them away a little bit.

Luster from some of the fireplaces in the Keep had been beacon**s** to fertile imaginations in their youth, just like this. Those most favored were covered in palladot. Early stone carvers had created whimsy for Keep dwellers seeking to withstand Soonayah's cold. Once eve fell, darkness saturated no matter the season, causing light from the flames to range off objects in the room and hit the brilliant palladot gemstones just so. If you squinted, you could picture them as the original meteorites that formed them. She had lain in pelts on the floor with the fire blazing before sleeping-time and reached out to the stones' vibrancy.

Chanting, "If I just capture them, I could fly away," as a girl who murmured her wishes at the fold of the altar of gemstones for many many moons. *And ride along on their odyssey of skipping across the skies!*

Their galaxy, Caelum, was one of two dreamed upon on moon-filled nights. A body could fly from the spiraling Caelum to the galaxy next door. Its twin spiraled an inconceivable number of kiloparsecs away. Yet, her mind's eye managed her whooshing between the two galaxies, clutching a cache of palladot from the Keep's fireplace between her two palms. Come morn, she'd awakened ensconced in her own bed where no doubt her mother had carried her after discovering her asleep upon the floor.

Her absence this day and the prior couldn't help but be noticed by now. Her mother would've begun asking for her a long time ago. *"Where has Tierahna, the perpetual wanderer, gotten off to?"*

Lu'nil, her cousin will have told her. Once Tierney gained distance from the Keep, that is. That's why word had been left with her. *"Off for a day or two's excursion to the borderlands—"* was the message left on Lu'nil's console. Leaving it that way had served a purpose for her cause. She'd wanted some time alone in the start of her journey, and had known Lu'nil wouldn't get the message until after her sparring session. When she required invigoration, Lu'nil deactivated all devices that could disturb her from her immersions.

Once, she'd told Tierney that while fighting, she could concentrate on certain moves—a level of reformation, she'd called it—and become one with her mind and body, then she could separate the two. The essence of who she was shifted from her body trapped by the ravages of time, then switched back as if tugged by some connective tissue when her cognizance would start to drift off.

An astonishing gift if one understood it. Tierney wasn't so sure Lu'nil did. She'd only dabbled with it up until now, not learning all its capabilities...or ramifications. *It was good she'd been out of it for a while when she'd left, though.* It'd been best not to concern her too much in the beginning. Best to make her move first, then answer the inevitable queries later.

Lu'nil would've retrieved the transmission after her session. And would've had a question or two, but ultimately, she'd look out for her as she always did. Which was what Tierney was depending on. Being her closest of confidants, she had an understanding of the need for Tierney's urgency and what all this running about was for.

Late eve here on the other side of Soonayah meant it was near morn in Dameerh. Their mother never slept. Not when Tierney went on excursion, according to Os'carah, the babe of the siblings. A discussion with the queen about what she was doing out here or rather what she was attempting to do could be started now. Especially now. The Keep in slumber was the perfect opportunity to slip in a reason as to why she'd gone away without announcing it. When the lights were lowered, the hive at home unwound. To drift through the halls put one in a wonderland. The furbishings, the open skies, the accouterments still there yet behind a shroud, like entering into a place that wafted between real and unreal, a utopian dreamland.

Yes, her mother might be quite a bit more amenable in the middle of the night. Who wouldn't be in those surroundings?

But I need more time to figure out how to push my agenda along.

Besides, the fire beckoned to her. The simple chemical reaction of fuel heated to combustion by a heat source. The common enough principle was the essence of life here in Soonayah. Without it, they'd all wither and die. In the beginning-times of their land, hundreds of thousands did die until they'd discovered their connection to the flame.

Each time *she* swayed toward the fire it flared, reacting. *Proximity to it makes my own skin unbearable.* As her hair moved with their convection, the flames crackled too high. The fire should be banked down, but it enraptured her. Never a truer Soonahyin to be found, it was only natural that she'd revel in it. *My ultimate comfort come to ignite me.* Innervation conflagrated at the core as it did for everybody, burned up the sternum into cords swollen on both sides of the neck, to tingling in the scalp. How she must look rooted before the fire, her frizz of a mane flying behind her like a wind-captured sail.

The queen's voice ringing on a loop inside her head told sermons to them over and over again in their youth, "*No good serves our people from long proximity to the heat of the flames,*" always warning them back from the flames.

Tierney ignored the mantra. Things shouldn't always be easy. Her mother couldn't keep them from every challenging thing. Even for instance now, her cords' engorging stung her neck. That she didn't release at least some of the soul-energy bit her with sensation.

But there was something there, just out of reach.

Inured to the feeling, she let it take its way, almost. Some conscious-ness she'd keep, less end up walking into the fireplace enthralled, burnt to a crisp. Now, *too many* stories had been told of teams and teams of people this had happened to. Soonahyins enraptured, sometimes nixed their own thought processes to veer toward a drugged feeling in an escape from the harshness of their environment. *And that, I definitely remember to avoid.* There was something else there between consciousness and voluntary delirium though. Something... different.

Something more.

If she closed her eyes the perspective was given reign as she'd teetered around the edges of these occurrences for days now. How stressful it'd been, her body in stasis between the tension it took to fight against the phenomena and fear of what would happen when she could no longer hold out. *Drat it!* After a few moments, she released her muscles. Giving in to the urge of what her own physicality seemed to be screaming for, she was torn about it now. Who knew what she should be doing in these circumstances? Nobody'd ever experienced this before. And for the first time, the different frame of reference freed itself inside her head.

Oh, wow! "People. People are everywhere." They were shone as globules of energy with beacons of light inside them. And every being around her struck an invisible field of *her* energy while her eyes were closed. *They're not even inside the room with me.* Yet, she could detect them.

The knowledge of it, *goodness*, the feel of it presented as the ultimate in intro-spection. Another person's existence. Feeling someone else as you would yourself and they somehow became a part of you.

Uncle? In the next room, he moved about, his energy palpable, anxious. Not retired yet either, Haarth paced his room from one end to another.

The wolf's energy silhouette slumbering near the bottom of her bed, she didn't just feel. *Bak'rah, my kindred, I think I can see you.* So, people weren't the only beings she could detect. *That was good to know.*

In a one-off, another energy signature struck her, but it wasn't in the room.

The Kalameshee!

How she knew on first instinct it was him, she couldn't say. But there wasn't a doubt who it was who skulked outside her terrace.

"Steady yourself," she murmured, clenching her fingers near bruising against the hearth. She'd expected this after all. No need in alarming Bak'rah. He'd rip out the Kalameshee's throat before she had a chance at him. Neither incite Haarth either, of course. Larza vexing his plan was a surety why he wasn't abed this late. He anticipated the next move as much as she did.

And then an even stranger occurrence happened while she was trying to corral the buzzing in her chest over the Kalamashee. An energy signature was detected near the Kalameshee. One that you couldn't discern who it was without seeing them. Unmistakably though, somebody was moving stealthily in on the Kalameshee from behind. As he hastened to his first move, everything happened all at once and so fast it was a wonder Tierney tracked each participant in the fray.

As though he was summoned from deep sleep, Bak'rah acted first. By a connection—that had never been able to be explained when she'd asked the Ministry of Science about their kinship—he sensed the Kalameshee gaining access to the room through the door off the balcony at the same time Tierney did. From slumber, he surged to a howling jump through the air.

Instead of the quiet entrance the Kalameshee had evidently planned, the glass door crashed against the wall. The reason? The other energy signature Tierney had picked up on had gained on him in a speed. Peetah Pearl in a diving roll flew in at his back. She righted herself with a frostfire weapon pulled taut over her arm and trained at his skull. Into the room tangled the whirling tsunami: a body the size of a mountain flung between the door and the frame, the sight of someone speeding...that wasn't quite a sight, couldn't be seen, but sensed and felt, and the aftermath of a blizzard that would never be denied in Soonayah. Squalls of snow trapped with the two bodies were ushered in with the cold too.

That new *inter-spection* Tierney had been experimenting with pulled at her. Her semblance of quiet imploded, she mustered some control to drag herself from its grip. "No killing, Bak'rah!"

Tingling had let loose up the cords of her neck, into her scalp, accessing the furthest extensions of herself, even along the ends of her hair. Sensation seized her, whirling and whirling her *hair* first. The sense of losing oneself separated a person a little when they began to speed. Bounding in leaps toward the skirmish, continual motion was necessary. *Here it goes. Here it goes*; that zinging down to the toes, to the hairs rising up on one's arms. And a *whole body* could be whirled from in front of the heat. No matter that she moved last, the kinetics that triggered speeding caused a person to disappear from view—faster than an average eye could follow, faster than molecules could be impeded by any solid—she landed with a thump, first on the Kalameshee.

A hand inside the arm-sling of the frostfire, the trigger pulled, Peetah Pearl pointed a weapon at him unwavering. She awaited the infinitesimal—the sliver of time the weapon took to sap moisture from the air and release. Lethal or incapacitating, dry ice burned through gristle and bone either way. Peetah Pearl balanced the frostfire underneath with her other hand on the trigger release. *How was this all happening so fast?* Maybe coming here against the rules in the first place was the omen something unmanageable was bound to happen.

From where he crouched on the Kalameshee's chest, Bak'rah salivated. Tierney's foot was the only thing holding him back, which may have been no better than letting him go. Her foot pulsed energy against the Kalameshee's throat. Then Haarth slammed through the adjoining door, bare-chested, in immediate fighting-stance.

They all squared onto the Kalameshee.

It was only Tierney who scowled at her uncle, unable to fathom why his aggression triggered her own. It caused a stronger pulse from her foot into the Kalameshee's throat, and he groaned aloud but didn't move one muscle. "Your next move or any words I don't like will make me crush your throat."

Every portion of the Kalameshee's body remained still except his lips. "I'm not here to do you harm, Princess."

Of all the things that could happen. You've go to be jesting me. The timbre in his voice strummed tremblings up her nerves, racing to the top of her legs, on to her mons. *The last thing I need at this point.* Awareness of him was a stupid involuntary response given the current circumstances. A great time to have a reaction to someone when she'd only recently sworn off men saying, she hadn't the time to invest only for them to eventually give in to pressure and be run off by her brothers. And a great person to have a reaction to! She pressed even harder against his throat. "Then why *are* you here? And a fine way you demonstrate doing no harm, Kalameshee. Should I think of you as the welcome party come to greet me in the dark of night, then?"

His decision to put this little set-to in play hadn't turned out well for him. It'd wrought him green Kalameshee eyes shimmering, tears flooding, his face tightening, turning puce-colored. He tried to speak but couldn't. Haarth, at her side now, squeezed Tierney's elbow, pressing her to ease her foot from the Kalameshee's throat. But their connection spurred another involuntary pulse. She shook off Haarth's touch, but did ease the pressure...but not all the way. Any Kalameshee should know better than to trespass against a royal in Soonayah.

"Leave him room to speak, Tierahna. How else will we know his intentions? If he moves, let the beast have at his throat."

Her breath heaved to the point she thought she'd never catch it up again. She wrenched herself free. Her body's inner pulsing was near uncontrollable. *Tierney innervates herself in the flames beyond what she knows is safe. Mother would love to know that.*

Her soul-energy seethed too high. Not that standing this close to Haarth's helped calm it any. She glared at him and pictured her mother's "*I told you so*" shake of her head.

What was going on here? *Aggressive energy radiates off Uncle. Is that why Mother exiled him?*

Tierney had never felt this much of a connection with anyone. Soonahyins could fasten to another's energy even through their clothes. But the attachment had never been this sharp even with her brothers during sparring matches when aggression and skin-to-skin contact were at their highest. She moved to the other side of the Kalameshee, and put some distance between her and Haarth too, so that when she was near Peetah Pearl, she tried to steady her system. Then the Kalameshee took that opportunity to shift too. *He* backed up from the wolf.

A baring of every one of Bak'rah's teeth proved he was barely contained as well. He lowered his head and snarled, not appreciating the Kalameshee's shifting. Accordingly, the Kalameshee reared back, ceasing his movements and just bore with the wolf's bulk crushing him.

His chest rose and struggled, stuttering for breath until at last, he spoke. "I'm here as an emissary of the Kalameshee Royal House. We wanted to speak with the Soonahyin princess. I bring declaration of peace in the King's own hand, accompanied by visual notarization. The king of Kalamesh would never send someone into Soonayah for foul purposes, Princess."

She didn't know that. Had no idea what their motivations could be.

What other purpose could he have to break in here, but foul? "I will see this declaration. But if sneaking into my quarters while I was abed is what you believed a proper meeting, I think your king has sent the *wrong* emissary."

He looked at them all from his position on the floor and managed a laugh, albeit, his wince attested to his circumstances not really being funny. "The beast is crushing my lungs. I can't reach the pouch on my back."

She hesitated one beat, "Bak'rah!" before she called Bak'rah back. And would've laughed too to keep from crying if the moment wasn't so serious. This was rapidly getting out of control beyond what a young woman with limited power had planned when she'd decided on this journey. And Bak'rah whined, casting his head to one side too. That uncanny look he got sometimes was surely him questioning her judgment. *She* questioned her judgment, for ever having come here in the first place.

Before shuffling off him, the wolf growled what was clearly a last warning at the Kalameshee.

The intruder himself demonstrated enough training and a realization of how compromised he was. He sat up and brought a parcel from his back waistband. He made a show of turning it over for each of them, then handed it to her. Slow. Easy. In the unlikely event, the wolf didn't get him first, the sure-fired hand of the lodge's proprietor would follow up just as nicely.

Tierney, with Haarth back at her side, reached for a silver placard from the parcel save, Haarth threw a question at Peetah Pearl at the same time. "Do you have all explosives detectors operable as they should be within this lodge?" Until she answered, he pressed a hand to Tierney's to stop her from releasing the placard.

"Yes. And they're calibrated on a routine schedule as any allegiant Soonahyin establishment should guarantee." Unstinting prideful purpose shone from Peetah Pearl's face.

Assured by Peetah Pearl's dutiful doggedness, they slid the placard's lid forward until it snapped open. Vellum inside peaked out. If, as the Kalameshee said, the message was meant for *her*—once Tierney touched the vellum, the declaration would render. The visual notarization portion couldn't be falsified. She will have accepted an official declaration from the king of Kalamesh.

The occasion was so momentous she stood rapt for a moment. *What have I gotten myself into? I have enough that I'm trying to make happen. I don't need Kalamesh adding to it.*

Haarth's prodding her prompted her to lift the vellum, finally. King Ocierus Coleman Beard then stood before them. He declared, "Good faith intentions," in furthering relations between their two lands.

He was a projection. Simple. A connection between the visual notarization and whatever biological remnant used. Yet, he appeared as though if you reached for him, you would encounter flesh. So, notarizations weren't falsified or reproduced. They could only be made with biological remnants from whoever sent them. She'd received contact from the highest echelons of Kalamesh.

The king would know she'd gotten the message too. She'd sent reciprocation when she'd lifted the vellum. Somewhere in Kalamesh on a synced device, *her* biological signature had been received.

There was no going back now.

Tierney's brow ached right in that nagging spot above the left eye. Her teeth ravaged the bulb of her lip. She hadn't initiated contact with Kalamesh. If she were being honest with herself, she had no confidence in any of this. Negotiating with foreign heads wasn't for her. *I need to learn negotiations with my own mother.* Actual diplomacy was best left to chancellorship members and chieftains...and the queen.

Tierney had set this meeting with Haarth to stir up border issues within her *own* land for her *own* purposes. Now she'd been preempted by the Kalameshee king?

A king determined to open dialogue, with bearing like the kings of old. Masterful. Tall. Unrepentant. Except he had skin several shades lighter than those Tierney'd known. That hint of the sun tint burnishing. Defiant, lion-like hair. His looks were well known amongst the lands. Although, now that she thought about it, she curved her shoulder to hide her face from the Klameshee's scrutiny. He did look suspiciously like the so-called emissary sitting, watching her every move and every thought chased across her features. The Kalameshee noticed her studying him and spoke with the bold assurance of someone of his station. "So what now?

Chapter 4

Dealing with the Kalameshee's behavior put her in mind of trying to capture a lemming when it poked its head up out the ground. *An infuriating predicament to find one's self in!* "What happens now is I get to be the one asking questions." Tierney winced. Hot, lusty soul-energy surged through her blood. It heated her face but was probably undetectable beneath the brown skin of a Soonahyin, only her whole body was flushed with heat too. Since he watched her every move, she hoped he read this Soonahyin's face real good. "If you be as you say, here representing a King who professes peace and diplomacy, then why skulk around the lodge, never presenting yourself before my uncle? And your crashing in here could have caused me to kill you! Setting off an incident that could have come to war!"

In the after-note of that accusation, Peetah Pearl shuffled from one foot, then danced onto the other one. One foot. Then the other one again. The jitter was a hesitancy everyone expressed a time or two in their lives. We all had second thoughts, even the staunchest of us. Peetah Pearl, presumably, the defender of Outliers, was no different. The staunchest of the staunchest, it seemed she was just a person too. And she and Haarth shared sideways glances with one another. The indictment released on the room's frequencies, still pulsed in the airwaves causing them to swing their attentions, brows raised back to Tierney. There was no telling what they thought she was talking about. Yet, Tierney's stare never wavered from the Kalameshee. She hadn't a doubt in her mind of the conclusion she'd come to. "Is that not right...*Prince*? If I killed the Kalameshee king's son, all good intentions would become moot, would they not?"

Like the good Kalameshee she figured him to be, once he stood, he measured the room in spite of the wolf still growling at him. From watchfulness he shifted to wariness. Calling attention to his full height, clearly, he deemed distance necessary between himself and the wolf. As he slid near her uncle, he looked even more like his father. The resemblance was remarkable. *How could I have missed it?*

As tall as Haarth, except his bulk overly bulged with muscle, fur on top of fur covered his proportions from head to toe. Known of the land of Kalamesh, was for the men there to be built like mountains. However, strapping anatomy didn't matter in the least with the churning starting to build inside Tierney.

A vision of the Keep's decorum: its welcome of fires in every room, its constancy of people everywhere, its assurance of safety exuding from the walls epitomized why what was happening here now was in jeopardy of pulling from her a reaction that could be irrevocable. She wasn't used to this type of provocation. Everything around her was kept well oiled, a predictable life normally.

Haarth turned the breadth of his body half-blocking the Kalameshee, and light glanced off his torso. Cuts, scars grooved his chest, across his arms, and rutted his back and shoulders. Another example of this situation's unpredictability. Tierney'd never seen Haarth half-dressed before. The scars had healed, but what'd happened to him? The pain of what he must've gone through to be disfigured like that distracted her, for a bit. The Kalameshee moving amongst them free was of more consequence. *I might not be used to this, but I must stay alert to everything going on in this situation.* "Peetah Pearl, kill him if he moves again."

Laughter threatened at the absurdity of the circumstances—this was unbelievable how it'd come about—except the seriousness of it all ended up choking her throat with something closer to panic. Poor Peetah Pearl, it seemed her psyche was contradictory in a similar vein. She adjusted her shoulders this time. Her feet's shuffling, which had been steadfast before, declared concern at shooting a prince of another land. At the same time, her unfaltered targeting of the Kalameshee demonstrated a resolve to do a duty *her* princess commanded and to see this incident hopefully to constrained conclusions.

Of course, *the Kalameshee* would chuckle at the scene. The m*uskox ass! The guy was insufferable!* "I'm not here to do you harm. I wouldn't have let it come to you killing me." The drollness in his voice grated along Tierney's spine, instantaneously, the heat boiling inside her like liquid fire flushed her veins to a point of no return. Her soul-energy battered her as prisoners would a locked vault door. Such arrogance in the face of Soonahyins was unthinkable. In essence, he was begging to be shown who was running this inquest, and as an answer to his wish, her tenacity sent her flying across the space between them. His back hit the wall after taking several steps backward, away from her aggression.

Tierney led with her elbow, popped her forearm into his throat, and pressed all her weight into it too. This should do. *What of that Kalameshee-lemming head now?* she sneered.

This close up, minute details of his appearance shone in relief against a background that for some reason, shrank in deference to her being right up against him. Every little thing about him was narrowed to a pinpoint.

A mole about the size of the head of a needle peeked from behind the curve of his earlobe. The flaxen hair at his temples and in his sideburns was that of a boy who hadn't quite rid himself of his curls once he reached adulthood. His irises sparked too, and weren't solely green but had a rim of hazel as well. In addition, they were flickering with strain because she held him captive, or was he reading her down to her bones as they stood there? That's why she'd been able to detect the green in his eyes across the reception. They gleamed—a tractor beam summing up the very crux of a scene in one sweep—keen in their assessment, coursing her face, tracing her skin all the way to her tunic's neckline.

The fascination was evidently with her tunic's felt material, unfastened from around her neck and its snood's scrunched flaps hung open as the fire had warmed her. He strained forward against her forearm, pressing closer to her, which had to cut his breath shorter. But he brushed his nose against her cheek...and threw her off utterly, which was probably his aim. Such were the ways of the Kalameshee.

Why *was* he doing that? He couldn't be expressing attraction when he was one fingerbreadth away from dying. Was he smelling her? He kept his hands to his sides. Open. Showing no retaliation. So encroaching into her space was enough then? Or who was to say if it was enough? He couldn't answer for himself because his breaths began to drag, and his face ran the gamut from red to puce again and darker. He never made another move other than clenching his fists. Of everything he'd done so far, this was probably the most prudent thing to do to save his own life. And of course, a Kalameshee would recognize that, wouldn't he?

Okay. Okay. I know I have to let him breathe. Haarth's hand shaking Tierney's shoulder urged her to ease up a little. She *eased* up a bit, only she didn't let up the full force. He hadn't proven himself yet, and with him being a Kalameshee, he probably never would.

He exhaled nothing but spittle, then he laughed. He laughed when she was on the verge of killing him. *Just fine for him when my stress hasn't allowed me any humor in this unbelievable situation.* As much as his position allowed with even more humor, he looked beyond her to Haarth and said, "She's an aggressive one, isn't she?"

"If you mean, is she lethal? Then yes. She can kill you and in very quick order. So, everyone here will ramp it down a notch...or twelve."

Tierney arched a brow at her uncle's tone. *His touch though!* She wanted his hand off her—and bad. He made slowing her racing heart impossible. It was so shot with her energy-quickened blood, his soul-energy may as well have been a live fire to her sensibilities.

"Calm yourself," he implored.

She was shook by her own behavior likening herself to a frenzied animal. It was best she removed herself from the provocateur, clear to the other side of the room. He knew what he was doing. A Kalameshee in the midst of a dilemma would operate in the prime of his abilities.

This was where she should be, on the wall—away from everybody else. Ferber wood curved and notched with a shine all its own, layered with one but-end at the corner resonating with the aroma of the wood that proffered rest for her back. Cornices made of exposed beams winked down at them too before they angled off to the joists in the ceiling. The shine like a torch when she glanced at it, like breaking up a scuffle in the dark.

Whoowee, this was way too intense! How grateful I am to get on this side of the room. Distance was always a good thing instead of killing. Away from the Kalameshee's face that *oh so* wanted to be smashed, with distance between herself and Haarth too.

Haarth's effect on her concerned her, sure. She'd think on that later. Alone.When she was the only one to provoke herself with thoughts on being this uncontrolled. She'd been having enough of a time with her control on her own lately. She didn't need the Kalameshee for that.

What was the Kalameshee's look about, anyway?

Sly from one to the other of them. *Does he sense this heightening energy between me and Uncle too?* His gaze zeroed right back in on Tierney, stalkerish in its study. Eyes on stems made of magnets with her as the only attractant.

"You could be none other than the son of a king because your arrogance is astounding," Tierney said, her voice bouncing off those cornices when in these circumstances it was best she regained some control. "If I had decided killing you would be justified just for trespassing too closely to my person, there would have been no chance for you to explain yourself to me."

The air in the room grew as thick as dust because she was right and everyone else knew it too. Her point already having reached the ears it was intended for, continued to throb in the crooks and the crannies, commanding a pause in their tableau. They *all* took one another's measure, except for the wolf of course. He growled often as he was poised on his haunches already riding Tierney's energy, ready to spring into action at the slightest inference she needed his attack.

If Haarth hadn't warned her from the beginning about what the Kalameshee might do, Tierney may well have taken catastrophic actions. Forcing the queen of Soonayah into staving off war, simply due to Tierney's need to determine her fate for herself. No amount of reasoning would have sufficed.

Deep, gustful breaths calmed Tierney's system for a few moments. She couldn't afford a high-strung temperament in as critical a time as this. Her land's border destiny could very well rest within her hands. She needed clear wits about her.

Peetah Pearl, unlike her, had a steadiness of hand as placid as the water of Serene Lake, even with the frostfire pulled-to-fire over her arm. *Cumbersome personified.* Tension in the room at detonation level. If ever her chilling presence and the presence of a dispute-ending frostfire were needed, it was now.

Of course, Haarth would stand at the center. Sideways on the balls of his feet allowed him an advantage over everybody else. Near as naked as when he was born, the ancestors rode his posture—ghosts inherent in the bones of a Soonahyin like him. Tierney slanted a knowing look at her uncle. *How deliberate he was.* Cooling the situation, he'd placed himself between her and the Kalameshee, his back to her. She'd defer to him. He possessed a far calmer frame of mind than she did.

And then they had the intruder, the cocksure Kalameshee, the very instigator of all this fuss, his eyes of sylvan raking them all down to their crevices, seemingly missing nothing. Fur on his shoulders unlike Soonahyin skins buffed him up as large as a leviathan. A testament to Kalemesh's interpretation on how to stay warm in Soonahyah, but which created stature that imposed itself over those of them who were smaller in the room. Gratefully, Haarth's stance counterbalanced his. Command was something some were just born with. It exuded from the pores and draped itself in no artifice to be well received by other landsmen, Kalemeshees alike.

Their faction of five, including the wolf, remained one lethal group at a standoff, and not everyone with an overt allegiance to one another, either. All of them were *right* to be wary.

The Kalameshee continued scouring everything. The room. Their faces. Their carriages. Tierney even caught him locking onto the pulses in their necks, reading them as he would manuscripts laid open for his perusal. "You're right, princess Tierahna. I'm Torhvald Coleman Beard. The third son of the king of Kalamesh." His voice breaking the silence projected a cadence expected to calm the situation. "I volunteered for this mission as emissary and never meant to make light of what might have happened when you didn't know who I was. But I have very little experience with females so fierce as you." Was he grinning at her? *Cheekily!* " I have seen your likeness. Still, *you* in person...?" He shook his head and talked with his hands out, facing up. A gesture used by those who hoped they appeared unalarming in a situation requiring delicacy. Usually, the receivers of such gestures remained unaware and biddable. Was everything a Kalameshee did, every gesture made, even eye contact used to disarm people?

And Flattery? Tierney snorted. *His audacity was fierce!* Veracity resonated from his voice. *But didn't he consider I might possess training similar to his?* "You say pretty words Kalameshee, yet offer no reasonable cause for your stealth. You lie with your omissions. Each time you've spoken, you've given no full answers to my questions."

"I had to take precautions. I'm traveling alone. And I arrived before Prince Haarth Kyuumbuck Soonayah Ahn'Trunkh. My father set a whole contingent for deployment here when we heard of your meeting, but I cautioned him against it. Although, we were sure the intel we received came from a credible source." Tierney cackled at Haarth's pursed face. Larza was the only possible source of credible intel the Kalameshees had access to. "I thought it better that I came alone because we understood on good authority, you two hadn't made it known to many you were meeting."

As she grit her teeth, it seemed to her she ground the enamel loud enough for everyone to hear. Larza had a lot to answer for. It must be nice to have a royal spy who was so thorough.

"It's our understanding this is unusual," he said. Unless he's visiting with his daughter, Prince Haarth's normal communication with your royal house is on strict routine. I thought intruding on your initial meeting was unwise, more subtlety was needed."

"So, you decided not to intrude. But you take us all for fools? Uncle, I think we *should* kill him. We shall face the consequences with Mother together. Risk of a Kalameshee spy trespassing this close to royals is too high when he still lies to us."

Waving frantically was the Kalameshee's attempt at staving off that end. "You're right, Princess Tierahna! Breaking in here was a stupid idea, but I needed confirmation of your identity before I presented you with the declaration. If for any reason we hadn't gotten your biological signature close enough, your touch could have destroyed the declaration." The Kalameshee slid a look beneath lowered eyelids toward Haarth then. "Evidently, the sample we used was a close enough relation."

"Why not send a declaration allowing for a common receiver?"

"This missive was meant only for you. If you didn't receive it, then no one should. This matter is too delicate. The declaration destroys its own contents if anyone other than you opens it."

"So, if you had been ambushed and the declaration taken, then at least no one would know of your attempt to communicate with me? That's a shortsighted attitude toward *your* life." Tierney would have great reservations about interacting with a land whose leader didn't value the life of his own son. He would surely take no care with his dealings with other people.

"As I said," the Kalameshee began. That smirk he'd carried on his face even when his life was threatened had fallen aside. "It took some convincing of my father to allow me this mission on my own. He gave me this duty of utmost importance to our land. Had he no confidence in my capabilities to provide my own security, he wouldn't have sanctioned it."

Quite clever too. The candor displayed sounded believable. Hints of defensiveness might have even moved a couple of those listening. Had he deduced her feelings on being one of the royal house's offspring and not the first or even the second in line for queendom? Did he understand what drove her here? Why she needed this so badly, then played on her feelings, likening his own situation to hers?

As a girl, Tierney'd worked hard for validation even though her mother showed no favoritism. She resented the possibility of the Kalameshee seeing all this in her, or of his having anything of the slightest in common with her. But her guard did lower some, shown in the slackening of her posture. Her pulse ramped down some notches too. A raptor's eyes hunted out the strain leaving her shoulders and keyed in on it. "Our coding for the biological signature worked so seamlessly. You and your...*uncle* must carry many alleles in common."

Why did he hesitate on the word *uncle*? Her gaze flew from him *to* her uncle. Haarth's eyebrows lowered at the Kalameshee making some insinuation, but he said nothing. Tierney couldn't let it slip by. She was far too confrontational for that. "Yes. He is my uncle after all." She didn't care for the Kalameshee's too-confident manner either. How had he flipped the dynamics of this situation to his advantage? A little while ago he'd been on the floor looking up at them. Now he held the balance? She would grant him being good at flipping a situation as only a Kalameshee could. Nothing more though. It was he who was the intruder here. "It should have worked if it was *his* biological sample that you *stole*, right?"

He shrugged as unflappable as ever. "Our technicians encoded allowances in case his genetic code wasn't close enough to yours. We expected the mechanism would expand once you touched it. Then retract and narrow in on specific female identifiers we included as a focus as close to your biological signature as possible. But it seems none of our extra efforts were needed. The device didn't hesitate. So...your family must have very similar genes." The sarcasm echoed. What was he implying? Her lack of control ran across her mind. She'd retained so little lowering her energy levels as she usually did when Haarth stood near her with his raised. Having a connection to Haarth like a tangible thing did disturb her.

"Whatever you're inferring, Kalameshee, you overreach. And your insolence is even more brazen than when Tierahna first choked you out for your laughter in such a critical moment as this. But your reasoning on your mechanism's response requires little explanation."

Haarth finally deigned to speak. However, his scowl professed that he wasn't at all used to explaining himself. "We *are family*. A family's genes are supposed to be close. And it has been many spans of time since Tierahna and I have been in physical contact. Our reaction must be due to our not having been in each other's company for fifteen or so spans."

So Haarth felt it too? She tried to gauge his thoughts as they looked at one another. And though his explanation sounded plausible, Tierney held an innate sense it couldn't account for so strong a reaction. *Wow!* She'd been out of her depth when she'd decided to come here.

She looked about the room for something, anything staunch to latch her mind onto.

The bed she hadn't had a chance to use yet hang against the far corner. A sculptured attached to the wall that twisted a trunk of uneven nodules to the floor was interesting, all the same, it faded into the background with this scene so prevalent. The door the Kalameshee smashed through was somewhat serviceable, and called attention to itself because they hadn't righted it to keep the snow from blowing in and piling around its hinge. Cold slithered its way in through its misshapen form on a course to compete with the fire.

And of course, there *was* Bak'rah too. Her reliable pup. His tail thumped against the planks of the floor. A faithful swishing. Her feet twitched, on the verge of taking up Peetah Pearl's earlier foot shuffle to the beat of it. Quite eye-catching, it'd been, *rhythm, as dependable as always. Far more dependable than how I feel right now.* For the first time in the ordeal, she wondered what the outcome would be. It was time to truly defer to Haarth. She'd let him confront the Kalameshee.

Haarth moved between them like an arbiter as he spoke already. He'd been sent away to the southeastern borderlands right as uncharted activity started over the borders. That's why she'd contacted him, in any case. For his reputation. He'd taken charge of the dominions there, aligning trade and securing the lands. *Who better to help me with my plans?*

She now realized what made his governance so effective. He used his stature as if authoritarian, communicating power while he reserved judgment and allowed certain efforts to play out. Thus, his strategy came from ascertaining the most knowledge first. Her father had been famous for his diplomacy too. *I will be mindful to study all Uncle's tactics from now on.*

Haarth's posture now could only be interpreted as overbearing though. Even Tierney thought his walking so close to the Kalameshee intimidating. Although his people practiced reading the emotions of others, the slight curl of the lip betrayed the Kalameshee's resentment of Haarth's deportment. His father, the Kalameshee king, was renowned for such tactics too. He should be used to this. Surely, he'd developed skills to handle the travails of royal maneuverings from his youth. But now he was here in his own right, taking on relations with a land that insofar as the recent past, could only be described as strained at best. His not appreciating Haarth having clout of such consideration showed. He'd gulped and the nubbin in his throat bobbed up and down. With his difficulty in swallowing, how ill-prepared he appeared in front of him.

Haarth's stare bore into the Kalameshee's forehead. "I'm no fool. I knew when Larza approached me in so forward a manner, she had her own agenda. You should know, I became aware in the beginning that she was of your royal house." A laugh erupted from Haarth striking the tension in the room with the stridency of a whistle. Tierney jumped and grimaced on witnessing the others flinch too. "But we had no intel she was considered a spy. Although spying is what she did for you, is it not?"

"No," the Kalameshee said. He looked Haarth straight in his face then. "My aunt Larza has always gone her own way. When she left Kalamesh, she said she was coming for a visit here in Soonayah to learn different things and a different people. She wasn't sent here as an infiltrator. That you and she found compatibility was of your own accord."

"But the intel she sent wasn't refused, was it? So, essentially you had a plant in place. I knew she reported back to you. When she relayed she was involved with me, your land would have been remiss of its sovereign duty not to question her."

"Then Uncle, you knew she would tell them we were meeting," Tierney interjected.

"No, Tierahna." A twist to his lips acknowledged her lack of faith in him. "Despite what you may think, I don't conduct business abed. Larza had to have meddled with the intention of finding out about our meeting. And come to think of it." He glowered at the Kalameshee as if ready to kill. "If she got my biological sample from—"

The Kalameshee's laughter cut Haarth off. "No! I know what you're thinking and we did ask her to retrieve the sample. All we asked for, and all we got was a tuft of your hair. Nothing more intrusive than that."

"That is intrusive enough! If she'd taken what I thought..." Haarth shook his head. "I wouldn't be blamed for wringing her scrawny little neck!" He glared at the Kalameshee. "Your people have gone through quite a few machinations just to gain audience with a princess with no determining power and her pitifully near excommunicated uncle. What exactly is it you want?"

Chapter 5

Haarth communicated well for someone who never really had been excommunicated. So well, a running stream of his voice blended into the background along with the Kalameshee's, Peetah Pearl's, and crackles from the fire.

All Soonahyins agreed on a few occasions that did require a person to sit. Some were camaraderie, possibly when eating, others were often times traveling, but always for negotiation and interrogation. You could take a person off guard when you made them comfortable. Whichever of the latter two instances this occasion was, wasn't apparent.

A Kalameshee royal in Soonayah.

One who'd snuck in under false pretenses and confessed he; "*Just wanted to be a part of your protocols to widen Soonayah's borders.*" Foreign influence in Soonahyin deliberations? *Yeah, that would go over well.* Tierney mocked. The queen would never allow it, even if she and Haarth ever got her to hold assembly on the issue in the first place. *Bringing a Kalameshee royal along to add to the upheaval in-store is a grand idea.* She sneered. They may as well make themselves comfortable right here at Outliers in the meantime, or else end up as shriveled as aged husks by the time it took to hash this out.

They'd moved their dubious party to sit around the fire. Outliers' attendant's efficiency had produced a whirlwind in activity to refit new terrace doors. They'd stoked the fireplace to an inviting toastiness too. *Quaint and cozy.* One side of Tierney's mouth lifted at the portrayal the scene belied. She sat closest to the fire, Bak'rah at her feet. Haarth sat adjacent to her. In spite of everyone else getting comfortable, Peetah Pearl insisted on taking stance.

She'd stationed herself to the back left-side of Haarth, posted up in attention on the wall. Her frostfire remained over her forearm but lowered, the trigger released and no longer aimed at the Kalmeshee's head. The fit of the frostfire looked to be perfect...and costly. The royal house commissioned only one group in Soonayah custom-fitted frostfires like that. Tierney's eyes met Peetah Pearl's at that moment. *Just who was she?*

From Tierney's periphery, the Kalameshee's glances burned the side of her face. It hardly mattered, she wouldn't be joining their conversation.

To her dismay, the Queen's mantra of their youth had proven steeped in truth. They'd had enough warnings about indulging for long periods in the heat of the flames. She'd lost control of her soul-energy's innervation because of attraction to fire like that of a suicidal lemming. Even now, it magnetized her. Every time she lifted a finger, the flames looked to be flickering in tune with her rhythm. Bak'rah's earlobe flicked in concert with the movement too. She lifted her hand in the act of evincing a sharper wave. *One. Two. Thr...* Her ears pricked up on the words "Tempeh Tu," and her gaze shot across all that coziness toward Peetah Pearl again.

Peetah Pearl abandoned her post against the wall and came and stood before Haarth. "Yes. I released from the Tempeh Tu sometime before you left for the southeastern dominions." Peetah Pearl nodded at Tierney. "Princess Tierahna there was just a young one then. I set out here and started Outliers. Been here ever since."

Haarth was the representative of Soonahyin authority here. Peetah

Pearl squaring her chest attested to her knowledge of his right to question someone who'd inserted themselves in the business of the royal house. In the meantime, her full thinking on the matter was portrayed in her actions. She glanced toward the Kalameshee. "I'm made aware of all who patron Outliers. I noticed the Kalameshee when he came. Kalameshees are rare here, though there have been some who have patronized before. But when you came, Prince Haarth, and the princess, I knew the Kalameshee's presence here at the same time couldn't be a coincidence. So, I watched. And I tracked him when you and the princess retired and he followed, but not through your entrance door."

"You were a Principal?"

Haarth's boring into Peetah Pearl with his inquisition didn't cause her to falter. "Yes. Principal Sect II."

He dissected every detail in her demeanor as he continued to question her. "You reached such ranks and must have been young yourself. Yet, you decided leaving a better option?"

"Yes. Since I wasn't babe enough to understand what the utterance of Tempeh Tu from my parents meant, the Tempeh Tu consumed my everlasting devotion. Once I advanced among the levels in quick form, I felt accomplished. Later, I undertook a lodge out here beyond the density of the populace." Peetah Pearl looked down and went silent. She raised her gaze after a few moments and alighted onto Haarth. Her expression was like an O, mouth opened, eyes rounded. "You recognized me when you first arrived, yet you didn't say anything."

"Yes, I recognized you." Unhindered by her revelation, purpose stamped his every inflection. "And I said nothing." He continued. "So, you released your assignment of the Tempeh Tu, the elite guard of the Keep, and still, you obliged us all by coming to the defense of the Princess."

"Although I did release from service, I will bleed Tempeh Tu all the rest of my days." Peetah Pearl had come to the defense of the princess. But to his defense as well. Yet, when she answered him, tactful truth showed she still retained the diplomacy she'd needed as a matter of course. The life of a Tempeh Tu. "And when I see the Soonahyin Royal House in need and I can help, then I will not hesitate to serve." Haarth studied her, his eyes tracing her carriage. Stout poise. Feet braced apart. Then he nodded and relented his questioning.

All eyes circled onward, inevitably rounding back to the Kalameshee, of course. It was a given that the focus would return to him. He was the only outsider in the room.

He made a face. "My presence here alone brings attention to myself, doesn't it? Leave it to me not to recognize that and proceed with stealth. I may as well have walked straight up to you both and introduced myself as coming here for your meeting."

His feigned humility was cute. Tierney was of a mind the Kalameshee's intentions required some questioning, in spite of the fact that she believed his land was genuine in seeking common ground with theirs. She switched her attention from the fire and looked him straight in the eye. "Might as well have," she said. Then swung away, once again, preoccupying herself with the moves she would make next, musings at the flicks of the flames.

"You're an empath, is that so *Torhvald*?" Haarth asked.

The Kalameshee's gaze flew to Haarth. Haarth's quirk to his lips neither attested to nor denied whether he was being snide, enunciating the Kalameshee's given name that way. His face revealed nothing but blandness. For all the Kalameshee's expertise in avoidance, was he even susceptible to it? The familiarity of someone calling him by his proper name, attempting to finagle him into revealing more? That might be too obvious for him.

However, if anyone could be successful at it, it would be Haarth. Tierney had poured over reports in study of her uncle's methods. They vouched for his ability to pull answers out of anyone. In one of his chancellorship dominions, Oxhild, he encountered every lie offenders dreamed up from those who attempted breaches at the border there. The Kalameshee scrunched his face, studied the floor, and said not one other word. Haarth helped him along. "After you admit your subterfuge has put you in a poor position with us, wouldn't truth be best?"

He shook his head. His lip did that resentful curl again. "My people's abilities are not empathic, no."

"Then how *would* you describe them?" Obviously, Haarth had no intention of letting up until he had satisfaction.

The Kalameshee opened his mouth then closed it again. "I...some of us can see an outline of a being. Their emotions, their connections are encompassed within this..." he gestured with his hands, "sort of profile." They all looked at one another, then turned their confusion back on him. "You may think of this as something like an aura. But for us, it's far more nuanced than that. So, when we attempt to explain it, most don't understand," he ended on a sigh.

He'd given in. Tierney could almost respect him for that. Almost.

"But that doesn't stop you from using this with others, even as it's unbeknownst to them, does it?" Haarth asked.

It'd been obvious, the Kalameshee's stalking of every movement they made. The tracking of them down to the tics of their faces. So, whether it was the Kalameshee's opinion that they would understand it or not, he was due for a full reckoning on his abilities.

Her scowl flayed him in his seat, the Kalameshee had folded his lips and his arms, hesitating for some time and only relented after Tierney'd turned to face him. "We do use it in our everyday lives, yes. It's not an effect that can be turned on and off. But we try to mute it so we're not completely guided by it or it becomes a substitute for all spontaneous interaction, most-especially, in our personal dealings."

He cut his eyes at Tierney first, then slid his gaze to Haarth underneath slit eyelids.

"If you attempt a softening of your details for Larza's sake, it's too late for her. She and I have been at odds as of late. And now, her duplicity has sealed away any possibility of an accord between us. You'd better concern yourself with reading Ana'Kehrah's white-hot profile you're bound to encounter when you present your request for more trade and free travel. The queen is inflexible in her opposition to these causes. She won't take kindly to your coming into our lands without notification under such circumstances, either."

How off-hand Haarth was when the Kalamashee sucked in his breath and stiffened at the announcement. "You will advocate for me an audience before your queen?" the Kalameshee asked. Haarth would if Tierney had anything to do with it. All under the guise of wanting open borders. She'd ease through them once they were more open along with everybody else, being committed to a frozen tundra sanctum against her will nixed. Forever.

"Tierahna and I discussed this and came to some conclusions. Though you did preempt us, this is in line with why we were meeting. And having an emissary who's as well placed as you in the echelons of your land is a gift we can't overlook. Though an audience with Ana'Kehrah is not something we can assure you," Haarth "har-rumphed. We must travel to the dominion of our high seat and reveal our reasons for our own meeting to the queen first. We must explain *ourselves* before promises can be made to you."

* * *

Haarth

"Prince Haarth?"

Haarth lifted a brow, wincing some as he turned from checking his satchel, the title being used landing in a soft spot of denial. "It's been a long time since people called me by that title. Haarth is good enough. I'm nothing more than a chancellor to those of my present region."

"You're still *Prince* to me." Peetah Pearl's stubbornness indicated unabashed deference to him. "I entreat you to allow me as an escort for you and Princess Tierahna."

Both Haarth's eyebrows rose then. He and Tierahna were capable of multifaceted security for themselves. Yet, accompaniment of a Tempeh Tu Principal in close company was a level of security he couldn't scoff at. "I do travel alone sometimes. A whole sect of Tempeh Tu is not always needed in close proximity. You think a day trip to the high seat dominion puts us at risk?"

He glanced toward the Kalameshee where he sat watching Tierahna as she prepared for departure. Intermittently, the princess tended the wolf with some attention while she ignored the Kalameshee. A homespun scene with the fireplace framing them as a backdrop, its crackles and logs adding the perfect touch of domesticity. The setting inspired for Haarth a reverie of a moment like this, with shared glances and soft-spoken words passed between the two instead of contention, except not in the present time. In the future, perhaps? *Utterly unequivocally impossible. Ana'kerah would kill us both, me spectacularly for having allowed Tierahna exposure to the Kalameshee from the beginning.*

Peetah Pearl paused in thought too. "For simple day travel over Soonayah? No." Her eyes followed Haarth's to the interaction between the Kalameshee and the princess. "These circumstances are quite different from an everyday trek. And as you know, you won't make the full distance before night falls again, either."

Haarth nodded his agreement. "Your diligence is most appreciated. But first I must find transport large enough to accommodate us all. Are there any leasings nearby?"

She smiled and as she did, with her high cheekbones and flawless brown skin, the former Tempeh Tu showed herself as quite pretty. "As a matter of fact, *I'm* a leasing steward. The next closest is more than eleven parses away." She laughed and gestured outside the windows. "His exchanges are robbery to travelers in a bind." My largest cruiser snowcraft is ours for the taking. No one has left this eve since the miserable blizzard passed."

Haarth returned her smile. "Then we depart come morn."

Chapter 6

When everyone was head-set on getting to the other side of the land as quickly as possible and animal migrations weren't projected beforehand, it was a good possibility they'd chance across the movement known in Soonayah as the white stampede. And being so lucky, the stampede marched south-westward, the opposite direction. Tierney huffed and leaned more comfortably against some window-glass.

"Just great." Migrating eland beasts bumped along the sides of Peetah Pearl's cruiser snowcraft. *A perfect lapse in judgment to start the venture home. Like I don't have enough to contend with.*

People spoke of waiting days for through passage of the mammoth, silver-haired, cloven-hoofed herd. Their only fortune was in catching the tail end of the drove of hundreds of thousands of animals.

Them inside the cruiser craft weathered collisions with the elands with little fuss. Tierney retracting tables behind the conductor's cab proved stable enough for her and Bak'rah. They alternated between the seats that resulted when she needed them or taking stance far away from Haarth. But mostly away from the Kalameshee. Such as now.

I need no more incitement by either of them after the upheaval I tamped down the prior day. Interaction with the Kalameshee revealed her as beyond excitable. *It's confounding how crafty his personality is.*

Her three older brothers, "*the utter muskox asses,*"—that perfect name for them and their foolishness always occurred to her on the heels of considering what actions she might take against them—conducted themselves as the epitome of obnoxiousness on any given day. Still, she'd developed ways of giving it back on par with them. Yet somehow, her capability of sarcastic composure eluded her when mixing it up with the Kalameshee. The experimentation with what she now thought of as her inter-spection, the Kalameshee's smugness, and her reaction to Haarth's proximity had defeated her usual approach to trying situations. An approach she'd learned at the hands of relentless brothers.

Now was a good time to switch that train of thought. No good would come of letting those nut-buckets rule her brain. They took up enough of a presence in her everyday decisions. She rubbed her forehead to wipe it clear of their oppressive faces, trying to fixate on something else. On purpose, she mumbled, "Uncle sits there like a sentinel," and was determined to grin at his posture as she observed him. "Even when he does sit he can't relax." He had assumed command over their little traveling party. Apparently, he felt compelled to keep vigil over the whole forward compartment of the cruiser craft's surprising trappings.

It was a common cruiser without the equipage enjoyed on royal transports, but its fittings did lend comfort for their journey. A craft that provided reclining and collapsible cushioned seats and a bubble of heat against the elements buffeting the cruiser *should* do. Short of what the royals were used to—individual stance and seating pods for privacy and size double that of cruisers that were part of convoys that carried whole families—were means no one could expect it to compete with.

Haarth's stare from the rear of the Kalameshee, near the bunk built-

ins (delegated for Peetah Pearl and the Kalameshee) *and the sleeping cabins* (reserved for Tierney and Haarth's benefit), *for sure drills a hole into the back of the Kalameshee's head.* Tierney chuckled under her breath, settling herself even comfier in the generosity provided.

At least the Kalameshee's discomfort with Haarth plays out as a time-filler. She had that. And swishing scenery. And the white stampede. They helped her stay preoccupied from the upcoming confrontation with her mother. Somewhat. Though nothing could effectively rid that specter of occupying the back of her head. The jostling of the hovering cruiser by the beasts created a diversion in itself. A monotonous instrumental. An accompaniment to…

"Star up high, oh so grand.

Open the sky, and implant the land.

Blazing to—

Agh!" A collision pitched Tierney off her feet. "Got you, my pup." Bak'rah skidded toward the back, hitting his head. She'd caught him just before he hurt himself against the seats. Outside, an eland beast had veered off at a gallop in-tandem with them, clattering right up on the side of the cruiser. His eyes rolled white in his head and pierced hers with their starkness. The visions and experiences that must have shifted across his corneas, across his consciousness: the clatter of his hooves covering the northern steppes, a roam of the flats for the sweet grasses at the beginning of the season of new life, sallies into the waters of Serene Lake, parses and parses of free running, the wind drying the silver hairs around the eland's mandibles. And now, he foamed at the mouth too.

Poor thing. He was getting ready to speed, but he would never get away.

They hunted him. Crashing against the barrier of the cruiser wouldn't save him. The hovering craft carried wards against anyone or anything that could speed. Nothing could just speed right into a snowcraft.

Faithful Soonahyins were tracking the white stampede, as always they pushed it along a migration path, unfortunately, right toward them. The hunters traveled in working caravans, filling their range coffers alongside professional hunters who kept the stampede's numbers culled by furnishing Soonayah's food stockpiles. No one went hungry in Soonayah. Fatty eland meat and scores of thick meat covered in blubber from the massive lommul fished from the raging seas of Telluric were staples for Soonayah's people. Tierney personally favored flesh from the fat-waddling fowl.

However, none of them needed to concern themselves with roasting these kinds of foodstuffs in the cruiser's roasting jets now. Peetah Pearl had provisions brought for them from Outliers' cookery. The spooked buck whose forward-curving antlers scraped the cruiser's window was under no threat to be butchered and eaten by them. Not this day at least.

A hunter on a snowcat craft rode steer on the buck. *Majesty ropes the brawn of the beast's stature. His sinew will make for bounteous addition to the stockpiles.*

As if a portent of his understanding of what was on the horizon for him, the eland beast jerked his head at the hunter drawing near him. While in the inside, Tierney held on as his big body clamored against the cruiser. His eyes radiated their whiteness, hair whirling long flashing it's silver.

Tierney mouthed at a hunter who threw a hand up at the cruiser for their entanglement in the work of steering the stampede, "It's *your* fault." The hunter's irritation should be directed at herself. Hunters were experts at using special equipment they were provided to direct the stampede. And especially, the predators that fed off stray beasts. There were scores of them that depended on the eland for survival. The predators that tunneled underground, the veryum, the most dangerous of them all. They were supposed to keep them away from populated areas.

As if to soothe against the down on the buck's throat, Tierney pressed her hand along the window where tremors beset her fingers. She surprised herself with her reaction to the eland beast's fate. The glass, cold on her fingertips, represented something elemental. The barrier between safety and freedom. And at what cost, freedom? With his hoof-strikes cracking the ground, his gullet flapping, the long silver hairs hanging refracting light, doom forebode the beast. His sudden disappearance from their side played right into the hunters' trap.

His fate was sealed now.

Her heartbeat raced for him, she imagined in sync with his, galloping, just about bursting from her chest. As the only other animal in Soonayah like its people, eland beasts speeded. For the sake of caution, people with the gift were warned about speeding beyond their vision. *"Never speed into the unknown."* The eland speeded no farther than three hundred paces, about as far as he could see. He landed within a predicted zone where hunters lay in wait and ambushed him.

"Oh, the blood!" Tierney closed her eyes from the butchering. Licitly preparing the meat kept it pure. It'd be dispatched onto larger cold-storage transports that trailed the stampede as a part of the hunting caravan. They'd subsequently supply ranges, hamlets, and enclaves with stores for all their stockpiles en-route. *Unfortunately,* the butchering caused a muster of other beasts nearby, a frenzy that nearly capsized the cruiser.

"We have no choice, we have to remove ourselves from the stampede's path," she told Peetah Pearl. Even more animals could try and hide in the safety of the cruiser now that they were agitated by the buck's killing.

Peetah Pearl directed the cruiser to pull out of the way to the top of a crest. And so, the stampede passed en-masse as hunters carried out a practice that had sustained Soonayah through time. Millions of hoof-claps thundered the ground they hovered over.

Oh, that was why they stampeded too close to populated areas. That same hunter who'd thrown her hand up at them rode too far off from the drove. The hunter was lollygagging. There was no way she could be guiding the stampede and monitoring for predators that far away. How many of the other thousands of hunters on this through passage was just as lackadaisical?

That was another portent too. One the hunter was undoubtedly not aware she was making. And sure enough, *their* snowcraft's hovering was off. The steady monotony of the drove's hooves was counterpointed by a heavier dirge so uneven, the cruiser teetered on its air blowers. Tierney and Haarth caught each other's gazes. *This was bad!* "Peetah Pearl!" She'd already started to reel them away...

Too late!

The negligent hunter was the first to go. *Oh no! She's allowed herself to get to far away from the stampede where she can be picked off too easily!* Tierney hadn't a clue how reaching her hand out for her was supposed to help her when she was so far away from the hunter.

Blocked by a veryum that came up out of no where, the hunter's snowcraft tilted on an axis straight toward the sky and was swallowed underneath the ground. "Watch out! Oh no! Oh no! Somebody help her!" The veryum exploded through the soil, its tusks cracking the hunter's snowcraft, then crunched onto it...and her. "No! I can't watch this!" No one could help the hunter now. One of the many dangers of traveling over Soonahyin land. The predators here took account for people's lives no more than they would the animal population's. Eland beasts tumbled all over the terrain the veryum fragmented too. And other hunters headed straight for the monster.

"We're in their way!" Tierney shouted. Haarth and the Kalameshee jumped up to help Peetah Pearl conduct the cruiser. The hoverer was so volatile they might roll if they didn't get it stabilized.

The veryum would use the crest they were on to escape. Veryum sought dense-packed ground where people couldn't follow or use their shock-rods through whenever there was a threat. The flesh-eating behemoth reached them. Tunneling beneath the crest, the veryum traveled too fast for stability and disintegrated the soil underneath them. It rose after the vibration of the cruiser craft startled it and toppled them haphazardly over its back. Their attempt at careening the cruiser away at the same time sent them cartwheeling over the snow, knocking them all about inside, with the intent of knocking them clear of their senses it seemed too. Them sitting on the crest, out of the way hadn't kept them safe. Anybody in the vicinity was at risk when the hunters weren't up to the carrying out their duties.

They crashed upside down, and just Haarth was left with *enough* of his senses to fly from the cruiser.

There was a difference in viewing the world from the bottom up. Through the glass out into the snow caused the landscape to appear askew and yet right somehow, tilted to let the elands run free into the sky. Upside down, mind you. There was still that. Tierney frowned, a sense of the apropos hitting a spot inside tender with the observation. *Everything wrong but right. Suits my life just about now.* The rest of them scrambled after Haarth...eventually, after they took quite a bit of time to find which way was up.

Once they were out in the cold and the snow, Tierney shook her head against a ringing inside. The elands' thundering stunned her poor brain ever more. She righted herself when the ground stopped its weeble-wobbling, speeding as quick as she could to a scene that was already too far gone.

The hunters had the veryum trapped and spiked it with their shock-rods. "Leave it be! You're going to kill i...!"

The mammoth worm undulated, frenzied. All its legs spasmed, then it went still. "No! That's such a waste! It'd only been trying to survive!"

While they studied the the veryum that was so large their party and twenty or so hunters didn't have the numbers to surround it completely, one of the hunters contacted the animal patrol who would come and harvest the remains for various uses in Soonayah's medical, chemical and textile industries. Other industries too—too numerous to name.

A veryum carcass had many many benefits. Thousands really which was why Soonayah tracked them, and if any did die naturally, the patrol would find them as fast as it could and determine if their remains could be harvest usually. And then another hunter who seemed to be in charge of this lax lot, could be heard reporting the incident to some faceless authority over her armset. Word of this incident was sure to get back to the queen now. "That tops it all," Tierney grunted. "I'll probably be hearing directly from her soon."

After quite some time later, other hunters-even more numerous in the numbers-walked in a slow processional with somber faces, like they'd received some silent command to come and pay their respects. They gathered the remains of their mutilated member—the negligent hunter—her arm, her head... Her torso? They'd gut the veryum and retrieve *it*. Spend days preparing her body, chiseling it up for carriage to her family. Starting the protocols for a requiem. The consecration of feeding her body as a supplement, her soul-energy as a sustenance to the Soonahyin soil.

Soonahyins didn't like waste. A people who'd had to forge a path in their frozen land couldn't afford to. Now, only a reduced team of hunters that we're left could continue to track the stampede. A relief for them wouldn't be timely yet. All because that hunter was lax. A person no less valuable all the same—the practiced tracker and Tellurician soul now gone. No matter that the hunter had some responsibility for the incident, Tierney shed tears for her and her family. "What a cataclysmic tragedy this was." Soonayah went out of it's way with security and precautions taught to everyone to avoid just this kind of thing. And still, the hunter had been killed. This was a testament to how dangerous things could be and how they could never take their security for granted here. She bowed her head for a few moments lost in sorrow for the poor soul.

After a while, Peetah Pearl used a remote to gyroscope the cruiser upright. And they all crawled back into the chaos that had been made of it.

Chapter 7

Once the cruiser was put back together enough to start its rush by again, Tierney sucked at the cool crispness synonymous with Soonahyin air. She filled her lungs with as much as they could hold after that catastrophe. Such a rarity it was, observing her surroundings while someone else did the conducting. That is, once she could calm herself some and fixate on people active in their home dominions.

Some repaired roofs of their homesteads, shoring up any gapes around the prerequisite chimneys. They also checked for cracks in the stone of their domes, the blasted blizzard having done untold damage upturning the length of the land.

People gathered excess snow at the edges of their enclaves and homesteads too. Those homesteads as big as Outliers, four or five generations would be housed inside. Meanwhile, youth from the enclaves delighted in pile-ons atop the snow. They flattened the mounds again, proving their parents' work moot. A sigh deflated all the air out of Tierney's chest, the tension still there, her lips quirked upward nonetheless.

People's interactions were so fascinating. Scouring through the woods, beyond the roads at the goings-on in the enclaves, became a game for herself. One of escapism from the animal attacks, the needless death of witless hunters...and oh yes, from a mother who'd control her down to her coping mechanisms if she could. *Can't ever forget that.*

Diverting herself from too much going on inside her mind, she intentionally eyed roofs of the homesteads made of chornyne stone tiles. They sloped steep angles. She blinked, refocusing several times at the light glaring through the clear tiles once eve fell. *There was one!* She persisted until she found the odd cylinder-designed homesteads made of the rich ferber wood so prevalent of Soonayah amidst the thousands of circular-constructed stone masonry. Both were domes designed not to resist air heated inside from bodies and fires and heating mechanisms. But ferber wood trees couched together in their growth, almost as if they knew they'd thrive with more impact on everything around them together. That made them hard to fell and rare and exorbitant building material. *And so easy to spot in my need for distraction.*

Her breath fogged the glass framing the panorama around her. How she missed this. Journeying alone required her to be absorbed in road signage. Her *own* security from the veryum and other threats were paramount with only Bak'rah for company. In royal transports, she was always in the company of her family and attendants. Here, Tierney had all manner of leeway to reacquaint herself with her land: Peetah Pearl conducted the cruiser, the Kalameshee squirmed in his seat, catching Haarth's eye every once and a while, and Haarth pinned him where he sat anytime he glanced back at him.

She chuckled at them. How her brothers would laugh at a Kalameshee so uncomfortable with Haarth, he couldn't use his abilities to stalk those around him. *Too bad for him.*

Otherwise, he'd have the time to study all the snowcrafts they came across. Unlike theirs, most other glass-topped transports could be peered into. Haarth had thought of added security for them. He had the entirety of *their* top turned opaque. They had sight of everything outside of the cruiser, but no one outside could peer in. Tierney hadn't argued. Turning the top opaque helped alleviate the need for constant surveillance while they journeyed back to the Keep. And if it afforded her a curiosity into the lives of people whose snowcrafts revealed themselves to her, then that was a bonus. *All the better for time-filling.*

Viewing young ones battling over seats while their elders engaged in the banality of daily life, she gasped aloud. *Someone forgot she would be seen as the sky issues in its darkness.* Her eyes widened as well at the naked woman bared by the portion of her glass top that hadn't been dimmed over her cabin as she slept. Soonahyins tended to be secure in their natural forms, and so the woman had probably not given a thought to being seen.

They traveled countless sights of Soonahyin hills and planes; many many enclaves buried within the trees of all the dominions they pressed through, lights from the homesteads pinpointing the activity of the people in them, stretches of snow so far out they dropped off the sides of the planet, snow-draped mountains edging the sky, woodlands stripped bare for the coming season, and some still flourishing laden with the most obstinate flora and the like in snow too weighing their branches. And they stopped once for power in an enclave called Halliope. Other people conducted their hovering snowcrafts on by, barely noticing them. Some stopped and powered up too. Tierney got out and stretched her legs and let Bak'rah relieve himself in a brisk walk, observing as people scampered back and forth wrapped in their furs in the cold.

Roasted fowl carried on the air from a dome building that had a turnstile of visitors. They carried packages under their arms that leaked the aroma. The busiest though was a stone dome with people seen through the windows raising their mugs as they stood around its fireplaces. Clusters of domed buildings ranged up to the end of the enclave and slanted downward to its entrance to temper creating the wind tunnels Soonayah's climate was prime for.

The day's sun had waned. Peetah Pearl's conducting the transport had them making good headway. After getting back on the road and going quite some distance, Haarth directed her to veer off deep into the woods.

Tierney called out to him, "Why are we detouring from the thoroughfare? From all the roads, Uncle? We're not on any course now." Though roads in Soonayah weren't physically traveled upon because of the probability of snow in all seasons, snowcrafts were attracted to them. As long as snowcrafts were close, there was connection. They received feedback, travel info, and even colloquial event info from the roads which were used for course selection. It was just too bad they'd traveled too far inward by the time they'd been alerted about the white stampede.

Haarth walked to the front and stood side by side with Peetah Pearl. He instructed her to input an up-sweeping path. "I saw an oddly lit fire here when I made my way to Outliers. I tracked back as far as I could risk when you didn't get there on time. But even on my snowcat, I couldn't come back far enough to investigate before I had to get back to you."

"Oh. That's why you weren't there when I arrived." It was a good thing he'd been on his snowcat when she was on foot, or he'd have had her waiting until the next day. "What's so unusual about a fire here that it would cause you a trek back this far? There are those who do still camp in the woods, you didn't know?" Many at the Keep delighted in camping in snowy woods as if it were the greatest highlight of all time.

Haarth answered, "Yes, Tierahna. I remember quite well about regular life, so I do know that." She'd heard he was known to enjoy the occasional night away from his responsibilities, camping beneath the stars too. It was said that was how he cleared his head when time allowed. "I saw this fire, but it was its color that got my attention.

It flamed a strange pinkish color." His lips turned down around the edges, implied he realized how his own description must sound.

Pinkish color? Peetah Pearl looked at him with her forehead wrinkled. Tierney paused in brushing Bak'rah's fur. The Kalameshee walked to the head of the cruiser and joined the other two. They all peered out the window trying for a glimpse at this fire. Haarth pointed to the right. "There! See there, in the distance?" Peetah Pearl squinted for confirmation and set the cruiser in the direction of Haarth's pointing.

Now that they hovered over the rubble littering a forest floor instead of the road, the cruiser jerked and swayed. This was no snowcat. The cruiser made a cumbersome job of traversing the terrain. Everyone held on as they plied their way upward.

Tierney surrounded Bak'rah's heat. "Can't let you go skidding across the floor again." *Oh wow. How odd.* The closer they got, they saw that there *was* a fire burning with a weird pink tint. Someone moved in and out of the light of the fire too. Glare escaping the cruiser was already dimmed, nevertheless, they jolted to a stop some ways beyond the person's camp.

Why would Haarth be so concerned about this? Tierney remained in her seat. She grabbed Haarth's arm as he went past after donning his cloak. "Uncle, why should we investigate such a matter when we don't know what we may come across? Let's contact a guard brigade while we move on. We have pressing issues."

It had taken spans of time for the issue she wanted to be this prevalent. Cross-border travel. The perfect cover. She *did* believe in it. Ancient prejudices were why the lands were so separated. Base, narrow-mindedness kept Tellurians from learning about each other. She scoffed. *How appropriate that helping to break the back of stupidity will net me my freedom too.* She never would have committed to a forbidden meeting with an excommunicated uncle, no matter how she complained to him about the changes needed in their sovereignty.

Not if she hadn't overheard her mother talking to her companion about herself.

"Why does Tierahna have this compulsion to rock her body and tap her feet that way? Is she manic, do you think? I believe she should be sent off to the frozen tundra sanctum and soon. She needs help."

"You believe it's that serious?" her companion had asked.

"It may be. She even does it when she's not aware sometimes. It has become like a tic she can't control. With everything she has happening now, the sanctum may be where its best for her."

The queen believed Tierney's behavior was unstable.

If only she knew about my accompanying sing-songs along with my need for rhythm in my most nervous urges. Aching from all the trials this journey had wrought so far, Tierney's shoulders slumped. And they weren't even nearly home. So what if she liked to rock a bit and tap her foot. She wasn't harming anybody. The borders must open to Soonahyins traveling. She was leaving the Keep come what may, out of her mother's shadow. *And all the better I will be for claiming my own life.*

Haarth's diligence, though conscientious, was a delay. Now that her agenda was possibly happening, the confrontation with the queen was riding on her. *It was well past time for it.* Besides, the risk to their security was stupid to take on. Hadn't they encountered enough on this trip already? A mal-funtioning snowcat in a blizzard, a rabid wolf, ravening veryum, and a gate-crashing Kalameshee wasn't enough?

"There aren't any divisions close enough, Tierahna. And those closest shouldn't be pulled away from their assignments. I'm here. I can determine what this anomaly is. You know as I do, no one camps this close to the Okehfey mountains because of the howling winds trapped here," Haarth said, his plans determinedly marching toward whatever there was to discover out there in that snow and the cold and said blistering winds. "Anyone choosing to settle this far up the base must do so with calculation." As he slipped Tierney's hand from him, he petted her arm. "It's altogether well, Tierahna. You wait here and we'll tell you what's happened when we get back."

Tierney stood and just missed bumping into Haarth's chin right as he moved out of the way. She'd almost caused him to bite his own tongue. The corners of her mouth lifted at the thought. Haarth smirked, shaking his head at her attitude. Off to the side, the Kalameshee chuckled on witnessing their interaction. She cut off Harrth's procession and huffed from the exit before them both.

Snow, snow, and more snow. Crunching onto the ground elicited Tierney's flex of her toes within her wolvien boots again. This would be a true test of their shukka-warming insulation. Her earlier trudge through the snow couldn't have done them any good. Were they still intact after the muck had gotten inside? The mechanism kicked on as soon as her toes stiffened from the chill. *The little buggers were sturdy.*

Wolvien carried a charged-static current used for suction climbing, enhanced like pretty much everything in Soonayah was. At their skinning, furriers tapped and harnessed the animal's charged static. Their temperamental mating and long hibernation gave them restrictive reproduction habits. They were only allowed to be hunted in limited numbers. Which made the boots a highly prized luxury she would hate to replace.

She grinned. *Much appreciations to the wonders of umbereen. I won't be going back on the waiting list for another pair.*

Haarth snapped his fingers in front of her face. Tierney, "Harrumph." *Altogether well with your impatience, Uncle, because we shouldn't be out here anyway.*

Gesturing everyone in different directions around the person at the fire, the Kalameshee, he ordered to a path to his left. Constant line of his sight. As far as trust was concerned, they had none for him. They all skulked off behind the underbrush. Peetah Pearl again had her frostfire pulled-to-fire over her forearm. The Kalameshee reached behind his back, from his pouch, he produced a hand-size hilt from a scabbard. The contraption wound an extension of its metal around his hand. While they watched, it clicked into place and flung another lit, rapier-size, metal piece outward. The hilt probably only opened to his touch.

Haarth gave the Kalameshee's weapon quite some consideration as he and Tierney moved out, hands raised at the ready. Bak'rah lowered his head in a prowl, of course, stalking at Tierney's side.

Once they were in position with the person at the fire surrounded, the conundrum became trying not to be heard. Tierney struggled as her chest burned with the effort of keeping the harshness of her breath from the air. She cinched the snood of her cloak over her face against the winds found further up the base of the Okehfey mountains. Only her eyes remained exposed so she could see while snow whipped at her lashes. Unfolding goggles attached to the inside lip of her snood, she covered them too. *Cold. Cold. Cold. Cold. It cuts against the skin like a knife up here.* It was so cold, she would include her eyes behind the warmth of her snood if she could get away with being blinded.

The air-frost could literally be seen. When Peetah Pearl had engaged the trigger to-fire on her frostfire, the air-frost had been a frieze on the air that swooped its way into the frostfire's pressurized pelletizer.

Your heat is my savior my pup. Crouched in the snow, Bak'rah came close to her. He nuzzled her and sought to provide her some comfort, and she returned the favor. She encircled his torso and palmed his chest and whispered to him, "Bak'rah, see." Her constant. Attuned as he was to her soul-energy, he used his oculusion as soon as they touched. Training her eyes forward, she arched away from the flash of his coat, and her vision joined his on an instant.

The campsite shone through a lens of illumination in the darkness, which highlighted every object they scanned. The camper at the fire had set camp in a copse of Telluric's tallest trees. The grouping of ferber trees was rooted in the clearing they all took cover in the bushes around. Straight shoots as they were from the ground until they grew their prickled blue leaves at their crown, fifty fathoms beyond all the other trees. One of very few trees that kept their foliage through the brittleness of the season of long dark nights. Their foliage-free trunks offered Bak'rah's oculusion an uninterrupted path over the campsite.

A covered fire was being tended to by the camper from the opposite side. The person's illumination glowed yellow, alluding to them being as benign a presence as Haarth and the Kalamashee. Tierney spotted those two too, glowing just as yellow, hiding behind bushes on the other side of the camp. *This camper is harmless.*

Bak'rah didn't even growl as she lifted from him and readied for the confrontation. *What are we doing out here?*

At that precise moment, a patch of air behind where Haarth and the Kalameshee hid blurred within her vision. Her eyes fogged. *Open space between the trees looks like...static?* She snatched her hand from Bak'rah to end her connection to his oculusion. "What was that?

Haarth showed himself first. Speeding. He reappeared at once in the middle of the campsite. Then everyone else crashed from the surrounding underbrush and revealed themselves too. The camper shrieked and staggered backward, and ended up tumbling over the fire, squealing at contact with the flames. A log fell and upended the contraption the person had fashioned to protect the fire from the winds. Pink sparks and pink-fired logs pitched everywhere. The person contorted into a perfect ball shape and rolled unnaturally fast over the fire. So fast, serious injury might just have been avoided.

Haarth chased after—a leap of the fire as the person completed the roll, menacing right where the camper righted. The person shrank back as close to the fire as possible without burning. "What reason do you have for your trespass here?" Haarth shouted within striking distance, looming right over-top of the camper.

Look at him. He might kill the camper before he gets the chance to get any answers.

"I'm not trespassing. I came through your border checkpoint. They approved me registry as a foreign visitor." A metallic twang rang from the voice, true as a bell, muffled some from the person being curled in on them self away from Haarth's menace.

"Uncle! Step back so you can hear the answers!" Tierney barked at him when it looked as if he would uncoil the person with his own hands.

Haarth shifted to one side by no more than a few paces. "Yet you hide out here in the Wilds of Okehfey away from any of the populace. Stand up so we can see you," he ordered.

Upon rising, the camper's height was no different than anyone else's. But a head so bald it appeared shiny drew first attention, except for a patch of blunt, blue-black hair standing on end at the crown shot through with a clamp. *Like a stalk, it stands.* And then came that shimmery skin. Tierney swore it gleamed pale pink or maybe deep blush better described its sheen. "I'm the first Lorgren to visit your land and knew your people wouldn't be used to my kind. I came and regrouped here when my transport conked out. After I repair my transport, I intended to continue my journey to the dominion of your high seat."

To Dameerh?

Haarth lurched toward the camper again. Recoil was the response he got. No aggression at all. "Uncle! Can't you see he's no warrior? Bak'rah found no hint of aggression. No evil intent anywhere near him. Give him space so he won't feel frightened of you. But I must tell you—there was an uhm...we *did* see something out there—"

"She. I am female." Limpid eyes like amethyst gawped at Tierney.

Pride had imbued that clang in the robotic voice as she'd said she was female, like being female was something exceptional. "Her. Give *her* room to speak, Uncle."

"And though I'm no warrior. I haven't had need to use them yet, but I am equipped with defenses." The upright hair bobbed as she talked.

How frightened she must be. To thwart them of any attack they might make, she gave up information she shouldn't. Really, they were strangers to her. *Aggressive ones at that, with Uncle trying to kill her and all.* "It's to your best discretion not to warn people you haven't used your defenses before. Or really that you have any defenses at all. Let them be a surprise to whoever you need to use them on."

Geez, those eyes. Under lifted eyebrows, they beamed and blinked at Tierney's gumption to offer her advice. Haarth grunted. "Tierahna, we know nothing of these Lorgren people's motivations for sending her here. And she said she was headed to Dameerh. Maybe her defenses are meant to be used there."

"*We* know them, Uncle. We have all learned of them in our lessons before. Though I never thought I'd see a Lorgren in *our* land. They never travel this far, and they *do not war*. They've never had a war in their history."

The Kalameshee stepped forward from the shadows almost as if an afterthought, just so he could back Tierney up and said, "I've encountered them before too. We have more interaction with them because their land shares a border with Kalamesh. Even though it's all canyon, we send flying razors back and forth. Tierahna is right. They're not a warring people." He caught Tierney's eyes and quirked his mouth up in reassurance.

Haarth threw his hands up. "So, our borders have more free travel than we thought. We have a Kalameshee coming as he sees fit and a Lorgren who has no need of even being questioned."

Tierney rolled her eyes from Haarth back toward the Lorgren, thinking. She was aware most considered her features striking. Honestly, her mother and sister's looks outshone hers by fathoms, but then everyone knew her as an intellectual too. The queen *was* her mother, after all. Beauty was a tool that could be used like any other perception people had about a person. Now, she needed to assuage the Lorgren from her fear. She maneuvered between Haarth and the Lorgren, then shifted her snood back so the Lorgren could see the features others thought so appealing. And she softened them with a smile. She softened her voice too and spoke to her in a tone she used on her sister when she wanted her nice and sweet. "Do you have a name?"

The Lorgren's shoulders went back, her chest puffed out. She announced, "I am Mlai."

"Mi...Mil-lai." Tricky. It would take some repetition to get it right. Where was this transport the Lorgren mentioned? She looked around. "My snowcat craft died a little time ago too, Mil-lai. What about your transport? Are you capable of carrying out its repair yourself?"

"A burner coil within the motor unit malfunctioned. I tried moving similar pieces from other compartments to replace it, but it didn't work. I fear I must brave one of your markets for a close facsimile replacement." Mlai's eyes widened on that suggestion. Did she fear traveling within the heart of their populace so? Then why did she come here?

Tierney nodded, then gestured to the fire Mlai had set camp around. "This fire is fascinating. I've never witnessed a fire burn with such color. What causes the...pinkness?" Tierney so soothed the Lorgren as she spoke, Mlai didn't balk when Tierney came nearer to her.

The Lorgren led her to her transport. It was hidden behind bushes with flora draped over it. She even allowed Bak'rah close enough to sniff her hand. She pulled some of the bushes away and pointed to the back of her transport that sported a lid still flapped open. "I reserviced bunting used as support for some of my transport's infrastructure. The bunting touches a lot of things inside the transport and some of the lubrication which is used for all our mechanics was transferred. The bunting is what turns the fire's color so. As you can see, our skin is a similar color because of the same lubrication."

Now that was surprising. No one spoke, fascinated into silence by Mlai's explanation. "All Lorgrens are part cybernetic with partial bio-mechanical anatomy. You must've noticed that my voice box is mechanical. So are varied other parts of my body. This is how we're made."

"How you're made is quite phenomenal, with that skin of yours gleaming in the starlight. I learned the Lorgren had part biological and part robotic anatomies in my lessons as wel—"

"Not robotics, bio-mechanics." Mlai's voice stiffened toward Tierney for the first time. "Our cybernetics work in tandem with our anatomies...most of the time anyway." And that fast, the stiffness was gone. But the Lorgren's attempt to share an inside joke with Tierney fell flat. Her bark of laughter was her own.

Tierney smiled at the remark, howbeit she had no idea what the Lorgren found funny. "Of course, bio-mechanical. So, Mil-lai, is your transport able to raise power?"

"Yes!" She said, her face fell as she continued. "But it will only fly so far before all forward momentum is cut. I banked it before it crashed several times on attempting to fly."

"Your transport is a flying apparatus?" Tierney asked. Mlai nodded. "Then perhaps we should offer a tow to the nearest market that will possibly have the equipment you need."

Mlai grinned as a gruffle from Haarth rumbled from the side. She looked from Haarth to Tierney and back again, then decided to step closer to Tierney. "Tier-rah-na? That would be most magnanimous of you. I have position to offer recompense for your help."

Everyone jumped, shouting, "Agh! What!" partially from a scream from Mlai right then, as much as from a shuffle in the bushes.

One moment they all stood there unthreatened and the next, Haarth was bellowing out orders to everyone. He and the Kalameshee sprinted toward the sight of movement slicing through the trees. Bak'rah started running too, not able to sense whatever it was and chased after Haarth and the Kalameshee. Tierney and Peetah Pearl shot out right behind them.

Leaves flew from the trees. Bushes split in two. Snow was mowed into the air. For all that, the *cause* of the effects on the environment was still hidden. Then Tierney stopped cold in the middle of the woods. "The air!"

That thing she'd seen with Bak'rah's oculusion blurred in her vision like it did before. Pressing the hem of her sleeve three times, she directed light from her armset and her snood into the wind. Her shoulder torchlights bounced off something solid too. Even in the dark, static differentiated the purple skies of night from one spot of open space. She blinked and blinked. It was there. The apparition made an intentional course correction. It circled back on itself toward the camp. "We left the Lorgren alone!"

Tierney ran so fast in its wake, her speeding was triggered sooner than she'd ever provoked it before. *Swish! Swish! Swishing* sounded from her sides and her rear, alerting her the others followed her lead. The Lorgren squealed again. "Agh! It has me!" Ahead of them reaching her, she rolled in that ball shape again, erratically this time, entangled with *the air?*

"Static rolls inside the ball with her!"

Like a lion in the wind, the Kalameshee bolted to Mlai first, anticipating them all, he'd outstripped everyone who speeded. He dove on top of the scatter-shot ball. Tierney entered the fray and latched onto the...*empty space with substance?* While Bak'rah yipped and tried to find his way in.

Whatever she was grabbing slithered. Well, maybe not slithered, but it moved like skin unattached to bone. Her clutching sank her nails into something corporeal, yet couldn't be seen. How was that possible? Haarth stomped its wriggling shape wrapped around Mlai and bound in a hold by the Kalameshee and Tierney.

The Kalameshee continued to drag Mlai and Tierney's clawing in the tussle with it too. Tierney pulsed it, and a burn flared through the nothingness in a contained explosion that gave the Kalameshee the chance to drag it from the crush. He flung what could only be called a visual manifestation of air from the Lorgren into open space. Peetah Pearl shot it with her frostfire. The static froze mid-frenzy and then shattered to the ground. As soon as they walked up to where it'd landed with Bak'rah sniffing at it, the static melted away.

With heaving breaths, they all looked at the Lorgren lying where they'd left her. "What fiendishness have you attracted and brought stalking you into our land?" Haarth asked aloud what everyone else was thinking.

There was no choice but to take her with them now. She couldn't be left here alone.

Chapter 8

H *aarth*

Through the window, the roads like serpents unwinding woke from their slumber. Every hundred parses or so, people were hitched to their sides and accessed excess burn-off for energy. Soonahyins not wasting anything used the energy to help heat caravans camped in lay-bys for the night to reserve their stocked power stores. *Beautiful when you looked at it in an abstract kind of way. Remove the practical applications of it all to just appreciate the ethos.* Free energy everywhere in Soonyah to keep the citizenry from freezing to death. Heated buildings left opened, unguarded for those who may need a lay-by. Food stores for anyone needing food. Habits of survival for people in the cold.

Their cruiser's hovering activated the roads to come online as a series of colors, signals, and borders in the dark. For their benefit, paces ahead, light led the way. People in the lay-by caravan camps were reflected in the light visiting from one cruiser to another, mixing over shared bonfires. Chornyne stone roofs in enclaves off a ways twinkled their light from between the trees. Villages and enclaves ranged right along the sides of the roads too. The effects resulted in momentary confusion for anyone never exposed to the culture before.

Haarth paid methodical attention to guides on the road. He called it *"busy work"* when he needed his mind engaged.

Surely, they think I'm angry now.

Stone possessed more pliability than his features did. Two seats to the rear of the Lorgren, his demeanor chilled the inside of the cruiser. *Good.* The presumptuous Tierahna, the Kalameshee who he had to keep an eye on constantly, and now the Lorgren could use the cool-down. Guarding them was done better when they were all quiet and quiescent.

In the course of a life, the wise learned not to be at the mercy of highs and lows in emotions when things were only mildly stressful. Vagaries in the royal environment had seen to teaching him that. His parents were long gone, but only after the one person who he'd had the most in common with, his brother had died. Not to mention, his love was denied him. A sly grimace to himself concealed that no anger tinged his temperament at all. These were easy times in comparison. Recent events knocked around his brain and clouded his vision as he uploaded relays from the road to the optiglass window next to him for details of any true issues while his thoughts were otherwise occupied. The transmission titled: **Removal of Trees by Mechanized Skidders,** blurred after reading about the issue for the twelfth time.

It was unfortunate the trees were immature. The blizzard had felled ferber trees more than any other kind. *No worry about those in any event.* Ferber wood commanded high value in Soonayah. As long as there were people like Tierahna's youngest brother, Ad'rihl who favored the trees like pets, they would be salvaged down to their splinters.

Once, Haarth heard tell that Ad'rihl made Tierahna avow to secrecy. Alas, she should have known better than to agree. *Especially with Ad'rihl as the party plotting the terms.* He'd admitted that a recent flight above the highest of ferber trees had lulled him into their majesty. As soon as she'd heard the reason for the pact, she'd wanted to renege.

Their mother *should* have been told, but she *did* tell Lu'nil. Haarth scratched his jaw. Which was how he'd come by the information. He'd been having misgivings about the trees for some time now too.

Ad'rihl swore the ferber's blue-blanketing depths had beckoned him in. They'd enraptured him into drifting and the drag of their thistles against his flying-razor's undercarriage was the merciful fate that shook him conscious.

And still, he loved the cussed trees. Haarth shook his head. Their mother had cursed Ad'rihl's pursuit of his pilot levels since the day he began them. Rightfully so. It granted him adventures of the skies of Soonayah most never experienced, however, his risk-taking was a scourge on Ana'kerah.

Haarth grunted with his thoughts tipping toward the queen. *Those were best left alone.* And he switched to the cruiser's progress lit by refraction from the road. Magnetic-floating lights above the roads chased back the darkness around them and threw the cruiser's shadow along the snow. They towed shadows of Haarth's snowcat craft and the Kalameshee and the Lorgren's transports too. Which gave rise to Tierney wheedling at him. "You see it too, Uncle? Our shadows like a convoy of Cordalai going to festival?"

"Uhm...hm," was the best response that could be pulled from him.

The Lorgren had no problem taking up Tierney's peace offering. *She was quite the chatterer,* he'd come to see. "The Cordalai is the collection of Soonahyin clans indigenous to its frozen tundra," she said. Haarth grunted aloud this time. He'd been enjoying the quiet. Now he wished he'd given a more thorough response to forego the whole monologue he was sure the Lorgren had in-store to regal them with. "They're known for their oscillating hamlets that move according to informed Starfall landings and the change in seasons. They're also known for their mining and multitudes of cottage industries." As if expecting a reward for her knowledge, the Lorgren toadied a smile about the cruiser at its occupants.

To the Soonahyin's the information was commonplace. The Kalameshee's jaw dropped open. He looked from Haarth to Tierahna. "There are people who live out there?"

Tierahna glowered at him and said pretty much the first words she'd spoken to him that day. "Of course, it's colder on the frozen tundra, but Soonahyins are acclimated for the cold. Every Soonahyin visits their family clans and stays for a time on the frozen tundra."

Uh oh! What was that about? Overly sensitive much? Hmm...That was curious. Would he have even more explaining to do to Ana'kerah when he finally got them to the Keep? Haarth had caught Tierahna's eyes trailing over the Kalameshee's physique earlier. Was her outward aversion to him a defense mechanism and she didn't understand why she might need one? And the Kalameshee was the unwitting clod pole? *Not likely.* A Kalameshee could never safely be considered unwitting in any respect. Did he manipulate Tierahna's interest in him then? Haarth's eyes narrowed on the two of them. Now that the Kalameshee had gotten her attention, he rushed her with questions. "But how can they know where asteroids will land?"

Tierahna's lip curled and she barely looked at him a second time. "Did you seek to learn nothing of us? Yet you volunteered yourself as emissary to come here." She pointedly turned away.

Haarth wouldn't have believed it if he wasn't seeing it for himself. So he was right. *Unfortunately, absolutely right!* This type of play, back and forth between man and woman had existed since time memorial. She was the epitome of a woman attracted against her will. He took pity on the Kalameshee, but he'd only get answers to his questions from *him.* It looked like he'd have to give Tierahna a few words of warning later. The Kalameshee had come here under cunning circumstances. Probably not the best person to think of having relations with. "The Astrophysicist Sect, who are a part of our

Science Ministry, they detect the exact trajectory of Starfall landings. The asteroids are calibrated and their size perfectly reduced for entry. Then they're directed to where they're most needed on Soonahyin lands," Haarth told him.

"That's astonishing. Starfalls must cause untold damage though. Why not destroy the asteroids that make it to the alluvial shield like all other lands on Telluric do?"

Because the alluvial shield that surrounds all of Telluric for its protection is perfect to be manipulated for our Starfalls, Haarth thought. *Because it suits us.* He smirked. Soonayah would use whatever was needed to provide the best possible outcomes for its people.

The Kalameshee asked, "And you inform the Cor-da-lai where not to camp, but you allow them to remain out on the frozen tundra? Isn't it simpler to ban them from it?" The Kalameshee's questions were the normal ones for Soonahyins too. The smallest of them still at their mother's knee. How incomprehensible the frozen tundra supporting a population must seem to the non-Soonahyin mind.

"The Cordalai don't camp," the *Lorgren* answered him. She knew enough, it seemed, to answer the Kalameshee's questions in-depth. "They're more than one thousand different sects of clans that move whole hamlets according to Starfall predictions."

When Tierahna swiveled in her seat, Haarth snorted. He'd known she would relent to the Kalameshee's curiosity. That was her nature. She'd revel in his discoveries in their land. "All Soonahyins are informed of Starfalls. We're taught about them in lessons when we're young," Tiernahna said. "In youth, some people are inclined to learn to calculate Starfalls for themselves. They're the ones who usually go to the Ministry of Science. And nearly all Soonahyins sojourn to live amongst the stars with the Cordalai clans at least once in their lives. It's a rite of passage. So yes, the Cordalai are informed of Starfalls. But any Cordalai you find can calculate them as well as any minister of science." Even in her youth, Haarth had known Tierahna not to tolerate ignorance well. She'd debated adults who hadn't been willing to learn new ways, and she treated the Kalameshee to the same derision. "We allow some asteroids to land because it benefits the land. We're good at this. We manipulate our portion of the alluvial shield just as we need to. Besides, the land repairs itself. And why do you think we haven't slaughtered all those veryum?"

"Veryum? That creature with the million crawling legs that just nearly killed us? You keep them on purpose?" The one thing the Kalameshee *did* understand was Soonayah's biggest menace. Haarth chuckled.

"Yes." Tierahna chuckled at his wide-eyed question too. "Secretions from those *"million crawling legs"*—as you call them—help repair the land too. Soonayah is selective in all that it does. But no hunter would get caught tracking the white stampede without training on repelling those predators. The veryum enjoy the flesh of people as much as they do eland meat." She used that wheedling voice again, this time she directed it at the Kalameshee. "I'm sure Kalameshee flesh would be a new delicacy for them."

The Kalameshee's gazed drifted beyond their conversation in the cruiser, beyond the closest landscape. His eyes searched the countryside as if he pictured the life in a Cordalai hamlet. "But what about people getting hurt out there?"

"There are medics and medical facilities amongst every clan. Infirmaries at every bay. People aren't *allowed* to live on the frozen tundra, it's their right. The Cordalai are the ones who've kept the tradition of living amongst the falling stars as all Soonahyins once did. After they grow up in their enclaves, some go live their whole lives out on the frozen tundra. Who are we to dictate to our people what they must do?" Tierahna's description of the hamlets *lingered* over the ways of the Cordalai, her words caressed the practices of the people as if she missed the airs of the frozen tundra.

"Tier-ah-na?" The Lorgren's eyes pasted onto her.

"Yes, Mlai." Tierahna worked her mouth, concentrating on enunciating the Lorgren's name just right.

The Lorgren tipped to the edge of her seat. The points of her fingers indented the molded cork seat-backing in front of her. "Will the market to which you're escorting me have an infirmary?"

"Uh…I'm most regretful, Mlai. Tems enclave?" Tierahna looked to the cruiser's cab. Peetah Pearl nodded back at her. "Tems enclave—where we're taking you is one of few enclaves that don't have its own infirmary." The Lorgren lowered her eyes to her lap.

Tierahna crossed the aisle. She sat on her knees facing the Lorgren. "Why do you need an infirmary, Mlai? Is it not only your transport in need of repair?"

Tierahna sat back on her heels and Haarth understood why she would. The Lorgren's eyes were like liquid pools of amethyst close up. He'd pulled back from staring into them a time or two himself. Making hard decisions called for one not to be influenced by the innocence of beauty. "I…am ill," the Lorgren said. "Lorgrens have no real diseases, but we do have rejection. We're created and then integrated with our biomechanics. As we get older, there can be rejection episodes. These are controlled with many therapies that'd always worked before, but now our bodies have evolved. We're adjusting." She smiled. "I am the first to start the rejection this early. I'm told I will die soon."

What she'd just said wasn't okay. Wasn't a passing thought to tug at the farcical. It was actually quite distressing, still, she'd smiled. *Agreeability was just her nature? Even as she tells us she's dying? Or is she deceiving us?* "Diseases! I knew something like this could happen. Now, what foreign disease may we all have been exposed to!" Haarth's bark from behind startled Tierahna in her seat.

Mlai flinched at Haarth's rumbling too, only she turned to face him.

He raised a brow at her squaring her shoulders. *Oh, so this was a bold one?* Completely contrary to what he'd heard of the Logrens' natures. "We don't have disease. My illness is *rejection*," she said, truth echoing in her voice. "Our body design eliminates disease. And even if it were a disease, our makeups are too different. Our constitutions are not compatible. Any disease couldn't be spread between us."

Uncaring of the possible disease spread that Haarth was so hype about, Tierahna reached out and touched her Mlai. He folded his mouth at her response to his blowing everything so out of proportion. He *understood* what the ramifications could've been if they'd left the Lorgren in the woods. To his estimation it just would've been better to have the guard brigade take possession of her. Mlai's hand covered Tierahna's. "Oh Mlai, I'm so sorry. We won't delay finding the nearest infirmary for you."

"Tierahna! You're to make no more promises. Your mother expects us in-Keep within a reasonable time of making this journey. As you well know, the queen isn't the best at patience. No other detours will delay us."

"Tie-rah-na?" The Lorgren looked between Tierahna and Haarth, her eyes stretched. "You're Princess Tierahna?" Tierahna nodded. "Haar...Prince Haarth is right. You must leave me and continue your journey. My rejection is the best it's ever been. Not one episode has debilitated me since I came to your land. You should leave me at this Tems enclave you speak of. I shall visit one of your infirmaries once I've repaired my transport and I'll request an audience before your queen myself." Mlai removed Tierahna's hand from her shoulder and squeezed it. "Your umbereen has shown itself as a practical curative to our rejection." There, her infectious smile came back again too. "We have a procedure similar to one used at your infirmaries. Treated umbereen can be injected right into our diffusive dissemination system, and this might prolong my life. As this was the only reason

I asked of an infirmary, Prince Haarth is right. There's no greater initiative than keeping an audience before your queen."

Tierahna bit her lips right as Haarth started a silent countdown. *Yeah right, she'll let this go. Ten. Nine. Eight—*

And sure enough, before he'd gotten halfway through it, her compassion for the Lorgren won out. "No, Mlai. Are you aware of why you're better since you traveled here?" The Lorgren shook her head. "Umbereen is profuse in our soil. Along with agate, moldavite, and all manner of other minerals and gemstones. Your body has surely soaked it up since you got here." She gave Haarth a glare that would quell any lesser man. "We *shall* go to Tems enclave only to power this cruiser to stock capacity. Then we shall travel to the East Tundra Bay Festival."

Mlai screeched, bouncing in her seat, but then she covered her mouth as she shifted to gauge Haarth's reaction. "No, Tierahna. We continue to Dameerh," he responded, not disappointing.

"Haarth...Uncle." Tiernahna softened her tone. "Think on it. We know we must answer to Mother. She's at full boar already. I defied her. And we come to her with a Kalameshee in tow, asking for favors. She will skin us like a wolvien for its pelt if we leave a Lorgren wandering unprotected. Not to mention, whatever that was in the woods might still be hunting her."

Haarth grumbled. No one else moved as he sat there determinedly following the night zipping past the window. "That's altogether well, Tierahna. But that doesn't mean we must go to the festival. We could attend an infirmary at a place beyond Tems enclave. Artees village is but six parses away."

"Oh...kay. The East Tundra Bay Festival is but four. They're sure to have any part Mlai needs for her transport. And I had intentions all along to travel to the festival on my way home."

Peetah Pearl came around the optiglass divider from the cruiser's cab. Their progress didn't falter. Snowcrafts mostly rode on auto-conductor anyway. A conductor was only needed for adjustments and corrections. "I need some items myself. There were several proprietors from Cordalai cottage industries that were developing products I had interest in last season. I could trade with them if we go. I'll have my purchases sent to Outliers from there."

Right, Peetah Pearl. You adding to this was just what was needed right now. Haarth's apprehension? The security logistics of a festival filled with milling people. Tierahna being his major concern. His brother, Stah'lief's death made his seeing to his niece's well-being his duty when she was in his company. He traveled often with but a small sect of his own guards. Sometimes if traveling without notice, as he was now, he traveled on his own.

But then I keep a low profile.

As chancellor, he was an agent of the people. That was the way he carried out his duties. Things were far less formal in his dominions than in the high seat enclave. *Just as I like it.* He employed inclusive management, encouraging a more relaxed and approachable atmosphere. The all-involved onslaught had been a balm to his bruised and grieving soul when he'd first gotten to his headquarter dominion, Oxhild.

Stah'lief had just died. He'd left his home forever. He'd found solace in the work of rebuilding the dominions. *Lawlessness had run amuck.* For some reason, his brother had been distracted, neglecting the border. Haarth had entrenched himself with invaluable delegates, coupled with shedding some of the formal protocols from the Keep. And found an abiding escape from what he'd come to believe an irretrievable tableau back at home.

Unlike Tierney, who possessed little experience with unpredictable situations, *sheltered by an iron-willed mother whose rule protects her precious progeny from the sully of the world.* He hated to admit even to himself, but lately, his comfort in his dominions had been waning. Anxiousness had settled between his shoulder blades. *I need to get back to the Keep.*

Dameerh was one of the destinations he traveled to on his own. He eased in and out of the dominion as he saw fit. No one the wiser. Only now, the anticipation for being inside his own home rode low in his belly. He pictured Ana'kerah's face when he would confront her. *She will be livid.* Yes, it was best that they go straight there.

Another detour didn't sit well, anyway. Not while having to keep account of the Kalameshee. Tierahna's instincts were right on only one thing here. Their current situation. Escorting a Lorgren gone astray. He hadn't been angry about that. Her wandering the enclaves of Soonayah alone lined her up for disaster. Whatever that was after her in the woods could find her again.

Somehow, she'd made it here by herself, which was an astonishing feat alone. *How old was she in the first place?* As far as he was concerned, neglect accounted for her journeying so far beyond Lorgr's borders without so much as a guardian at her side. He'd oversee the Lorgren's safe passage to the Keep, but was still not moved enough to detour to an infirmary ensconced within the belly of the world's largest festival. *And trail behind three females too? Not at all.* "For all our knowledge of this Lorgren, her curative could take days. Days we cannot spare, Tierahna."

"No, Prince Haarth. As I said, the curative practiced by your land's medics is like our own. Although we're not compatible, our anatomies are still as similar as any Tellurecian's. I wouldn't delay you long. The curative takes only a short time." Haarth wasn't a brute. The plea in the jewels of Mlai's eyes wasn't lost on him.

A chuckle came from across the aisle as the Kalameshee said, "It seems you're the only hold-out against this festival."

Haarth's scowl deepened. "All together well then, Tierahna." He pointed at her. "But it's you who must tell your mother."

There the Lorgren went screaming again, blanching their ears before she covered her mouth. Her eyes flew to Haarth. "I can pay recompense for your help," she offered, then folded her lips together. He cringed, hoping she wasn't on the verge of trilling their eardrums constantly. Instead, she turned in little flounces and peered through the window.

"So...what makes this East Tundra Bay Festival so special?" the Kalameshee asked when everyone had resumed their former positions within the cruiser.

Tierahna chortled and didn't answer him. She turned too and snuggled in against Bak'rah for the rest of the journey.

Chapter 9

The lead-in to the festival was choked as transport after transport chugged along. Far more arduous travel than was recommended involved a trawl up the Galen mountain. Formations—crawled to and fro and to and fro too. Not all the transports were operated by conductors as steady at the helm as Peetah Pearl either.

They secured the cruiser on a southeast tip of the lead-in. *The edge of a rift. Perfect.* Near a plunge of thousands of fathoms to the base of the mountain plateau. The spot was already dubious. Two tornebirds—as large as small people—competed for one available mate overhead. Their orange feathers streaking above were nowhere near close, but Tierney and the party ducked as they exited the cruiser as if beset by the scavengers. It was because they had to step with such care at the rift's edge that they felt the need to contend with the birds' swooping and chasing too. Even Bak'rah was skittish. He whimpered and blocked Tierney from falling on her turn. "Much appreciations, my boy." *Always looking out for me.*

On foot, they covered at least two parses back to the festival, mucking through the dirty mix of slush and ice and transports. The structure that materialized was a floating island on snow. The entrance?—open-air. The Kalameshee whirled around. "This is phenomenal!" Booths and stalls and shops and smells abounded, sounds of business, people haggling and laughing, and the bustle of the crowd was all disorienting. A practiced few used magnetized propulsion boots to wound their way over-top of the slower-moving crowds on foot.

Such a bazaar! Tierney loved it.

Sight after sight of every variation of needs and delights a person could dream stretched before them. "How is it possible to find any one proprietor in a place that doesn't end?" the Kalameshee wondered aloud.

Tierney'd help him out on this. She touched him for the first time ever on his shoulder. The heat from his body transferred to her, permeating through his furs. Confoundment with the festival was understandable. She'd had the same reaction as a young one. Pointing forward to the furthest place beyond them, "look there," she said, "it *has* an end." When you see the lights of the Solare Corona past the festival erections, that's its end. You're seeing the beginning of the frozen tundra."

Blinking several times, he strained his attention in that direction. Too much excitement surrounded them still. Tierney connected with that heat again. This time it was easier to touch him. Ever easier. Were her fingers fluttering because she wanted to connect with his heat more? This second time around maybe hold on a little longer? "Clear your vision."

Up this far atop a mountain, the sky presented itself as a dark comfort. White Moon shone its incandescence while Spare Moon's blueish tint intertwined—meshed, they drenched the land in silvery light. The sky's familiarity perpetrated a falseness, a grounding of a person's senses because your feet felt to be on solid ground, but the thin air nipping your face with ice told the true story. They stood fathoms and fathoms in the sky. She nearly lost herself as she usually did, dreaming of the stars, when in fact, the low-hung moons were elusive...the stars vast. "Follow the night sky between the festival erections until there is nothing but sky left." She lifted her face to his, exhaling her crisp breath over his skin, its warmth curling into his ear. "See there? Latch onto its path. Can you make out an open sky of changing light?"

He did as she told him and his eyes flared open. "The Solare Corona! I can see it!"

"He...can...see...it. He...can...see...it." The Lorgren mimicked him, sing-songing his discovery. "The Kalameshee can finally see the Solare Corona. The result of collisions between gaseous particles in the atmosphere with charged particles released from the sun's atmosph—"

"We must synchronize what we're doing here so we don't get disoriented and are lost to this utter nether-world forever." Before Mlai got going on a soliloquy of her knowledge of the Solare Corona, Haarth interjected some structure.

Peetah Pearl snorted because Haarth's inflection punctuated that he couldn't believe anyone would volunteer for what most of the people were there to do. Slog as thousands through what was pretty much a maze. She choked back her laughter though, the look he gave her quelling her lips to silence.

While the Kalameshee wandered off to the opening's metal edge and jostled it with hands the size of mitts, testing its support. "But if all the Cor-da-lai who assemble here come in convoys from the different clans of the frozen tundra, how could this structure be built? And what of organization? Who determines if they may or may not come if the weather turns foul?"

Tierney pulled on the edging as well, having followed him over. The edging was implanted as solidly as the mountain they stood on. Gratefully, the Kalameshee had the awareness of a babe just birthed from his mother's womb (or portrayed as if he did) about some things and hadn't an inkling that she'd veered to him like iron to lodestone. In this, she could appreciated his ignorance.

A mutually attracted Kalameshee would be a strain to her already tried psyche. Only she missed his smirk as his eyes made the trace from the frizz of hair puffed at her temple and tucked impatiently behind one ear to her fur boots for the thousandth time since he'd met her. However, Haarth caught the look just fine. "This structure is not permanent construction. Its footing is anchored leagues deep into the permafrost. But only after calibration for the staunchest support, once the previous season's anchor positions have repaired themselves. At some point, the plateau will not be safe for more anchors. The festival will be switched to a different locale then. But until then, we have the best possible view of the Solare Corona," she told him.

Without them asking, the closest proprietor took it upon himself to lift the top of a display of fur muffs. He winked at Tierney and the Kalameshee as he unhooked the whole display case, understanding what Tierney was explaining. He slid it back and showed them its smooth fabrication, pushing it forward again and slotting it into place. "Most appreciations." She winked back at the proprietor and gave him a smile that made him blush. To the Kalameshee she said, "Cordalai are not the only ones registered here. Any Soonahyin can register. They come and choose their design to be erected onto the structure as its being anchored and formed."

Tierney pointed to the festival's uppermost parts. A lip of roofing was partially pulled out. Technicians on erectors were working on it. "This entire structure is also extrapolated to include a retracting ceiling and weatherproof conditioning. All Soonahyins are educated on weather conditioning due to the nature of our climate. That blizzard we just had came through here. No doubt, the structure was weather-sealed and this whole festival was made into a self-sufficient enclave unto itself." The Kalameshee ran fingers through his hair, shaking his head. *He really does know nothing of our culture.* Even Mlai was versed on Soonayah and *her* people had never visited their land before.

Tierney didn't understand a people who chose willful ignorance of other people. At least he was soaking up the information now though.

"How do we navigate inside? As Prince Haarth said, one could wander aimlessly for all time."

"I know! I know!" Mlai interrupted before Tierney could answer. She lifted her forearm and a clear, lighted console, dripping pink fluids ejected. "We synchronize our movements within the East Tundra Bay Festival's agenda." People tittered about them. A pinkish being with a console erupting from her forearm made...uhh quite a sight.

Haarth corralled them away from the influx of passersby by huddling them in a corner, and said, "Tierahna, I expect you not to call undue attention to yourself." He opened his cloak and fiddled with the breastplate of his garment. After a couple of manipulations, another clear console sprang onto a stiffened contraption in front of him like a supplemental desk. Peetah Pearl had one also. To Tierney, the breastplate consoles were too fussy. She ran a finger over her armset. It shrilled. Then they waited for the Kalameshee to reveal his. He reached behind his back and produced a book-sized console. Evidently, the pouch he carried out of sight had an endless capacity.

Mlai instigated a touch of her forearm console to each of their devices. A beacon of light started from hers and arrowed to theirs and ended in one starburst, haloing a bright flash through all the clear devices at the same time.

"Synchronized!" she announced, then proceeded to wander off. Surely, her console directed her straight to the infirmary.

"Tierahna, accompany the Logren to the infirmary as you were the one insistent on bringing her here. Peetah Pearl, locate them to the infirmary and secure them there, then you may commence with your trade." Peetah Pearl gave Haarth a short nod. "And you are with me. We will imbibe in a bit of a treat. A well-deserved one while we wait on these others." Haarth's tone to the Kalameshee was a given.

* * *

Tierney's armset thrummed against her bicep. She felt it, yet ignored its signal flashing too. Pulling on the device, she adjusted its fit over the arm, the buzzing was irritating her a bit. *It can only be Uncle. Why couldn't it have worked this way when my snowcat put me down? Back when I really needed to talk to him in that blizzard?* The thing worked perfectly well now. Leave it to him to insist like this when she wasn't connecting. She rocked back and forth against a window, staring onto the crowd that milled through the festival below. Peetah Pearl had left a while ago with Tierney *nice and secured* while she'd *freely* gone about her trade. The room, situated off the private curative theater, was unimpeachable.

It was just...perfect. Feels like a preview of what I have to look forward to locked away in that sanctum on the frozen tundra if Mother gets her way.

Tierney had given the room a go-around earlier, replacing interesting-looking tumblers and a spouted, covered bowl of alkaline liquid in a more symmetrical order. The sculpture hung above a mantle was shaped... She turned her head sideways. *No shape. No artistic appeal at all.* "Blah." That couldn't have been intended for inspiration in this stark place. She'd held a pumis fruit, sucked in its fragrance—"*Pungent,*" and sighed, it hadn't appealed either—ending up back to hold up the window.

Everyone worked so hard to make sure she was secured, buttoned-up, perfectly aligned, and conformed to all standards. If she exhibited the smallest imperfection she must be sent away and fixed, everything always taken care of. Always provided for. "A better description of my life would be sterile...and controlled." Her pulse had raced with what she'd witnessed on her way here. One patron being attended for a burn from preparing food at one of the eateries within the festival. Corridors alive with medics and staff going about the business of healing. This so-called safety was too cut off. *Too quiet.*

Bak'rah and some packages were at her feet. She'd partaken in a bit of trade herself as they'd made their way to the infirmary, and now she had a bird's-eye-view as people swarmed for their own commodities. Every clan of Soonayah that was known was represented in the festival below: plaited heads of members of the Ahn'Trunkh clans, jeweled-toned scarf clad heads of Ahn'Creet, beads shimmered on the Ahn'Sirh as they moved along. She traced the braids of one Ahn'Rih to his toes. *Those intricate patterns are insane.*

An Ahn'Tupth male, his hair a free-flowing cloud behind him, propulsed in magnetized boots past her window and waved at her. She tittered a wave back at him. His interruption was only a moment, but she'd almost missed it; another bright Kalameshee head. Number thirteen so far amongst the thousands.

No matter her mother's stance, more and more foreigners were traveling across their borders. The commodities, especially the natural ones abundant in their land, were in great demand in other places. It behooved Soonayah to get ahead of the influx. They should streamline their trade for their own best benefit. Her mother couldn't stop the passage of time. People inexorably moved forward. And so would she.

Her armset zinged her again. She sighed but announced for it to connect. "Tierahna! Where are you?" Haarth's fierce countenance was cast onto the window before her. Strapped to her bicep, her armset's projector would find the best surface to display its subject. "I await Mlai's release at the infirmary. You well know that, Uncle." They were synchronized, after all. She cocked her head to one side as she answered him.

"She's still not discharged?"

Tierney pursed her lips. "I have gotten no word on her status."

Haarth's brow wrinkled. Hers too. With similar expressions, they resembled one another. "Did the Lorgren not say the curative she sought took only a little time?"

Tierney heaved herself from the window and trod to that pale sculpture, wishing for it to fall from the wall and break into a million pieces. It'd make it far more interesting than it remaining whole. Tiny pieces of curious sizes bouncing, bouncing about. She could practically follow one particular piece's path of uneven rhythm in her mind and then shook herself. *No time for that now. No escapism.* She had to stay here in the present to answer her uncle. Then back she went to the window again.

What *was* taking so long? Bak'rah came to her side, whimpering. She rubbed her nails behind his ears. *Scratch. Scratch. Scratch.*

"Tierahna!"

"Yes! She did advise so, but I've been given no update."

They both paused in thought, and Haarth said. "Be that as it may, I've been informed of your lack of communication with the queen as well."

"Might I ask from whom this informing came?"

"That's of no consequence. Though protocol *is not* inconsequential. You will communicate with the queen as I requested—"

The inner and outer doors opened at the same time. Peetah Pearl came to join her, just as a medic arrived with a paler-pink Mlai in tow.

"Uncle, I'll communicate with Mother in a bit. Mlai's here. We'll be with you shortly." She disconnected.

"Princess Tierahna, please accept our regrets for the delay. We conducted comprehensive research on the compatibility of the curative the Lorgren submitted. This took more time than we'd thought," the medic said.

"Was it compatible?" Tierney bent and touched the bald side of Mlai's head.

"Oh, indeed. The curative has proven an improvement on our own protocols. The schema the Lorgren submitted was so extensive, we introduced it to our Ministry of Medics. In-depth research is being put into play as we speak."

Tierney breathed and the medic followed her study of Mlai's pale complexion. "She's still anesthetized," the medic explained. It's our belief that after some recuperation she may *fully* recover. Can we be allowed follow-ups to test our theories—"

"She's no subject to be prodded for your experiments." The words were cut off before the insult could finish being voiced. "Her feelings are as developed as ours are. There'll be no follow-up tests—"

Mlai stood, ending Tierney's dressing down of the medic. Pained watching Mlai's exaggerated motions, so unlike the bouncing behavior they'd come to expect, Tierney stuck a hand out to catch her in case she fell. "Tierah...Princess Tierahna."

"Just Tierney for you."

"I appreciate so much what's been done for me here. I have permission to offer recompense for your help. And I would do it, by the way. Those tests. If it would help all Lorgr, I would do it. But I must report back to my *home* first any success the curative has produced."

"Then we require she be taken to our transport near the—"

"I can walk, Tierney." Although pale, her smile was bright. So Tierney relented. They exited on foot after some instructions on aftercare from the medic.

Chapter 10

She'd almost tipped over again, listless, like a drunk veryum who bumped into bedrock, schist, clay mineral, and the like, except Mlai's obstacle course was made of people. A circumnavigation that wreaked havoc on the ebb and flow in the festival crowd. Tierney wrapped an arm around her willowy waist. They had better stop...for the fourth time, at this shop's displayed tooled leather garments, satchels, and shukka boots.

It was best they kept her between them. Tierney and Peetah Pearl urged her forward as they walked on either side of her.

"Should I carry her?" Peetah Pearl asked.

"Be careful!" Tierney warned, simultaneously.

Mlai was weak, albeit her personality wasn't lacking. Her tug from Tierney's hold had Tierney reaching for her again. "Mlai? What is it now?" Only to find her turned back the way they'd come. Others around them were turned too. They gazed off at the East Tundra Bay Festival's opened ending.

Light from the Solare Corona refracted in the sky and transformed the sky's inky palate. A riveting sight for Soonahyins too who were regularly exposed to its pageantry. The setting of the market was a testament to innovation in engineering, with the festival's erections centered atop the mountain. A frame that overlooked the whole of mountain ranges that had snow drooped in cowls over their tops and stood shoulder-to-shoulder with *their* plateau, then angled and flattened and razed until level, where the frozen tundra laid its permafrost.

Several hundred parses beyond their location—the farthest north into the frozen tundra of all the settlements—an Ahn'Tupth Cordalai clan engaged a mirrored sphere in their hamlet. There they harnessed energy from the Solare Corona as Soonayah regulated them to do. Also, they were charged with allotting a small portion of the light energy to be reflected back into the sky.

Inconceivable as always. Aerials prancing colors across the sky weren't fantastic enough for Soonayah.

The Ahn'Tupth clan displayed a light diorama in addition to the vision of the Solare Corona onto the mist for all of Soonayah's splendor. Mlai laughed and employed that jaunty little bounce they had gotten used to. "Good." Tierney was glad her energy was rallying.

In just the right spot, the Ahn'Tupth male who'd passed Tierney's window at the infirmary had positioned himself to the delight of the crowd as well. He appeared as if he engaged with the Solare Corona itself, juggling and twirling light. Deploying amazing skills with his polarized propulsion boots, he looked like he lay aloft the sky on a bed of light.

Couldn't have timed it better myself. This'll make getting to the entrance more convenient. Tierney took benefit of everyone's stillness and signaled to Peetah Pearl, then she encircled Mlai's shoulders and wove them through the crowd. Haarth and the Kalameshee were already at the entrance standing off to one side when they got there. Of course, the Kalameshee would be as fascinated with the energy show as much as everyone else was. At present, he was looking toward the sky too. "What *is* the Ahn'Tupth male getting up to now?"

Curiosity won out and Tierney swung back around, then ducked down fast with the rest of the crowd. Jarring light screeched across the tops of their heads ending in an explosion of incandescent dew that landed in sparkles at their feet. They all clapped and laughed at being spoofed by the Ahn'Tupth male's antics. He'd reached behind his shoulder and pretended to pitch the light right at them, magnified by repeaters hung high to replicate his image. Tierney rose tentatively. Wouldn't want to tempt him in case he had more hijinks hidden for them, and she glanced over the crowd. *Of course, no surprises there.* Who would've had to guess who would be the only person to remain standing? Haarth hadn't ducked at all and just shook his head at all *their* hooked reactions.

She didn't mind that she'd fallen for the Ahn'Tupth's trickery. Admiration for his cunning exploits tickled her appreciation for pure innate ability, and he was masterful with those propulsion boots too. *All that talent had to be instinctual. Bet he couldn't put into words how he did it.* Just as he started gyrating the time-honored sikya dance, Tierney shifted to the entrance. *He is still in the sky. Wow!* He deserved all the applause they could give him. "Phenomenal!" she shouted. Nevertheless, it was the perfect time for them to go.

Best beat those who'd be leaving after the Ahn'Tupth male's final salute.

The...snow. "Umpf." She stumbled a little when she stepped out into the elements. *The...snow...the...snow...again...I...meet...you...where... you...are...* Sometimes the mind reverted to a monotony like a song by her most favored crooner or the rhyme from her youth by default. A sort of hum that kept her comforted and she would rock to it. Just like her mother said, she wasn't always aware when it was happening. A protective mechanism of a sort. Automatic in it's onset. Given the current circumstances, this time it was glaringly obvious.

She made an exiting gesture to their party so that they could get out of there. Outside with the wind wrapping around them, she fingered her armset no sooner than her feet crunched on the snow. They had a walk ahead of them to the cruiser. Which should she do during it? Fill it with concentrating on the cold nipping at any parts it could catch exposed while she sang in a futile attempt at more diversion or go ahead and do what she knew she needed to do?

Engage in some mother talk.

She had no excuse to put it off any longer. *Ugh!* She mouthed to Peetah Pearl and Haarth she'd walk ahead for privacy, then announced for her armrest to engage her mother. Who would want to hear the production that was about to take place? No one. *Not me either. I would rather skip it too.* That's why she'd relieved everyone else of having to hear it.

Point taken, they eyed her warily from paces away. *And then surprise!* Recriminations began as soon as the armset engaged. *Just as I figured they would.*

Through legions of transports, her mother's image caught, quite captivatingly in a perverse way, on optiglass windows. Soft and beguiling, her high forehead and dimpled cheeks contoured to the shapes of the glass. And each time her lips uttered a reprimand, a beam of Tellurician moonlight caressed a curve on her cheekbone, making her mother's presence a luminescent virago, pestering Tierney from on high. Tierney's actual thoughts on the matter had her laughing behind her teeth at the absurdity of it all.

Geez! It seemed a lifetime ago since they'd last talked. "I don't understand your itch to explore." She would bet her mother presumed her perfect life as a princess should've been enough. "Meeting Haarth secretly about the borders had been a radical act!" On and on her mother went. How could Tierney convince her to be open to something new when it didn't make sense for it to be like this whenever they talked?

And she'd never be able to confront her mother about what she'd overheard between her and her companion either. There was a blockade between them, fathoms high and leagues long with no meeting in between. She cringed at being as chastised as she'd been in her youth. Down and down and casted ever further down her head went, every word exchanged weighing her upper body until she was watching her feet crunch the snow and was paying no mind to the look of the land before her.

But I'm a woman now. I can just tell Mother, no. You can't put me away in some sanctum. Yeah. That would happen.

Of course, she wasn't walking anymore. Her scamper was just short of a jog, zigzagging through the transports crushed into the lead-in. And true to form, her canter was to the rhythm of their hot exchange.

Locked away in a sanctum.

Locked away in a sanctum.

Locked...away...in ...that...sanctum, the drum-beat bouncing around and around her skull. *Mother is the main one who pulls this so-called unstable behavior out of me.*

So distracted by her mother she was, for once she forgot her training. Routines that had been drilled into her since birth scattered from her brain. She should have been taking note of their surroundings right then. Goodness knew what developments lay in wait for a royal who was not on her guard.

Everyone else followed at slower paces. At the front of them, Peetah Pearl had her eyes peeled toward Tierney ahead.

Except, the queen blistered Tierney. "Mother! Not all Soonahyin families should live in the same homestea…"

Rounding Peetah Pearl's cruiser, Bak'rah yapped and yapped at her. All of this was coming onto sensibilities that had been bombarded as of late with the new introspection stressing her body's normal response system also. It was too much. An average person could maybe zone out some of the elements once their mind became overloaded, naturally, to protect them self.

Tierney wasn't average. The default into the rocking, the tapping and the singing was unconscious. Any other time, her mind wanted to grant everything its due, until sometimes....she'd check out automatically without meaning to. She'd take these little breaks into her own world when she felt overloaded. A place in the mind and spirit that allowed a solace within one's very own person. You just weren't supposed to fall into it without electing to go. The element of the process that had been a bit out of her control lately.

I'll just have to step around you Bak'rah. I'll give you all the attention you want in a moment, my boy. Let me gather myself for a time.

This was an unfortunate move she'd later come to regret.

His eyes! My sweet pup! She whipped back to him as she realized his eyes were turning that eerie yellow. His coat flashed bright too, whiter than the snow around them.

And the tornebird's swoop didn't make a sound.

Out of nowhere, an orange shadow rushing her vision was her second warning. Bak'rah's yipping, regrettably had been the first and she'd ignored it. Claws were aimed at her head now. Her loud talking had aggravated the tornebirds. The largest, the female, took issue with Tierney's disturbance of her attempted mating with the suitor she'd decided on, the smaller of the two male birds.

Furiously flapping a wingspan longer than Tierney's whole body, the tornebird whipped rushes of wind and squawked a cacophony of screeches, deafening them to everything else around them. Disorienting them. Bak'rah vaulted onto his hind legs and batted the hulking bird with massive paws. Its sickle of a beak took vicious jabs at them in a vortex of screeches and wind and wings squalling at every turn.

"Bak'rah, watch out!"

Bak'rah's diversion caused the scavenger to miss latching into

Tierney's head, but the bird's talons managed a heaving sting to her shoulder and clipped her off balance anyway. Her foot slipped. Righting herself between the confines of the cruiser and the rift proved an insurmountable feat with the bird's cyclonic intent set on ending her. She tripped over Bak'rah. By then he had contrived a push against her to help her footing.

It was funny though. *I don't think even the world's most adept pup can save me from this.* As if to prove her point correct, the pads of his paws found no better purchase than her feet had done a moment ago. They slipped over the icy snow as well. Tierney couldn't catch herself. She stumbled, ducking the scavenger out of necessity this time, and stumbled and…plummeted over the edge of the rift where the snowcraft cruiser stood.

Bak'rah tumbled too…or heedlessly jumped off the rift along with her. Who was to say? There was no telling which was the truth with his devotion. Peetah Pearl, Haarth, Mlai, and the Kalameshee rushed around the cruiser as she plunged. Everyone screamed, "Tierahna!" including her mother, who saw what was happening. Tierney'd still been talking to her on her armset.

"Great."

She was falling from a mount so high, she went through clouds that kissed her cheeks with iced cotton wool, and all she could think was, *another catastrophe to contend with—with Mother. She'd expect something like this of me. Maybe think I did it on purpose to distract from my true intentions.*

Belatedly, she calmed herself mid-air, and had better get it together before it didn't matter if she'd done this on purpose or not, and ended up as a splat at the bottom of a mountain.

Her stomach had finally made a lurch to her mouth. She flipped her body and scrabbled for Bak'rah, then set off her speeding from her core. Like lava, heat from her soul-energy innervated, carrying to the cords on her neck on to her scalp. *My ultimate comfort come to rescue me this time.* Her hair began its whirl. Her body blurred and disappeared only to reappear again on a small ledge with Bak'rah next to her. She gave a distraught wave of her arms. Hard to see with clouds in the way. Through shifts in the puffy whiteness, the clouds' drift, she made out the top of the cliff. *Hope everybody peering over that ledge is reassured because I most definitely am not!*

This was crazy! It reminded her of when she'd first found Bak'rah. Him prancing gingerly at the edge of the shelf they'd landed on. Hands grasping at his fur, tugging him tight against her. *And abject terror,* as a running theme. An attempted rescue that had ended with his near-death and hers as well.

"Be calm, my pup." Any move they made was a threat to them now. Morbidly, she tipped her head to peer into the fathoms and fathoms below. *So like me to want to see what I'm in for.* Ice, whiteness, a nothingness yawned up at her. No ground at all.

Bak'rah's paws continued to skid like *they* were on ice. Tierney's clutch of his fur was snatched away. He hurtled from their foothold that had been too insubstantial in the first place, making pure instinct take over in that place in her psyche where she lost the grasp of cognitive thought and just acted. That place that she'd resorted to so much lately. "I've got him!" In the moment that she was about to act, the Kalameshee's shout stopped her from jumping after him.

Her shelf of safety was already tenuous. Gratefully, others were there to help her this time. She needed help to curb that instinct that had been her undoing on so many occasions, which wouldn't matter really if she lost her sweet pup. Nothing would. Him sacrificing himself for her might just be the one thing that would call all the unstable behavior that her mother thought so enfeebling to the light for good.

She was lucky those with her acted instantaneously. Mlai, who had seemed delicate, almost child-like reacted like a shot, neon pink cords sent flying from her arm, directed to Bak'rah's howling form. The Kalameshee did a speed-skydive off the cliff with the cords. Resembling a bird of prey himself, he dove, spinning, maintaining complete control, and leveled out when he gained on Bak'rah and pulled Mlai's wet cords around them—as the ends of the cords gripped them like fingers.

It became clear that they had a major problem right away though. The Kalameshee and Bak'rah's weight jerked Mlai toward the edge of the rift. "You're too heavy for her!"

Mlai wrapped her hands around the cords and tried to back up from the ledge, but that wasn't working out too well. So Haarth stepped in front of her, and trapped Mlai behind himself, and blocked her from falling also. "Brace yourself on me," he said.

And he pulled then wrapped the damp cords over *his* forearm, and yet then, he started to tilt too. *Ooh wee! This was getting worse and worse by the moment.*

If Tierney acted, she could make things more disastrous than they already were. *Calm...calm! You must think first.* They needed her to stay on her shelf, relatively secure until they helped the Kalameshee and Bak'rah. Not a time to check out of her awareness either. Even though his wrapping the cords around his arms was ingenious—the cords would never have been able to retract back into Mlai fast enough—it was evident, Haarth couldn't bear the weight of the wolf and the Kalameshee *and* Mlai for too much longer either.

Peetah Pearl shouted at Tierney. "Do not move!" Where was she going to go? Besides interfering and possibly causing the deaths of everybody. They had one last possible grace. Peetah Pearl's presence stood between them all and the utter tragedy of a crash to the bottom of the plateau.

Peetah Pearl looked around for help and paused as if she saw someone approaching from a distance. Quickly it appeared, she deduced that they were too far away, so she then wrapped and crossed her legs within the step-footing of the cruiser. Then she flipped herself backward and hooked arms through Mlai's arms, her shoulder hinged into Mlai's back, and braced a locked hold around Mlai's and in turn Haarth's waist.

"What was *that*?" From the direction Peetah Pearl had looked, the blue light of a frostfire discharge shot across the sky, nearly reaching the circling tornebirds. The birds squawked because the hunting of them in their flight, the shooting at them dispersed them from circling overhead. *That was great a relief. Who could that be defending their party from afar?* Again, it seemed someone was right on her heels and she hadn't noticed them before.

The matter at hand though was the cruiser's metal squeaking with each effort Haarth exerted pulling up tension from the cords. That took her mind away from that glimpse of a thought about others following them. And Mlai's cords were biomechanical. It was inevitable they would stretch under the strain. The obvious most crucial worry currently from the looks of the cords.

For practicality's sake, the Kalameshee loosened the cords from himself in time to drop back down to the shelf where Tierney waited. *Good idea. That stands for a better chance.*

Only, their perch yielded too little room for them both too. In turn, they had to take hold of each other. What else could they do? How else could they contort themselves into fitting? And who could give a care about them being this close in these circumstances? *Maybe me...a little.* He smelled so good, like brisk air, and man, and testosterone, and...

The people chain—Haarth, Mlai, and Peetah Pearl made—slowly got Bak'rah back to safety. Horrendously slow! *Please, come on.* This was all she should be concentrating on. It was only when Bak'rah's paws scrabbled at the edge of the cliff until he was snatched in by Haarth, and landed on the snow-covered rock, that Tierney realized she hugged the Kalameshee like her life depended on it. "Uhm...much appreciations."

She patted his biceps, but his attention was arrested on her face now that the sense of impending danger was relieved. *Come on, now. He should know it was rude to stare at a person like that. Yeah...uhm really awkward.* She slid her hands from his shoulders, and was intent on pushing him away. He bundled her ever closer to his body. "We must get down from here," she stressed, wanting away from him so she could think clearly and figure them a way out of this mess."I speeded to this shelf with Bak'rah, but he's in sync with me. Everything happened so fast, I couldn't trigger my speeding before he fell again. I don't believe I can speed with you."

"No. Me either. I have rope. I can rappel down."

Thankfully, he was able to ready equipment he just so happened to have in his bottomless pouch. After she waited the time she thought it took to rappel half the distance to the ground, she jumped over the edge, seeming to pause in air. Her hair whorled, she flipped then disappeared from view—falling, falling, speeding through space and ice that rushed past her body, in spite of the fact she couldn't be seen. The physics of the speed buffering the air around her against the mountain's edges, the ice, and even the ground and the air itself—slowing, slowing—slowed her down progressively more, buffering her until she landed on the ground safely. She looked up to the Kalameshee and willed him to step deftly enough in *his* descent. "There's a foothold below you! Just there, to the left! Yes, you found it!" she shouted, once she thought he was within earshot. It seemed like it had taken half the night for him to get this far.

Horror struck in her throat after a long time of him rappelling and he'd reached at least seventeen fathoms above her. His foot slipped a foothold covered in iced snow. He started a freefall. Snow and debris dislodged. He just caught himself on his ropes about nine fathoms before he hit the ground. Debris falling with him cracked him over his head. He took a few moments and gathered himself, then began a slow rappel again. When he paused, Tierney called out to him, "What is it?"

He yelled, "My rope is at an end!" He'd come prepared for everything else, how could he not have enough rope? *I guess he wouldn't have thought he'd be climbing a mountain, especially not one this high.*

The risk-taking fool! What was he doing! She ran with all her might, her calves hampered by the snow. He'd released his rope. Pulling everything she had left inside her core in a speed, she launched herself at him before he met the ground in an attempt to buffer his landing too.

They both landed with a great *whoof* in a mound fat with heaped snow. She on top of him. Powder flying everywhere. *And all my maneuverings to help him gone in vain.* Somehow, he'd managed to break *her* fall.

A worm of fear sliding into her belly couldn't be accounted for as the snow settled around them. When she'd raised her head from his shoulder his eyes were shut. Little pellets of snow clung to his eyelashes. Ice was enmeshed in his brows, in the swathe of hair shown at his temple, his lips were tinged to a faded blue. "Torhvald?" He didn't move. The worm turned, sickening her insides now. "Torhvald!"

"So...you're aware I have a name after all. I must say, it sounds good coming from your tongue." His chuckle accompanied a slow opening of eyes glittering with *hazel* lights now. She pushed against his chest. He jested after they'd both nearly fallen to their deaths?

How they'd landed arranged them in such a way that his gaze

meandered an uninterrupted path over her face. Their heavy breaths mingled. She'd used an exorbitant amount of her soul-energy speeding them both. *Now I know I can do it.* It'd worked when she'd thought it couldn't. Thus, her payment for her over-ambitiousness was exertion that had her hankering after a slit at his neck, *her* energy having depleted for her efforts. The minuscule collar opening revealed a sliver of his skin and it beckoned to her. Their breaths now misted the air, making a tangible connection between them.

How funny he'd been, come into their land bedecked in layer upon layer of garments and furs. One layer between the skin and a shukka insulated woolen, then other outer garments heated a body just right. Yet, his energy hadn't diminished at all from their fall. Heat wafted off him, emanating through his furs. They were in a world of their own, staring at each other.

At some point, her nose burrowed its way into the juncture of his collar despite herself. Her savoring a wholesomeness on her tongue shocked her from what she was *actually* doing. *Really, Tiernahna? You need a taste of his skin, now?* Tierney raised her head. They were so close, she witnessed his eyes change to the greenest she'd ever seen them. A click of awareness registered in their verdant depths just as her own awareness of the situation kicked into high gear.

Hip to breast, her weight cleaved every curve of her body to his. She'd sought his warmth, pressed into contact with his jaw, her mouth mumming his neck. Her actions her own, yet she hadn't stopped them. Tierney knew better than to let her urges get the better of her. The need for innervation was a constant thing. Was it any wonder that his awareness would manifest as a resounding hardness against her hip? The slide of those hands behind her waist, anchoring her to him? The shift of one hand into her hair, pulling her face down to his? Her sputter was late on the uptake. She'd caused this in him. *What was I thinking, tasting the man!* She pulled back to no avail because he pressed on, ravaging her sputtering mouth.

I caused this—his grinding her into the impression in the snow his body had made. Tierney'd whimpered and squirmed, which encouraged him evidently and he'd flipped her onto her back aiming for deeper access to her mouth. She'd been kissed before, but the Kalameshee's talented tongue made her forget that they lay in a bed of snow, which stuck in her hair with her snood having fallen back, and slid like cold muck down the back of her neck.

If her brothers could see her now. Pinned to the ground like a feeble damsel, while some man...

She bucked like a crazed thing. One...two...then three times before she dislodged him.

Once they were on their feet, he chuckled. She wanted to rip the smile from his face with her bare hands. Alas, she couldn't risk the result of touching him again. "I'll forgive you this trespass once, as you did save my wolf's life."

They squared off like fighters. Tierney with her hands raised to ward him off and the Kalameshee circling her. "And what excuse will you offer for the second, tenth, and twenty-fifth times we engage in it then? You followed your curiosity with me and started this. But now that I've tasted you, I have every intention of indulging in it further."

They both blanched as lights approached. Peetah Pearl's cruiser had made its way down from the plateau at speed. *Good!* Tierney released the breath she hadn't known she held.

Chapter 11

Back on the cruiser, everyone was exhausted from the continuous travel. They were overwrought and quite bruised and battered from all their unforeseen ordeals too. Mlai most-especially was the worst of them. She already needed rest from the curative she'd undergone. Vital appendages of her body being tugged out of shape as well, she was now even weaker and needed a true recovery.

Tierney and the Kalameshee's entrance saw them lumbering onto the cruiser. They'd slumped into their seats. Everyone except Tierney registered a buzzing at the conductor's panels. Tierney only realized what it signified the moment her mother's face appeared in front of her. Peetah Pearl had sent a connection to the optiglass divider between the conductor's cab and Tierney.

Perfect.

She ground her teeth. They'd been connected when she'd fallen off that plateau. Her mother had witnessed her daughter's fall and she was sure not to have spoken to anyone until now. She would be incensed and more than a little fretful. *Ah great! A splendid mood to talk to her in.*

"Tierahna! You're safe after a fall from a mountain, but what effort was made to reassure me? An incident like that could require a whole sect of Tempeh Tu's deployment to your location."

Tierney covered her mouth as she scoffed. Only, she couldn't muster restraint to keep her eyes from rolling. What her mother really meant was that she had just stopped short of overreacting, expending the highly valuable assets of the Tempeh Tu on so small a matter as Tierney's fall. Surely, the queen was aware that if the incident had proven serious, someone in their party would've had to report it. Haarth most likely. Not only as her uncle but as a Soonahyin official it would be his duty. "Yes, I'm aware Mother." She answered, a slant to her lips. "We've just gotten back on the cruiser. I intended a reconnection with you once we settled in." The muscles of her face strained as she clenched her jaw to keep a straight face.

The queen rubbed a hand over her eyes. "That's altogether good, Tierahna. And though, to you, my concern may seem high-handed, I-am-your-mother. I carry out the business of Soonayah as a constant, but your well-being is paramount too. I can't let any of you come second. Especially as *you* insist on traveling from the furthest end of Soonayah to the next."

A mother's well-placed guilt was a beast that could quell the most audacious insolence.

In truth, the queen's words did chasten her. Tierney lowered her head. Her toe went to tapping against the baseboard. Beneath her lashes, she cut a glance at the Kalameshee where he sat across the aisle. He offered her a smile in return.

The queen always being so invested in her was meant to be caring. As Queen, she had a full retinue of responsibilities, which she was excellent at handling, and *still* she made time to dictate Tierney and her siblings' lives. It had taken dedication to prove herself worthy to the people of Soonayah. After the king's death, they'd questioned her capabilities. Soonayah's leaders had even held meetings on rescinding her ascension as the ruling queen. Soonayah's people elected those in line to continue to inherit its sovereignty. It wasn't a given. She'd been elected, so eventually, they'd let it be. Now, they cherished her. Leaders from other lands fawned after her. Unnecessary worry for Tierney shouldn't be something she had to deal with too. *So, I'm going to take myself off her hands.*

You deal with Soonyah and I will go to some other land, she thought.

To her mother, she said, "Of course, Mother. Truly, the next order of business was a connection with you." Tierney shifted in her seat. Mlai was listing to one side. "I must ask your pardon again. We need to settle Mlai after the strenuous events of the day. We're on our way, Mother. In several parses, we should be within view of Dameerh."

"Don't sever this connection, Tierahna!" The queen lifted herself and peered past Tierney's shoulder. Mlai moved with Tierney's movements attempting to make herself small and hide behind her. "That's the other purpose for my contact. Is this Mel...loy the Lorgren you spoke about? There's been contact from Lorgr. They're asking about the son of one of their High Council. The Ministry of Communication relayed our message of his arrival to our land. They were shocked. I don't think they expected him to survive the journey."

Tierney spun around, exposing Mlai completely to her mother's view. She was now not only listing, but her eyes were half-closed too. "Indeed, this is the Lorgren, Mother. But the High Council of Lorgr must be mistaken. The Lorgren's name is Mlai and she's female."

Tierney waved frantically at the Kalameshee as she propped Mlai up. He came, maneuvered Tierney out of the way, and manfully lifted Mlai into his arms. Tierney pointed him to the sleeping cabin that Peetah Pearl had assigned to *her.*

The sacrifice of the sleeping cabin didn't go unnoticed by Mlai. Though she was hard-pressed to keep her eyes open, she put up a fight. In the end, Tierney ran roughshod over her protests. As she and the Kalameshee laid her in the bed anyway, they both noticed the cords hanging from her arm. There was some shrinkage still needed, but they were mostly retracted. Part of the gape in her arm was nearly sealed. The skin once it had united had somehow fused back together again. The part not sealed exposed tissues, muscles, and the inner biomechanical structures saturated in pink fluid. Tierney frowned, pulling the skin of Mlai's arm together. She applied a healing bandage. *That should help it fuse faster.* The translucent sticky would dissolve once it was used up. *Hope she feels better soon.* As she worked, the Kalameshee squeezed her shoulder. She'd forgotten he was there for a moment. Of course, he would want to make sure Mlai was okay too.

Barely uttering words, Mlai's lips moved. Tierney bent to hear her whispers. She sighed, "They have always wished for a boy in me."

* * *

Even Haarth was bushed on the last leg of their journey. He'd sealed himself behind his cabin door, but only after he'd given Tierney instructions on taking first watch. He'd said, *"I'll take over after I've closed my eyes a bit."* Mlai rested now. Tierney'd stayed with her, stroking her brow until she'd drifted off. The cruiser's atmosphere had quieted, fatigue having stolen its way throughout the forward compartment and sapped its travelers. The Kalameshee and Peetah Pearl were installed in their bunk built-ins too, and the cruiser was set for auto-conductor. Only Tierney lay in the seats behind the conductor's cab alone with Bak'rah.

Even though he and she sprawled as best as the cushions afforded, it wasn't a comfortable fit. In her mind, she was experiencing the perverse reaction though: night blanketed her, and nestled her in its snug arms while an array of changing scenes played out on the optiglass ceiling of the cruiser. With an ergonomic roll beneath her neck and Bak'rah's heat pressed to her side, she gave her comfort no mind as she lay there.

The ceiling was a continuation of the window surrounding the cruiser. Optiglass. A forward down-sloping cap that took up the whole upper portion of the cruiser's outer shell. The glass tops were the norm on snowcrafts. Usually, she never paid them much attention. It was only that in her reclining position, the optiglass wrapped her in the velvet night's sky.

The last display on the glass was a familiar scene. The hills of Dayea. They rolled into the mountains by the same name that her late father *had been* and her eldest brother by five spans, Eh'kotah, *still was* so fascinated with. Her last excursion was to the base of those mountains. She'd stayed for a time in the enclave Kosnah nestled in the foothills there, carrying out short exhausting climbs that hadn't come close to the heights her father must have climbed the unfaithful day he died at Dayea. The view of Kosnah at Mount Dayea had been displayed in its most optimal light on the optiglass. The burgeoning season of new life. The only blemishes marring the scene were plots of snow, plopping from the surrounding trees, yet to melt on the heated roof. The snow gave the scene of Dayea a dreamy hue.

"Deceptively benign," she mouthed to herself, her smile sad... sleepy.

A few things about her father held prominent places in her memory since he'd died when she was so young. His face was a blur. The particulars stolen from her mind, replaced by more solid characteristics. Haarth's usually. Her father and Haarth were said to have favored each other in looks. Tierney retrieved recordings whenever she wanted to recall his exact features. But for her lack of memory of his face, she made up for in remembering his kindness. Even as King, he'd found time to spend with them on an individual basis.

The plops of snow onto the optiglass had a monotony to them. A rhythm she latched onto, of course. *Plop...plop-plop. Plop-plop.* The changing scenes and the cadence—*plop-plop*—jogged memories to the fore as she battled her drowsiness. She and her father running heedlessly through calf-deep snow with no destination in mind, laughing and chanting the Soonahyin Starfall rhyme...

"Star up high, oh so grand.

Open the sky and implant the land..."

Bak'rah flinched, his steady panting startled by her yawning and stretching. She resettled herself, murmuring the rhyme as she drifted off.

"Blazing to ground seeds Soo-nah-yin,

All in kind—plant, animal and man.

Star so rich, empowers everything..."

Chapter 12

Tierney was sure she dozed off and on because she had a succinct memory of a tap on her shoulder. Haarth'd told her he would take over. But at some point—just before day—the Kalameshee awakened her with noise of sliding into the seat behind her. He leaned over the back of her seat and in-turn her shoulder, also in a proximity to her face that was far too close. If she turned, she would essentially breathe his breath. *An intimacy I intend to forego. A little too close for comfort, if you don't mind.*

Maneuvering her seat too swiftly, she engaged the lever. She and Bak'rah plunked back to a seated position, which impelled her to rub Bak'rah beneath his chin when he grumbled. "Shhh..." she murmured to the wolf.

The Kalameshee didn't speak and just loomed behind her for several moments, long enough for the silence to develop into a pregnant force depressing her nerves.

But I can keep it going if he can.

Otherwise, she feared she'd lose her chance to keep vigil of the Solare Corona in the distance. The intent was to avoid a regurgitation of what happened between them while they'd flounced around in the snow.

His voice, near a whisper, breaking into the quite caused her to wince. "Soonayah possesses lands so rich, yet you still let Starfalls land to enhance an already overflowing bounty. It calls one to wonder about your appreciation of your riches."

If the intentions with his words were to get her attention? Oh, he'd achieved his aim alright. Tierney jerked in her seat. Her arm brushed his hair-roughened one and she didn't pull away. "Why would you speculate on our appreciation? We treasure all we possess and accord all things their due respect."

"It's a wonder then, isn't it?" He gestured to the aeronautics of light in the sky barely perceptible from the distance. "You see? The Solare Corona winks at you its dance of light fantastic. So awe-inspiring, I sit here straining in my seat for a better glimpse, yet you barely lift your head in acknowledgment."

Tierney gasped. "From this great a distance, it's not fully visible. We would need to travel far, further north even than the East Tundra Bay Festival's locale to have a proper viewin—"

"It's quite proper enough for me, you see. Just the glimpses I've had thus far have astonished me...humbled me really. I do know you think me uncouth, filled with ignorance of your land, while still coming here with hands outstretched simply to take from it." He shook his head at her perception of him.

"But isn't that what you *are*?" she asked.

He laughed. "It is. But I'm...more than that. Now that I'm here, I bear witness to the reasons your queen is so protective. You have an overabundance of all the things every land needs, but you're not charitable with it."

Although Tierney didn't agree with the position of restrictive borders and trading which her mother held for so long, she didn't like hearing it expressed in such a way from an outsider. One who didn't have an appreciation for the complexities of her mother's stance. One who also used words...and anything else as tools for his ways of manipulations. *I have to remember that then when I'm falling into those eyes of his.* "We allow some trade. And your presence here speaks to the issue of our borders being completely closed, doesn't it? Would you be here if they were?"

"As I said, I bear witness to your reasons. Protection of one's resources is inevitable with land so rich as yours."

Tierney huffed and shifted away from him, nudging his arm with her movement. She wouldn't argue against a point when her thoughts ran along similar lines. Her mother's policy on these matters was just *one* of the sorest spots of contention between them. The issue had come up for debate during the convention of dominion chancellors and clan chieftains as well as during the last assembly cycle and nothing had come of it.

What she and Haarth had instigated was the first real movement toward some addressment. *Finally, some action. As controversial as it is.*

They now brought a Kalameshee for an audience before the queen. He'd make entreaty for more trade and cooperation between their shared border. All because she'd snuck off and met Haarth. Had taken it upon herself to have some kind of discussion on a subject she couldn't even raise with her mother. Not the *most* important thing she couldn't talk to her about, but relevant for her cause. Being committed to that sanctum was the constant specter hanging over her, and drove pretty much every other action she took.

At the heart of it, Haarth was a chancellor of the very dominion boasting the border between Soonayah and Kalamesh, right there at the southeast border of their land. His word carried more sway than hers. *So here we are.* She'd met with the uncle who'd been removed from the family and *of* whom the queen never spoke. Like he was a specter hidden in a closet somewhere.

Tierney'd get a better read on her mother's anger when she was in her presence. The queen would have every right to it. Yet, Tierney'd had no choice. She could hear her mother now. *"Tierahna, you're so head-set on conquering some new place, but if you figure out what you truly want, you will see you can carve your own path wherever you are."*

Not if I am secured away in some sanctum, I can't.

If it weren't for that, in a way her mother was right. Sometimes her dreams were too big for her own peace of mind. She'd see where she'd settle once the borders were more open. Her mother was overprotective of them all. Particularly so of Tierney. Still, she possessed the wherewithal to allow them some individual exploration. Even letting Tierney sojourn across Soonayah on her own.

Hard-fought battle had attained her that right. Tierney knew if she mentioned going to the borderland, Haarth's dominion, Oxhild or just tip-toeing over the Kalamesh border, her mother would balk... violently. Maybe even revoke Tierney's capacity to travel anywhere. *Send me to the sanctum even earlier than she plans. No. I must maneuver this carefully to get out of it what I want. Little does she know, crossing the border is the ultimate goal.* She'd get to Kalamesh one day soon. In the end, a transplant to somewhere...anywhere else was the answer.

Tierney didn't understand why her mother held such a reluctance for any real interaction with her uncle and even with other lands. She'd heard about *Haarth* being kidnapped when he was a young man.

It'd happened to Haarth, so why is Mother the one with the unreasonable stance?

In their youth, they'd been told tales of raiders from Drundel taking Haarth and his party. Scaring little ones as a warning was the idea. Drundel bordered Soonayah to the mid-south and southwest. The Okehfey mountain range and the Sea of Ore separated Soonayah from the plunderers.

Haarth, on a sojourn of his own as a young man, had toured across the land of Kalamesh, and his whole party had been kidnapped by the Drundel. In those days there weren't all the restrictions on

Soonahyins traveling abroad. Those in talks figured they couldn't reason with the Drundel raiders. They couldn't meet their demands. Soonayah didn't negotiate. So they may never have gotten Haarth's body back to consecrate back to the soil if the Drundel had killed him.

They'd been proven right too. Soonayah had evidence of what the kidnappers were capable of. The fingers of a female of Haarth's party had been sent by the Drundel raiders to show that they had them and that they were willing to kill.

As a response, a planned recovery operation went into play. A ruse to get close to where they were holding them...and fell completely apart. The Drundel made no attempt at a good-faith exchange. They never brought Haarth to the designated meeting place in the first place. In a free-for-all, the Tempeh Tu killed every Drundel involved, save from one. The remaining raider had been an underling. They hadn't gotten any intel on the machinations of those who held Haarth or even who they were out of him, given that, he did go so far as implicating the presiding hierarchy of the Drundel land's involvement. When threatened with having to attest to this before said hierarchy, he'd killed himself in his vault.

Haarth's fate was left as a captive over a span of time. He escaped with trickery and his own brute force into the land called Olum. A desert between the borders of Kalamesh and Drundel, evading recapture through sheer cunning, snaking through the deathtrap of the Olum desert. A Kalameshee contingent deployed there found Haarth. They'd also found proof that the remainder of his party was dead.

Haarth hadn't cared. He'd stayed and scoured the desert, and had come up with pieces of his party's skin, scalps, a portion of a Tempeh Tu's leg. Any description of the harrowing events as gruesome was an understatement.

And this is what they told the youth as a forewarning.

Only, Tierney recalled well the scene that set the *current* impasse between her mother and Haarth. It'd been *Haarth* who championed better relations with other lands.

And he had been kidnapped.

She'd seen it all but never spoke of it to her mother because she and her cousin Lu'nil were doing something they were told never to do. Days after her father's passing, they made a pact to travel through the crawl space of air ducts littering the Keep from the passage opening near the youth quarters where they slept.

Her mother had made Lu'nil and Tierney swear never to enter the ducts again. A Keep guard had caught them exiting the ducts once exhausted, scared, and covered in dust. They'd been lost in them for an eternity. The queen frightened them with a tale of being stuck in them forever and no one ever finding them.

Nevertheless, that was over. They had been little then. They were big girls by the ages of nine and eight. Lu'nil was the fearless one who urged Tierney to take chances. Hence, their crawling through the ductwork commenced. And this time they weren't frightened because they planned the only "*surefire route to the very top of the Keep.*"

They giggled their way from room to room, peering through air slats, laughing, beside themselves at her brothers', Korrell and Adrihl's shoving match over their father's fastest flying razor, they were both too young yet to pilot. After crawling on to peer through slats into another room, they watched in fascination as one of the Keep's guards and their most favored caregiver stripped themselves bare. They humped each other until the guard wore himself out on top of their caregiver while she patted his head.

They instinctively stopped giggling when Haarth and her mother slammed into a sitting room, carrying on a fierce argument. Haarth had taken a position similar to Tierney's now. He hadn't backed down even though some said his captivity by the Drundel raiders was beyond savage. He claimed he was trying to carry out what he knew was one of his brother, Stah'lief's, last wishes. The encounter was enough for her mother though and ended up being the catalyst to Haarth's appointment to the southeastern borderlands as the chancellor there, and little to no communication between him and the queen. Even official business he did through an attendant. They conferred about Lu'nil, her comings and goings when she visited Haarth. That was it. Haarth didn't even travel to the high seat dominion for the convention of assemblies. His viceroy's attendance in his stead was the norm.

"She hadn't wanted him to go back to Kalamesh. She feared for his life," Tierney murmured aloud a discovery she hadn't understood until now. That's when the queen had tightened the borders so much, Soonahyins rarely leaving their own land.

The Kalameshee scowled. "Who's going to Kalamesh? Who is *she*? Your mother? Mlai?"

Tierney shook her head, unable to explain. There was something she didn't understand between her mother and Haarth. She had no answer for the Kalameshee about a thing she just didn't get herself. He didn't seem to need any, anyway. He was easing toward her, his eyes on her lips.

And she watched him musing, *this is so not good.* Still, she leaned in to meet his mouth.

Then toppled forward, missing the connection with him. He'd jumped to his feet. Glad he hadn't noticed, she grimaced at her own behavior. His attention was taken by something far more fascinating than herself.

"My eyes have taken in so much, I'm not sure I can stand anymore. And this is your home!" he said.

Tierney laughed. It was inexplicable why the Kalameshee's amazement with her land pleased her so. "No. This is the Frozen Folly." He *was* asking if they lived inside the Frozen Folly, right?

"What's a Frozen Folly?" he asked, eyes wide at the sight of the monolith of ice looming from its perch inside Dameerh.

Peetah Pearl walked past and chuckled at his reaction. She took her usual position in the conductor's cab. "During its excavation, it was dated as the most ancient monument on the entire planet of Telluric. Formed far before Soonayah was ever founded, when Starfalls were still not controlled," she told him.

The Kalameshee went and joined Peetah Pearl at the conductor's panel as she regaled him all about the Frozen Folly. Scrunched into her seat, Tierney watched him with Peetah Pearl and leaned into Bak'rah. *I'll just close my eyes for the time it takes to get to the Keep.*

Something jostled her from behind. *Great!* Haarth, sliding into the Kalameshee's vacated seat. She stilled. *He might want nothing.* She groaned when he touched her shoulder. Bak'rah grumbled his own sentiment. *I couldn't agree more, my boy.*

"I watched your interaction with the Kalameshee from the door of the privy closet and I believe I witnessed you find...an understanding with him." Haarth took duty *way* too far. She pouted with the thought of him leaving the privy closet door open. Some things crossed the lines of propriety. In the meantime, his words were a statement. His raised brows told her he expected her to answer him.

Understanding? How was he defining the concept? He stared at her, waiting. Tierney's mouth opened, then closed. "Uhm...not so much an understanding, Uncle. More an appreciation for his plight. He did, after all, jump from a mountain to save my wolf. What benefit would keeping outward animosity toward him get any of us?"

Haarth glanced to the cab of the cruiser, jaw clenched as his gaze moved from Peetah Pearl to the Kalameshee. Tierney couldn't blame him if he still didn't trust the Kalameshee. After her conversation with him, she was starting to suspect he hadn't begun to reveal his true angle.

"He watches every move you make, and you seem to have come to accept it. Maybe even enjoy it."

"I can't say it's acceptable to me, Uncle. I'm more...not concerned," she answered. She couldn't say she had an aversion to the Kalameshee either. Not after their dalliance in the snow. She wouldn't lie to herself. She had no delusions about the fact that she'd instigated it too.

"That's altogether well, Tierahna. The hope now then is that your mother will have as little concern." Tierney frowned. "Now is the time that we'll discover if it's so. We're here.

Chapter 13

ome.

Dameerh, the enclave. The high seat was Soonayah's most populated, hence considered a full dominion in its own right. Roads narrowed through enclaves, coupled with thoroughfares teeming with people that caused blockages. They slowed for one.

Mlai made her way from Tierney's sleeping cabin when they stopped. Domed buildings constructed from tan, cream, rock-colored stone masonry—because of the Ministry of Architecture's Historical Sect's development restrictions—gave off an old-world feel. *Quaint and charming.*

The Kalameshee's eyes trailed every nuance along the streets, the cobblestone walkways, the people everywhere and more, taking in all the ambiance. Since his words earlier, Tierney would commit herself to see the abundance of her land through his eyes. A foreigner's eyes. *Now, all I have to do is figure out how to do that.*

"Renewed appreciation." Mlai's eyebrows raised at Tierney's mutterings.

Tierney shook her head to the question on Mlai's face and really examined her. Her pink skin was still wan, but she smiled from ear to ear as she looked around. *Hopefully, she will be back to her vivacious self again soon.* Tierney squeezed her shoulder.

Maybe the excitement of being in the home dominion could replenish Mlai's good health. The picturesque Dameerh could convince a person they were still in times before any advancement. If it weren't for the flying apparatuses and hovering snowcrafts everywhere.

The cruiser's optiglass was still opaque, Haarth having never deemed their passage secure enough to change the setting. They observed the dominion unobstructed with no one's attention on them.

The high seat was a sight, always busy with people. And thus, a girl no more than a babe walked on a walkway, paying no mind to her steps, covered in mink fur from the hood on her head, down to the tops of her toes.

Those little feet are surely warm, sheathed in wolvien shukka boots as they were. Tierney scowled at the memory of her own nearly ruined boots. Her trek in near blizzard conditions two days earlier pained her to think about it. Looking at the babe transformed her from those thoughts at the picture the babe made. A little like an overstuffed warbler. She waddled, encumbered in her mother's efforts to assure she felt not one chill. The mother walked a ways behind laden with packages.

A stencil on one of the packages stood out. *The Rising Bun. They made gorgeous confections.* Mother and daughter were coming from the direction of the eatery, the little one's attention absorbed by the sticky bun she carried that her mother must've just indulged her with. Her boots peaked from beneath her parka, the more she tottered along. She took one step too close to the corner and Tierney lifted from her seat.

"I have to catch her before she's in the thoroughfare," she announced to no one in particular or anyone who might be paying attention.

But on instinct, the mother—though burdened with packages—seemed to sense the babe's wayward movement. She pinched the back of her snood, making the babe's parka shift to reveal a little face concentrating on her treat. *Aww...* Tiny babe-sized braids strung with beads obscured the babe's vision. *She will be fine with that mother.* The mother was guiding her daughter with the pinched snood. She had no need for Tierney to rescue her. *How was I thinking I could get to her in time, anyway?* So Tierney retook her seat. When the babe shook the offending hair, Tierney laughed. "She's determined to consume a bun as big as she is."

"Who?" Mlai asked, and Tierney gestured to the little one.

The mother crouched, then righted her daughter's snood and pointed to a flying razor, and appeared quite practiced at this diversion. Tierney followed her misdirection too, although, the transport *was* flying too low within the dominion. Tierney almost missed the mother tearing off more than half the sticky bun her daughter held. She wrapped it. An adept hand slid it into a pocket within her own pelt without the little one ever taking notice.

And Tierney barked out with laughter. Everyone in the cruiser shifted to look at her. She explained to them what she'd seen and the Kalameshee came and took his seat near her again. They all laughed too...even Haarth.

Why were her eyes drawn to the Kalameshee when she was wondering if she could ever be as uncanny a mother as the woman on the street? Continuing to chuckle, he kept the girl and her mother in his sights as they moved along. "The joy of life is found in a babe."

A tingle shivered up Tierney's back upon hearing his words, settling right beneath her breastbone as leaded as a weight.

At first, the transport's shadow moving across his face didn't register. "Hold on." She strained for a look at the sky behind them. "That flying razor is well below altitude within the dominion. It abides by no flight route."

Tierney moved from one side of the cruiser to the other. Along the outskirts of Dameerh, structures were allowed taller dimensions. Flight towers controlled flight from there. She would contact the Ministry of Transport about the flying razor once she got settled at the Keep.

On the outer range of the Frozen Folly, the flight tower to the east always drew her attention first. Whatever the weather conditions, it blended in with the Folly's appearance. To see the tower, you would follow the lines along its base to its precipice to a darker outline. At night, the two became one, and no matter how discerning the eye, the tower couldn't be detected.

The Folly sat off a ways to the east, presenting itself as a backdrop, presiding over the enclave that had been built around it. The Kalameshee and Mlai's gazes were caught by the Frozen Folly as well. Delighted in their wonder, Tierney laughed again. If they were enraptured by the enclave and the Frozen Folly now, she couldn't wait for them to see them come eve. While the Folly captivated their attention, the cruiser sailed on to the most southern end of the Dameerh enclave, on through the gates of the Keep.

"We're here," she said.

The leaded weight in her diaphragm hardened and dropped to upset her stomach of its own accord. She'd never been this apprehensive to face her mother before. Although the queen was fierce, she was nothing if not pragmatic. Tierney felt a crippling kind of foreboding that stunted her feet from moving. *I'm hesitant to step into my own home.* She just *knew* that once she did everything would change from this day forward.

As usual, the Kalameshee rushed a million questions at her. Anything he asked, she was more than willing to help with, the barrage from him a welcome delay. *Gives me a little more time to prepare myself.* He paused after they disembarked from the cruiser and attendants took it away. And ran a hand over the rectangular blocks on the outer wall of the Keep.

"What nature of rock is this? It's as translucent as ice but warm to the touch."

"It's chornyne stone used in Soonahyin architecture because of its insulation. The Keep is schemed for a maximization of inner heat. The chornyne stone allows for little to no added insulation." Tierney rubbed the chornyne stone as well. It breathed, or well it seemed like it did, like it was alive. "It has quite an effect in Soonayah. I'm sure you noticed we use it for roof tiles too. Chornyne stone is enhanced from the land. The stones mesh together. They never leak either. Perfect for our snow."

The Kalameshee nodded as if still contemplating the stones. "The effects of leaving your gates unattended could be the welcome of any scoundrel with mal-intent on a clear path to your royal seat." His gaze, leastwise, swept through all the people wandering the courtyard, past those in Keep regalia tending to transports and visitors, on over to the courtyard's gates.

At first, Tierney'd had almost no patience with him at all, but she was starting to understand him a little and was willing to help him along with his misconceptions—his thought processes. As he *was* willing to change his ignorance of their culture. All the questions were proof of that. "They're open because all Soonahyins are welcome to the common areas of the Keep. Isn't it as much theirs as it is ours? Although no person is allowed inside carrying arms as you are. Those who aren't authorized, anyway." She had softened her air the more she interacted with him. Her manner, her skin resplendent toward him when she smiled. When she talked, he watched her lips and tongue and teeth form the words. "Once we cross the threshold, your weapons will be confiscated. Because you're traveling with us, clearance was waved through. Had you not been, the unengaged moat may well have activated. Mother's first visit with you could've been through a reversible pier-glass as she tried to discern your level of subversion."

Bak'rah's muzzle brushed against her. A move of his head underneath her hand to pull her attention from the Kalameshee. She looked down at him. He was restless to get to his special place within her quarters. "I know, my boy." She curled her fingers behind his ears. The rest of their party had moved on into the Keep. So, regardless of whether she was ready or not, into the Keep she was bound.

Chapter 14

The Kalameshee's pouch he carried in the fitting on his back *was* never-ending. It harbored near enough gear to fit a trunk.

Tierney stood to the side engaged with an elder of an Ahn'Sirh clan and his family. They'd made the journey to Dameerh for their mid-time Ritual of Ume for revitalization. Every Soonahyin everywhere had to revitalize. The elder had insisted on visiting the Keep out of nostalgia. His speaking to the young of his clan was what drew Tierney over.

"In my days as sentry, we never had one successful incursion through the outer gates," he told them. "Me getting older and the young ones getting quicker is why I returned to our hamlet." Having been back in his Cordalai hamlet for the last thirty spans, life as a chronicler should be his second calling with the way he spun a tale.

How old he was? Tierney was loathed to guess. He looked as if he could be no younger than a hundred spans, but stood tall and spry, and as a sentry, would have been the epitome of vigor in his time. And as he'd made it to the high seat dominion under his own volition to maintain his Ritual of Ume, his age was probably far beyond a hundred. But Tierney wouldn't be asking.

He introduced her to his family in first respect, the "Princess Tierahna Haareth Soonayah Ahn'Trunkh." Like *he* was family.

"Oohs" and "aahs" came from the young ones on meeting the princess.

Tierney basked in the familial camaraderie she had with her people. While she touched the beaded heads of some of the youths, she sank to a crouch and marveled at their short hair. For traditional reasons and mostly for warmth, Soonahyins rarely if ever cut their hair. Well, that and kinetics. The soul-energy of Soonahyins—intensely so for those who speeded—partially released out of the hair. *Goodness*! This would be the most of what she missed when she left. Her people.

She'd decided she'd plait the hair of any of her own young as most Ahn'Trunkh wore theirs. Experiment with the beautiful glass and stone beaded styles the Ahn'Sirh clan were so adept at weaving too. Rubbing a smooth bead between her finger, she touched the braid of one babe. The little one covered her mouth. Before bringing her irresistible face close to hers, Tierney lifted her into her arms and they grinned at each other.

On instinct, she turned to the Kalameshee's hold-up at the garrison pass-through. Of course, *still hemmed up.* From there he was watching her interactions with the babe as she'd suspected he would be. His eye's imprint on her body left a passage that lingered...in intimate places most times. She'd felt them burning all the way to her spine on several occasions. After handing the little one back into the fold of her family, she said her farewells.

What's taking him so long? Maybe she could hurry them along if she headed to the stanchion to hasten his clearance.

They had his pouch, no larger than the span of an average man's back spread open. Most of the items she knew he carried inside were laid out and cataloged. There were many more she'd never seen.

"Each time the pouch is re-examined, another item is found," the garrison guards told her.

She scowled at the Kalameshee. "What manner of material is this?" Hefting the pouch, inside the plain valise were ordinary compartments. How could it be a minimal size and hold enough garments for days of travel and all the gear a tactician could need? "What type of technology works this way?"

The Kalashee's hand covered hers, and their eyes connected. Something else connected too that she couldn't put a name to. Whatever the frisson was called, they both felt it the moment they touched again. Had to have. An electrical current that strong could fry the nerves if one didn't pay attention to it. Oh, and he paid attention alright. He eased in closer to her, encircling her shoulders with his other arm, he then lifted her fingers right into the lip of the pouch and stalk-size fingers manipulated hers until she depressed distinct nodules within the material. After a specific pattern input, the scabbard he'd produced when they were in the woods emerged. Because of the scabbard's true bulk, it was pushed from the pouch into her hand. The scabbards hilt was still warm like he'd held it recently and it retained the residual heat from his body, and her hand curled to latch onto that heat signature of where his hand had imprinted.

Her mouth gaping like a fish earned her a chuckle from him. "That should be all the items." He took the pouch from her limp fingers and handed it and his weapon to the garrison guards. They confiscated the scabbard and re-examined the pouch with the scan detector for any further surprises. "My pouch is made of nanomachines. They communicate with and distribute all the like-kind bots in my equipment. They're expanded and retracted to their best configuration until I need them." He winked at her while she was still giving her best impression of a blowfish. "I guess my people must not seem quite so unsophisticated as you thought, huh?

Once they finished its examination and had reinserted the allowable contents, Tierney seized the pouch from the garrison guards. "We must submit this for analysis by the devisers in the Automation Sect..."

The Kalameshee, with a soft touch mind you, took the pouch from her pliant fingers and moved it out of her reach. Almost like she was a skittish animal who he was afraid to spook. His smile didn't take the sting out of those actions though. When she went to grab it again, he fitted the pouch into the slot on his back. Meanwhile, his urging her onward with him into the atrium threw her off briefly. *Wha...what are you doing?* This allowed him to keep her hand in his as they walked. *Smooth.* She had to remember he was good at this type of thing. "That's why I'm here, remember? Kalamesh's request for trade with Soonayah."

Was that the only reason he was here? From the look in his eyes, quite a few other reasons, far more intense came to mind. Or was she seeing things—seeing the actions and the interest that he wanted her to see? Entangled by a Kalemeshee's machinations.

In the atrium, he stopped in his tracks and looked up, causing her to bump into his back. *What now?* If they didn't get to her mother soon, the queen would surely send out a search party for them, even though she *did* understand why he was so distracted.

The clarion dome atop the atrium drenched the tiles they stood on in sunlight. Dazzling angles bounced off the mosaics. Wall carvings and benches were arranged in an open perimeter around the atrium too. And rainbows and sunrays danced all over the people filling the benches and the artifacts and the attendees studying the walls. The Kalameshee gasped.

Everything, including the people, was made participants in the diorama bombarding the senses in the atrium. One beam of sunlight arrowed at such an angle it caught a corner of mosaics of blue and purple, gold and teal, and orange that formed a sort of portal and jumping beam. Young ones skipping around, burst through the color spectrum, throwing the colors in relief against their brown skin. "Sweet heavens! Are they literally playing with rainbows?" Lifting his eyes to the dome, "And is that more chornyne stone?" he asked.

"No. It's the mineral lonsdaleite sanded to its crystal shine. Chornyne stone is not pliable enough for a dome and could never shape rainbows pretty enough for them to play with. The density is too high for clarity."

"But you use it on your outer walls?"

"Yes. But not for its translucent appearance. Did you not notice the outer walls are still yet fortified from within? You can't peer within the walls. And even the dome, though impenetrable, has bulwark fortification." She was short with him and she realized it. Her mind hadn't yet moved from how he'd used her attraction to take that pouch away, so she hadn't noticed as he had, her brother's approach from behind. He ruffled her hair by putting his whole arm into it and flailing her head about. Even before she saw who it was, she knew who would do such a *detestable* thing.

"Ad'rihl!" Hampered from turning to him, her shoulder jerked in its socket because the Kalameshee had hold of her hand. And had tightened his grip when she tried to get to her brother with the expected retaliation she knew he hated: jumping on his back, tangling her fists into his plaits, and riding him like an animal until he bucked her off. Although that dreaded answer hadn't been able to be deployed for her own hated taunting since they'd been young because of Ad'rihl's adeptness for countering her, she would have given it an audacious try. But for *one* fact; the Kalameshee had hold of her hand.

Her brother grinned upon seeing her. His crossing his arms and cocking his brow told her he noticed the hand-holding too. "Why, Tierney. Mother will be beside herself with how welcoming you are to our new foreigner here."

Though he didn't hurt her, the Kalameshee held her with enough force that she struggled to remove herself from him. Her soul-energy flashed within her body and pulsed from her hand into his. Still, he didn't let her go. *Wow! How had he withstood that?* Tierney never changed her expression, because she didn't want to alarm her brother, but it was amazing the Kalameshee had absorbed a pulse like that. A Kalameshee's retention of their soul-energy must allow for them to have stronger resistance. Her brother's eyes moved from her to the Kalameshee of their own accord, a glint hardening inside them. A gaze that had marveled after the young ones prancing around before, clamped to her brother's and returned his stare. She looked from one man to the other until they seemed to come to some unspoken understanding.

That was it!

Her patience gone with the both of them, she sent an even more strident pulse into the Kalameshee. Giving her hand one last squeeze, he held onto her a moment longer, then broke the stare-off with her brother and finally let her go.

And the skin there felt bereft now that his heat no longer touched her. Her jerking her arm, then wrapping it around herself, ended with her unaware that she was rubbing it against her tunic. "I just toured the Dome of Clarity with the Kalames...with Torhvald, Ad'rihl. And he, of course, had to give up his weapon. It took only a little time." Mush must've been made out of her brains, with her offering up excuses to her brother like he had some authority over her. Like he wasn't only two spans older than she.

"Oh, I see. Come now, then. I've been sent for your delivery without delay to the Hall of Covenance. Mother's patience has been short as of late." So here was the search party to deliver her back at her mother's beck and call.

Tierney cackled at her brother's back. "As of late? More constant,

I should think. And what need is there for us to meet in the Hall of Covenance? Wouldn't one of the more informal reception halls serve just as well?"

Ad'rihl whirled back to her and had dropped his smile. "She must contend with a whole *docket* of critical matters, as you well know, Tierney. You should be of a mind not to line yourself up to be added to it. And we're meeting in the Hall of Covenance because of the chain of events you set off. This Kalameshee and even the Lorgren's business are official sovereign issues. A convening of the dominions' chancellors and the Council of Chieftains has been called. Assembly shall be held here within a short amount of time."

Oh boy. That mass from before stuck in the base of her throat this time. It was back again, the weight, leaded now with about fifty stones more. Ad'rihl chuffed her under her chin with his knuckles. "It's altogether well, Tierahna. What you have envisioned is at hand." His encouragement made her feel no less sick. As she pondered how to negotiate these new revelations, Tierney followed him by rote from the atrium. They stepped down through the well of people and artifacts to a concealed corridor that led to some restricted sections of the Keep.

"There is the beast!" Ad'rihl called, lowering himself to ruffle Bak'rah's coat. The wolf wallowed in Ad'rihl's attention. Probably a little lonely now, her beautiful pup mugged it up, prancing in circles for Ad'rihl. It was best practice to keep him away from the common areas, so Tierney had sent him to the corridor earlier. Most people were afraid of him on sight, especially the young. But he hadn't left the corridor when the Kalameshee hadn't let go of her hand.

That was different. He never hesitated to come if he divined she needed him. Tierney considered that for a moment. She *had* been miffed at how easily the Kalameshee handled her. Ad'rihl walked in view of a detector that scanned his whole body. They were scanned too and granted entrance to some secured areas of the Keep. She'd known though, that the Kalameshee wouldn't hurt her. And Bak'rah had sensed it too.

Chapter 15

Tierney grinned and shook her head at the realization she'd just come to about her and the Kalameshee. No faster than the smile appeared, it was wiped from her face quick enough though. The first person she encountered when she entered the dazzling embellishment of the Hall of Covenance? The queen, of course.

"Why Tierahna, my daughter, the perpetual wanderer. I'm so glad you've found entertainment while we all wait here with great patience for you and the Kalameshee." Her mother had a knack for making her feel like she'd only spent about nine spans on their planet Telluric circling its sun. The queen was upset with her and she had reason to be.

"Mother." They joined arms, forearms to elbows. She bent to kiss her cheek too as she and her siblings always greeted their mother. "I was just thinking on my happiness at being home."

"That's altogether well, Tierahna. What purpose would there be to wander from one end of Soonayah to another, if a home wasn't being kept for your comfort to come back to?" Tierney winced. *And so the reprimands began.* And her ending up an escort to a Kalameshee, who carried unsolicited requests—on top of all the undercurrents between herself and the queen—was just her due. *Whatever gave me the notion to act on my own opinion?* She pressed her lips together to keep the scream inside her head from spilling from her mouth. She would only display herself as the youth-filled girl that she always felt she was when in her mother's presence.

Her mother smoothed a frizz of hair behind Tierney's ear, her touch soft on the downcast head of her eldest daughter. Tapping her under her chin made Tierney meet her gaze. Her mother's eyes searched hers. *Always, always searching.* "To what avail was involving Haarth, Tierahna? Did you think his clout would convert me?"

"I was involved, Ana'kerah, to allow her expression." Haarth's baritone resounded before Tierney could ever answer. Everyone in the hall gave him their attention. "Tierahna spoke to me on issues she has strong feelings about and on those she believes she can instrument change in." His words echoed throughout the hall.

Though the rich red and blue velvet tapestries that draped the walls and the short pile, royal-blue carpeting helped mute sound, Haarth's voice bounced around the vaulted tray-ceilings. They were fashioned not only to inspire awe at the diaphanous gold-inlaid art on them but in perfect roundness for excellent acoustics. Which allowed speeches from those given on the floor to resound up to the patron's galleries, situated in the highest balconies, surrounding the whole hall. The Kalameshee and Mlai's gazes traveled the room to its farthest recesses. All who attended assembly here were expected to participate in whatever that took place between the decision-makers who would occupy the closest tiered seating to the floor. Tierney and their whole party *held* their *silence*, awaiting a response from the queen.

By not a tic of a nerve did her mother's expression reveal one thing. Still, the tension in the hall grew thick. The queen *did glance* at Haarth, but then quickly away. Haarth had spoken up for Tierney and now the queen had to answer. "Do you feel removed from me so much that you must seek counsel from others, Tierahna?" But rather than address Haarth himself, she addressed her response to Tierney.

"Others? I'm now other?" Haarth laughed in direct challenge to the queen's misdirection. He took a step toward her within the cluster they were all standing in. Tierney's brothers, Korrell—whom Tierney had noticed standing near her mother when she first entered *and* Ad'rihl—both angled themselves subtly forward.

Haarth barked out with laughter again, revealing he hadn't missed her brothers' positioning. "So, I really am an outsider here? Tierahna came to me because she could find no quarter here amongst her immediates." Opened arms, hands out, he moved back from their group. "Have no worry. I would die before I allowed any harm to befall your mother."

The *queen's* laugh was forced out with her stepping up onto the first tier of seats. The seats were positioned in an arrangement for conference. All the room's rises of tiered seats were swiveled by a control hidden on an outer partition. They focused around a staged lectern area with the patron's balconettes around the top of them for extra seating. The queen could now look out over their group. Everyone else had pulled back too.

Ok. More relaxed. I never expected this kind of tension. Tierney worried her lips. *No need in revealing that I know about Mother's plans with all these people around. Looks like Haarth had plans to confront Mother too.*

The queen's smile seemed grateful, directed at Haarth for stepping back, lessening the tension. But his visage was pinned to her, hawkish in it's nature. And she looked away again. "Ana'kerah, my nephews are strung tight enough to kill on reflex. When was the last Kulumdeh Vy organized? Or are they barred as participants in combat preparations? Smothering restrictions in that area too?"

Korrell, Tierney's second oldest brother by three spans, broke into the tension, his mannerism intense on behalf of their mother. "We train and compete for regular Kulumdeh Vies, Uncle. At present, our alert is on high." Korrell spoke while looking undaunted into the face of his uncle, so he missed their mother's shake of her head. "Mother was attacked while we hunted in the wild reeves of Okehfey. Ad'rihl and I had split off to climb the slopes further up for fresher kills. Mother was then surrounded by insurgents—"

"Okehfey? Where we were? We encountered something in the woods there too. Though it was hard to tell if it was an actual person. It was invisible. Hard to tell *what* it was. We should have been informed that you were there at the same time. And why was she left alone just so you could climb further for more daring feats—"

"This is what has always been done, Uncle. Even as boys we dared to climb further in the face of the winds of Okehfey. You question if we train. This is proof that we do." Korrell's timbre never changed, yet the words he spoke were filled with strength, employing a match for his uncle beyond his experience.

Haarth's anger was manifesting as energy that radiated off him, ratcheting up tension already at a breaking point in the room again. "When this attack happened, why did Eh'kotah not reinforce your mother's—"

"Eh'kotah travels back from his trek up the Dayea mountains as we speak."

"Eh'kotah too?" Tierney muttered. She hadn't known their eldest brother was off on another of his harrowing treks while she traveled across Soonayah in the midst of a blizzard. Oh, that was what prompted Ad'rihl's warning about staying off their mother's full docket. The queen may well have gone for a relaxing hunt in the Okehfey wilds to temper her mind's worries for them. Only to be attacked by marauders in her own land.

"So, your mother was abandoned—"

"She wasn't abandoned. She had a whole sect of Tempeh Tu at her defense. We could see the blue lights of their frostfires discharging.

Their clashes are what alerted us to fight our way back."

"Frostfires?" Tierney recognized this habit now. Haarth pacing like he had at Outliers when his mind was racing, analyzing things from every angle. He stopped and speared Korrell where he stood. "So deadly force was used. You talk of fighting your way back. How many insurgents were there? Was your mother injured?"

"No less than fifty were there and yes, we killed them all. Mother's shoulder was dislocated. An insurgent devised a slip through her guards." Korrell's look bathed his mother in admiration. "She pulsed him nearly to a crisp in hand to hand." In extension, the queen gave him a weak smile in return.

"Mahtah!" Tierney cried out the moniker she had given her mother as a babe, as Bak'rah whimpered somewhere beyond her sight. *This is what I get for being so intent on myself.* Even with Bak'rah's carrying on, Tierney didn't falter getting to her mother. *Mother was attacked and I never even knew.* She rushed to her mother's side and with a gingerly touch, looked for lasting harm, causing her mother's mouth to lift. Tierney made sure to take care with her shoulder as they embraced.

"We think mother's collected soul-energy released too high when he surprised her." Ad'rihl continued Korrell's recount of the event. "It's rare for anyone to pulse out so much energy in one go that death is the result. Rarer even for a female. Yet, Mother managed to subdue another one too. The insurgent attempted to break her hold and the Tempeh Tu eliminated her on the spot. So no interrogation was done, as none of them survived."

Haarth, motionless now, watched the queen with burgeoning regard. Still, she wouldn't meet his gaze. "Fifty rebels across our borders, and were beaten back with your party of...?" He looked to Ad'rihl.

"Fifteen," Ad'rihl answered flexing wide shoulders in a not-so-subtle swagger.

"Fifteen." Haarth's cocked eyebrows relayed his pride in them himself. "Then it's demonstrated that your training is far more than up to par, rather it's commendable. But through what gap did they cross? My dominion's border, Oxhild is held sacrosanct. I interrogate anyone who attempts incursions myself. I would've been advised of any breach."

"I reported some disturbances on the border to the queen and the Guard Council some time ago." The husk of Peetah Pearl's voice startled Tierney when she answered Haarth. For a while there, she'd forgotten their whole traveling party was in the room. "I became aware of unusual activity taking place at the Licome Passage. That's one of the reasons I insisted on escorting you back here. This must be where these insurgents came through. There's no other undetectable entrance into our lands." Korrell nodded in agreement with Peetah Pearl.

"Who is the chancellor there that has allowed this incursion? Pominor!" Haarth pounced on the name of the chancellor of Lehquate. The dominion stood at the mouth of the Licome Passage, the small, nearly inaccessible strip of land that resided on the one open aperture where Soonahyin and Drundel lands met. "He must be brought here to answer to what he allowed to happen."

The queen cooed to Tierney as she extracted herself from her daughter's clinging, patting her hair while she made the little noises so her daughter would loosen her lock around her neck, then addressed Haarth directly for the first time. "Pominor Prehmtor Olehor Ahn'Bangh will travel here within a short time. The chancellors of all the dominions shall come for the convening of the assembly in the course of deciding the very matter you two have brought to the fore. We will debrief him further then. Strategic countermeasures have been put into play by the Guard Council and me already. Pominor was integral in those plans."

"Not before a pack of insurgents crossed the passage and lay in wait to ambush you while you hunted. His custodianship is lax! Why wasn't I told about this to be put on guard for similar occurrences at my own border post? For that matter..." Haarth looked around and found the Kalameshee. Naturally, he stood only a few paces from Tierney. The Kalameshee's eyes tracked everyone and everything that was going on in the room. Probing each other for several moments, he and Haarth's gazes stuck like magnets. "Where was the communication when a Kalameshee was cleared through my border while still armed with his weaponry? It's impossible that he and his scabbard came through undetected. Only you could have approved his entrance into our lands without my knowledge, Ana'kerah."

Unthinkable! Mother would never undercut Uncle!

Haarth's voice lowered, paying deference to the revelations unfolding. "Was he allowed in to see if I had turned treason to our land...my queen?" he delivered a question that no one else would have dared ask the queen. For if the reason for the question were truly a possibility, no less than death should be its response.

Chapter 16

Tierney shot back from everyone inside the little cluster group they'd formed. "Uncle! What do you speak of? Mother would never think you capable of treason! There's no one more loyal than you. Even we here know all that you've done. The sacrifice of living away from your home to secure the southeastern dominions to prosperity. How could mother have let the Kalameshee through to rendezvous a meeting that she didn't know was taking pla...?" Her voice tripped all over the looks—from the grimace on Haarth's face to her mother's lowered lids.

Tierney bowed her head, her face crumpling until she had to turn away. *There is no way Mother could know why I was meeting Haarth, is there?* "Uncle? Mother...she didn't know about our meeting? You would've told me of her knowledge if you knew...right, Uncle?" As Tierney spoke, her voice wavered. Everyone in the room looked down and avoided its appeal. Everyone except for Ad'rihl who had the sensitivity of a goat.

Ad'rihl shifted out of the way as Bak'rah passed him. The wolf whimpered on a weave, bumping anyone in the way of getting to Tierney. Stepping onto a tier of conference seating, she slumped on one of the red, rich-textured seats so that Bak'rah could come into her arms. She whispered, "Shh, sweet pup," and nuzzled his neck.

"Calm yourself, Tierney," Ad'rihl derided. "Before you have the beast howling down the Keep. You can't be so young you still believe you've been allowed to traipse all over Soonayah on your own all this time? You have Shadow Guard who keeps Mother abreast of your every move. Peetah Pearl informed her of the Kalameshee preceding Haarth to Outliers. By the time the Kalameshee trespassed into your quarters, we *all* here were gripped to your Shadow Guard's watch of you through the walls. We were on guard as reinforcements." Ad'rihl cackled at their exploits even as his eyes found the Kalameshee's. That glint of steel from before returned. "You should hear the tales from the Shadow Guards themselves. What they must do to keep you from detecting them." He shook his head. "All so the innocent Tierney may feel some sense of independence. You should be far beyond needing those youthful reassurances by now."

"Agh!" Ad'rihl yelped at the slap Korrell cracked across the back of his head. His capacity for insensitivity was legendary. Even Korrell knew him as such, and he understood him better than most. Ad'rihl returned Korrell's glare with a glower of his own and shrugged, mouthing the silent question, "What!" Completely oblivious.

As Haarth approached Tierney, she turned her face further into Bak'rah's fur and rocked against him, her nose wrinkling in disgust with herself. The wetness clinging to his fur came from her.

"Tierahna. I knew you weren't allowed to travel the length of our land unaccompanied when we talked in the beginning. I never realized how unaware *you were* until we spoke that last time before we went to Outliers. This is why I insisted you communicate with your mother. Basically, that was one of the major reasons why I agreed to meet you all the way out there at all." He rubbed a hand over her frizz and brushed fingers over the knuckles she'd tucked into Bak'rah's fur. "For some time to talk away from here with you. You're of an age to assert a stance with your mother. I wanted to impress upon you to speak up. And maybe she would start treating you like the adult that you are and stop keeping so much from you."

Tierney laughed. "So, everyone here operated in knowledge apart from me?" *Yet, they have no clue about Mother's future plans for me.* "Laughably inexperienced Tierney? I walked around in foolish arrogance, utterly ignorant. The one saving fact is that I at least wasn't being tracked for fear of subversion." Now, little things niggled her memory that she should've noticed before; like the figures she'd seen crest the hill behind her at Outliers, the frostfire discharged toward the tornebirds, a sense of being watched wherever she went. Even when she'd thought she was alone, she'd attributed that to the constancy of the Tempeh Tu, believing the instinct was just the residual effects of being under ever-present eyes.

"And neither was Haarth, Tierahna. As you already stated, and everyone here well knows." The queen's soft voice compelled them, imbued with an undeniable force of character. "You headed so far west, I received notice that Haarth had left his post and traveled west as well. I was of a mind you two would meet." The queen's gaze went to Haarth at last. "We allowed the Kalameshee prince crossing the border to play out. We surveilled *his* intentions, not yours for meeting your uncle. And not Haarth's whose loyalty I've never once questioned." The queen and Haarth exchanged a long glance for the first time since he had come home to the Keep.

"Peetah Pearl was speed tracking him when he broke into my quarters. Did you put her on guard?" Tierney asked.

"I didn't, but I'm grateful, all the same. The Shadow Guard posted in a nearby corridor to your suite in case they were needed. The Kalameshee's weapon had already been neutralized when he'd come through the border gate, it couldn't fire. But you all handled the situation yourselves."

Everyone pivoted to the bang of ornate doors opened suddenly, slammed against the wall. Tierney's sister, Os'carah intruded on their little scene, head held high, their cousin L'unil behind her. Their entrance disrupted the unfortunate quagmire from vaulting forward with relentless revelations. "Tierahna Harreth Soonayah Ahn'Trunkh, you finally decide to come home? After nearly five full days away. You promised you wouldn't go on one of your long excursions!"

Lu'nil and Tierney smirked at each other behind Os'carah's back. Her greeting was the norm of brattiness expected.

Lu'nil, far more self-possessed, had a bit more maturity than her young cousin, and as required for a bit more maturity, her demeanor cooled, inducing a wave of lament at the thickness in the atmosphere that would send Lu'nil on a straight line to her father. Joining arms, she and Haarth hugged and kissed each other's cheeks. Lu'nil hadn't visited him in his dominions for some time. Their missing each other was evident in their pleasure in seeing each other now.

Tierney always wondered about the dynamics of father-daughter relationships. She and Lu'nil were raised together like sisters. Of course, she was close to Os'carah, the babe of the Keep. Yet, the very fact of her sister's young age of eighteen lent to Tierney having a closer relationship with Lu'nil. Lu'nil's relationship with her father, Haarth, confounded her though. They seemed to have great camaraderie. He encouraged Lu'nil to follow her own mind. She spoke with unabashed pride of her father's fierce chancellorship. *Yet, she'd chosen to live most of her life here at the Keep with us.*

The circumstances of their youth cultivated reverence at having someone so like her with whom to grow. Lu'nil was her kindred in looks too. Tall and built, unlike Os'carah who had their mother's slighter, more rounded build. And although she was grateful to have Lu'nil as near a sister could be, Tierney would never live separate from a father such as Haarth. *Not if given the choice. And maybe then I wouldn't be on the verge of having to run away from my own home.*

Os'carah strolled to the queen and wound herself around her and took no account of her sore shoulder, missing their mother's wince of pain. Tierney stood to go to them and unwrap her from their mother because she knew their mother never would. The queen indulged Os'carah's demonstrative nature. But she wasn't feeling particularly charitable toward their mother, was she? She had probably not even told Os'carah of the attack at Okehfey out of some misguided attempt to shield her. *I think I will remain right where I am. Mother can take care of herself.*

Os'carah tugged on the queen's ear. The white ornament hanging from the bar, wrapped around the queen's upper lobe tinkled. "Mother, should we take offense? Tierney, gone for days on end, returning without your onyx ear-wrap or my wolvien shukka boots that I've been subjected to waiting two whole seasons for!"

The pout on Os'carah's face worked as well on Tierney as it did on anyone else. "I haven't been gone five full days Os'kie. You exaggerate. And your assumption to dispatch me for your whims is quite snobbish, anyway. Yet, would I dare show my face here without your boots when you know I've been to the festival?" A smile pulled at Tierney's lips despite herself. "Even I'm not so bold. The never-ending sorrow from you would make my ears bleed. The boots and my gear must have been delivered to my quarters by now."

A belly laugh escaped her as she braced to receive her sister who ran full tilt toward her. Os'carah flung herself into Tierney's arms, screeching. "You retrieved them, Tierney? You get so absorbed in discovery and so on, I was fraught that you wouldn't remember your promise to get them on your next excursion. Not that you told anybody you were leaving anyway." Os'carah pulled back within Tierney's embrace and put a finger to her chin. "Should I regret my doubt of you? No, I shall not. You leave me too often for any regret. It's only right that you feel compelled to indulge me. Otherwise, what good is to be had from my elder sister? I must try them right now!" Preparing to run straight to Tierney's quarters to scavenge for the boots, she jumped away from Tierney. "Come now, Lu'nil. We should see how fitting the auburn fur looks against my skin."

"Wait! You should meet our new friend first. Mlai?" Tierney held out her hand and Mlai came and grasped it. "She's Lorgren and needs a rest. Will you show her to the guest residences on your way to *raid* my quarters?"

Os'carah greeted Mlai and took her hand from Tierney's, pausing to sum up the delicate Lorgren. Then she shrugged. If Tierney found the retiring foreigner decent, she could be trusted. "Your skin has such beauty," Os'carah said. She skimmed the back of one knuckle over Mlai's cheek and walked to the door with her. "It must be so grand to match attire to it." Looking down at Mlai's dark, utilitarian tunic and cape, a moue pursed her lips. "I have a far more flattering pelisse. With your frame—"

"She must rest, Os'carah!" Tierney called after them.

"Of course she must," Os'carah answered, wide eyes mocking Tierney.

Tierney shook her head. "Bak'rah go. Take Bak'rah to my quarters as well, please. He's weary from our journey too."

The balm of Os'carah's vivacity had dispelled the contesting energies in the room. Her whirlwind of a departure with Lu'nil and Mlai stole the zest from the air and sealed it behind the closed door. Tierney regretted their absences as soon as they were gone.

Chapter 17

This needs to be over! And I haven't even confronted Mother about her plans to commit me yet. A glance at her mother revealed a queen staring after their departed family members too. Her face looked like how Tierney felt, like one's brain writhed inside its own skull with a body that literally vibrated heightened energy.

The eldest of the siblings, her brother Eh'kotah's energy struck Tierney as if he were there in the room. Probably because a spar vy with him right then would expend some of the anger hoarding inside her. *And the perfect time for a vy?* Right now. If he landed a blow maybe it would knock her free of the angst razing her brain.

She'd knock him back of course. No matter how skilled or how fast or how powerful everyone else was, her tenacity made her a competitive contender. Tierney would quite relish removing that lopsided grin the many females that Eh'kotah courted thought so handsome. *Rip it right from his face.*

Figuring Eh'kotah's breadth of body for about as broad as the Kalameshee's, his height the same as his, all her brothers and Haarth 's as well, her thoughts manifested him. Just like that, he was there. One moment her mind captured a feel of his soul-energy, the next, he stood there next to the Kalameshee. He came from the opposite doors that lead to the under passageways of the Keep and stopped.

His shoulders squared within the same frame as the Kalameshee's. He spared him a once-over before he proceeded to Haarth.

Brandishing a pallet of tanned wolvien over his shoulder, his plaits twisted and pinned out of the way in a ball on the back of his head, the hoisted hides didn't detract from his entrance. He was *her* brother and even she admitted the swagger in the flow of his gait oozed confidence. Her eyes rolled automatically. Hefting the hides from his shoulder, Eh'kotah dumped them onto the backs of the beautifully-textiled seats, flinging melted snow and tanning gook everywhere. Tierney squawked and flinched back, the freezing mess sluicing everyone anyway.

"Eh'kotah! For all things proper!" Far too late with her warning, the queen had held her hand out to stop him. "Why didn't you leave them at the Keep's transport landing? You could've had the furrier summoned to take them to her foundry."

Eh'kotah cut eyes to his mother with a grimace one of a naughty boy caught by his mother's presence. "The guards advised me that you all met here. I brought them to show you the near infestation of wolvien in the Dayea mountains. Their numbers in that ecosystem are such that they should be culled for the safety of the people who brave the mountains for a climb." *Eh'kotah would think that.* He was the main instigator who climbed those wretched mountains. After kissing their mother, he searched amongst their faces until he found Haarth, and they joined forearms, embracing, Eh'kotah pounding Haarth's back. "Uncle! Finally! You've returned home."

Tierney cringed for Haarth. He had returned to Dameerh, to the Keep, not as a homecoming, but as her escort and no doubt, to see the Kalameshee and Mlai delivered without incident before the queen. Haarth's carriage had none of her awkwardness though. He didn't falter in the affection he returned to Eh'kotah.

The two had formed a strong bond over the spans of time. As

the eldest and the one most interested in carrying out the sovereign practices of their land, Eh'kotah consulted with Haarth on domestic affairs. Oftentimes, he used this leeway to visit Haarth in the dominions he governed and accompanied Lu'nil when she traveled there too. "I'm only here to bring this Kalameshee to an audience before Ana'kerah...and uhm, cover a few subjects that need some clarification for myself."

The smile on Eh'kotah's face dropped and he looked into the faces of everyone else in the room. "Why should a Kalameshee need an audience before our queen? What business could he have here?"

Silence greeted his questions, the perfect opportunity for an inter-loper to ingratiate himself. Unfortunately, the Kalameshee stepped forward. "I have true business for your queen. I'm an emissary of the Kalameshee royal house and bring tidings in a declaration of peace and good faith intentions to further relations between our two lands. We advocate for a summit on trade of some of your rich commodities. We could negotiate for some of *our* cybernetic analytics."

A nuance in reactions rippled through the Soonahyins occupying the Hall of Covenance in response to Kalameshee's gaffe, which started at suspicion in Eh'kotah's tilted head and ended in annoyance with the pleat on the queen's features. The Kalameshee's pitch? Too overzealous. Tierney made a face herself. *His tongue must have thickened in his mouth.* "Tierney expressed..." He stopped himself short. His eyes stuck on the queen's flattened lips, brows raised too at his casual use of her daughter's name. "*Princess...Tierahna* expressed a desire to see one of the pieces of my equipment, my pouch analyz—," he got out.

Tierney folded her lips when her mother's voice climbed above his. He was too eager. Now the Kalameshee's inexperience outweighed his judgment. And the queen would eat alive anyone without the savvy to hold stead with her. "You may take your declarations of furthering relations between our lands back to your father, Ocierus. You tell him *my directive* that good faith intentions be carried out in plain sight with concise dealings. Not through covert measures of crossing our borders to besiege my daughter, who has no official capacity in our sovereignty other than princess. Your actions have likened you to a subversive and if ever attempted again, will be met with unilateral redressing."

"It wasn't our intention—"

The queen chopped her hand through the air and sucked off his flow of words. "Your intentions are moot. Your actions speak for you. I'm not of a mind to hear any of your justifications. You do well to be allowed to stay in Dameerh this night. Any more words and you'll be escorted to the border now."

The Kalameshee on the receiving end of her mother's temper wrenched at Tierney's own pique. Only those with intimate relationships with the queen knew how to navigate her nature. It was her mercurial characteristics that tended to make her diplomacy so effective. She was loyal and sympathetic, but had the ability to discern how much of this to put on display. Her protectiveness was deployed at will when negotiating from adverse positions for her people with chancellors and chieftains and officials from other lands alike. The queen's respect was well earned. Tierney'd spent a lifetime watching as those given the opportunity to enter deliberations with her, bustled to anticipate her edicts, leaders of other lands courting her to elicit her favor.

That's why I'm doing neither. I will make my plans on my own. The foreparents chose well when they chose Mother to match with the king.

The Kalameshee wasn't on caliber with her. And he'd entered their land under hidden circumstances rather than with an official announcement, an egregious act to the queen. "Mother, I'm sure he came as he did to gain footing with Haarth and me first. King

Ocierus—"

"So, you speak for Kalamesh now?" The queen slanted a look at her.

"No. I'm speaking for someone whose actions have made his position irretrievable with you. I must speak for that *position*—to open the borders more—when it may have lost more sway because you're already opposed to it." Haarth was right. It was past time she asserted herself with her mother.

The queen canted her head at her daughter's tone. Tierney's willfulness had manifested in many ways from youth. This was no different. She held her breath as she waited for her mother's reaction. "The convening of assembly has already been called for your so-called position, Tierahna. When you left here for your venture to seek counsel with Haarth, I knew it was time I opened discussions. Any conclusions that come from the assembly will be a matter of record. So, your *position* has lost no ground."

A "harumph," grumbled from Haarth and bounced around the acoustics. "Hasn't it, Ana'kerah? But what about the *position* she never knew about? What of those who were never made *aware* of *their positions*? *You* made the decision to wipe *the ground* completely from beneath them."

The queen whirled toward Haarth's voice and gawped at him. Their first real steady connection with her guards down. His eyes branded her in accusation in return. "Haarth—"

"Yes, Ana'kerah? Should I think you've been making decisions for everyone's good or in service to yourself?"

The queen's lips opened and formed a perfect "O" before closing. "Haarth...we may speak in private. There's no need—"

"There's every need! This will no longer be held." He shook his head, and his shoulders drooped, his spirit was in a way that Tierney never thought to see. "Is she my daughter, Ana'Kerah?"

The question dropped into the hall like a softly delivered bomb.

The topsy-turvies Tierney'd dealt with all day lurched vomit to the back of her mouth. Her fists went to her belly as she swallowed the bile back down. Haarth's use of the word "*daughter*" struck a chord so deep inside, it strummed against the essence of who she was. And her clenched knuckles kept her from covering her ears. *I don't want to hear this! I can't hear thi…!*

Good grief! My reaction to him! That should've been the warning that this was coming. If Tierney could've staved off the answer to Haarth's question, she would have. This was too much for one day.

Her father was dead. Had been for so long, she didn't remember all it was like to have one. Everything in her said the "*She*" he was referring to was *her, Tierney.* Whatever her mother and Haarth did to make it a possibility that she might be his daughter was beyond her capability of processing right now. *This whole farce has been enough! Being committed to that sanctum. Followed everywhere I go. This…this is absurdity about who may be my fath…!*

"Haarth! Please. We mustn't do this here." *The queen of Soonayah pleading? Shocker!* Queen Ana'kerah did not beg.

"Why not, Mother?" Tierney's sick belly threw up the rush of words. "You know what's best for us all, right? The answer to all things resides within that crafty mind of yours. Why not answer him here? You were groomed to be queen for these very—"

"I was never groomed to be Queen! I inherited the mantle by default. The one groomed for this was killed out there in that desert when Haarth chose to run away and abandon me here!" *Now the queen shouted?* Blurting what obviously had been held inside her all this time. Even the rafters were quelled from echoing after her. Tierney could never remember once hearing her mother shout. Weeping when her father died. Yes. Perturbed with her and her siblings. Always. But shouting? Never.

"Ana'Kerah," Haarth broke in, his voice fraught, passionate. Just her name on his tongue held tumult that obviously their intermingling had wrought throughout their lives.

A few people at the Keep still remembered how distraught the queen had been when Stah'lief had gone for days and days on end with no communication. How weak to his desires and angry Haarth had gotten when Stah'lief went on another of his sojourns into a raging blizzard to his precious Dayea mountains. A very few, maybe including Bernehvelle, the queen's most trusted companion knew Haarth had taken the queen to his bed. Afterward, ripe with inappropriateness the situation forced Haarth to stay away from the Keep from that day onward. The queen keeping the secret of who fathered Tierney was inconceivable, but who could blame a psyche in complete protective mode?

People said nothing good had ever happened for them since the day Haarth traveled to Kalamesh. They'd been mostly right. Except Tierney existed now.

Haarth's face though. Pain etched into his features, causing an aging to creep in his robust physicality had kept away. "I never abandoned you. It was a sojourn, Anah. I needed to see a different place than what I'd always known."

He was just like me.

'I asked you to stay! Yet you went with that...woman, Irdulon." The queen's face pinched just forming her name. "For adventure before you both committed yourselves. Off for a sojourn of Kalamesh," she mocked him using a cadence similar to his own voice. "But I have been here!" She pointed to the royal blue floor at their feet. "No matter how many times you've left!"

Haarth stepped forward and Eh'kotah blocked him by placing a hand on the sinews of his chest. Collected soul-energy emitted right on the cusp of release. Haarth looked at the hand that blocked him from the queen. His gaze rose. He and Eh'kotah shared a moment. "Maybe Mother is right. This is a private matter between you and—"

"No, Eh'kotah! There's no going back. He's revealed enough that you *all* will have questions now."

Eh'kotah turned to his mother and gestured to himself and his brothers. "We have always known, Mother. You even gave Tierney the feminized version of Haarth's name. Even as boys we understood the significance of that. The dynamics between you all were always off. We were of age enough to understand when those around us still spoke about the happenings before and after Haarth had been taken. You need have no worries about our thoughts."

"But what about me, Matah!" Tierney's constitution cracked a fissure as wide as those wretched Dayea mountains—down to her very being. "*I* don't understand! What all have you kept from me?" She hid her face in the crook of her elbow. Nobody needed to see her torment.

"Tierahna?" Her mother's hands pulled her arm from her face. "Tierahna come, my daughter, we must speak." She tugged her into her embrace, and they walked away.

<h1 style="text-align:center">Chapter 18</h1>

She didn't see where her mother took her. All she knew was that they were moving because she'd covered her face again while she was in her mother's arms. Only when a door opened and they were ushered into an eerie quiet, did she lift her head.

My most favored.

Though her mother said she'd never been groomed for her role as queen, she was using manipulation even now. Tierney shook her head. *Underneath it all, she's always plotting.*

The muted sound Tierney's skimming feet made over the rug comforted her...briefly. She loved this place. Her mother knew that. The stillness of one of the few communal rooms in the Keep with covered floors, the observation deck greeted them. This was their *special* place. She made a straight line from the small landing to the stairs and took them down in-between the short aisle of seats. Her hands trailed over the backs of the seats until she stepped down onto an optiglass floor.

Down and down and down. Through the glass under her feet, fathoms yawned between herself and the ground. Every first step onto the deck a notion formed about it breaking. There'd never been a recorded case where Soonahyin tempered optiglass broke while in use, as a given. Still, she pictured the glass shattering, her body falling as she screamed and screamed through the depths. Usually, she laughed at herself. Now, the oddity could only muster a lift to one side of her lips.

A further amble out onto the deck brought her to its end where it curved up into a seamless glass wall. From the outside, the observation deck looked like an elongated bubble along the side of the Keep.

Inside, a luminary appeared where her fingers touched one spot on the wall just above where she could see the Frozen Folly through its glass. A lighted depiction showed the Folly in various stages of excavation, listing all its various historical facts.

Over her shoulder, her mother had followed her down and had taken a seat on the lowest level of seats before the observation deck started. She'd watched Tierney and not interrupted these quiet moments in her most favored place. "You turned off the auditory?" Tierney asked.

"Yes. When we entered. I think we can go without a sound-recording accompanying what we must speak of."

Swinging back to the glass, a scowl formed to Tierney's self. Her mother presumed that they both wanted no sound-recording. She would have welcomed the distraction of the monotone voice that accompanied the exhibits. The wall lit again at another point she touched and a dance theater luminary appeared. The real dance theater shown through the glass was framed by the luminary. The exhibit opened its doors and turned around and around. Without the accompanying music, the dance theater appeared loopy...erratic.

"So clumsy looking. Nothing like us Soonahyins," Tierney muttered.

Moving on to spot after spot on the optiglass, nearly all the exhibits were displayed. Each time her fingers met glass, historical facts about places of interest within Dameerh came into sharper focus. Eve fell over the dominion and affixed the luminaries with a backdrop of night. *The season of long dark nights*. Weak sunshine didn't stand a chance in

Soonayah in this season.

One of the few vibrant memories Tierney clung to of her father, Stah'lief, was them laughing together here as the enclave came alive on another early nightfall. The enclave, a jewel in the night around the beacon of blue light arising from the Frozen Folly. She'd teased him about the name he'd inherited from two of their far passed ancestor kings. His mother'd told him that when he was born, he was given the name of one of the particular kings—the Lief part of Stah'lief—because his head reminded her of that kingly ancestor's distinction. He'd indulged her amusement with his name and revealed that he'd always believed his mother had just thought he had a big head. Her giggles had been uncontrollable. He'd told her he'd made sure to take care in naming her and her siblings.

An echo of them singing the Starfall rhyme and watching a Starfall together as if it was a novel fascination until late into the eve, slipped in a sense of déjà vu. She lay her forehead on the glass, cold seeping into her bones, and closed her eyes against the liquid pooling from them. "Was it Father who gave me Haarth's name?"

The queen breathed heavily, eyes assessing the droop to her daughter's shoulders. "Yes, it was your father who named you. Come sit here with me, Tierahna."

Tierney came and slumped into the seat her mother patted next to her. "I may never understand this, Mother. But I had a right to know. Why have you kept so much from me? I haven't been a babe for a long time."

"You must think on it, Tierahna. It was more than about your being young. I've never spoken of it to anyone. Not Haarth and not even Stah'lief. Once I started the telling of it, I wouldn't have been able to stop telling. Everyone, the people of Soonayah may have deemed it their prerogative to question me too."

"I'm not people, Mother. This is my life. Now that I've *thought* about it, I can almost understand why you never told me the Shadow Guard followed me on my excursions. You meant to allow me a sense of freedom. Room to explore me. But a princess traveling alone could never be allowed." Tierney's face contorted. "I have only to think of myself when I first started taking my sojourns to know your way was right. I would've fought like an unreasonable thing if I'd known." She sneered at herself and of course, her eyes began to fill again. The queen grabbed her arms and drew her back when she went to turn away. "But Father not being my father and Uncle...Haar..."

Her mother let go of Tierney's arms and captured her face in both hands. She used her thumbs to wipe the tears that overflowed. "I'm grateful for your understanding." Tugging her tighter against her, she gave Tierney's cheek a hard kiss. "Me and Haarth lived a long, convoluted history. I can't tell all the intimacies that have gone into it. Just know that he was the first love of my life. And I've never, no matter the effort, been able to depart from that love."

She loved him even now?

Tierney wanted to look her in the face and witness the conviction of the words. She shrugged at the hold her mother had on her. However, the queen wouldn't let her move far. "You and he were first matched?"

The queen pulled at Tierney, pressing her down to lay her head across her lap as she nodded. She ran tender fingers through her hair and Tierney's body just went limp. The solace of it. The welcome of it. Giving in to her mother's ministrations, she breathed deep. Most people didn't know that the queen had taken the time to plait the hair of her own sons and daughters when they were young. When Tierney's turn came, she always chose to come here where she would lay her head in her mother's lap. Some of those rare moments when she was pliant, and as sweet as a babe, and had let her mother tend her. Just as she did now.

She sucked in the spice of the bergamot and Boswellia tree oils her mother liked so well. As she used them liberally to moisturize and scent her own skin and dress their hair. On some occasions, Tierney remembered drifting off to sleep watching the lights of the enclave come alive through the optiglass. Closing her eyes, she nearly lost herself to sleep in her mother's scent wafting to her and sweeter memories of moments like this. *Please...just be a dream.* Her heart begged for a reprieve.

But the queen began to speak again. "Haarth and I *were* pledged to be matched. And well pledged we were because my mother and father moved here from our Cordalai hamlet for the match to be natural when I was but a babe. We grew together and knew nothing of other possibilities because we'd been chosen for each other from the cradle. As you know, I'm from the direct line of the Chieftain of our Ahn'Tooht clan and I had shown strong abilities as I grew. Your foreparents were quite pleased with their first match. But they never gave thought to the chaos they would cause if one of us were to die young. And that the switching up of their progeny to match with a different one was not like switching out one snowcraft for another."

"So...you never loved Father...Stah'lief? I'm confused as to what to call him now."

"He was the father you knew him to be. That hasn't changed. What you and Haarth pursue from this day forward is the future. He now is your father too. And yes, I did love Stah'lief. We loved each other in our own ways." Tierney winced as her mother's fingers tightened in her hair." Early on, we learned to cling to each other in our grief after we thought both Haarth and Irdulon were lost to us." She didn't dare move for fear that her mother would stop her overdue account of her and Haarth's hidden love affair, so she clenched her teeth as the fingers got agitated more, caught on another tangle. "It was only when Haarth returned home alone and alive, that there was no disguising who held my heart."

That made no sense. Tierney shot upright then bored into her mother's eyes, and after a few moments of the connection, stood up. The movement dragged her mother's fingers from her hair. She walked onto the optiglass again. The luminaries lit up in rapid succession behind a pass of her hand over the glass. Soft light that shone through the frizz of her hair, frazzled from her mother's fingers and that haloed behind her silhouette, lended her an appearance akin to a sprite. An ethereal in mahogany skin sent to walk on Telluric amongst the mortals. And the glass wall exaggerated her vivacity which almost burned the corneas. "You may not be aware of this, but that's the first time you've admitted outright that he's my father." Tierney shook her head, disheveling her hair more. "Listening to your story, Mother, calls into question this love you claim so true. If it be as sure as you say, no matter the consequences, Haarth should've been told far, far before now. And so should I have."

"Tierahna." The queen reached out to Tierney. Tierney ignored her and ran, taking the stairs before her two at a time as she blocked out her mother's words.

"Tierahna!"

When Tierney hit the landing, she speeded to the door to get there fast enough to stop her mother's voice from reaching her ears. Once on the other side, she leaned against the door after closing it on her mother sitting alone in the dark still calling her name.

* * *

"Where has everyone gone?" Empty, the Hall of Covenance greeted

Tierney with an echo of her question back at her. Shadows menaced the earlier vibrant room. She turned all about as she did whenever she entered through that door and encountered a different arrangement of the space. Tiers of seats that had been positioned for conference before, were now swiveled back toward a standard lecture formation. High over the hanging tapestries, up to the gilded terraces of balconette seats, the lights were lowered.

A Keep attendant had rolled the vaulted ceilings open and exposed the center inlay of chornyne tiled roofing. Even with it opened to the clear tiles, no real light shone through. An intentional design created to, "*Alight sunrays on all those in the Hall of Covenance with truth,*" now only bleached the darkness.

When they were young, her siblings had treasured sneaking and hiding within the vast recesses of the Hall of Covenance at night, traipsing through the darkness framed by the night's sky. The silvery glancing of the Tellurician moons had caught glimpses of them running from one hiding place to another in the hall's alcoves.

Tierney? *Not so much.* She hadn't ever told them there were too many dark nooks. Retreats too narrowed from the voluminous tapestries and ornate apparatus to her liking. The *corners were too deepened with night shadows.*

"Agh!" Tierney jumped into fighting stance ready to maim the owner of a hand that touched her.

"Be calm. It's only I." Haarth stood back to allow her to see his face.

With trembling fingers, she rubbed her forehead. "I had just decided that returning to a changed, darkened room after only leaving it as a different space moments before is quite chilling."

"I waited for your mother and you. Is she not with you?" He looked beyond her shoulder for the queen.

"No." Opening her mouth to say...something, whatever she could come up with to Haarth, she lowered her head instead. *What can I say?*

Haarth lifted her chin. "You need have no awkwardness with me. We're still family. We're still the same."

"Yes, we're family. But family that has had no true interaction beyond a communication console in more than fifteen spans."

He squeezed her shoulders. "This will be remedied by us beyond this day." He bent his knees, lowering himself, and peering into her downturned face. "Do you agree?"

Clumsy to have the moment over with, a jerk of her head was the response she gave. "I agree. Where has everyone gone? I intended to help the Kalameshee find provisions and lodgings for the night."

And also, would be glad of the escape from a room that was a ghost of the place it had been before. She didn't tell him that, though. In contrast to *her* reaction, Haarth stepped back for a *connection* to the glances of silver through the chornyne stone tiles that broke the darkness in the room.

When did he make a habit of avoiding someone's eyes like that? The hairs on the back of Tierney's neck sprang to attention. Where *was* the Kalameshee?

"I think it's unwise to be found cavorting with the Kalameshee alone."

Tierney guffawed. "Found cavorting? Just who'd be taking account of any *cavorting* I might do? Where have the rest of them gone, Unc... Fath..." Tierney wrinkled her brow, tongue-stumped on the two words that weren't interchangeable in her mind.

"Just Haarth for now. We'll work our way up to Father."

"Please don't think I'm unaware you distract me with this conversation. Where have they taken the Kalameshee, *Haarth*?"

He looked away from her again to the door this time. "Your brothers felt the need to have a few words with him."

Tierney flew from the Hall of Covenance. She knew the only place they would've gone to have a few *so-called* words.

Chapter 19

The sparring arena. No place for a Kalameshee and brothers bent on unreasonable protectiveness.

There was an aura of a spotlight honed in on the Kalameshee the moment you entered onto the bumpered floor. He stood tall facing Tierney's brothers who baited him. Around them all, a group of spectators circled a match where her brothers held sway.

I must be seeing things. There's no way they would do this. This *has* to be wrong. She wouldn't have believed it if she weren't witnessing it with her own eyes. Every Soonahyin rocked in rhythm to the calls and responses the group chanted. They were partaking in a vying match for standing—three against one—with a Kalameshee royal, who had no idea of the full-out acumen he would need to take on just one of them.

A Kalameshee royal whose well-being rested solely at their feet too. He'd been in their custody since they'd discovered he'd sneaked across their border. Sparring with her brothers meant any real harm he came to would be at the hands of Soonahyin royals. Tierney deemed it her prerogative to rescue the Kalameshee from the inevitable fate of the match. *I'm going to help him be delivered unblemished back to his homeland. The least I can do.* The brothers with the stage of the arena behind them, standing as warriors at the gate, didn't deserve the rush that came from giving someone a good thumping.

Besides, if anyone deserved a match to release their energy, it was her. She sponsored vies for standing more often than any of her siblings, contrary to the fact that she possessed the least skill at sparring than them all. Of course, *she* had the most tenacity. A workout with her eldest brother would do her energy good. *I could skewer him right now with what is raging inside me.*

Lu'nil, hands down, fought with more skill than she did. Her cousin was like a freaking animal when it came to applying an innate sure-footedness and flexibility to their sparring and competitions of vies for standing. The ultimate goal? The tournament of Kalumdeh Vy. Lu'nil's prowess prevented even males from challenging her until the very last levels of a tournament. But Korrell's acumen surpassed even hers.

As they say, "*watch those who are quiet and stand to themselves. It's their reserve that may harbor a ferocity like no other.*" He fought as the ultimate sparrer that all other contenders vied to upset, even Ad'rihl.

Ad'rihl's strength lay in harnessing his speeding gift. He and Korrell wielded this same ability. Speeding and pulsing in competition were outlawed from the early vies on after people were accidentally killed. A people discovering their intrinsic gifts necessitated tempering their strengths when dealing with one another.

For Ad'rihl, the harnessing effect gave him the advantage of fast movements. He never shifted from view, stopping short of a full speed.

Yet, *he* wasn't faster than Os'carah, the babe. Os'carah, expected to be practiced in sparring as well, raced through her competitions, "*If I can't be caught, how can anyone land a blow?*" as her mantra.

Oh, but for the indomitable Eh'kotah. *Keep that arrogance and test him if you will.* The most powerful of them, he didn't need to speed or pulse you, any blow he landed only felt as if he'd socked you incapable of breathing. If he could get enough people to agree to a match, he'd probably be on par with Korrell. Most tended to avoid fighting him. Who could afford the recuperation needed after a bout with Eh'kotah had taken its toll?

Uhm...me, actually. It was a state Tierney'd welcomed in times when fighting was the only thing that would rid her of her frustrations. Hopefully, if there was anything to be gained from this, it would be that the Kalameshee could at least excise some of his pressures.

All of a sudden, one of the spectators surrounding the match gave a cry from the belly incited by Ad'rihl's jump without warning. He turned swiftly in the air, his leg outstretched, vaulting himself from the bumpered floor, he may as well've had feathers. At which point, Tierney lunged, except she could never reach them *duly* to stop this brutish behavior. And Ad'rihl continued to whip his leg around, swooshing his foot near the Kalameshee's face.

These fools would actually risk doing harm to a *royal* from *another land.* The Kalameshee shifted in time for Ad'rihl's foot to just miss his eye, then centered himself again. He kept her brothers in sight, but turned in circles so that neither of them could end up behind him. *Smart move.* They'd blindside him and end him quickly if he let them take him off-guard. Perversely, which would be better though? His being blindsided and ended quickly or to watch him be pummeled into submission? Tierney was loathed to pick, both options were on the losing end for the Kalameshee.

Eh'kotah and Ad'rihl were posted off to his sides with Korrell, the most lethal, in front. Pushing through the spectators, Tierney came just short of reaching them before Haarth held her back and gave a shake of his head at her interference. "He's holding his own. Are you *trying* to diminish his stance?" She wasn't. But how much of a stance would it matter if he ended up with a broken neck?

Eh'kotah whirled so fast with his feet aloft that she didn't see the hand that windmilled behind them. His fist clipped the Kalameshee's shoulder, nearly toppling him over.

The Kalameshee didn't go down. His movements were jerky and perspiration saturated his hair and coated his brow, yet he didn't let his guard down either. *How long had this been going on?* The Kalameshee looked to be unwilling to concede, which she'd admire more if he weren't setting himself up for a defeat by damage that Soonayah might have to answer for later.

He watched her brothers' every move in anticipation of the next. Tierney quaked in her strain against Haarth's grasp. *Cussed!* The Kalameshee could hope to withstand this challenge for only so long. He'd made no move to defend himself yet. And though they didn't converge on him all at once or move in consistent motion as was usual in vies, there was only a matter of time before one of them scored a lay-out blow.

A side door opened. The spectators' calls setting the rhythm to the match quieted. When they resumed the chants again, the timbres and cadences echoed. The rafters here provided the perfect acoustics for the Soonahyin fight chants as they were designed to. And as was only right, spectators were eager to set the tone for the fight. This being a royal match merely made them keener to participate to fulfill their parts as witnesses.

Tierney didn't risk turning around to see who entered. The ultimate contender hadn't moved yet. Korrell. He watched the Kalameshee as steady as the Kalameshee watched him, then fainted forward. *Oh no!* She'd been hoping his not moving signaled a concession—him figuring the Kalameshee'd had enough. Woest be to the Kalameshee now. With Korrell's sights on him, he would go down for sure.

The Kalameshee, already anticipating Korrell, shifted to avoid him. *Oh!* Whatever technique he was using might be his saving grace. The constant shifting as he tracked her brothers' smallest of movements kept him from the brunt end of their fists.

As Korrell swayed back to his original position, he dropped backward. Fast. Into a handstand. *Hmm...* She might've given the Kalemshee too much credit too soon. A form of Korrell's body could still be seen where it'd been before. His foot kicking around showed up out of nowhere. Korrell's gift of harnessing his speeding allowed for his body's movements to appear to be completed in more than one place at once.

Evidently, the Kalameshee's dogging of each of her brother's movements failed him too. "Watch out!" she screamed. Korrell's foot caught him on the side of his head and sent him smashing to the bumpered floor.

You could practically see the stars spinning around his sprawled form. Try as he might to get back to fighting stance, the Kalameshee shook his head and lay there, dazed. Then he pulled himself together enough to kick to his feet again. Haarth had released her when Korrell's blow landed and Tierney took that opportunity to run and stand in front of the Kalameshee right as Korrell and Ad'rihl advanced on him again.

The Kalameshee gripped her. Senses being wrecked, bobbing around as if he was a willow in the wind, he might not have realized he held her too tightly when he pulled her to his side. "No!" She confronted her brothers and dared them to go through her. "Stand down! You won't carry on this farce to prove your masculinity on my behalf!"

They all stood before each other now, searching for the next moves. And it could be seen there—in Ad'rihl's bobbing from foot to foot, cackling, chafing to continue the vy—proof the brothers had no intention of letting up. "Remove yourself from the match, Tierney. He accepted our challenge as is fair." he said to her.

"What's fair about the three of you against one? This won't continue. Not if I have anything to say about it."

"Unfair would be for one of us to match with him unleashed." So Korrell needed to cant forward too, a march of him and the other two miscreants to make what point? The only concession to his recent physical exertions, beads of sweat dampening his brow? Okay, he was an iceberg. What was new? "He stood for the challenge not knowing whether we would hold back, as he should've if he expects to court you. Be glad that he has substance to withstand us." Korrell answered.

"He's not courting me!"

"Then you may want to tell him that. He was well aware of why we made this challenge.

Tierney's soul-energy levels climbed so fast she thought she might explode her head. The Kalameshee's hand skimmed her forearm to wield her on over to his side.

"No!" She wrenched from him and confronted her brothers again, the world around her started to spin—which was only fair. The inside of her head may as well match her thoughts. "You have no standing to demand this of anyone. He at least has had the wherewithal to stand up to you three." She pushed at the breadth of Korrell's chest. It didn't budge him, but it did flush her with a minute satisfaction, however fleeting it was. "Can you not grasp how many suitors have been turned off from me after they learned how you three behave?"

"Then they failed you miserably and were never worthy of you from the beginning," Korrell said, his intonation flat.

She resented his breathing not even being altered while she panted like a dog with its face in the wind. Tierney's anger burned fiercest against the eldest of her brothers, Eh'kotah though. More protective of her than any of them, his participation in this confounded her. *Eh'kotah is usually the fair one.* "Eh'kotah! You above these two nut-buckets should know better than this. Only time can gauge someone's compatibility. How else can I ever get close to anyone?"

"With Father gone, I'm charged to determine who courts you."

Eh'kotah jogged up to her too as if the three of them in the consistent motion for a match would cow her. And leave the Kalameshee open for whatever they wanted to do to him? They could think again. "No *closeness* will be had by anyone who can't stand for you."

Tierney stomped her foot and caused Eh'kotah to snatch his away before her heel landed on his instep. "No one will be willing to stand for me if they're never given the chance to know me."

"Knowing that you are the first princess of Soonayah, from the ancient royal lines of the Ahn'Trunkh and Ahn'Tooht clans before they ever think to approach is enough. If there is no thought given to the possibility of being appraised as a prospective suitor, then as Korrell said, they were never worthy from the beginning."

Only going right up to Eh'kotah and standing on her toes to get in his face would do if she weren't going to hit him in his mouth. "You muskox asses!" Drawing Ad'rihl's cackles at the term Tierney knew their mother hated, she flung her arms round to encompass all of them. "You three dally from one woman to another as you please, never taking a match, not even a consort, and you think to wield your whims over me! This comes to an end this day!"

An arm wound around her waist and swooped her off her feet. Ad'rihl had snuck behind her. "It doesn't come to an end until we say. Now remove yourself from the match—" Tierney kicked her feet as he carried her away from the Kalameshee and stopped short of pulsing Ad'rihl. Over his shoulder, she spied her mother. She must've been who'd come through the side door. She disapproved of them pulsing each other as much as she disliked them calling each other profane names. Instead, Tierney took Ad'rihl off guard pincering her fingernails into the arm he'd banded across her middle. He loosened his grip and she punctured ever deeper into the offending flesh. *Need to get him good to have an effect.* With it slack now, she braced his arm and twisted it up behind his back. He countered, reversing her motion, moving, turning, not relenting until she had to let go. Movements like how'd he'd done all their lives. Her youngest brother was relentless at everything and an opponent gave up sometimes, just to be rid of him. *Wish I could be rid of him now!*

They squared off at each other. *Muskox ass!* Ad'rihl, with his mouth over the wound her claws had punctured. "So, it's the Kalameshee who needs you to stand in his stead?" he garbled around his hand.

"I stand for myself! If anyone fights, it's me they'll face." She turned in a circle to confront every one of the brothers at the same time.

"Calm yourself, Tierahna." Haarth strolled forward to cool the situation. "This match is at an end. All the points needed to be made have been proven on all sides."

"No, Haarth! This has been allowed to go on for too long." She turned to her brothers again. "I challenge you all to a vy."

Ad'rihl laughed in her face. Eh'kotah just shook his head as if his confidence in his strength should've been a warning to her not to challenge him. But Korrell turned his back and walked away. Oh, what did he do that for? The back of him sauntering from her was like waving eland meat at a starving snowcat. She ran, jumped his back, and wound her arms into his plaits tethering herself to him. It took him some time to peel her off too. "Look at yourself, Tierney! This isn't new to you. You say he doesn't court you, but you are ready to rip my head off for him." Korrell honed in on her ragged breaths and heightened energy. "You must question your own motivations."

"I know what my motivations are. Just fight *me*, if you want to fight." Tierney's skin buzzed with her soul-energy elevated so high. She needed a release. A good scrap would do just to expend the energy from overwhelming her. "Come on, Korrell. I will give you a true test of your status this day."

With a pitying look on his face, he slanted his head to one side. "No,

Tierahna. You would sear my skin to chalk in this mood. I won't fight you."

"Come on now," she taunted them. "One of you must be up for the challenge. After all, you were all ready to unite against the Kalameshee just on Ad'rihl's instigation. Surely, you can withstand my proposition. There's but one of me too."

"Ad'rihl didn't instigate this. The challenge was called at my direction for what must be done. We make no apologies for it and the Kalameshee understood the need of it as well." If Eh'kotah sneered anymore his face would fold in on itself, his patience was long gone. "You may want to go and take some repetitions in the Frozen Folly. You won't be given the satisfaction of a fight with us this night."

"Will no one accept my challenge then?" Tierney tore around at all the men and women who gathered as spectators, her craze to relieve herself of some energy agitating her voice as she did her hunt. Ok'nuh, Principal Sect I of Eh'kotah's Tempeh Tu guard, stood head and shoulders above everyone else. She stalked to him and hauled him into the center of the match. He shot a look toward the queen who sat in the raised section of arena seats for royal attendees.

The queen's expression gave away neither approval nor denial. But Eh'kotah had come to stand near her and he didn't demure. Haarth nodded to Ok'nuh. Someone in the crowd gave a long caterwauling bellow, signaling for the evidently approved match to begin. The spectators rocked to their calls, "Impi!" and responses, "ngomumo!" until they encircled Tierney and Ok'nuh, setting the tempo for the match. Tierney removed her boots and ripped the outer layers of her clothing from her body until she was attired in a thin under chemisette and leggings; her first layer. "Was it you who shadowed me, Ok'nuh, my friend?"

Lowering his eyes, Ok'nuh saluted her before he took up his fighting stance. He never raised his gaze to look at her, obvious he didn't relish the position she'd put him in. "It was not I, Princess Tierahna."

Tierney glared at the top of his bent head, hating that he wouldn't meet her eyes, only in that instant it hit her. "But you know who did?"

His eyes shifted to direct contact. He raised himself tall before her for a moment. "I do. If I wasn't Principal charged to Prince Eh'kotah's sect, I would have volunteered to act as your Shadow Guard too. But as all the Tempeh Tu must synchronize any cross assignments, we *do know the special* missions that must be coordinated. I'm sure they would like to reveal their identities to you themselves. So, I will say no more."

Tierney moved so fast, she wheeled herself onto one arm, continued the motion, brought her feet round, and caught Ok'nuh on his chin.

Any match in Soonayah needed the competitor's full participation or you could be killed by mistake, whether the competitor was going against a princess or not. Ok'nuh dropped his demeanor of deference to Tierney. He windmilled his whole body off the floor in a spectacular feat for a man his size and came down in a pass of arms and legs that clipped the back of Tierney's leg. Her knee buckled. Righting herself, she ignored the pain already radiating in arrows up to her knee.

Lurching, and ready to swing to the next position in hopes no one noticed her favoring her leg because—*for goodness sakes*—she required this not to be over too soon. The anger inside her from everything that had happened that day demanded a release. Ok'nuh aggressed again, whirling all the way to the floor, he swiped his leg beneath her. Tierney saw his intentions in his eyes. He was attempting to lay her out, pin her and end the match before any more damage could be done.

That's going to be a big "No," on that my friend. I need this so as to not scorch the hair off my own head. She jumped his leg and rolled near him, chopping the side of his neck before either of them stood.

Ok'nuh pivoted with one leg still on the floor, the other one he whipped up and around his own body and Tierney's. She spun her leg to deflect. Both their legs crashed into each other, but this time her sore leg buckled and sent her crashing to the floor.

"Tierahna!" Her mother rose, shouting from the royal box.

Mother? No, no. Not now. Gratefully, Eh'kotah grappled with her to hold her at bay. "She welcomed this. She let her heightened energy push her into this. Let her finish this heedless challenge," he said to their mother.

"What honor is there to be found in fighting a mountain? You and Haarth shouldn't have approved." The queen jerked her shoulder from Eh'Kotah's grasp.

The feat of getting up from the floor barely got Tierney to fighting stance. The pain in her left leg burned so, it beat now in tandem with her heart. Its rhythm possessed her and she rocked to it. *Oh great.* Outweighing the calls and responses of the spectators, the beat's heaviness thrummed. This wasn't the best time to lose herself to rhythmic lulling as she was one to do. But it put her inside a haze, at a tempo all her own anyway. Like one did sobut metimes and entered another mind when there was a carnival of activity going on outside oneself. And a stillness took over her. Everything seen through the eyes like windows viewing the world, but not of it. A clearer vision actually. A once-over of the crowd found that the Kalameshee stood between Korrell and Ad'rihl as they held him back. His face was all red and galled at her brothers' physical restraint of him. She almost smiled. Maybe if he could out-maneuver them he could slip in a lick on Ok'nuh and give her the upper-hand.

But focusing again on Ok'nuh, she judged him, *fit and ready to go until daybreak.* Her energy levels were crashing, elevated too high, too fast after traveling most of the day. The tornebird's assault still pulsed in her shoulder too. *Attacking wolves and man-eating veryum isn't enough for me. I get myself into a vy with possibly the largest Soonahyin on Telluric. Mother is right on some things about me; my impulsiveness is asinine. Sometimes I just can't think, I react. And look where I end up.* The bout's main skirmishes loomed ahead. She was bound to end up in an unconscious nap on the floor if she let Ok'nuh land one more blow.

When he rocked right, then left, he raised his arm too high and telegraphed his next attack. She met his arm with a roundhouse kick that he caught mid-move. *Uh, oh.* He flipped her feet over head like she weighed no more than a babe. Remarkably landing on her feet, she lifted her left leg immediately to take the weight off.

Not allowing her time to gather herself—*just a moment… please!*—Ok'nuh reeled himself through the air again. *Oh yeah, big boy? He really was trying to put an end to this early.* This time, Tierney countered with a slackening of her own body and used the momentum of his weight to pull him off balance. While he struggled to stay upright, she grasped his arm and swung herself onto his back. She braced her forearm beneath his chin and locked a choke hold. *Sleep. I beg you to sleep so maybe I can sleep too. I was way ahead of myself when I let my anger get me into this.* But he flipped her—over his head this time. She landed with a crack of her back against the floor and he fell on top of her.

In a blur of movement, he was thrown off. The queen had stood, ducking Eh'kotah's arms in the heat of her daughter and the mountain's match. Jumping from her perch on the royal box, in continual motion, she speeded into the match, landed with her foot in the sensitive spot on Ok'nuh's back, and plucked him off her daughter.

"Mother! You can't intervene on a fair match," she said while struggling to stand, so her mother grasped her arm and helped her up. Once on her feet, Tierney yanked on her mother's clutch. "It's not done that a match is interrupted!" Tierney's intent was to walk away as she turned her back on her mother.

The queen hauled her back so fast, she could have mistaken it for a speed. Her grip tightened until Tierney winced. "What is done is what I see fit to do. You must not forget that *I* am still queen here." She let go of Tierney's arm and Tierney knew better than to say more to her in this mood. She bent and retrieved her clothes. With her head lowered, shoulders sagging, she limped from the sparring arena. And the Kalameshee followed behind her.

Chapter 20

Tierney donned her attire again. The temperature in the corridors chilled her now with sweat dampening her skin. She latched onto the Kalameshee and dragged him down to the Keep's transport landing. Hurriedly. Running away as was her usual. Away from her mother's shadow bearing down on her. Away from the skein coiled in her brain always...always pushing her too far. "I have something that can refresh you," she said breathlessly. Determined to separate herself from this bent of her soul-energy raising too high, too fast to support a calm state of mind. A bent that had been reoccurring over and over again lately. She had to get a handle on it. Look where it was landing her. Running away from a situation that had gotten out of hand...again. The same exact feeling that'd had her ready to kill the Kalameshee when he'd broken into her room at Outliers. A kind of rousing inside her that as it gained momentum became frenetic and for instance, instigated a rush to the other side of Soonayah in a blizzard.

The Kalameshee followed wherever her soft hands urged and the two of them curled through warrens of security stanchions, barracks, rushing past the stone walls and halogen lamps that comprised the underpassage and whole hives of interconnected attendant's facilities. The secured inlet was busy with passersby who crossed from the landing where the transports were kept. The attendants coming into the Keep from there watched after them as they raced toward the only access to the underpassage conveyor.

Tierney braced the Kalameshee at his back once they were there. *If he's not careful, he will fall over me.*

He balked at stepping onto the conveyor. "Come on, now." Then without hesitation, he took the hand she offered. "One big step and you should be fine." She steadied him, her laugh strained a bit as he held both arms out and lunged onto a conveyor that shined up at them. It bore their steps forward.

Each footfall on the conveyor produced an iridescence that outlined their footprints. The Kalameshee walked back and forth to the effect of an array of colors between his feet, and Tierney and her issues. *A person couldn't ask for more, could they?* Not when the pressing thing was to get away from the fever in one's own mind. This was perfect for that. The conveyor was like a tube. Circular walls mirrored their handprints placed to steady themselves too—to the extent of engendering a calm to the psyche. Ideal for settling an over-active spirit.

"This tube mimics reactions just as your roads do. They wake up when you touch them." Prisms of color trailed behind his eager Kalameshee hand. "Is the tube the same mechanism as your roads?"

"Not exactly. They both make use of Soonayah's optiglass." Tierney heaved a breath and tapped the wall twice. A terminal appeared. It moved apace with the hand she kept on the wall. She fingered a pattern over the terminal and chuckled gratefully for the Kalameshee's behavior. His artlessness was helping her and he didn't even know it. He'd ducked when an appearance of shooting stars dashed over their heads and all around them along the tunnel. She never looked directly at them herself. Their shower effect could be dizzying. Instead, she fingered the terminal again and anointed him with her smile. He'd earned it, helping to take her mind off the culmination of things that had happened that day. Especially, the cataclysm that had just taken place in the fighting arena.

A woman standing at a translucent desk appeared, filling a portion of the wall with her hair tamed back to one giant puff pulled behind her. It outlined an arched brow and long neck that emphasized her apparel. All white was her background and attire, while people in white bustled about behind her.

"I'm your directory agent, Sholah. You grace me this eve to facilitate you, Princess Tierahna."

"Pleasantries to you, Sholah. Inform the Ministry of Transport to review the airway reportings, please. A flying razor flew far too low within the dominion earlier and the pilot should be penalized. If the Ministry of Transport should need confirmation, have them communicate with me directly for my testimony. Also, clear the airways over the royal alcove."

Sholah's eyebrows first rose, then she lowered them again and stood straighter with her shoulders back as if she'd remembered herself. The royal family's hands-on involvement with everyday occurrences was well known throughout the land. The agent shouldn't have been surprised at Tierney's willingness to involve herself in the minor air offense. "With fidelity I serve, Princess Tierahna." Sholah saluted in veneration to Tierney.

Tierney bent her head slightly in return. "Much appreciations." Sholah disappeared. One swipe and the terminal flew along the wall until it disappeared too.

"You must have strong feelings about poor piloting." The Kalameshee said.

"We all do. Our land can't run flying passages like other lands because our weather is too extreme. All flying journeys are on strict governance in Soonayah out of necessity. Only a few reach the special pilot levels to fly more than short, routine distances. My own foreparents died in a crash a long time ago." she answered him, her lips turned down for a moment with the memory of her family members' deaths. "On simple flying travel to the borderland dominion, Lehquate, a snowstorm cropped up. They arrowed straight into a trap of ferber trees when I was young. The legend is that the ferber trees beckoned them in. Add the weather to that and they never stood a chance."

The shower of stars was reactivated, albeit, Tierney grunted when she bent her knees some. Despite the pain that radiated from where Ok'nuh had targeted his blow in just the right spot, the effort was worth it.

Side to side she slid, careful with the leg. She'd been doing this since she could remember. Imagining herself skating on the underpassage conveyor. When she'd keep the Starfall just in her periphery, she'd float with the meteors, taken away to another galaxy. *Away....away... away.* Skating produced a kaleidoscope in her wake, painting the conveyor and subsequently the skies in her own exhaustive art. Flying, twirling, proximity to the stars brushing her hair into a cloud around her. The present lost with the actions to the point that she ended up at a clumsy angle on her last twirl, and was lucky the Kalameshee was there to catch her.

Awkward much? Geez! Flailing at him like that? Perfect, Tierney. She eased from his arms now that she was back on planet Telluric. *Now, what had we been talking about? Oh.*

"Flying journeys—coming across mercurial weather is why our placement and maintenance of our roads are essential. But the process used in the roads *is* a bit different from the one used in these walls and the conveyor." A rainbow swept the wall behind her hand as she activated it again. "The road's optiglass is embedded with quartz transmitters that communicate with each other and the technical devices they encounter. Some things can be accessed by hand on the roads, but very few."

She slowed the shower of stars. The Kalameshee's stare at the wall made him look dazed. "These walls here are quite different. As you can see, no technical device is needed at all. However, *this conveyor* is tempered, metallicizing it with alloys, so the glass is supple enough to move."

The Kalameshee smirked at her and jogged ahead a ways. "Am I allowed to run? Will it enhance my speed beyond what I'm capable of?"

Tierney shrugged and shut the stars off. His attention was taken with the Starfall and his punishment for being so hooked was to list to one side as he ran. "You may try. But did you notice Korrell's ability to harness his movements without speeding, looking like he was in more than one place at once?"

He snorted. "I had no choice but to notice it when he used it to smash me out of my senses." Grimacing, he rubbed the spot on his head that Korrell had caught with his foot.

If I weren't so fair, I could almost think you deserved it. With a sniff, she turned her back on him.

His behavior in the fighting arena with her brothers still aggravated to no end. In defense of him, she'd portrayed herself as a shrew in front of everybody, nearly getting herself pulverized in the process. *Haarth* had been a witness to her behavior, her new father. She shook her head. *And* she'd been under the scrutiny of her mother's exacting eyes too. *More fuel for her to send me away.* "For all things proper, what cause can you claim for taking on the challenge by the three of them?" she demanded of him and paused and waited for any possible explanation he could come up with. "There's nothing shameful in declining a challenge. Soonahyins do it all the time for more training if we don't think we stand a chance. Or if we're simply not inclined to be beaten to a pulp." He just gazed at her after her statements and volunteered not a word.

Her steps snapped as she walked off, shoulders stiffened too. "You may risk running if you want. I wouldn't advise it, though. Ad'rihl has a similar gift to Korrell's. Once when we were young, he challenged Korrell to a race here and harnessed his speeding to such an extent, he lost control and bounced along these walls until he concussed that soft skull of his. Mother even called them muskox asses to their faces for their foolishness. They've been banned from speeding along the conveyor ever since."

The Kalameshee's burst of laughter echoed around the tunnel.

It *did* make quite a picture. A young Ad'rihl bopping his brains about in the tunnel. And the queen, in her worry, reduced to profane language crossing her precious lips. The corners of Tierney's mouth lifted as well. Amusement at her brother's expense was always good.

* * *

Torhvald

The conveyor sidled upward and Tierney stepped off as light beamed from under her feet. Torhvald yanked his hand off a wall of ice material. *What was that?* It had been black optiglass tailing colorful patterns a moment before.

His gaze wandered over Tierney's figure moving ahead and he sped up to catch up. Her pace barely hinted at hitches of the pain in her calf. "We're inside the Frozen Folly, aren't we?" he asked, trailing the walls up and up to an open roof, as they meandered through the course of ice.

She turned and smiled at him. "We are at that." And the smile slipped the moment she saw what he was doing. She snatched his fingers from the wall. "Don't let its beauty lull you. The ice can burn if touched too long. Come. We have a ways to go yet."

Really? He rubbed the tips of his fingers. Numb, even through his gloves. He'd hate to lose a digit or two. *They did come in handy.*

Shapes of people muted through the walls navigated similar courses toward destinations no doubt like theirs, where Tierney led him along a maze of an ice arcade. Excitement echoed from the young, mingled with older more sanguine tones.

Torhvald chuckled under his breath. Since he'd come to Soonayah, he was like the youth in his enthusiasm for different experiences. Tierney's uniqueness alone was unsettling enough, coupled with his wheeling from one unknown thing to another, which had him acting all out of character. Those at home would be astonished at some of the things he'd taken on.

His father for one, would ask him, "*Did falling from that mountain addle your brain? Or did that Soonahyin's foot loosen your cerebral cortex from your convoluting skull?*"

Chortling to himself, he realized he hadn't done the minimum to set into motion what he'd been sent here to do. And accepting a challenge from three Soonahyin royals? *Just foolish.* Even he knew Soonahyins were prolific fighters. The royals who trained alongside their Tempeh Tu guard personified the most elite fighting on all of Telluric.

All told, a sense of fate had punched him in his gut since the moment he'd first watched Tierney walk into Peetah Pearl's lodge and had thrown him off his purpose, utterly. It hadn't occurred to him to back down from her brothers' challenge on his fitness to court her either. Never mind that he hadn't fully formed the thought himself. Hadn't expressed this desire to her, let alone her parents, who now included the ever-watchful Prince Haarth. He sighed at his own behavior. *Just inexplicable.* Tierney swung around at the sound. "Don't fret the walk. We're here now."

She entered the center-right side of an opening. Their course through the maze of the Frozen Folly had led them to an alcove. She placed her hand flat on a panel on the lip of a grouping of stones. A fire flared, nearly reaching a wall of ice from within the circular pit. "Whoa!" he said. Tierney moved her fingers in a closing motion and made the fire recede.

Torhvald then followed her toward the Folly's inner wall. He was starting to wonder if he would follow her anywhere she led him. "Is that light I see?" Haunting blue light glanced off the walls from below. She stopped, thankfully. They'd walked upon a river lit from within. "What is this?"

"It's an aquifer. They run like a maze of rivers through the Frozen Folly just as the walls of ice do. They measure about twenty-six parses, a bit shy of the Folly's ice that's a staggering forty-five, but remarkable nonetheless, right? Come now. We'll bathe in the Folly's river for a much-needed refreshing." Tierney's eyes lit at the prospect, but Torhvald doubted he'd be capable of swimming in the below-freezing temperatures.

"I'm not acclimated to your temperatures as you are. You'll likely pull out a Torhvald-cicle if I get near that water."

She crouched, removed her glove, and ran her hand through the water, then stood and touched his cheek. "The aquifer's water is kept warm by the sediment and the effects of the deep-deep crevice leading to the gem farms at the bottom. You need only go to the chamber there."

What chamber? She pointed to a place in the wall that he couldn't tell from any other part of the ice. "Once you don a water costume, run and submerge yourself in the river. It's no different from what we all must do. Soonahyins come here to bathe for revitalization in the aquifer. We don't flout the cold any more than any other people do."

She left him there, apparently retreating to *her own* invisible chamber. So, he headed in the direction of the one she seemed sure was there for him, and rounded a curve of ice and sure enough, he found a chamber tucked away stored with water costumes and put one on. A length of expandable material stretched across his nether regions. Once he had a linen around him too, he sprinted to the edge of the aquifer. "Cold...cold...cold...cold," he wheezed before he gingerly jumped in.

Tierney was right. As he swam the water lapped warm against his skin. *It tingles.*

A few moments later, Tierney's shriek caused him to shift so quickly, he sank. Recovering from dunking himself like a downed stone, he spluttered water and gawped at her. He'd jerked above the water's surface before he drowned in stupor. *She made me forget to swim,* on witnessing her run to the water's edge in her water costume. Tiny toning scraps wrapped around voluptuous breasts and the generous curves of her bottom. *She may as well be naked for all the good the costume did.*

He hadn't stopped coughing water, and still, he swam enraptured toward her. But she laughed at him and splashed his face, then dove deep, avoiding him, showing off her splendid bottom as she went.

They played games of seek and retreat for some time in the aquifer of the Folly river. Her body cut clean through the water with Tohrvald's faithful lumbering after her at every turn. After a while, him chasing Tierney became him chasing his own tail, and so he gave himself a respite.

"A well-deserved one," floating on top of the river, "nothing but pure blackness," his tone was in deference as to not disturb the experience. The night sky stretched as a curtain through the ceiling of the walls of ice. "A surreal sensation." Freezing air braced over top of his body while his back portions were submerged in the hot silk of the river. *Like undergoing two different worlds at the same time.* He'd stopped chasing Tierney. She took in and held enough breath to explore the very bottom of the aquifer. The fluorescent fish—happily nipping along the rocks and the exposed areas of any swimmer's body who dared enter—were her company now. Fascination with the iridescence of the gemstones along the floor of the crevice only took his heavy body and untrained lungs so far.

In the midst of an idle in the water's warmth, floating and drifting, a sky of stars his only concern, a frisson of alarm came along. It jarred him out of his tranquility. Something dire was urging his empathic abilities from their normal steady hum to lurch into a frenzy. The hairs on his arms jolted up and chilled panic screeched along his spine too. He looked below, futilely trying to swipe water aside to search for Tierney. Dragging in a breath, he filled his lungs and dove as fast as he could to an outline of her body balled in crisis.

Chapter 21

A true release could be found at one's very fingertips. The wellspring of the aquifer flowed through the ground's pores, filtered with the sediment of minerals and nutrients, and residuals of umbereen were all the spa a body needed. Tierney forayed deeper and deeper into the depths until she touched the river's bottom where a host of gemstone farms lay. Each time she swam further down, she closed her eyes and pictured clearly the clusters of gems in her mind: the luster of black diamonds, gleaming greens of moldavite. The grotto enveloped her, loved her as Soonahyin soil did its people.

All that bottled-up contention with her mother lessened some with contact with the water. Oh, but the Folly's enkindling did more too, traversing to the bone of the body. The stuff you were made of recognized a kin in the water. There as the ultimate nurturer for sinews rent asunder, ligaments and thews ruptured to be synergized through conjoinment with the elements around them.

Her smile was a breathless one as she laid against clutches of palladot, a bubble of her contentment escaping between her teeth. *My most favored. Palladot.* Its emerald hue and striations of gold fascinated her so for some reason. "Hmpf..." Maybe that was why she was so fascinated with the Kalameshee's eyes.

When she rolled into a jagged cache of hibonite, on a whole *other* route pitiably, she began to struggle to keep in her once easily-held breath. *Goodness!* Was she sensitive to the point now that anything set her off? Just a touch of the blue stones, couched right next to the palladot, shining so brilliantly sent a clamorous coil ringing straight to her core?

Tierney doubled over underneath the water. Exhaling. Gut-wrenching. She coughed all the wind she had trapped in her lungs to sustain her. *I burn inside. This so-called inter-spection is starting to get the better of me. It's as easy to trigger as a ripple across water.* A contentment she'd needed badly was seethed away by her own actions. Her own burden. On account of something happening within her that she didn't understand. Images of other people's energy signatures who were inside the Frozen Folly with them crowded her brain. She opened her eyes, and...there they were...still.

Contrarily, once the Kalameshee got her above water her breath became normal. *Really? As though I hadn't struggled?* She snorted. Except the incident had her clinging to him close like he was someone as intimate to her as could be, with whimpers she couldn't keep from escaping her lips that gave away her distress. "I thought you were drowning," he said.

"I almost did," she muttered underneath her breath, her attempt at a snicker trailing off...a pitiful sound. The strength to fully express the scorn after that episode had leeched away until she had none left, and deflation settled on her like a winded sail. *Can't even muster the bother to be disgusted with myself.* A half-hearted smirk softened some of the exhaustion from her features. "A Soonahyin drown? That would be a tale to tell little ones for entertainment."

"You weren't in distress?"

"I...it's not something I can explain."

"You're brutally direct. I believe you capable of an explanation."

Tierney ruffled at his tone. The Kalameshee lifted her underneath her armpits and forced her to look him square on. But who was he to question her? "I may be, but I have no obligation to explain myself to you." Now, that was an odd statement to make, given she'd forgotten herself and had clung to him like a limpet.

For all the world she couldn't understand her stomach's drop when a huff puffed from him, and his back straightened and he put her away from him. The ramifications of why it would escaped her, but it did bother her if that was disappointment deepening the lines in his forehead. "You looked to be in distress, Tierney. I swam to get you. Just about bursting my lungs to do so. Don't I deserve an explanation of what caused such a reaction in you?"

What explanation could she give that a Kalameshee would under-stand? It wasn't as if Kalameshees had gifts similar to theirs, or at least she'd never heard that they did. "I don't refuse to tell you out of choice. I've had no good explanation for this phenomena since it started."

"Then describe it to me."

Wading water, she turned away from him. With her back to him, she did a waffle between *should I tell him or should I not? What good would it offer? Can he have any insight into what's been happening with me?* She whirled to then float herself toward the sky, her hair spread behind her. His being Kalameshee disassociated him in a way that made confiding in him somewhat removed. Set apart from everything going on and everyone else around her.

But uhm...did it really though? Was her mind even now altering him from someone unattainable to someone here and accessible? Morphing him into a position that made it more palatable to tell him her business.

In the end, a magnet had less attraction than the Kalameshee had for her. His closing in on her, hands supporting her beneath her back and thighs swayed her more than anything else did. His touch, silken on her body. Her breasts glistened from the water. Erect nipples pointed by freezing air pouted for his attention. She felt starved for it. After a lifetime of brothers blocking every attempt at sensual exploration, the Kalameshee's interest was a feast to the senses.

To his credit, he did try valiantly to keep his eyes away. The scrap of material tied around her failed to cover her completely, and he failed miserably too.

He'd been right all the same. She *had* been in distress. That was no mistake. Since he'd discovered her curled in on herself, his heart thundered against her side.

"You're aware that I bear you no ill will, right?" he asked.

Tierney snorted. "You wouldn't dare for fear of losing the closest thing to an ally you have here in Soonayah."

He chortled also, yet the curve on his mouth tilted toward self-deprecation. "That may be. But my care for you is genuine though I haven't spoken it." If only he would stop holding her gaze with his, then maybe she could think clearly. Try to see if talking about this was what was best. The inclination was there, but the act of doing it felt foreign to her. "It would be a privilege to share your confidence," he said.

And his words *sounded* sincere. They truly did. Only, a fluorescent dot nibbled at his arm. The speck of a fish took tiny pecks at him, backed off then came back for more. The fickle creature reminded Tierney of herself. A Kalameshee with potency—she couldn't deny. He attracted her like no other. But his behavior. So much caginess. Fully trusting him was a serious doubt.

No one else knew what had been happening with her. Soonahyins tended to shelter their gifts from the eyes of others instead of exploring them in the open. Safety. Self-sufficiency always at the forethought. One's gift could be a weapon if ever there was need to use it. You didn't broadcast it before you had to. She'd never even heard of anyone experiencing anything close to her *new* one and the extra stress it was causing. *If I told this, I'd probably end up telling everyone Mother is sending me to a sanctum too.* She'd wanted to talk to someone. After nearly drowning, anyone would do. And the Kalameshee was here.

She dithered, swirling the warmth surrounding them around and around, flapping her hands in the water. The words of her plight swirled around and around too, around and around, around and aroun...then fell from her tongue on a sigh.

"When I was below, I bumped into the hibonite gems and my mind opened to others here in the Folly with us. It's this...*awareness* I call my inter-spection for lack of a better name for it." After all was said and done, the pressure lessened some from her sternum once she opened up to someone, anyone. Even if she barely knew him.

"You had a premonition?"

"No. I can't see actual people or what they may do. I can't really see them at all. Their energy, it's alive to me. I feel them as they are."

She moved to begin swimming again. "No. You shouldn't resist. You're causing yourself harm when you don't have to." The Kalameshee stayed her. "You must stop fighting. You're going against a part of yourself. Now tell me. When did this phenomena start?"

Although her instinct was to melt in his arms and curl into his support, that was the opposite of what she did. Her body in contrast to the buoyancy of water around them had the pliancy of a piece of wood. She didn't have the luxury to be too much of herself with him. Not yet. "Quite some time before I journeyed to Outliers," she admitted. "There, I could detect you before you ever smashed into my room and caused such mayhem. And in the Hall of Covenance earlier, my brother Eh'kotah too. I practically saw his energy walk through the Keep before he joined us." Tremors shook her body. "But...in the water this time, I…" Tierney tossed her head and the Kalameshee stayed her again. "So many people came crashing into my head when it had only been gradual before."

"Trust me. Coming into our gifts when we are young is like this. I understand. Just close your eyes for a moment." His heart had returned to a regular thumping. "Relax." Against her, his lifeblood's rhythm was catching. Soothing her. *Bump-bump. Bump-bump.* She so needed to get a handle on what was happening, she'd try to do what he told her. "Now, you say that you can sense others." *Bump-bump.* "Don't resist them. Reach out, rather than fight their energy. Seek them, make them a part of you." *Bump-bump.* His biceps tightened against her body, disturbing her for a moment. He drew her closer, but then everything relaxed. His muscles. His breathing. His presence. Offering stillness.

So many people though. What would detecting them all at once do to her?

"Open yourself."

If she focused on the Kalameshee's closeness, he would distract her. *Okay…Okay. Have to find a way to concentrate on something else.*

Tension drifted from her body on a gust of frigid air. The sky's blackness stretched above, a bruise of purple. The Tellurician moons blazoned their silver. Arrows shimmered from the gemstones below, erupting from the aquifer. They glanced off the Folly's ice and leached it with color. An overpowering hue of hibonite dominated them all, charging the Folly walls with blue. They were surrounded in the colors of the Folly.

Below, she'd danced among the rainbows cascading from the gemstones. Whirling in waters so clear, she'd kept her eyes open. A water's restoration that tingled the body it revitalized. Whorls of glimmers scintillated her curves and caressed her lissome grace, innervating the Soonahyin soul-energy embodied from all the generations past, who'd latched their very beings onto the nucleus of Soonayah feeding them from its soil. Then energies of the others in the Frozen Folly had crippled her.

It was a given that the luster of the gemstones on the river's bottom was attributed to lava-like flows of umbereen beneath the crust where the Frozen Folly was implanted. Soonahyins treated the Frozen Folly as no idle monument, but as a place of revitalization. Those who didn't live close, visited on planned sojourns to Dameerh. They came twice in a span to keep their Rituals of Ume within its richness.

Tierney flexed her calf. *Little pain from the match with Ok'nuh remains.* The stab the tornebird managed to puncture stung less too. Bumps and bruises from the veryum and the wolf assaults, the fall from a mountain, the fight with some unseen thing in the woods, the residual effects of just trudging through all that snow were fading. The aquifer's waters were already having their effects on her body and she wasn't *carrying out* a ritual.

A sense of a whole family partaking in their ritual in the aquifer is what possessed her, the babe of the family slicing into her core the strongest. Soonahyins performed their Rituals of Ume accompanied by the hollow sounds of a tympan drum, and long mystical laments from a pumis tree flute, along with ritual chants crooned in deep tones by the family participating. Chords of Ume keened on the air, haunting the alcoves of the Frozen Folly. *Echoes off the ice. A mournful process.*

How frightening it must be for a babe who'd never been submerged. Deep dives into the river were done out of necessity. Revitalization of one's vigor girded them for sturdiness against the cold. One's inner soul-energy was steadied by reinforcement to the core. The babe approached his first span of life. *He needs to attend his first ritual.*

Tierney's connection to him shone in his energy's light so bright he blinded her. He wailed as his family suspended him in an Ume hammock while they worried the waters around him. He didn't settle with the actions foisted on him until they lowered the hammock and his father climbed in. The father tucked him into his chest and the babe and the father hung suspended on top of the river surrounded by the rest of the family who billowed the hammock in the waters. They chanted tones of Ume and crooned the little one's fretfulness away. The hammock took one great dip. The father plunged beneath the surface, swiftly he stroked below the river with the babe in his arms.

When they broke the surface again the babe's energy was ebullient. Tierney laughed in its infectiousness, dunking herself and the Kalameshee too. Water burned the backs of her nostrils and she snorted it all out. She'd taken the Kalameshee's hold of her off guard with her delight in the babe's bliss.

"You spoke aloud of the family ritual. I take it, the babe is well?"

The thrill Tierney got from the babe's joy sang inside her own skin. She nodded to the Kalameshee. "Yes. But only after the father held him and took over his ritual. Is there any greater wonder than a parent's protection of their young?"

Such an ironic statement was a provocative thing.

The Kalameshee raised one eyebrow. "Even if that parent holds the position of queen?" The thrill in the babe's triumph skittered and died. A pinpoint of brilliance snuffed out in the wink of the Kalameshee's suggestion. His touch to the side of her face, his thumb's caress to the corner of her lips failed to coax the joy from them again.

She turned and swam from him, her steps stammering on the way out, muck squishing between her toes as she exited the water. "Come. We have delayed in the Folly long enough."

The Kalameshee caught her and halted her progress to the river's edge. "We've done everything according to your directions. I'm not spurred to leave simply because I mention your mother." He held her slim waist, maneuvering her back against a shelf of polished rock off the river, the bend curving to their bodies just so. "I now desire exploration of a different kind."

Desire for a different kind of exploration was buried inside her too. Not even deeply. It was kindled easily by his touch, his attentions, forcing a will of its own in connection to eyes as clear as green glass, their reflection from the light from the aquifer compelling her even more. She'd been denied this fire all her life. For once, shouldn't she be free to act on it? Her brothers' meddling curtailed any exploration she'd attempted before. Yet, this man had stood up to all three of them, his stature proud as he'd taken them on.

Her hand, of its own accord, drifted to skin slippery with the aquifer's water. A caress of musculature defined so, it suggested impenetrability, yet his skin stretched hot and supple over it. She traced the backside of his neck too. She'd itched to explore the nubby extensions extruding from his spine the moment she'd seen him without his tunic. He shivered and she realized touching the extruding spine of a Kalameshee may well excite this one's arousal too fast. Instead, she raised her hand to a tuft of bright hair, now darkened by the river. Jaw bristles scratched the tender fingertips she caressed down his cheeks.

Taking her hand in his after a kiss to her palm, he then kissed the inside of her elbow. Bristliness tickled her skin. She shrugged with a giggle. Opening the space between her neck and shoulder, his hand palmed her into submission. He placed his lips there, nipping her distended cord. *That's too sensitive!*

He licked the little hurt he caused, the thrill whisking her giggles away. His mouth opening over hers captured Tierney's moan. There was no sweet introduction to his appetites like one would expect of new lovers. He'd been voracious during their romp in the snow. She should've been prepared for this dive into hedonistic tasting, but she wasn't. He ravaged her mouth, suckled her tongue and Tierney again began to lose where they were just as she'd done in the snow. *I can't do that now.*

They were still in the water of the Folly aquifer. She needed to deliver him to his lodgings this night because her mother would never allow...*Mother!*

He'd defended her mother. Folding her now puffed lips, Tierney pulled back from him with a groan. She rested her forehead against his chest for some moments and basked against his heat, dragging more of the heat into herself before she made a move again toward the river's edge. "We must retire from the water and dry ourselves. There are linens for us warming near the fire. Come now. And let us be quick."

The Kalameshee turned her back toward him as she started to move. "Why must we retire from the water? Because you have your mother in your brain always?"

"It wasn't me who introduced her here. I was content to ignore what happened earlier."

"But that's what drives you. Even when you're unaware, she's driving you. Ignoring it has no purchase when it has such prevalence in your mind. It must have. After what happened between you all this day, all your lives have changed forever." *If only he knew the whole of it with Mother, then maybe he would leave this alone.*

"I chose to let it be for this eve so that I could enjoy my connection in the Folly. Yet, you bring her presence here and defend her actions, which are indefensible!" Tierney pushed at his shoulders to move him from her path. His bearing held the fixedness of the trunk of a tree. Obviously, he had no intention of being moved from her so easily.

"You carry your self-determination from her like a badge. And see yourself in the young because of their likeness to that self that was shaped by your relationship. I don't defend her. You do in your self-belief alone. And refuse to look at her reasoning even as you laud the virtues of parenthood. I simply put words to it and...uhm there's something else too. You're hiding something from her. From everybody."

He crowded her against the bank of the river again. "Don't read my mind, empath. I'm entitled to privacy within my own head." Tierney searched desperately for reasons to balk.

The Kalameshee lowered his head to peer into her face. Effectively locking her to him, he encircled her shoulders with his arms, sliding his hand beneath the wet carpet of hair. "I don't read minds. But I'm attuned to you as if I can read yours. Doesn't that show you the connection between us? One deserving further discovery?"

This time when he lowered his mouth to hers, Tierney opened for him without hesitation. She had no true reason to deny him. She didn't want to deny him. His tongue wreaked havoc with her wherewithal. It shuttered away issues she hadn't equipped to address. She liked that. She welcomed it.

His slick chest contoured to her breast, earning her murmur of assent. "Yes." Rough hands devoured their permission to explore her body. As he cleaved to her against the bank, his manhood pressed her intimate parts. Apparently, this wasn't enough for him. He smoothed a hand up her thigh, around her buttocks, then lifted her limb over his hip to accommodate himself between her legs. He sent his hand back to the fullness of her backside, molding her against his erection. Tierney moaned into his mouth. He lifted his head. "I'm sorry, but I must taste you."

A mutter escaped her as she was a little out of her head now, "You're doing a pretty good job of tasting me alrea..." A cry broke from her. He'd slipped his hand from behind her back, brought her top down with the movement, exposing her turgid mahogany nipples to the cold and his hot gaze.

It was his turn to groan. "You are sublime." The words were garbled.

He'd pressed her hips harder against his, lifting her to his mouth at the same time. When he latched onto her nipple and laved it with his tongue, Tierney's head fell back. "Oh! Oh goodness!" Her shoulder plopped against the bank. The Kalameshee eased his hand between her skin and the stones poking her from the river's bank and pressed her deeper into his mouth.

Tierney's fingers went clutching into the Kalameshee's hair, stroking the nubs of his spine that extruded from his neck. Lost to the sting of his mouth tugging on her nipples, she held his head to her breasts. *This is finally happening for me.* Exquisite little tingles arrowed straight to the juncture of her hips and his, opening new worlds of sensation for her.

They were pressed tightly together, and they weren't pressed tightly enough. Tierney's body trembled. Poised. *His fingers.* Below the water, they teased the edge of her water costume's bottoms at the juncture where hip met thigh. She increased the pressure of her hips against his, grinding on him.

Suddenly, a loud "Whoop" pierced the silence. Laughter reverberated harshly throughout the alcove. Great, heavy splashing into the river yanked Tierney and the Kalameshee from each other's arms violently.

Chapter 22

A d'rihl, slick from the aquifer, shot above the water, another of his "Whoops" echoing. The loudness boomed off the ice, off the cruxes, the crannies shaped where ice met soil before it swooped toward the sky and set free the howling that deafened Tierney and the Kalameshee. They managed their heaving breaths while they tried to orient themselves with what was going on. Sounds pulsated in their ears, and made them fall under the water searching about for the source of the disturbance. Discombobulation eddied the waters around them, then something streaked right past them.

Of course, it was Ad'rihl diving, ripping through the water as unabashed as a boy, and bumping against them like a sleek silverfish. "Korrell!" he called to the other of the siblings who stood on the bank, and who disturbed the peace just as much as he did just by his presence. Korrell was wrapped in his linen against the cold, sneering at his brother's antics. "Come," Ad'drihl shouted. I'm replenished already. I challenge you this night like Tierney did earlier. But to a race to the gemstones. I wager I will best you by twenty paces."

Korrell dropped his linen and sauntered to the point on the river where the ground rose as an embankment over the water, positioned as a shelf before it curved around and flattened and became the river's bank that met the outer wall. He jumped high above the water and arrowed his body straight down. Once he flipped and started stroking, it was too late for Ad'rihl to catch him. Only, it wouldn't be Ad'rihl if he didn't try, right?

Her brothers' constant need to best each other irked to no end. *Idiots!* Always around. Always with the foolery, especially Ad'rihl. After a while, you'd think they'd grow up. She had. Tierney turned up her nose. She rolled her eyes beyond them back to the bank. Mlai was there, dropping linen too. "Mlai!" She raised her arms to ward Mlai off before she dove in. Mlai sprinted to the river, not another care in the world lending to her intentions other than hijinks. Her willowy form covered in a water costume similar to Tierney's, jumped high. Curled into that perfect ball shape as she'd done in the woods, her plop in the river caused barely a ripple.

She has metal in her body. Tierney held her breath until she reappeared. Whatever type her bio-mechanics were made of had to be heavier than sinew and bone.

Giggles bubbled above the surface before Mlai popped up, infectious hearing them come from her after she'd seemed so worn. "Ad'rihl pulled Korrell back by his ankle and beat him to the gemstones after all!"

Tierney sneered. *The patently Ad'rihl move was just like him. And I could care less what he does as long as he leaves me out of it...Korrell too.* Their interference in her life had worn a groove into her nerves over the spans of time. Her only concern right now was for Mlai's well-being. "Mlai, your biomechanics. Should you submerge yourself like this? Will you become too heavy to wade water after a time?"

Mlai laughed again and quirked her head as if Tierney's question was absurd. "When it's needed, our bio-mechanics are perfectly ballasted with hot air according to our weight. I swim well, Tierahna. I love it." Water ran down Mlai's body. Skin already endowed with a shade far from flat, more brightened by its natural essence like a Soonahyin's now, glistened in the Folly's light.

Okay then. No need to worry about Mlai. Just dandy! Though deflation settled on Tierney's spirit, pretty much rendering her done for good this time, still, she couldn't forget that the moment she'd been sharing with the Kalameshee was gone. *Forever.* There was no telling if they'd get to have another one either. And she was no further along in confronting her mother.

Hauling herself from the river, unlike before, she was able to go unhindered. There was no halting by roughened fingers impatient for more loving. And that spot right between the shoulder blades nagged, lamenting the loss. The drag to her footsteps and glance over her shoulder, confirmed the Kalameshee was exiting too. Her lumbering this time mimicked her state of mind, a blanket of white-hot exhaustion in mockery of a soul now truly, truly blinkered.

Several fleece-padded linens, their linings warmed, awaited them. *Most appreciations! Some heat! Good! Something positive to latch on to.* They dried themselves at the pit. The Kalameshee jerked the linen over his body and hopped from foot to foot. Tierney grinned as he groused. He expected the cold to drive him to seek cover. It was unnecessary. "Relax. You would be surprised at how toasty we can make it here in Soonayah."

She ushered him into a warmth wafting from the fire pit. Once his linen's insulation trapped his own body heat, he would settle fare enough. The silk of the banquette surrounding the fire pit, soothing to the skin, would mollify him some...hopefully. Unfortunately, the luxury couldn't make up fully for the abrupt dousing of passions. With her brothers here, their moments together had been taken away and couldn't be brought back.

Just thinking of what they had been heading toward made *her* arousal reignite. And quite suddenly she was ravenous again, mostly not for sustenance though. She had better feed some of her hunger with food seeing as how no other appetites would be fed anytime soon.

Of course, with my luck, this is how our first real loving would end. It follows too that a steaming goblet would tilt, Tierney balanced it underneath with her fingertips while handing it to the Kalameshee. The Keep's conscientious attendants must have placed this smorgasbord around the fire pit when they were in the Folly river. The food was still hot. They'd been too absorbed in each other to notice anyone enter the alcove, her brothers included. She cringed at what they might have witnessed them doing.

Busying herself with the food helped her overcome the heat in her cheeks some. There were minuscule servers placed to the side of the food arrangement, on a ring, and were picked up by the one attendant remaining and used to sample all the dishes, drinks as well. His and her eyes held over the lip of the beaker she drank. He hadn't tasted it yet. Tierney'd covered her tureen with her hand before he'd tested hers. If he fell to poison then so would she. He inclined his head acknowledging her actions before he left after he'd ensured all the other provisions were safe for their consumption.

Broth rich with fatty eland meat still on the bone and chunks of some blue root vegetable spilled over the Kalameshee's goblet as he gulped at it. A plank of buttery bread paid the perfect complement to meat roasted just right. The hunk he nabbed from the buffet arrangement would crumble in the mouth when bitten, along with the crunch of a mildly sweet root vegetable.

Handing him a dabbing towel for the broth that dribbled to his chin, Tierney pursed her lips. Her own sips were dainty. She retrieved a tined ladle for her more unhandy portions. And chewed bite after bite, beat after beat in accompaniment to her thoughts, feeding the one appetite that she could at the moment. It was some compensation for being hindered from their lovemaking. Poor compensation, such as it was, but she'd have to live with it.

Suddenly, shouting erupted from the river, Ad'rihl, Korrell, and

Mlai frisking and splashing in the middle of their swim. So even her thoughts about what she and the Kalameshee had been doing were to be interrupted too.

She couldn't have her daydreams to herself with her brothers around. Ad'rihl and Korrell engaging in raucous sport with Mlai in the aquifer sucked up all the attention toward *their* behavior. *Not surprising at all.* Reflections on her and the Kalameshee couldn't be done here because it deserved undivided considerations, and goodness knew that couldn't happen now. She'd smother it with all her attention later, alone, with no brothers.

After some time, the aforementioned brothers came and dried themselves in front of the fire. They too partook of the fare before them.

Pats, gruff and fast, finished Ad'rihl and Korrell's drying. They filled platters with goblets of bone broth, bread, butter, glass beakers of a hot beverage, brewed and blended from the roasted roots of the Chicon tree and powdered nuts.

In time, everyone's actions slowed as they noticed Mlai tending to herself. The density of the pink in her fine-boned leg was a marvel to them. *Utterly, notably inappropriate,* them goggling at her like she was some specimen, flayed open, on display behind glass. Even with chagrin heating her face, questions nagged at Tierney though. "Mlai. You seem recovered, but you've gotten so little rest. Do you think you've given yourself enough time to recuperate?

Tierney guided her with care to a seat within the banquette around the fire after helpings from the buffet were heaped upon her platter. "I feel well, Tierney. So much so, I enjoyed a romp in the water. Something I haven't had the energy to do in ages. My only fear was that the cold would hamper my recovery. But the river's waters run hot. And here it feels as if I'm in an enclosure of heat."

She nodded at Mlai's statement.

"You *are*," Ad'rihl answered. Tierney was grateful he interjected. Her interest in science and technology didn't come near to as much depth as his. His mind possessed the capacity for intricacies on the subjects, and he had a habit of being able to expound on things others barely knew about. "Essentially this *is* a heated room," he said. "Where the flagstones end, the area fifteen paces beyond the fire pit, there is a perimeter of ionized air that keeps the nice toasty heat inside. Before the air becomes stale, when the alcove needs airing out, attendants release the heat at regular intervals."

Mlai sipped her beaker of hot beverage, her eyes unfocused on the fire pit, her mind looked to be preoccupied elsewhere, only her physical presence there with them. "Why are the alcoves aired out? Wouldn't this melt the Frozen Folly's ice?"

"That's pretty much what we want. The Frozen Folly's chemistry is...a bit unique. Each fire pit within all the alcoves is aired out often at every chance the attendants get to check that the rivers are clear. They must be or the ice walls will reconstitute themselves. If left alone, the Folly can regenerate back to a solid block of ice." Mlai leaned against a bolster while Ad'rihl talked. Plush within her linen, she lifted her legs into the covers too, mimicking Tierney's recline in the sumptuousness around them.

At this time in the eve, a partial day of the Folly's wall's reconstitution loomed overhead in this alcove before it could be let out again with air. The stars, a brush of purple sky, a glimpse of White Moon peeking between them, the walls towered stark with their charge of blue shining from them. Sconces with lights affixed to them placed in nooks, counteracted the blue and commingled amber in, enfolding them inside the Frozen Folly alcove, and created a cocoon of ambiance that allowed the alcoves to be lit, making it better for seeing.

Faint strains of Ume ritual chants echoed off the ice. The walls remembered, you see, and latched onto the highest potency in the blue from the hibonite. One might have thought the faint murmurs that echoed were the people in the Folly now. That wasn't always so. The walls replayed every ritual chant ever uttered having imprinted them all on the ice's molecules. An imaginative mind could picture a soul enclosed by the walls of ice. Trapped. Languishing forever to the sounds of Ume chords consoling them.

"Blocked ice is the condition the Folly was found in before excavation ever occurred. Even the rivers were frozen solid before the Folly's underpinnings were scaled back and the natural aquifer allowed to seep." Korrell slanted a look at Tierney and they smirked at each other. Once Ad'rihl got going on any of his favorite subjects, it was a good bet he'd go off on a tangent if he wasn't stopped. "Only the multitude of gemstone farms on the floor of the crevice have been left as they were found. We imported fish to help the ecosystem stay clean and thrive. And we arrive at the Frozen Folly that we have all taken benefit of this night," Ad'rihl finished.

Korrell then put his finger to his lips. A surety was that it'd been Ad'rihl's droning on and on that had a drowsing effect. He pointed to Mlai swathed within her linen against the silk of the banquette's bolsters. She'd nodded off. The young Soonahyins had an ease with themselves that fostered an inclusive environment for the Lorgren.

Mlai stirred after some moments, gruffling. Furrowed brows accompanied her sitting up, adjusting herself as straight as if a pole was in her back. "I wondered if the gemstone beds were imports or if they occurred through nature," she said, her speech only a little slurred. "The ground the Folly is embedded in must be alive with all the processes taking place down there."

"You are altogether right, Mi...Mil-lee." Ad'rihl beamed—his demeanor looked to be one of delight in a neophyte showing interest in the fields he so loved. *His stumble in pronouncing her name was an atrocious attempt though.* Tierney rolled her eyes at his poor effort.

"The chemical and geological processes taking place below our very feet have been enough to keep our Ministry of Science occupied for eons," he said.

Crystal steins that smoked were being handed about like favors for the good boys and girls. Mlai's slim belly looked about ready to burst. She waved away the libation from Korrell that fogged up the sides of its beaker.

Mlai had already eaten more than Tierney guessed her slight body could handle. The drink in addition could be as good as a tonic for her recovery. Korrell pushed a frosty stein on her anyway, with it she'd sleep the innocence of a babe once she was abed.

Heavy drink wasn't a favorite of Tierney's. She declined. Unperturbed, the Kalameshee stretched for his. "If this is the smoking ice brew Prince Haarth introduced me to at the festival, then I can say now, ready another stein. For this one won't last long."

Korrell's chuckle accompanied the placement of another stein on the rim of the fire pit before the Kalameshee. The performance the Kalameshee had subjected himself to in the sparing arena had evidently garnered him some currency with her brothers.

Many had sought for an *in* with them. Any who were not willing to meet exemplary standards were turned away. Forcefully. Some Tierney hadn't known about. They'd failed on the most basic level when they heard of the gauntlet of her brothers. She'd learned about them once they'd been long gone. Those who thought to try an end-round pass her brothers straight to Tierney lost their respect. They put themselves at a disadvantage from the outset. Any man serious in his pursuit of the First Princess, Tierahna of Soonayah should expect and welcome a vetting. Her brothers had a saying:

"The victorious proof of a suitor's worthiness shall be exalted."

Leave it to say, no one had ever been exalted. Tierney began her rocking routine again. The surrounds, the sumptuousness of the banquette, eating staples of Soonahyin fare lost their diversionary effects for her. Thoughts of what all had happened that day, the vy earlier with her brother's most especially, tainted the atmosphere.

Ad'rihl must've informed her brothers of the Kalameshee's interest. Their stare-off in the atrium had been Ad'rihl's issuance of a silent warning. One the Kalameshee hadn't backed down from. The next step, *of course*, a bout in the sparring arena. Tierney was sick of it. Their reign over her life would come to an end soon enough when she left, *but I want them stopped now.*

She doubted all three of them taking part in the match was even planned. It probably stemmed from them thinking they sensed some weight in the Kalameshee as a prospect. What they didn't know was that their efforts were premature. She and the Kalameshee's moments together were skimpy at best. There'd not been enough time alone to explore each other fully. Look at them now.

The pooling of her feminine nectar from their foreplay was useless. She sat here now with brothers...Mlai. *The Kalameshee's presence as good as a muskox's ass!*

Defying all that, he was still here just the same. He'd stood strong against her brothers using his empathic gifts to anticipate their moves. It was obvious neither of them had worked out exactly how he was doing it either. And still, he was here after the dressing down he'd taken from the queen, instead of heading back to his home. Back to his cosseted role of prince in his own land. The queen would be incensed if she too believed him a serious consideration for Tierney. *That may have her wanting to commit me ever sooner. His presence here could be affecting a faster send-off for me. One dilemma after another.* She frowned into her cup.

"You shared smoking ice brew with Haarth while you and he were at the East Tundra Bay Festival? Is that right?" Korrell and Ad'rihl shared identical shakes of their heads. It took special men to brave through the frightening ordeal of a festival, with the press of the jovial horde trading and all. Her brothers would have flayed their own skin to avoid it. "That was right before Tierney dove headfirst from the plateau, is it not?" Korrell asked.

Even with anger for Korrell still simmering inside her, that asinine question *forced* her laughter out. "I did no such thing as dive! Bak'rah came underfoot. We slipped when tornebirds—"

"He *did* dive though." Korrell nodded in the Kalameshee's direction. "As Haarth recollected, the Kalameshee here dove without a second thought after you when you...*fell.*"

Tierney's mouth quirked at her brother's hesitation on the word fell. There wasn't a Soonahyin alive foolish enough to dive from a mountain. Not when they didn't know what waited for them beyond the cliff. Korrell was right. The Kalameshee hadn't hesitated *to dive* when she'd needed *him.* Underneath her lashes, she gauged his reaction to her brother's teasing. He merely shrugged. "What thought was there to be had? She and the wolf had fallen. A great man I would be to wring my hands from the safety of the plateau."

Ad'rihl sat forward, including himself in questioning the Kalameshee too. "You deem it your right to protect Tierney then—"

Tierney's sigh interrupted the exchange. "This high-handed behavior is over. I don't need protection!" She said. "I am more than capable—"

"I do." The Kalameshee's unequivocal assertion stopped her defense of herself in its tracks.

Chapter 23

"I *do*." Forceful. "*I do…*" Unrepentant. His affirmation echoed across the silence. "Your Soonahyin men are a mystery to me. I know Tierney can protect herself. I know personally how strong she is. That's one of the things I like about her the most." He grimaced at Tierney and rubbed his jugular just where the point of her elbow had obstructed his breathing. She frowned considering the reminder. Outliers seemed a lifetime ago now.

"But I take this as a privilege. This care I have for her. She has been utterly stunning to me in so many ways since I first met her. And though I know not why no man here has come up to par for her, I'm grateful for it," he said.

Tierney's stomach somersaulted. She made it her business to look busy sipping on her Chicon root beverage. Everyone else was quiet. Her lips stubbornly mummed the edge of her beaker.

What do I feel about the Kalameshee's declaration?

Her eyes stuck to the steam from her drink that warmed her nose, away from her brothers' prying. Their presence here intruded on something private. Such words from the Kalameshee required time on her own to think about what they meant for her. *Yet, here they are in the mix of this too.* Her long-attached chaperons. Forever blocking decisions she should be making. Could she carry out a full exploration with a man if her brothers stepped aside? Without their wall of defense would she even have the nerve to follow through? The knot that'd been resting in her belly the whole day stewed. It *hadn't* left. She'd known something else was coming, but now the knot twisted up with a throb of anticipation. Her eyes lifted over the rim of her beaker and clashed with the Kalameshee's green focus. He'd already been watching her. Waiting.

Unapologetically, Korrell and Ad'rihl's attentions caught what should have been the private exchange between them. Then they had a silent exchange with each other. Korrell gestured to the second stein he'd passed to the Kalameshee. It smoked in the same spot on the fire pit. "Your second beverage is untouched, Kalameshee. What put you off our smoking ice brew? The thought of what possible accommodations you'll find this late in our foreign land? You two were so lost in each other when we entered that you didn't hear us. You will never be allowed a room in the Keep's guest residences. Though they are cordoned off, there is no promise you could make we would believe of you not attempting to coerce your way into Tierney's quarters." The jocularity Korrell had shared with the Kalameshee had disappeared, driven away with the Kalameshee's declaration. The planes of Korrell's jaw were back to their solemn mien. "Rest assured, Mother will not be providing any accommodations to lay your head this night Kalameshee, lest you get a babe on the precious First Princess of Soonayah."

The Kalameshee wretched, his coughed-up brew spewing every-where, smoking, it sizzled the flames. The fire pit's hissing forced everybody into flinching back. They all ended up coughing as the libation's frost smoked more coming into contact with the flames. A rare occasion of undemanding Soonahyin lounging was ruined by Korrell's meddling.

"There is no babe getting being gotten on me! You must think me an utter fool. What concern of yours should there be about my potential for being gotten with a babe, anyway? Turn your attention to your own virility and any possible addled-brained females who'll let you realize your progeny on them some day. Reproduction taking place in my loins is not to be spoken of again!"

Her brothers already believed she'd flip to the Kalameshee's defense at the slightest provocation. She'd proven as much earlier already. A few moments of anger here? *For what? Calm yourself, Tierney.* It wasn't worth the cost of the torment they'd deliver on her in the future. Her over-reaction in the sparring arena helped fuel this harassment *now*. Tierney pulled back from the edge of her seat and copied Korrell's cocksure sprawl.

"Such dramatics," Ad'rihl drawled at her outrage. Yet, he and Korrell kept their scrutiny of her and the Kalameshee going. "But I had been wondering about something along those lines too. Mil-lie?" He shook his head, failing at pronouncing her name again. "First off, I deem your name must be shortened. This whole Mil...Mil is entirely too much of a mouthful. Milly fits your manner far better." Mlai shook her head weakly, but stubbornly in rejecting the shortening of the name she seemed so proud of. "I have a curiosity I would like to put to you."

They all regarded Mlai, sympathetic to her doggedly propping herself up. She had begun to wilt and lean into the bolsters that were plumped around her, drowsiness overcoming her again. Amethyst sparked underneath the half-closed lids she turned on Ad'rihl. His propensity to jest even in serious times was one of his most commendable features. The Lorgren people possessed the reputation amongst the lands as stoics in the best of times. Utter aloofs and stubborn pragmatics in the worst. Tierney'd learned in her lessons that, "*joint empirical preponderance*" reigned supreme in their land. Rarely was anything beyond a collective of intellectual enhancement pursued and never was individualism encouraged.

Ad'rihl never took himself too seriously, though he presented as the most scholarly of all the Soonahyin royal family. And Mlai seemed charmed by his personality. Since she'd met him, she'd laughed at his quips when no one else did. Yet, not so much when he tried to change the name she took such dignity in. It seemed, under no circumstances did she want it diminished in even the slightest of ways.

"You may express your curiosity...Addy," Mlai said the new diminutive of Ad'rihl's name with a flourish. "But be aware that I shall return any shortening of my name with the same of yours."

Tierney snorted. *Quick-witted, I see. He deserves that.*

That shortening of Ad'rihl's name had been a favored of their older brothers, used to put him in his place in his youth. He hated it. Yet, his demeanor became more animated with Mlai rallying the energy to banter back with him. Tierney'd noticed that she'd tired quickly in her romp in the Folly river. Trying to hide their concern, the brothers had probably retired early from the river so that she could too. In a lean forward Ad'rihl got to his questions.

"Altogether well, *Milly*. We shall move forward with pretty monikers for each other then. But my question is about the reproductive capabilities of the *Lorgren*. Am I correct in understanding that you're all joined with your biomechanics at birt—?

"No, we're not. The development of a babe outside a womb is too risky for interruption by materials foreign to its organic incubation. Our biomechanics are not introduced until after all the babe's early developments—*far after* simulated birth. The courses are run on a routine until full integrations of all biomechanics are fulfilled in the *latter* spans of youth."

It was fascinating how the Lorgrens put biomechanics in themselves like it was a commonplace practice. No other land exercised such drastic changes to the body. In early times Lorgr was subjected to proof trials by The Tellurician Regulatory Body on the need for their biomechanics. Ad'rihl, no doubt, relished delving deeper into Mlai's brain about the hypotheses used to regulate her society's protocols. Such matters were just his tastes.

"And though you don't carry your babes in your wombs, can you... are you still capable of natural gestation and delivery of them?"

Mlai shook her head quickly and looked down at the fleece underside of the linen she wore. She turned the tail end up, exposing a swathe of pale pink calf. She pushed the points of her fingernails through the textured material.

* * *

Mlai

Ad'rihl asks the questions I have asked all my life, Mlai thought to herself. Since my youth, my fantasy has been to birth my own babe and hold the sweet babe in my arms.

When prescribed, Lorgrens donated their reproductive cells to their Fertility Commission in randomly-scrolled lots of twelve. Cells of twelve males were mixed then fertilized with the eggs of twelve females. Most were successful and gestation of the Lorgren babe began. Sometimes, rarely if you want the truth of it, the same cell and eggs that had just been donated. If any were unsuccessful, the donating Lorgren females and males at the latter end of the list were then added to the beginning list for the next round of lots. They were assured a resulting babe from that lot.

Fare and concise. The perfect convention for a society such as ours. Mlai guffawed.

Reproductive stunting had plagued them for eons beyond their recorded history. Desire to carry one's own babe wasn't exclusive to her. Particularly for her though, the dilemma couldn't be passed so easily for entering into the lots.

Her diagnosis of extreme rejection episodes early in her youth was a death sentence. Most in her society didn't begin to experience moderate episodes until they were well into their mid-to-late adult spans. Her people reached old age. Had prodigious lives, normally.

No babe of hers should be subjected to her death and absence. Mlai dreamed of defying their societal norms and smothering her babe with care and encouragement. *Mother did no less for me. It would be the least I can do for my own babe.* The babe would deserve better than to be left to whomever the High Council—the utter emotionless governing body of Lorgren society—deemed fit to be its mother.

She'd indulged in these fantasies during her many spans of tests and therapies with her mother always at her side. And they'd tracked her genes then. *Mother letting me in on Lorgr's little secret has been the driver for almost everything ever since.*

Her mother had revealed to her that she was a descendant of a great many of long convoluted lines of High Council patricians. An absolute rarity had been found too. Mlai had lineage from her own mother and father who were assigned to her. Her pedigree of so many of the High Council from now and generations past meant that they were so inbred, it was nigh impossible that the High Council ascribed to the reproductive strictures of randomly scrolled lots imposed on everyone else. So, she hadn't ascribed to them either.

Since her last spans at school, she was asked to input into the lots. They had waved away her youth, assuring her that because of her early rejection she was being encouraged to experience parenthood in case her time to indulge in it was shortened. Mlai wouldn't have believed them even if her mother hadn't already let her in on the secret of her genealogy. *Since when did the High Council of Lorgr give any thought to the desires of a single female?*

They wanted her genes reproduced. When she'd embarked on her journey here, there was the risk of her death before its completion. The High Council had attempted to take her in to the Fertility Commission by force before she left. Had it not been for her mother stopping them, they would have succeeded. They would even now be fertilizing her eggs with a male donor they deemed fit. Gestating a babe would have commenced whether she returned alive or not. Mlai had no plans to reproduce a babe into the lots.

And I will fight until I do die if I must to assure that.

"Do you have any intention of answering my question?" Ad'rihl asked.

The brothers had put *Tierney* through a lot that day. You could see Ad'rihl's insensitivity toward Mlai scraping Tierney's nerves too. Her lips peeled back from her teeth. She whispered fiercely to Ad'rihl's unaffected face. "Leave it be. She's already shaken her head "*No.*" Can't you see that the subject is sensitive for her?"

Korrell jumped toward Mlai in the nick of time and caught the nearly full stein slipping from her hand. Replacing it on the fire pit, he stood and looked down at her cheeks ruddy now in sleep. "She's drifted into slumber after racking her brains over Ad'rihl's intrusive questions."

Korrell bent to lift her but Ad'rihl shouldered him out of the way before he could touch her. "Leave her." Ad'rihl rearranged her linen. He then tucked the cloth around her and lifted Mlai himself. He preceded Korrell from the Frozen Folly alcove. Glancing over his shoulder, he said to Tierney and the Kalameshee, "Tierahna, I'm sure the Kalameshee will appreciate your escort to find lodgings within our fair dominion this night. Korrell and I will wait up in avid anticipation of your prompt return to the Keep."

Tierney stood too but didn't dignify Ad'rihl with any answer. She turned her back on echoes of laughter chortling from the Folly's corridor they'd gone off to. "Come now and dress," she addressed the Kalameshee. "As he said, I'll see to it that you have lodgings for the night. But I will take my dear time doing it as I see fit."

Chapter 24

E *h'kotah*

This is too decadent by far.

Eh'kotah luxuriating on his mother's lounger, one leg propped over the arm was the first seat he'd taken since he'd gotten back to the Keep. *May as well make use of this contraption covered in cushions and pillows, completely out of place in Mother's quarters.* Having taken stance nearly the whole journey back from the Dayea mountains; his mother took stance more often than *he* did. He'd never seen her partake in this frill of a seat. *Someone should break it in and I've earned it, waiting on her.*

She and her most trusted companion, Bernehvelle, quibbled over what attire she would wear to bed that eve. The queen took umbrage with a slip that had no more a mauve color in it than sheer material to cover herself. "I won't wear this ridiculous frill." Patience constrained her temper at first. The family could always tell when she was straining to exert it, her voice rose and cracked on certain inferences. She with a slow tone asked Bernehvelle for her lined bed leggings and long tunics.

After Bernehvelle said, "They're all being cleaned," Bernehvelle then excused the need for surely the endless supply of his mother's night attire to be cataloged and decommissioned at her will. That patience was no longer cracked, it splintered in two and back and forth they went.

For crying out loud, Bernehvelle may well not leave until Mother is tucked abed!

He could end up with no time alone with her. He'd asked his mother for this visit with him in her quarters because a discovery the likes of which that he'd happened upon in the Dayea mountains shouldn't wait.

And, of course, revelations churning up old secrets as they had in the Hall of Covenance that day were a scourge on everybody. He hadn't wanted to overburden the queen, but duty to his sovereign was sacrosanct. She'd consider him negligent if he didn't tell her what he now knew. It was because of its implications that he was missing out on a bout in the Frozen Folly with his brothers and the Lorgren.

After Mlai'd awakened, Korrell had advised them in an aside the good the Folly water would do her. But instead of going with them, he languished in his mother's outer lounge as she and Bernehvelle argued. *Patience.* Now it was his turn to constrain himself before *he* cracked. *For the love of—!*

His armset buzzed. It was Korrell telling him that the Kalameshee and Tierney were in the Folly's royal alcove along with them. Only, Eh'kotah's hand itched for his other console. The one in the side-slit on his calf, *for private matters only.* He fingered it through his animal skin trews. Intimacy had to be held off. Nyoma's feverishness for him would make for an exhausting night ahead. His climbing the Dayea mountains with only the rough-hewn Tempeh Tu for company had made him impatient too for the scent of Nyoma's sweet skin.

"If only these two would get past this stalemate," he muttered. It was funny, that was the one thing Tierney had gotten wrong about him, lumping him in with his brothers and their relations. Eh'kotah's fastidiousness outweighed his other penchants in one area in life: women. His tastes ran to the beautiful, of course. But his relations tended to dealings with one woman at a time. No consorts all over the place. Nyoma was the perfect example of that. So, unlike what Tierney thought, he *had* chosen consorts of a sort…in his own way. He and Nyoma were as close as two could be without ascribing any labels to their relationship, though they would never match with each other. He couldn't foresee any woman his mother would ever approve of.

Privately, he suspected this was why the queen hadn't tried to match him to some chieftain's nubile daughter. Without a doubt at all though, she and Nyoma would be at odds if they met. The dancer possessed a stubborn streak that would most definitely set them up for a clash.

Gone were the days Eh'kotah had sought his mother's approval with his women, anyway. Nyoma and he weren't matched because they preferred it that way. He had no urge to match with her. And she would laugh in his face at the prospect. Being matched to the next in line for king of Soonayah and all the encumbrances that came with that mantle stilted independence in a woman like Nyoma…a bit.

The argument between his mother and Bernehvelle lengthened. *There will be no accounting for how long I will be delayed from some much-needed time with the woman who I know will welcome me if these two are not stopped.*

"Bernehvelle?" He interrupted them. "Why can Mother not wear what she wishes for bed? It's she alone who must sleep with herself, is it not?"

Quite clever if I must say so myself. Eh'kotah chuckled. Neither Bernehvelle nor his mother's face creased in humor, though they *did* stop bickering at his interruption.

Lowered eyebrows and a glower on Bernehvelle's face accompanied a march toward him. *Uh, oh!* Once at his side, she slapped his leg from its unfit drape over the arm of the lounge seat. She thumped his head and proceeded to push him in his back. Her attempts were ineffectual in getting him to stand. He hunched and covered her hands when she pinched his ears with her razor nails. "Aww, Berneh! You will break skin if you continue with that!"

"It's skin that I aim for on a young man with such lax manners! You have some insolence to call me by the shortening of my name! That's reserved for my peers, not the fledgling want-to-be successor. What business do you have in your mother's quarters this late in the eve, anyway? Come. Remove yourself." Bernehvelle pushed his shoulders again and again to no effect. Her picking at his ears, now there she had success. She kept at it. He stood and towered over her, his ears stinging from her assault. *Can't reach them now, huh?* He smirked.

"It's a critical matter I must speak of with Mother."

"When is it ever not? If it isn't life or death, then remove yourself," she said under her breath. "Your mother's day has been fraught with affairs. Allow her a little peace before sleeping-time. Leave it be for just now, Eh'kotah." Bernehvelle begged him with her eyes, and he wanted to comply. The tumult of the day *had* to be wearing on his mother. She carried insurmountable responsibility, but he had responsibilities too. His mother wouldn't take kindly if he delayed once she learned what he needed to tell her.

Though Bernehvelle's face beseeched him, he searched over her head for his mother nonetheless. The queen no longer watched them. Evidently, she was assured Eh'kotah could rescue himself from the accosting he was taking Bernehvelle. He wasn't so sure about that. She'd gone to her privy closet. Its door was open. Through the archway, the antechamber comprised of glazed alabaster used for cleansing one's self was empty. She must have stepped behind the inner-privy door designed for private ablutions. "Can't you see that she's depleted and weary?" Bernehvelle whispered in another fierce undertone.

Eh'kotah looked toward the door again. Depleted? His mother? *Unheard of.* But the thought did give him pause. If anyone would know, it would be her caregiver from her youth, turned her most trusted companion. He couldn't imagine his mother wearied to a point that it affected her physically. But...what if she was? He had better defer to Bernehvelle's superior knowledge on his mother's present state...*for now.* He would be sure to get some time alone with the queen the next day.

He left with no further fuss.

On to Nyoma. Heady times awaiting. Out in the corridor, he rubbed his hands together then reached for his armset to order a carrier dock, and ended up dropping his hand back down. Glad, he had no need to signal for another polarized platform deployed from its centralized hub, Eh'kotah walked to the compartment in the corridor as the door of a carrier dock already there swished up. Haarth stepped out. They paused, greeted each other but proceeded on. Eh'kotah pondered if he should have warned Haarth of a poor reception from Bernehvelle. He thought better of it. The carrier globes serviced all the areas of the Keep. That Haarth had summoned a glass compartment and it planted on his mother's landing meant he had security permissions to do so. Maybe he could relieve Bernehvelle of her zealous guard of his mother's quarters. Eh'kotah couldn't think of two people who needed to talk more than his mother and Haarth at the moment.

* * *

Ana'kerah

Ana'kerah re-entered her bedchamber attired in the slip Bernehvelle had foisted on her. "This thing is ridiculous," she said, flicking the edge of the diaphanous trifle. She sighed and stretched the ache in her back. After all the turmoil of recent days, she was willing to give in to Bernehvelle. Maybe she'd leave her in peace the last few moments before bed and sleep and another dawning day of her mantle as queen. She did cover herself in the dressing coat that matched the laughable excuse of night attire. *Who would wear this in Soonayah?* The dressing coat was no longer than the slip. *It* at least was made of more substantial material and could not be seen clean through to her navel.

"Eh'kotah?" He'd gone. A sigh expelled from deep inside her. First, her eldest son thought it amusing, not insulting to assume she always slept alone. *And then he'd had that look about him—so like his father.* He was determined to conquer some new thing, she was sure of it. Whatever it was, she was sure she wouldn't like it either. But he'd gone. "Good." Now, once they finished plaiting and dressing her hair, she would remove Bernehvelle too. Then maybe she could well look forward to an early eve alone with a cool draught of her favored berry elixir and a nutty confection from the Rising Bun. She'd saved them for just such an occasion as this. A punishing day, and too many revelations to answer to—to count.

Let me hurry. She quickened her steps to retrieve her crock of bergamot and Boswellia tree oil. Then she heard Bernehvelle holding conversation with a voice too deep to be her regent, who had the easiest access to her chambers next to Bernehvelle. The strength in her shoulders shriveled up and disappeared. She had only thought to have a few moments to herself before daybreak. *Apparently, it was not to be.*

"Haarth!" She caught the crock of oil before it slipped right from her fingers. "What has possessed you to enter my quarters so? I may answer to a great many things as queen, but having domain over who enters my quarters is one of the few I retain as my choice."

Floundering, Haarth looked from Bernehvelle to her. Words stuttered in his throat. When she came further in past her privy chamber archway, his hard eyes swept her appearance from her face, then lower. "I...Bernehvelle...what has possessed you to wear such an ensemble in the icy temperatures of Soonayah?"

He was dumbfounded and that threw Ana'Kerah. Haarth rarely had to fumble for words. She glanced down at the amount of her toned brown legs on display. There wasn't a decent enough amount of material to reach halfway to her knees in the attire Bernehvelle had mired her with. "I...Bernehvelle made me...gave me this..." she trailed off. All the gumption she'd had a moment ago gone.

Haarth manned up and somehow found a way to turn his eyes to Bernehvelle. He lasered her where she stood. "It was Bernehvelle who summoned me here with a message of some urgency."

Bernehvelle sent her shoulders back straight like a hanger with angles poking the sleeves in her tunic and lifted her chin. "I spoke only truth of the urgency of the situation for which you're needed." And spoke down to him as if he were the mischievous boy she had censured on many occasions in his youth.

Haarth swung a look about him. "What urgency, Bernehvelle? The urgency of dressing your queen in her suggestive attire to ready her for her latest consort?"

Bernehvelle answered him over the gasp that came from the queen. "The urgency comes in the form of knowledge. The knowledge *I have* upon learning what transpired in the Hall of Covenance this day. I have watched the two people I think of like my own, considering I helped bring you up when I learned I could have no offspring. And seeing you two run from each other and savage each other and abandon each other over feelings too deep to ever leave you be. The urgency that comes from knowing it was far past time you knew you fathered that willful girl with abilities nearly identical to yours coming out." Bernehvelle tapped his solar plexus, right where it was said one's soul-energy was kept. "You don't have to use your gifts for her to be connected to you. There are plenty of people still here that remember them." Then she poked him in his chest too. "And the urgency of knowing you both may well attempt to bypass the events of this day... *again*. And never own up to grievous actions you both must take an accounting for."

What was Bernehvelle doing? Ana'kerah's heartbeat hiccuped inside her breast. She loathed to reprimand Bernehvelle. Her friend, whose opinion had been a guiding force throughout her life, but this was not her place. The slightest misstep could cause irreparable damage between herself and Tierahna. Not to mention Haarth's and her own impasse had never even been spoken of before. "Bernehvelle, you speak out of turn. These are matters whose boundaries you shouldn't overstep."

Bernehvelle looked to Ana'kerah. She swooped her arm out cross-wise of her body, palm upward, performing the perfect salute of veneration. The queen folded her mouth, instead of bending her head in acceptance. "Am I here out of no more necessity but to serve you? Or am I the friend who has attempted with all that she has to aid you in your growth of transformation as the queen of our hearts. With the fullest love in me, you are my truest daughter in spirit."

Ana'Kerah went to her and clutched her hand. "Bernehvelle don't dare let the suggestion of your being my servant leave your lips again. You know, as I do, that I ask nothing of you but your company to keep me sane in the constancy of my reign. You're my foundation on which

I'm latched. You keep my feet steadfast. It's only at *your* insistence that I let you run the attendants mad over upkeep of my attire. And it's *you* who savors dressing my hair in my plaits because it reminds you of my youth."

Bernehvelle ran her hand over a sprig of hair that lay against Ana'kerah's cheek. They hadn't had time to plait it as she favored.

"It's altogether well that I hadn't started on your hair then. We could still be plaiting it to your backside, stopping Haarth's visit."

Ana'kerah looked at Haarth with one eyebrow raised as if to ask, "*Is it me who's lost here?*" "Bernehvelle, you know you asked him here without my permission, right?"

Bernehvelle waved away her suggestion. "What permission was needed? It's proven that both of you are more stubborn than muskox asses. I couldn't wait until the end of all time. You must take a true account of your actions now before no more time remains."

Ana'kerah's stomach dropped. Bernehvelle had the optimism of a newly-birthed babe, and had lifted Ana'kerah's spirits on many a hard-won day. The pessimism in her voice worried her, for it was so unlike the Bernehvelle she relied on so heavily. "Berneh, are you ailing? Why do you speak with such fatalism?" Ana'kerah tried to pull Bernehvelle to her, but Bernehvelle shooed her away.

She moved to the bed hanging suspended from the ceiling in Ana'kerah's bedchamber. The lavender-draped contraption was the luxuriant standard expected of a queen. She lowered its bed clothing with a little too much room to accommodate only Ana'kerah. She stoked the bedchamber's fireplace and banked the fire for the night. The whole of the queen's quarters she tended as Ana'kerah and Haarth waited and watched her dawdle about. She lastly reached the outer lounge chamber. And then the lighting was reduced until the only remaining beam turned Ana'kerah's bed into a sultry island in a sea of darkness. You could almost hear a melody of flutes and harps and the like, luring bodies to wreck themselves together on its shores.

"Of course, I'm not ailing. My lineage is from the sturdiest of stock. But my man, Lorneam is being pressed to settle as a full-time seasoner in the Petery Harvest Strip. His homestead there has been flourishing yields of oxen and buckwheat. We're thinking a permanent residence there may allow him to plant a covered forest of Goncalo trees. Lorneam indulges my love of tigerwood so, he's committed to growing a whole forest to please me."

Whimsy laced her smile. Her affection for this Lorneam was that of a girl with her first-ever blush of love. "But l mean to set my conscience straight before I depart this Keep and leave Ana'kerah on her own." The playfulness could be seen sliding from her mouth through the lowered lighting as she looked at them both. "I knew that Haarth was the father when you grew too big too fast carrying Tierney in your belly. You and Stah'lief had too recently reconciled from one of your abstinent spates for her to be conceived by him."

"Berneh!"

"It's only the truth! You both must confront the past issues between you. Back then, Haarth should've been told, but it wasn't for *me* to tell him." Her smile in that moment was sudden. Devious. She turned it on Haarth. "Haarth, don't concern yourself that Ana'kerah is dressed as she is in preparation for a visit by one of her consorts. I haven't known her to have any such visitors to her bedchambers since *your* last visit before you left to your precious dominions." She slipped from the queen's quarters and left that gem in the air between the two in the room.

* * *

Bernehvelle

Outside, after she secured the door, she pressed her hand flat on the panel next to it until it recognized the hand print. She then drew her finger over the program that opened and input a bulletin that the queen was not to be addressed by any sovereign business the whole of the next day. Bernehvelle's last order of business that night? To set the two inside the room on course. *Forward.* She deleted a reminder that alerted the queen to arise come daybreak. *Hopefully, she will be too worn out to awaken with the sun.* She snorted and left them to it.

Chapter 25

Ana'kerah and Haarth

"Agh!" Ana'kerah cried out. She shook her hand, blew on it, and grumbled. After compressing tightly against the crock of bergamot and Boswellia tree oil, the crock's edging dented her skin. "I can't believe Bernehvelle's audacity." She slid her eyes from Haarth's.

Really, how could she think to hide her reaction to Bernehvelle's tale of her non-relations with imaginary consorts when her skin heated like fire and her shoulders bowed too, blaring her embarrassment to the heavens? Her face though spoke her thoughts loudly without any words, saying, *"Will this day never end?"*

Haarth measured the level of Ana'kerah's temper by the number of times her hand flapped. *When morning came, Bernehvelle could expect a stern talking to.*

He came further into the bedchamber and removed the crock from her, setting it out of her way, he pulled her hand away from her mouth to examine it. "There's no reason for you to cause yourself harm." When he turned her hand over, a whip of puckered skin showed red and angry. He rubbed his thumb over her skin to soothe away her rough treatment. "Don't worry that I'll put any truth in Bernehvelle's suggestions. I'm not the boy of my youth with belief that a woman's purity is saved for my pleasure."

Ana'kerah tugged at her hand. His grasp flexed but maintained its grip on her. "Whatever the status of my relations is none of your concern, Haarth."

"True. I'm just reassuring you that I don't believe Bernehvelle. The queen of Soonayah traipsing consorts in and out of her bedchamber at regular intervals is no one's concern but her own."

Ana'kerah wrenched at her hand. Haarth's grip tightened just short of pain. "You're all together, right. I'll have any man I see fit to have in my bedchambers at any time I please. Now let go of me, Haarth. Ad'rihl may have thought it a one-off thing when I caused that insurgent's death with one pulse, but you of all people know better than that. He had a blade at my gut. I released the pulse at power enough to put him down for good or else I might not have lived to tell about it." Their touching was having its due effect. Her skin on Haarth's burned him at the seam. "They don't know about the blade he had hidden in his boot. I chose not to alarm them. But you know me capable of turning you to ash where you stand. So, release me before you force me to do just that."

Haarth wished he could chuckle at her audacity, but his stomach roiled at the thought of someone getting close to her with a blade. Her safety far overshadowed any pleasure he received at this one woman of his dealings who never showed any compunction about standing up to him. Aware she could kill with one pulse, he pulled her to him anyway, trapping her hand against his chest, grateful she hadn't plaited her mass of hair into her usual practical style for bed. He basked in this intimacy with her. And lowered his head automatically as he sucked in the essence of Ana'kerah that had been denied him so long.

The heat between them, the scent so unique to her wove around them. It delivered him back to a time she *had* killed before. That ability of hers to kill with one pulse was imprinted on his brain. He'd witnessed her do it when he'd been just as enraptured as this.

Unripened in love, they'd lusted in their experiments of discovery in the differences between man and woman, one late budding day in the season of new life on a field of flowering grass. The rarity in Soonayah provided a richness around their loving. Afterward, they'd watched a fledgling snow owl attempt first flight a bit too early.

Snow owls of Soonayah historically, like everything, were enhanced. The birds grew fast and flew early. Cross-patterned migration required sturdy birds to withstand the climates of certain areas when the land turned too cold. Ana'kerah had shifted from him and watched the fledgling fall from its perch and crash to the ground, to her dismay. She'd told him before how she'd had this nagging urge within her. Rather than cause harm with her gift of pulsing, she'd felt she could harness an instinctual regression. Something burgeoning inside her at that time could produce the opposite effect. She'd felt she could heal.

Trying it that day on the broken owl, she'd near incinerated the poor chick within her palms. *The pitiful bird.* Haarth had held onto her while she'd cried wretchedly. He'd tried his best to assure her that it wasn't her fault for trying to help it. Having shared the intimacy of things like that with her gave him insight some would never have. She took to heart hurting any living thing. Even now he was sure she dealt with inner torturings over the insurgent's life. *She'd had no other choice but to defend herself.* Ana'kerah couldn't harm him any more than she could stop her regret for having taken any life. And he was starting to reconsider something else too.

Maybe Bernehvelle's suggestions shouldn't be dismissed out of hand.

Ana'kerah applied extreme considerations to most her actions, especially those focused around her role as queen. She may well have avoided the position of receiving a consort into the bedchamber of the queen. And he couldn't fathom her making assignations at some random lodge. His fingers flexed on the suppleness of her skin. Trying to remove the picture from his mind of her stealing away to some consort's homestead, he shook his head. *She'd never do that.* "Calm yourself, Ana'kerah. You could no more hurt me than I you. But whether it be my concern or not, I think it best not to let me learn of any man visiting you in your quarters, availing himself of you in your provocative night attire. Not while I'm here in the Keep."

Ana'kerah took him off guard...right then. She pulsed him. With ingenious expertise, she directed a flash in the perfect spot of vulnerability beneath his ribs and above his solar plexus. And gave herself the chance to snatch her hand away and put some distance between them. "Then it's altogether well that my night attire has no bearing on you, Haarth. Because we know that no matter how I dress or for whom, your truest interest lies in the cornucopia of women you avail yourself of on the regular. Do we not?"

Ana'kerah flounced the frilled edge of her ensemble almost revealing intimate parts of herself. Haarth's eyes latched onto the movement. "Don't tempt me, woman. You have no idea why my actions are what they are." The turn this conversation was taking was a mistake. And Ana'kerah's bedchamber was the worst place to be having it. His scour swept the darkened outer chamber of her quarters. *Now, where was that door?* "I'm fair to those I become involved with. I don't deceive them into believing me capable of committing to them. It's for their own good that I don't tarry long within their affections. For I can never match with them or even make real consorts of them."

Ana'kerah laughed in Haarth's face. She shook her head pitiably. "It's for their own good? Oh, how I know the feeling. The charitable Haarth leaves out of deference for the woman's position. How little does she understand his sacrifice. Is that what eased your mind each time you left me too?" She spun away from features hewn in granite, looking about her, searching, her focus on everything else within the bedchamber. She retrieved the crock of oil from the bureau where he'd placed it. Not glancing back at him, she missed the confirmation to her question in his eyes.

Very similar to their daughter, Tierahna—with whom at some point—Ana'kerah would have to approach and come to some kind of understanding, he had followed a path of his own direction since their youth. Whether Haarth's path coincided with his entanglement with Ana'kerah or not, he forged ahead if he thought it best. Him saying he'd gone from one woman to another for the good of all those involved, was probably true...in the convoluted way he went about doing things. Excluding his most recent interest. Larza retained the longest haven within Haarth's interest besides Ana'kerah.

"Oh but, Haarth? Although you have kept Larza close and fed her false information that you and the guard council have formulated, she *is* a true consort. If ever you've had one, she is it. And you had best leave this Keep this eve as per your usual if you think me so submissive that I would let your presence here stop me from satisfying my needs." Ana'kerah's face contorted. Her thoughts obviously torturous on his relationship with a woman that had persisted for over a span of time.

"Larza's and my involvement belies what one may see from outside. I know her as a woman with independence as her main objective. She knows my unavailability will never resolve itself. Our circumstances allow for no true entanglement." Haarth rubbed a hand over his own plaited hair, dragging a path down his jaw. "But you think I'll stand by while you take some unworthy consort into your bed? Watching you with my own brother wasn't enough? I will surely rip apart any man I see approach you for the smallest of trifles."

He stalked her then, stood menacingly over her, his stature swallowing hers with his mere shadow. Ana'kerah was never one cowered by his passions. Daring him toward a loss of control, she met him glare for glare. The transformation from the contemplation of her crock of oil to readying to meet him blossomed, firing. Animation took over the thrall of her features. The intimate portions of his body tightened as he witnessed it and he grimaced. To hide his condition, he recoiled from her as fast as he'd stalked her.

Bernehvelle baited this trap well.

He'd known the request for this meeting with Ana'kerah was rife for trouble. Regardless, the urgency Bernehvelle had relayed had him there with no delay. Now he was on the verge of taking unsuitable actions with the *queen*...again. He swung away on a march toward the lounge chamber, his eyes peeled to where the door should be. He would stumble his way through the dark if he had to—to find his way out. *Sanctuary...* A crash stopped him in his tracks.

Ana'kerah's crock of oils splintered against the archway next to him. He hadn't made it beyond the bedchamber. A sliver of glass pricked a bead of blood from a tiny slit behind his ear, but he flinched only when the keening of Ana'kerah's voice hollowed out his gut. "Run away, Haarth! Run! Run again from me as you always do!"

Haarth kept his back to her but shifted to catch her in his periphery. "Anah, you are a party to my appetites with you. I have little restraint with you as a given. With my passions elevated as they are, my energy is too high! So yes! I leave you as is appropriate. I leave as I always have, so as not to always be taking advantage of the queen!"

Ana'kerah's shoulders slumped to her toes. Any animation activated by their back and forth gone. Her hair curtained a face drawn now, seeking about for...something. The palm she'd carried the oil in clinched as if she missed the crock's weight. Haarth's unblinkered bolt for the exit seemed to have caused a break in her. A rage she hadn't controlled. She stared at the splat she'd made. Some of the thick green oil dripped in rivulets to the floor. Bernehvelle would let loose when she saw it and Haarth's face didn't look much better than that splat.

"Of course, you must leave, Haarth. You think I don't know my own mind. But have I ever once said I thought you to be taking advantage of me?" She let her arms drop. "No, wait. Far more importantly, have I ever asked you to go...ever when you've left?" A laugh burst from her. Strained. Painful. "Even now, no one knows it was you who chose to leave when you no longer had to after Stah'lief's death. They think it was me, the unyielding queen who exiled you to your precious dominions."

He'd never heard this in all the times he and Ana'kerah interacted. The convoluted travails of their relations wrought them everything except this. *Defeat?* He faced her now, uncaring if she witnessed the effects she had on his body. In fact, he welcomed it, preferring her disdain than to see her defeated. Drawn as he was to her, he approached her and lifted her chin. "You don't understand my position. Your perspective comes from that of the desired woman. But I've never left because I chose to. I leave because I must. And every time we were together after my kidnapping *was inappropriate* because nothing more could come of it. And advantage *was* being taken because you're the queen! No *regular* consort could ever be made of *me*. As I am the very brother of the king! Stah'lief's death made no difference. Even as I took you to this bed that last time before I left to my dominions it was a given that I must go."

"You could've stayed."

"No, I couldn't have! You still grieved him and rightfully so, because I did too. And no matter the time that passed you wrapped yourself in aloofness as his match until there was no meeting with conversation or either my visiting you here at the Keep. Nothing could take place between us."

All their latter adult lives anger played the constant state of being between them. Yet, Haarth had the audacity to lay the bulk of the responsibility for the tatters their relationship was in at Ana'kerah's feet. But as he said, she had the perspective of the woman.

"I wasn't aloof, Haarth. I had been hardened. By you. You think me unaware that you *do* come to Dameerh, not availing yourself of your home in this Keep because you must return to your woman, Larza. Your truest consort."

"She is no true consort!" Haarth speared her with his eyes. "And must you know why? Because of you! I won't commit to any woman, but for you!" He looked her up and down, the lines of his face tightened like there were no soft feelings in him for her. He acted as if she should have been privy to the details of his relations already.

Still, Ana'kerah's eyes thrilled at his announcement. But then she muted her reaction. When he and she came together, their appetite for each other was insatiable. Evenly matched, they fed off one another until gorged on greedy sensation. Sometimes to such an extent, they would need outside stimuli to pull them apart. Which always came. Everything *did* continue to churn outside their momentary stasis. And when it hit? A stunning sobering every time.

"Your relations with Larza likens to a commitment of a consort." She held up her hand to stop his words. "But I'll let that be and bring to mind a commitment of another kind. One that can't be denied. You will have an everlasting commitment to the mother of Lu'nil. She birthed your babe. That's a commitment you *chose* to share with her."

A coldness wafted from Haarth for the first time since he'd walked into her chambers. He lowered himself to look her straight in her face. "As well I should have. You and Stah'lief have multiplied with offspring in abundance. One of them mine, whom you chose for me not to know about. And I was to have no progeny of my own to know and love in my life?"

Ana'kerah spun toward the fireplace. With no oil and trembling fingers, she portioned her hair and began to plait it herself. Haarth followed and stayed her hands from the task. He preferred her hair as it was.

"You don't realize that you left me then too, do you, Haarth? She looked up at him but didn't deny him his claim to unravel the plait she'd started. "We loved here together as we did in our youth and within moments you had turned away from me again. You didn't talk to me. You didn't look at me. You became more a stranger than I'd ever known. After a time, I would search for you and became convinced that you had left the enclave for all time. When I finally learned that you had entrusted Celia to carry your babe for you—within such a short time of me growing heavier and heavier with Tierahna too—by then I was crazed with *Stah'lief's* absences."

In an action that was crazed in itself, she ran both her hands through her hair. It surely hurt. The movement snatched her hair from Haarth's fingers. "I was never sure if he had killed himself in his reckless pursuit to reach the peak of those wretched mountains. And you had abandoned me again. You know I don't begrudge Lu'nil one iota of life. She is as much a daughter to me as my own. But this time I lost you to the birthing of your own babe. When in this was I to feel capable of telling you about Tierahna, I ask? How much sanity was I to call on after only just birthing Stah'lief's brother's babe myself?"

Haarth slammed his fist against the bedchamber bureau. A crack formed. An ominous creak sounded as it climbed the wall. *This was all happening at Bernehvelle's instigation. She could well deal with the mess that came of it.* "You project onto me more forbearance than I am capable of, Anah. Your distress at Stah'lief's absence was mine as well. Although he was only my brother, I *did* love him. And even as I knew that I shouldn't, I took comfort in yours arms as I've never been capable of keeping from you when I'm close to you. Only to have Stah'lief return unharmed every time? I couldn't stay near you and act as if all was to my liking any longer. I'm not the man to stand aside as your consort while you remain matched to my brother in contentment. When that match was mine to have!"

In tune with their exchange, their heightening emotions rose to level of no return. Choices in their lives were made as best they could be in the circumstances. What could be answered for the choices now? "You compromised our match when you left here that very first time at the behest of that deceptive woman, Irdulon."

"What can come of shaming the dead, Anah?" Haarth shook his head at the introduction of Irdulon's name.

"But it's true. Stah'lief never agreed that she should go on a pre-matching sojourn with you to Kalamesh and neither did I you. But at least you told her of my disapproval. She hadn't gotten Stah'lief's permission as his match to go. She lied to you when she convinced you to let her accompany you. And you went and they took you both. And killed her and tortured us here with their threats to your life unless we agreed to an exchange for what they asked! After that operation went foul Haarth, we believed you truly dead."

Ana'kerah looked through the windows of her terrace into the night, her eyes glistening lost in the pain of the past. "No matter how many times we scoured that desert, only parts of your party were found. Even your skin and pieces of *your* scalp were found. Your parents never gave up searching, but as we approached a span of time, they harped on Stah'lief and me to do what was logical." She opened her palms as in offering to him "I had nothing left of you. I had no future with you in sight. Everything I had been groomed for since I could remember was ripped from me. I loved Stah'lief as a brother and so did he me, as his sister. In our grief we let them lead us to the match as if it were a natural thing." It was Ana'kerah who went to move away from him then. He grabbed her forearm and twisted her back around. "I had no care if I matched with Stah'lief or not. I was distraught in my loss of you! What else would you have had me do?"

"I would've had you not be matched to my brother, after trudging through that death trap of a desert with getting back to you as the only thing keeping me. After I finally fought from the *true tortures* they were delivering on *me*, I would've had you not be filled with my brother's babe when I finally crawled my way back to you!"

Tremors from inside Ana'kerah exploded from her core. Impossible to turn away from Haarth as he still had hold of her arm, she lowered her head and wept.

Chapter 26

Ana'kerah and Haarth

Her crying unmanned him. If there was one area in life that Haarth conceded to in weakness, it was Ana'Kerah distraught.

I must comfort her. I have to.

Any other time he'd thought about comforting her had ended, without fail, in him taking advantage of her. He lifted her and sat with her on his lap, anyway. The edge of the hanging bed bore them and moved a little. He rocked to its sway with her in his arms.

She wouldn't raise her face to him. Not cowed, never that. Rather, he allowed her her heartache for the moment. This thing between them had *enough* heartache for the both of them. Moisture stung the corners of his eyes too. Wariness, disappointment, desolation... and anger had fed the dearth of their ardency not just for the spans of time they'd spent apart, but forever, it seemed. Somehow, this thing between them spanned further than mere time could contain it. His chest rose and pushed against Ana'Kerah, expanded to seek connection to her in any way possible. One big breath, and release. *I always do this to her.* The rest of the world believed her face of the indomitable queen her truest self. He knew better. *Because I'm set-*

"

upon by images of her that raze my brain if just a hint of our relations is touched upon! "Berneh was right. We have savaged each other in this life."

"I longed to share the birth of our babe with you. But how could I? Stah'lief was here and...you weren't. And soon after, I heard of you celebrating the birth of your own babe." Sobs racked her frame. "It may seem perverse, but I took to myself and mourned at you having a babe with another. The situation could never have redeemed itself for me if you hadn't brought her here and let me help you bring her up." She looked at him, then lowered her head again. The brown of her eyes were drenched pools. "I was jealous. I craved her as another part of you."

Haarth lifted her chin back to him. Her face contoured—every curve of it pleased his idea of beauty—even if her puffy eyes and sniffling nose made him ache. "Lu'nil could have been with no better person. In no better place. Her security was uppermost in my decision, as she is a royal too. I wanted her *with me*. However, she needed to learn the protocols of her status as a royal. Both of which would have been substandard had she gone with me to tame my dominions. She deserved better than that. The woman you are made her home here akin to being one of your own."

He lowered his head to her hair and rested there, a solace settled on him just in being able to hold her. That dissatisfaction he'd experienced as of late filled—this was what he'd been hankering after and hadn't realized it. Hadn't allowed himself to realize it. "No woman have I ever met has had that kind of generosity. You're a greater mother to her than that fickle Celia has ever dreamed of being." Their breaths mingled in the intimate little cloister they'd made. He raised her chin again and this time pressed his lips onto her plump ones. Lips tasting of tears. He swiped them with his tongue, intermingling the drops of salted anguish on both their tongues. She'd opened for him.

They gorged on their first tastes of each other as they always did, kissing engrossed in their feasting after their long deprivation. Haarth sat back and arranged her astride his lap and pressed her mons against the erection that hadn't subsided in the least since he'd first tried to hide it from her. She wore nothing underneath the ridiculous guise Bernehvelle had pushed on her.

He was losing his head already. *And I have only just started to taste her.* His hands went beneath the frill she wore. He flexed his fingers in the globes of her buttocks, pulling her free of the dressing coat that blocked his vision. *I have to see her.* Her nipples were already distended for him beneath the gauze of material. The cloud of her scent wafted between them.

Still...his mind. He couldn't settle with so many of the things they'd said writhing within it. "Did Stah'lief know Tierahna was mine?"

A bald question in the middle of their intimacy.

Ana'kerah blinked back to reality and leaned away from him which was hard to do. No room was allowed between them. Neither of them wanted separation after the drought in their loving had only just been relieved. He pressed into the small of her back, bringing them ever closer. "I never told Stah'lief. I never told anyone. We didn't speak of it...but I have no doubt that he knew. It was he who gave her your name. I believe it was his way of showing his understanding...his forgiveness in this situation we all were in."

Haarth swept both palms up her waist and gave her breasts a hard squeeze. He was rough with her, the way he sent his hand to the back of her neck, pulled her mouth to his and delved between her lips with his tongue. He had wanted no forgiveness from his brother for his dealings with Ana'kerah.

Had no appreciation for Stah'lief's understanding. In his mind, they weren't needed. *She has always been mine.* His hands weren't gentle as he dragged the diaphanous slip up to her armpits either. Large palms wrapped her rib cage, smoothing lustrous brown skin. He plumped her breasts and pressed his face into them. Ana'kerah finished removing herself from her slip. He was too preoccupied with reacquainting himself with everything about her.

Filling hands with her breasts and suckling them, he went from one to the other. Lost in passion, Ana'kerah tossed her head and ground herself upon him. Her naked skin inflamed against his clothed form, inciting him to press his manhood for relief against her. It was crazy, but as she threw her head back his mind flipped and perceived her as the young woman she'd been before. Dewy skin and unbridled optimism for the lives they had to look forward to, all wrapped up as an offer at his pleasure. The set-up for disaster. Warped that a sovereignty, other people, an arrangement could decide how they lived the rest of their lives, or who they lived them with. Even trying the same tactics with his brother when they'd thought *he'd* died. Shouldn't people with good sense, at some point, have realize how stupid that was?

After working her nipples into stinging points of sensation, their mouths came together again, suckling tongues and nibbling full lips. Her *woman's body* wrapped around him now. All of her touched much of him. Standing with her in his arms, he lifted his head, and speared her with his glance, then he put her from him and began to remove his garments. "Like I said, every time I come near you it's like we're younglings in a field again. There's no return from this, Anah. There'll be no room for recriminations afterward. At *this* stage in our lives, we are both of age beyond the need for them."

She reached for his tunic and helped him remove it. "Do I seem like I'll have regrets?" Bent to the floor—his heated trews and undergarments were hung on his boots—she jerked at the offenders and growled. Raising her head to his shaft that sprang above her, it begged her to latch onto it, she soothed its length.

Haarth's growl outdid hers. But he tugged her up, slipping her touch from him. As ready as he was, he couldn't take too much of her soft palms stroking his erection if he wasn't to explode. The spans between their last loving dropped away and they were as they once were again. Lifting her and wrapping himself within the embrace of her legs, their mouths opened unerringly for one anther. Haarth entered her in one deep thrust straight to her core.

Home, the most exquisite place I've ever been.

A keening ripped from Ana'kerah's soul as she reared back. Haarth couldn't catch it with his lips. He held onto her hips to keep her bowed back from separating them. They rocked, braced against the support of Haarth's thighs, his member seated deep.

However, his legs were weakening to the feel of Ana'kerah's body cradling his, *tight,* as she had always enveloped him within her sheath. Clasping him, her body saying what her lips had never revealed; that *"I will keep you with me always."* He moved closer to the bed while he still had strength, and lowered her to its edge. Balancing her there, he continued to plunge inside her. The use of his feet against the floor as leverage, with the hanging nature of the bed, gave it a swing, meeting him with every lunge. She whimpered into Haarth's neck. The cords there hummed in the rise of his soul-energy. "How are you able to cradle me as tightly as if your body has never birthed a babe? I'm losing my hea—"

Ana'kerah's cries heightened and Haarth paused on the chance his passions might be too much. When he went to lift himself, she gripped his buttocks with nails that'd sunk into his muscle each time he thrusted. "Don't move from me."

"I couldn't, even if the Keep were falling down. I mustn't hurt you though." His body began its dance again of its own accord. The essence of Anah wrenched sensations to ride at the very edge of his control.

"You haven't hurt me. I want all of you," she murmured against his neck and put her feet on either side of his hips, and pushed back against him. Her feet slipped their purchase on the edge. Moving the bed's gossamer drapery aside, Haarth lifted her and shifted them both up onto it, maneuvering himself and Ana'kerah into the center, completely veiling them in its den of sensuality. "Don't hold back," she groaned.

And he didn't. Her encouragement in his ear, while she licked the engorged cord on his neck, sent the infinitesimal control he grasped splintering. Haarth shook his head, blinded. White-hot heat surged from his body.

Their separation from each other fated Ana'kerah to receive Haarth's loving into her body over and over. Again and again, they loved well into the night. She slept when she could, but he would awaken and reach for her each time that he did. He wasn't the boy of their youth with limitless vigor. Yet, him slaking himself on her was inexhaustible due to the perfect storm of conditions.

He preferred simple support for his own bedding. Not so was the sumptuousness of Ana'kerah's bedclothes. The drapery hung created a lavender conclave surrounding them while they loved, and instigated lusty passion of the voluptuary lying next to him even in his sleep. That last time he'd awakened from the unfamiliar plushness to roll into the mahogany vision of his dreams—her scent welcoming him into her body—was probably the most hedonistic experience of his life.

Soonahyins connected to another being's heated soul-energy when in contact. Little was it known outside of Soonayah that they cheated a being of a bit of it when they touched. Wasn't enough to mention. This phenomena occurred most often after speeding, pulsing, or sparring activity, and during sex in heightened skin-to-skin contact. There was always the consideration that they might deplete their partner of more soul-energy than they could spare, so caring for them afterward was the convention.

Haarth hadn't been with another Soonahyin in so much time it didn't matter how long it'd been. His last time here in the Keep with Ana'kerah was the only one prevalent in his brain. He'd lost touch with his connection in the heat. Larza, as a Kalameshee, didn't require the undergirding of one's soul-energy. Kalameshees were the exact opposite and stored excess heat in their bodies, making losing some of their soul-energy negligible to them. An unexpected treat with the overabundance of energy Soonahyins were able to siphon off them when the two peoples were involved with each other.

But for Haarth, the pushing back and forth of soul-energy—all the while engaged in the act of pushing back and forth during intercourse as a Soonahyin did with another Soonahyin—was a glorious act if there was a true connection as it was for Haarth and Ana'kerah. After loving her non-stop, being inside her body produced a transcendency.

He lay atop Ana'kerah spent. Their last bout of lovemaking may well have satiated him enough to leave her be...for a time. With her fingers clutched in his hair, her other hand rubbing over his buttocks, he rested sated, though still semi-erect inside her. His face pressed into the fragrance of her bosom. He was as replete as he could be, having taken his frustrations out onto Ana'kerah throughout the night, who had given it back to him as only the stubborn Ana'kerah could.

His mind, albeit, wouldn't rest along with his body. It wouldn't leave him be from thoughts of Stah'lief and Anah's life together. He mumbled against her breast the ruminations bumbling around his brain. "Stah'lief being so magnanimous, I wonder if he forgives us this transgression in his soul's rest this night?"

Ana'kerah's energy heightened against Haarth a heartbeat before she pulsed him. Because of course, he was still buried inside her, he felt it build before she did it. But he only chuckled at the violation. "Woman, you know pulsing while intimate isn't done." He groaned and surged deeper inside her. Her pulsing him only served to excite him in her temerity, engorging his member again. When he'd thought he could go no more, leave it to Ana'kerah to wring every vestige of his wherewithal from him.

"It's only you who brings Stah'lief's presence into this bed with us, where it shouldn't have a foothold. If he could have material thought, I believe he would be happy for us finally finding some even ground." She raised her hips fitfully against his but turned her head in a slow move away from him. The shift was evidently, in hopes he wouldn't see her eyes becoming wet again at his ungracious behavior.

Haarth lowered his head and licked the portion of her neck she'd exposed, goading a hiss from between her teeth. Her body clenched around his and the soft clutching she had been doing at his buttocks turned rough and stinging with her nails. His laving the extended cords of her neck was a surefire eroticism to her. He knew that. "Maybe you should remove yourself from me. I'm sure you've had your fill by now."

Haarth began to surge strongly into her drenched heat anew. "You should be prepared. For I shall never remove myself from you again. I shall never have my fill." He grabbed the slim wrists that were limiting his hip's movements. She'd been pincering his buttocks. He trapped her hands above her head. Then he turned her face back to his so her tear-drenched eyes could then witness the meaning in his. "Should I stop?" She shook her head *"No."* And he proved his intention with his body onto hers into the wee hours of the morn.

***

A chill awakened Ana'kerah. Quite bracing it was across her nakedness. She shifted. The effort was stiff after Haarth's loving. *Only my beloved of my youth can wrest from me these passions that have always lain in wait for him.* Her hand fell onto empty covers, but it was of no concern. He was there. Not far away, in a pensive posture. A shift of the beds draperies revealed him standing on the terrace. From one shoulder pitched to the other one, the straightness in his back bent no more to satisfaction nor disappointment. The glass door was slid up, letting the cold seep in. *Neutral.* An interesting state to be in after their lovemaking.

He spoke as soon as she approached him from behind. "I'm entrenched now, Anah." He twisted so that their eyes connected. "I'll no longer stand aside. You must be sure of what you seek with me. If what you want is permanence. For I will not come to the Keep and dally back and forth with you as if we're casual. I can't be casual with you and it won't be that easy an ordeal to surpass."

Hmm... It seemed his mind twisted and turned the things that would have to be considered if we continue with any more of this. "Even those who knew us in our youth will look askance at us. The assembly of chancellors and chieftains will think you're attempting to make me king. And your over-protective sons—though they say they knew of our involvement—may prove the most obstinate on *principal* in memory of their father."

Ana'kerah couldn't resist touching Haarth. Sympathetic to the musings that had chased him from their bed, she smoothed his shoulders, then kissed the evidence of his torture at the hands of the Drundel, a deep groove scarring his back. Her nerves settled into a humming evenness because his words ran along similar lines to her thoughts. "If you're here with me, I believe we can meet every challenge as it comes. Even with my sons here, I should think we'll find time to share in quite a bit more of what we just did." She laughed against his back, but he gripped her wrists and tugged her around to face him.

"You jest. They already challenged the Kalameshee. Still, they followed him and Tierahna to the Frozen Folly to continue their interrogation and break up anything those two could get up to in there as well. They sense his seriousness, I think. As do I. They're tenacious and of one accord in their duty to protect her. As they will be of you too." He probed her with his eyes. "They'll hold their line strong against us matching if they don't believe in it, Ana'kerah. But I won't settle for less. I've waited long enough for you to be mine. They'll stand against *us* and the Kalameshee too if they don't feel he or I meets their standards. We must be careful how we handle both these situations. Will you even allow her some exploration with the Kalmeshee?"

"You and her brothers read more into their interest in each other than is there. She has always been willful." Ana'kerah squinched her nose. "She won't settle easily into commitment with her first real consort. She's only just met him."

"I have different thoughts about that after I witnessed an almost instant connection, but I won't push you on it. You'll have have to come to terms with that yourself. My concern is what will happen between the three of us. You...I think you may have been too harsh on her in the sparring arena." He brushed her hair from her shoulder. "I couldn't believe she initiated that vy with Eh'kotah's Principal either, but she was overwrought with what she'd just learned. It may have served you better to soften your approach for once, just for her sake."

"The father speaks from his *long-lived* experience with his daughter. As I said, Tierahna has always been willful." Ana'kerah's laugh this time was through her teeth. She canted her head to one side as she peered at him, loving him for his arrogance even though it grated against her own sometimes. Which was what she needed, anyhow.

She recognized that her will needed tempering every now and again. "Now, *that's* something you have expertise in. Willfullness. She takes it after you, after all. And unlike Lu'nil and Os'carah, I've had to stand as strong with her as I have her brothers. She has a future of great consequence. They all do. It has been for me to try as best I can to help them prepare themselves for it. Me being soft on her won't do that."

Haarth skimmed his fingers down her cheek to her chin. "And then who stands strong for you? You haven't gone for a bout in the Frozen Folly yet. After the night we've just had, we're here deliberating on our offspring's reactions and what's best for them...and everybody else, but you're still favoring that shoulder you hurt in your fight with those insurgents." He spun and pulled her into the bedchamber from the terrace. "Come on. I will see to you then. Let's get you to the Folly before all the Keep comes alive with the first light of day."

Ana'kerah went with him after they quickly dressed. "Gladly! The terrace is still too cold in this season though it's closed off with its ionic barrier." She glanced at him while they laced fingers on their way to the Frozen Folly. "And Haarth, you must be sure of what you're seeking with me too because I have every intention of making you my king." She walked ahead of him. He'd stopped behind her, stunned by her words.

Chapter 27

The cookery hopped providing provisions for the Keep the next morn. Tierney sent attendants to retrieve the Kalameshee from his lodgings of the night before and they brought him to the nourishing room. She'd saved her hunger so that she wouldn't be secured off, taking her provision in her quarters—away from the bustling roasting jets set ablaze to produce mounds of food, and the clamor that was the standard for the larger space of the nourishing room. *Now I can share in the Kalameshee and Mlai's company.*

Her brothers' entrances didn't surprise her. They ate in the nourishing room often to be amidst the camaraderie of the Keep. Crisscrossing the room, they made it their business to socialize with everybody. Stopping and speaking with people eating at the mantles attached along the walls, this type of fellowship must keep them attuned to everything going on in the Keep.

Tierney's belly rumbled and she was led by a nose filled with steam from all the vittles straight to the cookery on the left side. The ladies were there too. Lu'nil, Os'carah, and Mlai loaded up on provisions proffered hot from the roasting jets. They chose crumble bread, soaked nardle eggs, lommel blubber at random themselves, so had no need of food tasters for their provisions. Peetah Pearl left them to it and circuited the room to get reacquainted with the many Tempeh

Tu and attendants she still remembered.

"I knew I would find you wherever the Kalameshee was allowed within this Keep," Lu'nil teased and pulled Tierney to one side. They both stood there at first, staring at one another for several moments. Tierney didn't have words yet to cover what you would say to someone in an abnormal situation such as theirs. She left it to Lu'nil to break the stalemate. "So...we're sisters in blood now." That was it. She'd heard what had happened in the Hall of Covenance the last eve. Lu'nil—a truest sister, needn't say more.

"I can only imagine the discussion between you and the queen. And for you to challenge all three brothers in the fighting arena—who would have thunk running away to Outliers would bring you this? Just how strong *are* your feelings for this Kalameshee? They are strong, even if you don't realize it," she said when Tierney avoided that Lu'nil look that proclaimed, "*I know your mind better than you do.*" "Have you been intimate with him, yet?" She promised she'd squeeze the answers to her gazillion questions out of Tierney once they had some time alone.

Tierney ate her first provisions with the threat of a confession to feelings she couldn't explain to herself hanging over her. Her brothers' raucousness, visits from one fire pit filled with guards and Keep attendants after another was a good distraction. They finally found their way to them, partook first provisions for that morn too, just before Bernehvelle and her man, Lorneam entered and greeted them.

It was a rare occasion to have all the siblings except Eh'kotah there. The family came together often, but still usually went about lives of their own. Interests varied amongst the siblings and their mother, making for an effort to be made to have time together. Though they lived in one domicile, they weren't on top of each other and that was common in all Soonahyin homesteads, residing together for the convenience of heating and resources, just not in each other's laps.

Therefore, Ad'rihl telling jokes at everyone's expense at their pit shaped a lively family gathering scene. *Forever the lewd dolt. Ugh!*

"She fell and splat her rump in a mound of snow this high," he gestured, holding his hand shoulder high, joking about Tierney's fall from the mountain. "And the Kalameshee here jumped after her with her rump the only thing in his sights." Everybody laughed.

"What else would spur me to jump from so high?" The Kalameshee proved himself as handy at the sporting and proceeded to banter back and forth with Ad'rihl. Her brother's eyes lit in the exchange. He respected anyone who could be as wicked with words as he and the Kalameshee laughed easily at himself.

Time passed eating, sharing in each other's company. Os'carah interrupted all the rancor and asked, "Where's Mother, Bernehvelle?" It was notable the queen wasn't there. She wasn't one to lounge about after the dawn of the rising day.

Bernehvelle said, "The queen is taking a much-needed restoration and shouldn't be disturbed."

Now, that sounded odd.

The explanation seemed to satisfy Os'carah and pretty much everyone else. *Mother never allots time aside to rest.* She was robust and trained in the fighting arts at the highest level. She lived and ate in moderation, and so had prime conditioning. Tierney glanced across the fire pit ruminating and caught her brother, Korrell's eye. He wore an expression like hers. Evidently, she wasn't the only one who had doubts about Bernehvelle's explanation.

The camaraderie settled down after a bit of time. Once they left the nourishing room, Tierney cornered Bernehvelle in the corridor. She asked politely to remove her from her man to have a few words.

"Is Mother ill and you cover for her in your vague explanation?" A tightening in her gut started up. Even if anger remained for a mother who had done what hers had—who was probably plotting her being committed to that sanctum right now—that anger couldn't outweigh her anxiety. Her mother was intrinsic to her. *The Kalameshee had gotten that right.*

Bernehvelle hedged. Her wizened gaze assessed Tierney. She'd heard what had happened in the Hall of Covenance and the sparring arena the previous day too. Tierney suppressed the urge to hide her face, a flush heating her skin. Then on second thought, she realized herself and straightened up. It wasn't *her* who others should be wary with. *It was Mother.* "Of course, your mother isn't ill. She's with Haarth, but he hasn't run as if scalded from her bed for once. My hope is that they finally contend with all the upheaval they've made of each other's lives. They must come to some realizations about what they want in each other. And I intend for them to have all the time they need to do so."

Korrell sidled next to them as if his horning in on Tierney pinning Bernehvelle down was a given. Apparently, he was as interested as she in a better explanation from Bernehvelle. She continued, "Stah'lief's presence overhanging them, the births of each other's babes, Haarth's leaving, and the ongoing demands of their offspring aren't their first priorities for once. This may be the chance they need to reconcile." Bernehvelle finished her statement and squinted at Korrell whose features lay passive.

His presence though...his hovering oppressed the conversation. The Korrell aura he wore about him like a shirt affected people this way in his most jovial moods too. Mostly, *they* were used to it. Ever-present, the power fairly overwhelmed any situation by several degrees. At the moment it was stifling. He must be really concerned about their mother. "Why a reconciliation? They have gone on to live separate lives now. Why revisit old hurts that can never be repaired?" he asked.

"You speak from the convenience of inexperience." Bernehvelle stood on her tippy toes and got right in his face or as close as her height would get her. Power or not. "One blissful in ignorance of ever knowing real love besides family. No *real* responsibility other than what you choose either. When there has been the kind of hurt those two have had and still they can't help but feel for each other, then they must confront it to repair themselves wholly...finally. They deserve the chance at it. You shall come to see the same for yourself one day, I have no doubt."

Korrell appeared unmoved but made no further comment for Bernehvelle to slap down. One of his cronies contacted him and her shouts could be heard beyond Korrell's armset, informing him that they were tracking a pregnant veryum to help it with its birthing if it needed it. With veryum being so large, they sometimes squashed their cocoons once they shed them, destroying any fertilized material that usually only contained one viable egg in the first place. His interests were taken now by the operation going on, he bade them a fair day and left them to their discussion.

The matter at hand. *Mother and Haarth?* Although Tierney'd just learned of their involvement the prior day, the thought of those two together did something to her. She placed a hand over the knot forming in her belly...again. For her mother this time.

The queen carried an aloneness about her. In constant surroundings of people, she still did. Tierney'd always reckoned she needed some companionship. Maybe that would help curb her concern for Tierney's doings, the lives of her siblings too. *Keep her from sending me away.* If Haarth could aid her to some fulfillment, then Tierney loved it. *Especially with my plans.* She had no thoughts for adhering to her mother's strictures anymore. Maybe she could figure out a way to go with the Kalameshee when he returned home. Stay out of her mother's detection for a while until the borders were officially widened. *Then I could travel anywhere, as far away as I want to.*

Who better for her mother to have than Haarth as her companion? It settled well with her when she knew her presence wouldn't be a constant for the queen to dwell on. *Haarth's clout and character are more than a match for Mother.*

Bernehvelle took Tierney's hands between hers and Tierney sighed. *Skin on skin heat.* Nothing more intimate than to share soul-energy this way, and Bernehvelle was counting on that, she was sure. Maybe this was where the queen had learned such tactics too, at Bernevelle's knee. The master manipulator. Bernehvelle then asked, "Will you allow them this reconciliation?"

Tierney blanched. "It isn't me who must allow—"

"It *is* you. Ana'kerah will never move forward with Haarth after everything you all have gone through if you don't approve."

Bernehvelle rubbed her fingers with more heat emanating over Tierney's cheek too, to soften her up even more probably. "Then have no worries," she said. "I most definitely approve of a match with Haarth." Bernehvelle's smile then lit the corridor. They both laughed as she bustled Tierney down close, the heat of a furnace between them now. She squeezed her cheeks and kissed them both before she patted her shoulder, and left her.

Bernehvelle rejoined Lorneam with a jaunt in her step now where he stood conversing with a sentry just relieved from the Keep's outer gates. From the archway of the nourishing room, they must have been watching the cookeries burn and people socialize. The two men were distinguished with grey peppering their temples and grey streaks strewn down the plaits on their backs too. Their heads lifted and followed smoke plumes from the many fire pits on their journeys drifting upward within their ionic air barriers, that only allowed most of the heat to disburse to those partaking of the *fire pits.* Dancing, the plumes were then pulled into vents and exited recesses in the ceiling. Outside, the smoke's *retained* heat helped warm the Keep's roof and clear it of piling snow, as was done on all roofs. Again, Soonahyins wouldn't want to waste even the heat from a firepit's smoke. It could be used.

Lorneam grinned as he received a big kiss on the cheek from Bernehvelle. They bade the sentry a fair day, and the sentry moved on to enjoy his first provisions.

Tierney smiled after the older couple as she left the corridor too in search of the others, and she found them, alright. She walked up on the Kalameshee complaining to Lu'nil and Mlai about his trusty pouch. The one that never left its fitting on his back.

"It was rendered unusable," he said. She sniggered as he described the pouch's misshaped lines. The deformed thing could no longer hold his equipment. Lu'nil chuckled too. They cut their eyes at each other, sharing a look underneath their lashes. He'd been "*scanalized,*" *a* victim of the Keep's detectors when he entered. The pouch's foreign technology would've been scanned, diagrammed, recorded. Its irregular capabilities neutralized for security purposes.

Tierney needn't try to have his pouch analyzed any longer. The thing was probably being reproduced as they stood there. But she didn't tell the Kalamshee this. She petted his arm and grinned at him. "Your pouch should recover its shape. Your land's technology must surely be robust enough to withstand a little trip to the cold of the Soonahyin Keep."

Lu'nil chortled at Tierney mocking the Kalameshee as they formed a little pack, Mlai in the middle, and organized a view of the enclave. Of Domes. People. Shops. Sweet cravings drew them to the Rising Bun. They nibbled its famous nutty sticky bun as they toured and swept along the cobblestone paths. Mlai scarfed hers down first to all their surprise. She wheedled them with those eyes of hers into traveling back to the baker's shop. Another full packet made its way into her possession. *Geez, Mlai could eat.*

The sticky smell of sweets followed them from the shop as they walked along the cobblestones. The stones' path ushered them to the dome of a coinage filled with people who were researching and conducting transactions for their silver mints trade accounts, too busy with currency in mind to look up and distract themselves from their business.

Flattened out and leading into a dome further along the way, the cobblestones were filthy at an open front with its rollable glass partly pulled down. The glass framed people repairing hoverers and other transports inside. Just when they were stepping past the shop, one flying razor got loose unmanned with the technicians scurrying behind it. *Their* party all scattered too, laughing because it looked as if it would break the glass and veer straight toward them. And had the Kalameshee grabbing her arm and skittering her toward a woman pitching hot water over the stones lining the pathway to another door. Running from the errant flying razor may have gotten them hit in the way of one of the many hoverers traversing the surface roads. To dodge the hot water that rinsed tanning solution from the cobblestones was a safer bet.

Tierney nodded at the woman she knew as the proprietor. Felia was her name.

Through her tannery's windows, a variety of skins hang on display. More was folded on shelves around the room, furs too. Felia's daughter, Chemen worked atop a table in the back. It had a million drawers of all sizes with brass drawer pulls that faced the street front. Short and stout with a large flat top, its wide surface was sturdy enough for Chemen to stoop over the table as she shaped the form of a wolvien shukka boot over a mold. Inside out, the color of the boot's fur, a rich red peaking out, nearly made Tierney stop to inquire about its size.

The cobblestones entries into the quaint buildings giving away to roads made of glass, signaling this way and that to hoverers were the marriage of two different worlds. The traditional and the modern.

Many many people coursed through the enclave on both surfaces. Too many to safely bring Bak'rah out on the streets for the day. Tierney had delegated her aide as his companion inside the Keep. She would have to make do separate from him for a time. Without a wolf around to limit interactions, she and Lu'nil were able to give warm greetings to Soonahyins who approached them with hearty wishes. And to the proprietors and shopkeepers. The locals neared them, some of them coming from their dome's locales, just out of curiosity for the foreigners they guided.

At one point a woman tried to actively waylay them. She and Lu'nil's Tempeh Tu stopped her before she got too close. Their perimeter had appeared casual until this woman's motivations were unclear. Giving a salute out of deference, her head stiff, still as proud as ever, her shoulders did drop to a straight line. She turned from them to continue on her way. Tierney's eyes traced her plaits that almost touched the ground, a shear never having been taken to them. They softened trailing over the woman's traditional Ahn'Trunkh tunic-styled overcloak and fur leggings. *She was Cordalai.*

She hastened her closest guard to hail the woman before she got too far. "Find out her business."

When one of the Tempeh Tu escorted her back, she took Tierney's hand in hers. She lowered her forehead to Tierney's gloved knuckles and saluted her *and Lu'nil* again. "You grace me with your compassion, even to allow me a little time within your schedule."

Tierney acknowledged her salute with a slight bow of her head in kind. "The guards tell me your hamlet is being overrun by thieving snowcats?" Then she inquired about the happenings taking place in the woman's hamlet. "Come." Taking the woman's arm, she brought her with them into an eatery where they took stance at an eating mantle close to the door. "Although I have yet to learn your name, I commend your initiative to approach me. Please, what actions have your chieftain taken to turn the snowcats away?"

"I'm Wilowah Tordum Litem Ahn'Trunkh, a daughter from the direct line of our chieftain. She ails now often with the malady of the bones. She and the clan elders have become overburdened as of late attempting to decide who will succeed her. The effects of her ill health have taken their toll. They decided our hamlet should move to our settlement reserved for the season of long dark nights. It was too early for our move there as we are not yet in the full flush of the harshest Soonahyin weather, but this was what was decided in answer to the threat of the snowcats." The woman, Wilowah, looked about her. She alighted on an arrangement of provisions displayed on the hearth of one of the eatery's fireplaces. And so they all partook of the food on offer as was done in Soonayah after Tierney made a gesture of assent. *"Eat often, even the fat and the gristle to flesh up the Soonahyin frame. Run fast, disappear and burn back the cold. Under-gird the soul-energy, innervate the essence."*

A virtual image of silver mints popped up for trade with the eatery's proprietor above Lu'nil's armset. She waved Tierney back to finish her conversation with Wilowah after the proprietor with her ring of minuscule servers had tasted the food.

Wilowah took a few moments to sort her selections. Elegant fingers placed cleansing bowl, cracker urn, butter crock, dipping saucer, and slipped a hot beaker in-point round her platter of blubber meat lommul pottage. *Customary arrangement.* Tierney hadn't witnessed such manners since her foremother's lessons at taking provisions. Her eyes moved from Wilowah's smooth, tactile hands to caress her hair. Shiny plaits stopping just short of brushing the ground. Wilowah curled the mass out of her way, tucked it under her elbow and over the mantle, and covered the gathered sinuous mound of hair with a dabbing towel.

As accustomed, the snood of Wilowah's overcloak, now lowered, would nearly cover her whole face with just eye holes to peek through. A bulkier silhouette meant for the harsher frozen tundra climes. The thought of its fit elicited treasured memories for Tierney of her and her siblings in similar dress frolicking about the frozen tundra. And that family name Litem was the same as some of Tierney's cousins of the same line. She hadn't seen them for ages. Willowah's clan name Ahn'Trunkh, meant of the Trunkh clan, and attested that *they too* were actual family, connected somewhere far far back and had descended from the same clan leader, Trunkh of the original twelve clans that founded Soonayah. It had been many spans since Tierney last went and lived amongst the stars with the line of her *own* family's Cordalai clan. She sucked in the air around them. Icy winds from the Frozen Tundra drifted off Wilowah's furs. *How I would love to sojourn to the tundra for a time if I wasn't threatened with being locked away there forever.*

"The brace of the tundra."

Wilowah rested her hands on the sides of her platters after arranging her food and waited out of custom. Her deferment to Tierney spurred Tierney to the courtesy at hand. She submerged her hands into the cool, tingling, clarifying liquid of her own cleansing bowl. And arranged her place setting *in-point* convention too, belatedly mimicking Wilowah's traditional behavior. She took up a hunk of bread, dipped it in the butter and spices in the dipping saucer, and took a bite. Only then did Wilowah follow suit, partaking in her own provisions.

Wilowah frowned for a moment into her platter. Clearly, her mind was occupied by thoughts other than the fare before them. Her next words she spoke with some care. "I'm sure the snowcats have followed us to our new settlement. There may even be a whole pack of them that have trailed behind us for our easy pickings. Which is understandable. It has to be far preferable to steal food than hunt for it. But with such proximity to us, time will cause an inevitable clash between people and predator."

"Have you informed the clan chieftain and the elders you suspect the snowcats have followed?"

"I have. They don't agree, as there have been no new sightings. But incidents like those that took place when this all began have started happening again. I fear if the clan is complacent, the snowcats will grow bolder." They finished their provisions as they talked. Tierney could only agree with Wilowah's sentiments. Proactive measures needed to be taken before any serious incidents befell the clan. That would send the whole hamlet into disaster.

Tierney assured Wilowah she would take the matter before the queen. The Animal Watch should set actions to rid the clan's hamlet of the pesky snowcats once and for all. Hopefully, without the cats having to be put down. Wilowah wrung her hands, then clasped them together. "Much, much, much appreciations for taking a few moments for my clan's issues. I must go and check at the infirmary on the chieftain now."

A small troop of her Cordalai clan had accompanied their chieftain for her Ritual of Ume to Dameerh. The chieftain had professed that her, "*Bones no longer ached as deeply.*" Her bone's malady reduced within moments of her deep dive into the Frozen Folly. Medics were helping her recovery along with more comprehensive curatives at the infirmary now. Wilowah cinched her snood and prepared to take her leave, but told Tierney in a happy aside after she had taken so much time out for her that so had her brother, Korrell. "He presided with honor over Chieftain's ritual this day." She asked Tierney if she would give him her appreciation. He had left quickly afterward. She hadn't had the chance to express it to him herself.

Wilowah left and Tierney and her group began their tour again and much to her surprise, their outing ended up at the dance theater. "It was your idea," Lu'nil reminded her. She'd been distracted by Wilowah's Cordalai clan's problems to an extent that she'd forgotten she'd wanted the theater to be their last stop.

Once they entered the ferber wood dome, they took it for empty. No one greeted them as was usually done.

The rich wood of the dome actually resonated, welcoming them into its large oval on its own. Silence and the redolence so like a mixture of other elements—peat, redvine, sarsaparilla—stuffed the air. Onto a landing, they circled and overlooked a wooden floor. Other doors branched off from the landing toward all directions. A few steps to clear the landing lead down some stairs to the dance floor. Tierney slid across to the floor's center. The glossed surface drew some faint moves from her, mimicking rhythms the dance theater compelled when in full swing.

Soonahyin rapture. Other lands believed them to be sybaritic in their dance. Hedonists. The dance was a tool that ensured life in the desolate cold. They had little care for those who cast aspersions on how they survived. Soonahyins answered to Soonayah.

In the center of the dance floor stood a stage. A large cylinder column distended from its middle was used as a dial to set the dance theater into play.

Tierney's body thrummed, the core catching up memories of her soul-energy triggered by the heavy beat that rode any tune sent through a dance theater and the heat generated by the bodies and pressed onto the dancers who moved as one. She tread one stair that led to the stage so that she could engage the dial in a demonstration for Mlai and the Kalameshee.

Her brother Eh'kotah appeared out of the shadows. His breadth blocked their view of the course he'd come from around the dial. They could just make out the dancer, Nyoma behind him. Tierney blinked. "Eh'kotah? I had no idea you were here. We figured the dance theater for empty when no one greeted us. Is that Nyoma beyond you? Have her come to meet our guests."

Eh'kotah walked forward and revealed Nyoma sporting puffed lips and fluttering fingers, untangling a mussed mane in an attempt to smooth her hair. A grin pulled at Tierney's lips. "Oh, I see why neither of you came to greet us. You were otherwise occupied."

Nyoma strolled from the back of the stage in her fluid dancer's way. "Please forgive. I wasn't aware you entered. And you've brought guests. I must give them a tour through the theater."

Trailing a hand down Nyoma's waist, Eh'kotah halted her and shook his head, and gestured to Tierney and Lu'nil. "Answer any questions they have, but remember my reasons for heading Tierney and her little party off here in the first place. Their Tempeh Tu informed us that this was their next stop. I must have them back at the Keep in a short time."

Though Tierney's brows rose at her brother's statement, the Kalameshee broke in before she could give voice to any questions. "I have but one curiosity. And it's why a dance theater would be given a place of such prominence in the dominion of your high seat when it's meant for an activity of leisure?"

Nyoma glided forward and went to spin the dial in the middle of the stage. It began a fast tune. With a theatrical flourish, she stopped it then placed her hand nearer the top of the dial. Another spin and a grumble meandered its way into the theater. A somber *thump thumping* beat its way into Tierney's heart, triggering her rhythmic reliance. Nyoma stopped it again and Tierney grimaced at herself as she missed the thrumming in her blood just that fast.

Likely held captive to Nyoma's evocative nature, the Kalameshee's mouth hung as wide as his eyes did. If she were closer to him, she would've closed it for him with a smack of her fingers under his chin. Instead, she rolled her eyes. It was unseemly for him to have his mouth flapped open like that. *Looking like a gulping fish,* she sniffed.

"All the heat shared when a dance theater is in play can be addictive for a Soonahyin," Nyoma lilted, her voice inflecting her passion for the dance on *them* too and they were used to her. "One's soul-energy is on a high constant when we share in the dance, which *is* an activity of leisure. But which once was the primary way we Soonahyins girded our energy. However, for some who must put off their Ritual of Ume, the heat within the dance sustains them. So, the dance theater is given a proper place of prominence as is its due."

Eh'kotah chuckled at the Kalameshee's stare at Nyoma. "Come now." He pounded his back and caused him to cough up an awkward gulp and chuckle too. "We can't tarry here. You've been summoned. Which you two ignore as usual. Check your consoles."

His scolding them earned him a shrug from Lu'nil. She waved her hand over the armset on her bicep like it was an afterthought. A beacon sent the bright red word "*ALERT*" blinking. The word dissipated from the air when her gloved fingers swiped through the flashing alarm. "The Lorgren High Council is inquiring about the success of Mlai's curative. They ask to *witness* her recovery and question Soonayah as to why she hasn't been returned to her land yet."

As everyone turned to Mlai, amethyst blinked back at them like an alert in itself. When she lifted an arm, her console erupted, emitting a sharp beeping sound as it did. She nodded, sending her stalk of hair bobbing. "There isn't a doubt. They're anxious and may believe me surely dead by now with no proof I'm alive. I felt them summoning me. I only thought to ignore the High Council this once as I was attuned to Tierney and Lu'nil's armsets buzzing and they ignored their parents too.

Chapter 28

Tierney had taken pride in acquainting her companions with sights of her dominion. She'd enjoyed their little tour. Unfortunately, now they all trooped behind Eh'kotah back to the Keep. Duty had been put off well long enough. *Reassuring Mlai's people? Priority number one.* They bumped into Korrell as they went and she hurried to catch up to him. "Guess who we just ran across?" She slapped him on his back, teasing him, and tugged at one of his plaits. "Wilowah Tordum Litem Ahn'Trunkkh." Tierney recounted her interaction with the Cordalai woman. "She sent her appreciation for your presiding over her chieftain's ritual."

As he took Wilowah's high regard in stride, his reserve was steady as always. Poise shed from his pores like sweat in such excess, a redolence of it trailed in the space around him. Only, Tierney remembered him growing from the boy of their youth as eager to please, anxious for acceptance, learning to develop into a whole person like all the rest of them. And so she asked him, "What interest do you have in performing Rituals of Ume?" Since he seemed to possess such nonchalance about the scholarship. "Do you consider yourself a curist?"

Korrell shrugged. "I preside over rituals as a service to those Soonahyins that I can. Not as any furtherance of any personal aspiration of my own."

Really? That made no sense.

Curist spent spans of time studying the practices needed to preside over rituals. Learning about the effects of the cold and restoration during a ritual and Soonahyins' need for regeneration of their soul-energy required dedication. That Korrell sought any knowledge on the ways at all meant he had personal interest. Yet, he wanted no acknowledgment of this from her or maybe any of the family. Tierney'd never heard talk of it before. *He takes his brooding ways to the limit sometimes.*

Upon them all walking further into the depths of the Keep, restrictions stopped neither Mlai nor even the Kalameshee's progress. The greatest surprise came when the doors of the transmission center swished up. No hesitation? The Kalameshee encountered no impediment to entering this deep into the Keep at all? *Now that was curious too. Even land leaders were only allowed so far.*

Closing silently behind them, the transmission center's doors engulfed them inside a room of white. No corners. No walls. Even the door they'd just come through couldn't now be differentiated from white space. Designed so that no foreign decoding from outside could penetrate, the white on everything, including the people acted as a kind rebuffer. If any sort of decoding was attempted, the would-be pirates encountered a stasis of white noise devised to capture the decoding and possibly trace it back to its origination. Or deliver in reverse whatever it was they were attempting to deliver onto Soonayah. Alive with lights and visual terminals on translucent backgrounds, the transmission center had people in it scuttering about, interacting with displays that were invisibly suspended in whiteness.

Sholah, the directory agent Tierney had talked to previously—decked out in all her white too on the far side—saluted Tierney and her party. All the royals bent their heads in acceptance.

The Kalameshee gravitated to a technician who operated a workstation that winded through views of the Keep. Scrolling at speed through one room after another, each room on the display recognizable. Yet, no contraption within these said rooms—that documented real-time accounts such as this—was detectable. He'd scoured for them. "I see that you take note of some of our security measures. I wonder about the debriefing King Ocierus will receive once you're back in your own land, Torhvald," The queen had walked up on him, appearing from a consultation with a technician.

He flinched only a bit, except he held his gaze steady with hers. "I will, of course, report back to my father all I have encountered here in Soonayah. The information I tell him will have more in-depth detail now that you've allowed me a sliver more access into the intricacies of your land." He shifted away from the technician's work with the security feed. "Which is why you relaxed the restrictions you had on me. Why you let me this far into your Keep. And really, it was one of the reasons why I was ever allowed into your land at all, isn't it, Queen Ana'kerah? I'm to deliver back to my father my great impressions of Soonayah and all I've seen that you want him to know." So, the Kalameshee's affable demeanor and emphatic gift helped him cover a cleverness that he deployed with purpose...of duty. His Kalamesh allegiance had been tested, clearly being no lesser than the queen had thought.

Converging on the Kalameshee was a surprise approach by the queen with Haarth at her rear. She had acted as if she'd had no use for the Kalameshee when they'd first met. Although she schooled her features, it seemed that her patience for his presence in Soonayah might be useful after all. Her white teeth flashed at him. The queen didn't deign to deny or confirm his conclusions. She addressed her son, Eh'kotah instead. "You retrieved them. Where did you find their little pack? Wallowing in their disobedience at the Rising Bun?"

"No. I intercepted them as Torhvald here became entranced by Nyoma as all men do, at the dance theater." Though Eh'kotah pounded him on his back again, a smile on his lips, his eyes regarded the Kalameshee with a glint of hardness inside them.

Everyone laughed at Eh'kotah's quip. Only Tierney scooted over to the Kalameshee's side to help him out. "Don't be deceived because Eh'kotah jests with you. He's involved with that dancer, Nyoma. He'll not take kindly if you pursued real interest in her."

The bemused look on his face spread into grin. "She was just so beautiful it astounded me." He shrugged a helpless gesture. "So *many* here have. The light in your people's skin alone entrances and can take a person's senses off guard." Lowering his head to peer into her eyes, he nudged her and grinned. "I have no real interest in her other than wonder. Does that settle better with your temperament?"

Tierney sniffed. What made him think his ogling Nyoma would have any effect on her? They needed to join the rest of her family who'd move on. She'd taken to showing him a stiff back whenever he irritated her. Now was no different. Turning her nose up too, she walked away with him right behind her as he chuckled. They stepped beyond the technicians, onto a circle delineated on the white floor in the room's center. Everyone surrounded a round mirrored dais. Suspended on the ceiling above the dais was a cone covered in mirrors too.

The regent who saw to the queen's communications stood next to her and touched his armset. A command was input. The outline of the mirrored cone above them blipped into focus then flipped a barrier field of blackness to join the line that they stood encircled within. Once the barrier had engaged, they heard nothing and saw no movement outside. Then a vision of a group of Lorgrens, so profound they appeared as though they were in the same room, opened between the mirrored dais and the mirrored cone above.

The queen made a cutting gesture to her regent. He dampened the Lorgrens' image, then she accessed her own armset. The black barrier shimmered then thinned. They could see outside of it now, however, the people in the white room continued their work, ignorant of the change in the barrier. "We want an impermeable barrier to keep *our* actions private, not so we can't detect what is happening outside," she reminded her regent.

He bowed his head and frowned. "Please forgive, Queen Ana'ke—" Gesturing for him to resume with the Lorgrens, she waved away the regent's apology.

The connection restored. And the Lorgrens didn't bother with greetings. They'd been in repeated contact with the Soonahyin royal house all day, apparently. No Mlai had been produced until now. So their first reaction bordered on the abrupt. The three in the communication had the prerequisite Lorgren pinkish skin, a bit redder stung now with irritation. Each of them sported swaths of blue-black hair pinned or smoothed in different positions—per that Lorgren's style—on otherwise bald heads. They all had slender bodies. The female of the three more so, albeit, hers was decidedly feminine. Huge eyes framed by ridiculous lashes as long as Mlai's clung to Mlai. "We see that you've finally made Meloy available," she said.

One of the male Lorgrens shuffled. His image became so large they all reared back from it. Once he settled, he had angled himself in a maneuver so he was the most prominent of them. "How unfortunate in this continued contact with your land, you've thwarted us by not producing our patrician when we asked," he said.

Just as the queen opened her mouth to respond, Mlai stepped forward, and she nodded to Mlai to continue when she saw her bite her lip to stop from blurting out an answer. "I'm here and well, as you can see. Mother? Didn't we decide together that I would be called by the name that I chose for myself before I left?

Love beamed from amethyst eyes so like Mlai's. Her mother's face lit in a smile all for her daughter. She pulled at the shoulder of the male Lorgren that blocked her whole sight of the healing Mlai. "You're very right, my daughter. Please forgive. Your look is vibrant compared to your condition when you left. Has the umbereen performed as well as the meager amounts we were allowed to do tests on suggested?"

The male Lorgren glowered down his nose at the genuine show of care displayed in front of the Soonahyins. His movement this time almost blocked Mlai's mother completely from view. He interjected, "*Meloy*"—pouncing on the name Mlai had evidently held prior to coming to Soonayah—"needs to travel back to our land, as that is what should have been done in the beginning. Courses of tests must be run."

Highlighting their fragility, Mlai's shoulders shot back, her forehead wrinkled, and her cheeks and mouth pursed ready to burst out with undoubted resentment. "Her weakened state after she completed such a serious curative stopped her from immediate travel. Travel the length of which could take days on her own." It was the queen interjecting now. One glance at the young Lorgren had the queen raising an eyebrow. No one could miss that this type of exchange was probably the long-lived course of the young Lorgren's life. "Though the High Council of Lorgr may consider travel by one of its gravely ill patricians over the whole length of Kalamesh—into the depths of the unfamiliar, cold Soonahyin lands, in no more than a short-distance flying apparatus, without guardianship or protection—appropriate; we here in Soonayah do not. And Mlai...is that correct?" The queen looked to Mlai for the *correct* pronunciation of her name. Mlai nodded profusely. "Won't be sent back to your land unescorted. She's still in recovery. In her condition, she deserves uneventful and quick transport over the arduous distances home."

If it were possible, the male Lorgren's face flushed an even deeper pink. "We...she insisted on going when she was forbidden. We had no reason to believe she could survi...rather we expected she wouldn't—no...no, no. We couldn't speculate on her chances—"

"And neither will we. Though her health must have been precarious when she set forth to come here, care should have been taken for her."

Mlai's mother elbowed her way out from behind the male Lorgren. She gave a firm nod to the queen. Her stance, smaller than the male Lorgren, bore a regal bearing that far outshone his. "I'm Corsene, her mother. I'm responsible for enabling her to travel in circumstances so fraught with risk. Here in Lorgr, she was being forced in a direction the abject opposite of her wishes. And she was so ill, the High Council sent no scout with her thinking she *would very well die* in the course of her journey." Corsene's eyes dropped a moment after a once-over feasted on her daughter's appearance. "It *is* deplorable that so little care was taken for one of our own."

"Mother! I'm not a babe," Mlai again spoke up. Her show of fearlessness was telling of their mother-daughter relationship. "My insistence in this journey brooked no argument. At the possibility of being forced into the fertility lots, neither you nor the High Council could've stop—"

"These actions are all in the past! What is in question now is her return to Lorgr. Pushing for her location, Corsene, one of our *Capstone-Tier* council members has connected in repeated discussions with your Ministry of Communication. The whole of Lorgr wants Meloy's retur—"

"I shall personally make sure *Mlai* is delivered back into the bosom of the Lorgren land," the queen said. The male Lorgren's tedium was unneeded after what they'd all just witnessed. "You'll receive communication as her journey is carried out."

So, *this* was how the Lorgren High Council operated. How desperate Mlai must've been to embark on such a treacherous journey knowing she could die during the course of it. Tierney watched the queen *watching* Mlai's mother as the male Lorgren rambled on. Corsene put her hands together then tugged them apart. Together again, apart repeatedly. Mlai's mother's posture bowed as if load-bearing, weighted and weighted the more arrogant the male Lorgren's tone bent. The queen's face loosened as she witnessed Corsene's reaction. *Mothers. The queen* more than anyone would understand Mlai's mother enabling Mlai's travel even though she could very well lose her daughter. A mother's plight was to make such dire decisions. But what the queen didn't have to do was indulge the male Lorgren's self-importance. She signaled for her regent to disconnect the communication while the male Lorgren was in the middle of another dictate.

A perfect Soonahyin salute was Mlai's payment in veneration to the queen. The queen tilted her head in acceptance. It took great courage to do what Mlai had done. The queen, it seemed intended to honor that courage by doing her part. "A whole sect of Tempeh Tu shall be appointed to conduct you to your land," she said, offering the young woman the support that she could.

"And *I* shall accompany her too, Mother." The bite in Tierney's voice reverberated around the black barrier.

The queen grimaced as she said, "I see... Honestly, I expected this would be your stance, Tierahna."

How could she have? Her words, the resignation on her face made the stiffness in Tierney's spine wilt some.

No. Not this time. This was her method. Always catching me off guard. That way she slides her edicts in before you know you're at her bidding. Me putting off this confrontation has played right into the whole problem. Tierney straightened her spine again. *Now is the time for it then.* "I know about what you want to do with me, Mother. I overheard you planning to commit me to that sanctum as unstable."

The queen cocked her head to the side. "You overheard me planni—?"

"Yes! As if the other secrets between us haven't been enough. You would send me away against my will? From my home! Away from my family forever!"

"No, I wouldn't." Breathing out the weight of the state of affairs between them, the queen folded her lips. "Your eavesdropping on a private conversation got you what you deserve; misery...over nothing. I think you're overwrought, Tierney. Your new gift is taking its toll, as is natural for anybody adapting something new within their body." She then pursed her lips as Tierney's eyes stretched. "Yes, I know about that too. There's little about you I don't know. The question is why you never came to *me*? What has happened that we can no longer talk? In your youth, you never stopped yammering at me."

Wait. No way! Tierney didn't understand. She'd been sure her mother was trying to undermine her maturing. Her gaze flew across the barrier to Lu'nil. The knowledge of spending nights together plotting the actions she would take scorched between them inside the barrier's space. They'd come up with intricate plans to counteract her mother, certain her dependency was because of the queen's dominance. Her own insecurities due to not being allowed to be herself. When her mother was now asking why she hadn't talked to her.

Sheesh...I've had no confidence in myself. All of this has been caused by that very thing. *Did I hear only what I wanted to hear? Then all my actions could be blamed on her. Am I never to take ownership for anything? Even behaviors I knew were getting out of control?* She lowered her gaze from Lu'nil, ending up skittering it all over everyone else in the black barrier, skipping over her mother too.

"You could've just come to me. Instead, you let all this build up inside you until you're making rash decisions: running away in a blizzard, overreacting to the slightest thing. You could unintentionally kill someone in this condition as your body is changing and you have no idea what to do with it. Your rocking and tapping all the time is a manifestation of what is happening inside you. And it's gotten worse. Far worse." She opened her hands toward Tierney. "The sanctum is to help you. You love the frozen tundra. I thought a little time out there would help you settle. Even if you never came to me, I intended to ask you about it when the time was right. Maybe...go with you. I've been there a few times myself when I needed a bit of an asylum, a place away to regather myself—to allow my body and my mind just pure openness as changes were happening inside *me* too." She lowered her hand. "I can't believe you thought I would commit you against you—."

" Mother...I..." Tierney's head fell back and she blinked several times. She wouldn't cry. She couldn't cry. *Not here.* "I believe you may be right, Mother. I *have* been overwrought. Too much going on at one time."

"And now you're determined to leave." The queen looked toward the white ceiling too.

"Now, I'm not sure I should go—"

"No. You *should* go. Your first sojourn abroad. This might be what helps resettle you. But no Soonahyin has traveled to foreign lands in many spans." Tierney's mouth just flapped right open, about as big as her eyes, goggling at her mother. The queen pinched her lips and kept a smile from forming "You must have a full garrison of Tempeh Tu assigned to you and your brothers shall go too."

"Mother," Korrell spoke up on the matter Tierney had told him about. The Cordalai hamlet stalked by snowcats. "Their situation is dire." He told the queen of some practices he'd learned that he could put into urgent use there. "I shall join Tierney's party after I leave from helping the Cordalai hamlet if they still remain in Lorgr."

The queen nodded her agreement. Snowcats on the prowl amongst the Soonahyin people was a disaster waiting to happen. Leaving in such haste, the hamlet might not have even replenished the frozen tundra ground they'd just left. And had they informed the Ministry of Cultivation that they were leaving early to their settlement for long dark nights? The queen would no doubt find out.

Eh'kotah also surprised everyone with his refusal. "Mother, if you recall I wanted to meet with you last eve? It was due to us discovering people hidden in the caves of the Dayea mountains."

"People!" was Haarth's reaction.

"That's impossible!" the queen exclaimed. Everyone began to talk at once.

"It *is* so," Eh'kotah announced, the resolution in his tone silencing everyone's disbelief. "A woman chased a child who had escaped her care. They weren't of some outlying clan that lives in the wilds as we know of either. Her hair was shorn nearly to her scalp. And they wore no overcloaks in the icy winds at such high elevations."

"What clan did she claim as her own?"

"We didn't get a chance to question her. We frightened her and she ran and disappeared as quickly as she'd come. My party could no longer remain up there in the elements to search for her when we'd been climbing off and on for days. I must return with more men and equipment and track these people while our memories are still fresh."

"I agree." Subdued now, the queen's glance shifted to Tierney, then away again, a frown marking her features.

"Have no worry for Tierahna," Haarth said after the queen was quiet for a while. "I shall attend her and the Lorgren on their travel to Lorgr and back."

The creases in the queen's brow calmed some then. She scrutinized Tierney, weighing her like she was appraising everything about her: her maturity, her decisiveness, her very femininity. Her mother's gaze was so piercing, it made Tierney want to cover up any vulner-ability that might be naked to the world. The cast on the queen's face eased after a time as if she'd concluded something—that Tierney wasn't a girl anymore. And, without a doubt, the Kalameshee had noticed every little feminine thing about her too. The queen's study had moved on to him now.

She's quite right. I am my own woman. I have to claim that right now and be it!

If Tierney and her mother didn't come to some accord, their relationship could be strained forever. However unnatural it was, the queen had to loosen her hold. It looked like she was trying. Tierney was developing her own ideas about who she was and she would try too. "Then Tierahna," the queen said. "I'm at ease that you will take this first travel abroad like you've always wanted. Ad'rihl, Haarth, and the Tempeh Tu will go with you."

The queen and Tierney continued to gaze at one another. In an overture to her mother, Tierney raised her hand. "Matah—"

"I have position to offer recompense for your help. I'm so appre-ciative of all the many actions you've taken for me here in Soonayah. The use of your medics and infirmary for my experimental curative can never be repaid. Will you please accept my offer?" Into the critical moment, Mlai entered the same curious refrain she had spoken several time since they'd met her.

"Mlai, you're healing now. On behalf of Soonayah, we're proud that you progress so. We need no more exchange for your recovery. What is this other compensation that you insist on offering, anyway?" Tierney asked.

Mlai rubbed her hand against her forearm. As she manipulated the skin on the area where her console usually came from. Tierney's cu-riosity peaked. Through the skin, Mlai's slim fingers made lightning-fast inputs before her console ever erupted. Once it did, she balled a small fist against it and flung her arm outward. A neon hologram of their planet, Telluric, the alluvial shield surrounding it, with a portion of the ominous asteroid ring that circled so closely shone vibrantly against the background of the black barrier.

To the surprise of everybody, any who'd believed it was a hologram were mistaken. Mlai interacted with the thing. She touched a finger to the vision. No hologram reacted that way. The alluvial shield shuddered, opening wider closer to all of them. She tapped inputs into a part of the shield near her. It whirled, changing to reveal the portions of Telluric it surrounded. Using her hand, she sent it spinning, scrolling until she reached Soonayah. With one finger she zeroed in on the streets of the high seat enclave, Dameerh.

People roamed in real-time in front of the inescapable specter of the Frozen Folly. Those in the barrier "oohed" and "aahed" at the present spectacle in front of them. "We just finished programming this focus-scape on our portion of the alluvial shield. They initialized this demonstration and its programming onto my biomechanics for exchange before I left. It's meant to help further relations between our two lands. Really...the offer was to entice you for more of your umbereen from your abundant supplies *if* I made it alive and my procedure proved successful. Your technicians will have much to do to initialize it onto your own portion of the alluvial shield if you want it.

Walking about the barrier, the queen examined the Tellurician lands from different angles. She touched Drundel and said, "It took our medics quite some time to analyze your biomechanics during your curative, Mlai. Afterward, a comprehensive study of them and you were done, and we were able to get a finished dissection of everything inside you once you entered the Keep through our detectors. I've been assured that they're already working on this technology discovered when the medics performed the curative on you."

"*Scanalized, again!*"

"I doubt it will take them long. Though *it is* a wonder to see in person." The queen offered no apology for the methods Soonayah used to protect itself.

Mlai shrugged. "I do believe my land's High Council thought I would never make it here to exchange it. But I did. It's yours now.

Chapter 29

S o...you're leaving me again?" Os'carah's pout made her face no less charming.

Tierney tweaked her sister's nose and brushed hands through the hair Os'carah loved to wear big and loose in puffs that swung past her waist. The tresses silhouetted around her royal skin made quite a sight, even for a Soonahyin. And Tierney's fingers didn't tangle in her hair like they did her own frizz. She turned and smirked at Lu'nil.

And we'll...that was a non-starter. She wasn't met with the exchange they normally shared when mollifying Os'carah. *Lu'nil wasn't smiling?*

She sat there as she indulged herself, sprawled as it were on one of the few lounge seats found in the Keep, with her head lowered. *Was that much concentration really needed just to pick at her fingernails?*

Taking stance always made for better boosts for Soonahyin metabolisms. Keeping their body heat innervated was an unconscious state of being for them...always. It was natural to eat fatty protein often, constantly burning up the fat by staying warm, speeding, sparring, hunting, and a myriad other ways in highly active lifestyles. Therefore, an occasion of the three princesses of the Keep lounging in the warmth of a salon while they shared in each other's lives, was a rare treat. One to be cherished for its scarcity.

The cushions and luxury might as well not be there for all the good it did Lu'nil. Her shoulders remained bunched. She made no effort to lift her gaze to Tierney's with the snicker expected for Os'carah's badgering.

So, Tierney would have to reassure Lu'nil too along with Os'carah. That was the reason she'd wanted them here for some time together. "The word leave is too strong a term. I'm going away only for a short time and I shall return straight away."

"I can't say that I wish to see you gone so soon again either, but I cheer your chance at the experience you've long craved. Especially now you know Queen-Mother is not trying to send you away." Whether quiet about it or not, Lu'nil *did* have an opinion on what was going on, apparently. She switched herself from her feigned absorption in her own comfort. "Your recount of what Lorgr is like may well be documented for all Soonahyin records. The first in-depth impressions of that land." Lu'nil looked at Tierney, an eye-to-eye connection finally.

"And that strapping Kalameshee is going with her, no doubt. She had better tell of more than just the land she visits. I want the ins-and-outs of every little thing you get up to. Pun intended," Os'carah added, wiggling her brows.

The fire's crackles suddenly captivated Tierney. It was she who glanced away from Lu'nil *and* Os'carah then. Reaching out, she soothed her hand over the pallodot on the hearth, golden-green glimpsing between her fingertips. Why were Os'carah's expectations always so suggestive? Was it really necessary to infer innuendo into everything? She may as well be lumped in with the brothers too for the annoyance she caused sometimes. "He won't attend this journey with us. I dare say, he'll probably return to his own land when we set off."

Inseparability reinforced by their spans together bred insight in

Lu'nil. Tierney recognized it touching her, probing her even when she wasn't near her sometimes. Often when she was intentionally avoiding her. When a need for a little time alone won out, another sojourn to the farthest reaches of Soonayah would conveniently call her away. Now, her study of Tierney bored into the side of her face. Irritating now and again how much she could see just by looking at a person. Tierney often believed Lu'nil could read a person's soul. Especially hers. What convinced her to relent on the questions she'd promised for Tierney's comeuppance? Tierney didn't know, but she didn't need it right now and was glad Lu'nil hadn't pushed it. She didn't have all the answers on the subject of the Kalameshee. On anything really, anymore. "Do you regret him not going?" Lu'nil *did* ask.

"In truth, I must say I do. Though our acquaintance has been short, I was...excited about what could become of it."

The younger two clearly understood when a woman shouldn't have her disappointment shoved in her face. The three women spoke not again of the possibilities with the Kalameshee. Os'carah went on to list items she deemed necessities for Tierney's journey. Once again, Tierney obliged her sister. She confirmed what she possessed of this mandatory list: "Yes—I was imbued against disease. My body is positively swimming with nutriments. No—you well know I can't take more than one pair of wolvien shukka boots. I only have the one. No!—I have no inhibitor against being gotten with a babe. You're about as bad as our broth—

Os'carah "tsked tsked," before leaving the room after saying, "I must supply my sister with all she needs for travel to a foreign land, for she can't be expected to understand the nature of these things as I do."

Tierney laughed as she left and this time, Lu'nil shared in the laughter. "Despite Os'carah's ridiculous list, are you wholly prepared for this passage to Lorgr?" Tierney understood what Lu'nil meant. Tierney-and-Lu'nil-speak activated as a codex file automatically in their conversations. She asked of more than the physical things.

She couldn't be sure that she *was* actually ready. She'd asked for this. Felt like she'd been waiting all her life for the freedom to explore as she willed. To be the Tierney of her dreams who set guides for her own life without using her mother as an excuse. But now that it was upon her...was she even more afraid? She dropped her eyes from Lu'nil's and muttered, "I...simply await communication for when it's time to go." A flutter in the solar plexus did suggest that apprehension lingered a stroke too long.

Lu'nil eyed her for several moments more and said, "Then I wish you a speedy journey and return. And know I send my goodwill with you, though I wish I could go with you beyond our strictures as well." Lu'nil reached her arm out to her and they clasped hands to elbows. Warmth spread between them as they held on longer than usual.

That phrase had been one of longing for discovery beyond what they'd always known, and was surprising in an obscure way. She stared at the door behind Lu'nil's departure too. Sure, Tierney was the more vocal of the two. *Lu'nil had probably never said anything before because I'm always whining, pushing everything to be my way.*

That recent argument with her mother, she'd asked to be allowed to travel beyond the dominion of Lehquate on to the Licomme passage to see the wild seas of the west. To see foreigners trying to navigate the seas and migrate to Soonayah, as they were being turned away. She'd wanted to ride with Soonayah's Sea Force and work the seas with them. Full off of having been allowed to sojourn so often, she'd had no idea then her every step had been followed. Tierney "harrumphed." The queen proved unmovable in her refusal, of course. And within days her *feelings* were hurt upon listening in on her mother and Bernehvelle's private conversation. *As a result, off I ran to meet Haarth at the other end of Soonayah.* Her cousin...her sister, a second thought.

I've been so negligent. If I hadn't been so set on blaming Mother for everything, blindly using her as a catalyst to do the things I was afraid of doing under my own will, I may have recognized similar desires in Lu'nil.

Her belly's contents clenched inside and her eyes were unerring in latching onto the convection of the flames. Drawn as was her wont to them, she stretched her hand out and moved closer without thought. Heat began as a rhythm through her fingers, thump-thumping up her wrist. Her body caught it up and beat inside to the pulse of the fire. She didn't entirely forget herself. Her awareness remained brooding over Lu'nil's predicament. *She will have as much opportunity as I do. I'll make sure of that.* All the same, she edged toward the flames just short of burning her skin. The fierce heat took its hold of her and moved up her body to her core. Pushing sensations to her head, her sternum screamed in intensity. Whirling hair was her only release of the energy starting a breathtaking assail of her.

Inside, her mind began opening into her intro-spection. "Okay... okay, learn control. Control. Be open to those around me." *Maybe because my head is hung up on what to do about Lu'nil, that'll be my anchor from losing control. Half of me will stay right here in worryland.* She sighed a welcome to the sensations at this point. May as well get used to them now. On the edges of her perception, the first impressions of people near her within the Keep were creeping in. The one closest touched her!

Startled, Tierney hurtled the interloper across the room. A pulse had released from her soul-energy arisen so high, she was too late to stop it. She opened her eyes to the sight of the Kalameshee cracking his back against the wall, and bit the skin inside her cheek in a rush toward him.

Except, the queen got there before she did. *Of course!* Unfortunately for her, her mother had entered just as she sent the Kalameshee sailing. Her mother swallowed laughter at the scene. By the time the queen reached the Kalameshee to help him up, he'd already jumped to his feet, shaking his head in a stunned fashion.

"I see that you don't listen to my words of caution even as you prepare to travel far away from this Keep. We don't have complete control when you're out of our reach, Tierahna," her mother said as she and the Kalameshee approached. "Do you understand that?" The queen pursed her lips and squinted between the Kalameshee's steps as they faltered and Tierney.

Her reply was murmured offhand to her mother. "Of course I do, Mother." She had thoughts only for the Kalameshee after sending him flying. He looked dazed. And if it weren't for the high retention of a Kalameshee's soul-energy that buffered him, she may well have smashed his body beyond a quick return. *Mother is right. I must get control.* His rebound was admirable and his puffed-out chest should've warned them both what was behind the speed of his recovery. "Queen Ana'kerah, I shall accompany Princess Tierahna on the journey to Lorgr and back. Afterward, I shall return—"

"Oh, is that so? Now you dictate to me what will go forward in Soonayah, I suppose?" the queen questioned him as all their gazes clashed.

The Kalameshee's shoulders lifted. Standing before the queen, he looked her straight on. But what was that smirk her mother still wore from when she'd first entered about? As a master of diplomacy, her mother maintained a face of steel when dealing with land leaders when negotiating. "The *Impassive Queen*," she was often called. "And if you're not allowed to travel in accompaniment with my daughter?"

"Then I shall follow her party to Lorgr. Even if I can't attend them in the same transport, Princess Tierahna shall have additional backing in me. How I travel is no concern."

"I have no doubt you would be dogged in a watch over her, no matter how you got there." The son of Kalamesh carried himself in true prince fashion. Proclaiming from his bearing that arrogance inbred from his nepotistic position could serve him well in his pursuit of Tierney.

"So it looks as if I must wish you a speedy journey in our royal transport too." The queen was relenting? A softening in her expression now toward the Klameshee shaped her lips.

The Kalameshee barked out with laughter. Tierney's eyes widened. *Was Mother actually smiling at him?* "Though I know you two are going to want to celebrate this *momentous* occasion, I must ask for a little time alone with my daughter."

The pulse in Tierney's neck went hectic, her features fervent and her mother's stare made them worse. Regardless, her gaze tracked after the Kalameshee and lingered on his limp as he got all the way to the door. Her mother wouldn't know her like this. Mooning behind a man. Her eyes skittered away when they landed on the queen. Away from her mother's searching, she swung toward the flames again. *Mother! Always searching...*

"What you carry inside for the foreigner and heedless flirtation with the perils of the flames are one and the same, you know. You have to remember who you are. Take your time with your first consort, Tierahna. Enjoy him. But be wary of claiming commitment too fast. Something that flames so hot so fast can be mercurial by nature and as destructive as tempting fate with this fire. You must temper this enthrallment you have with the man and the fire alike. Besides, no good serves our people from long proximity to the heat of the flames."

By rote, Tierney's lips moved, silently mimicking her mother's words. The queen sighed then put her face right near Tierney's. "Credit me with knowing you and your siblings think my cautiousness too much. But I speak with the knowledge of what has gone before. *Take* these flames, for instance." She pointed to the fireplace. "They move as you do. But don't ever believe you control them. They enrapture you with your inescapable attraction to their heat and they are enhanced as everything is in Soonayah. You should know that. The gift you have is just like Haarth's. He once described the effect of the heat of the Olum dessert similar to that of the flame, and he lost himself for days out there until he could shake off his stupor.

The queen—as knowing as always too.

I could have talked to Mother about this days ago. Should've known she knew what was going on with me. When doesn't she know everything anyhow? All that time wasted over things so trivial.

These feelings as of late, this newness in the changes in my body are... simply uncontrolled. I'm addicted, drugged interacting with the flames. Unusual even for a Soonahyin as I've been trying to avert all my life. Only, I ran straight toward what I'd been avoiding. It was only a small percentage of them who got hooked. Her mother's mantra in her head had spurred her on instead of warning her away. Look what she'd just done to the Kalameshee. *When I come back, I think I will go for some time in that sanctum.* "How is that possible, Mother? Our people have no domain over fire."

"We don't. But it's not just that the fire is responsive to us. It acts as any natural thing would. *We* cause it to unsettle. Our connection to its heat enhancement is elementary." The queen flipped one hand open. "Action." Then the other hand. "Reaction. That in no way implies control. Think on our behavior in the dance when energy is pushed back and forth between us. We practice in a dance theater surrounded by fire. A receptacle encompassed by ferber wood inviting all that energy, circulating and collecting it, and keeping us safe. You're not the only one, and you won't be the last whose enthrallment has pushed them to the edge." The queen swept Tierney's body. She ended by pressing her hands flush against her belly. "You are in a transformation of the gift that has always been inside you. It's said that in the beginning times when the dance was our only support to gird ourselves, plenty of fires leaped, attracting those gifted, burning them and others while they were in stupor."

From the beginning, her mother could have guided her like this. She might've been further along in handling her gift had she just said something. Which spoke to the conversation she'd eavesdropped on between the queen and Bernehvelle, instead of speaking up for herself as well. Communication after communication between her and Haarth hadn't caused her to act until she'd overheard that conversation. "I've been so arrogant. I believed myself special. No Soonahyin could possibly have experienced what I've been going through." Tierney guffawed thinking about her own behavior.

"You *are* your father's daughter. Haarth thought the same and acted in kind. And I've never heard of him using his gift again since he returned from the Olum dessert. You have the benefit of learning *beforehand* to temper yours and your exposure to heat so you can wield some control.

The queen moved her hands from Tierney's belly and brushed a frizz of hair back from her temple. "Tierahna?"

Oh no, please! Not that tone. It scraped along Tierney's nerves. She'd hoped to be well into Lorgr before her mother's voice possessed that tenor again. *If only I had such fortune.* Her mother wanted to tackle her negligence about who fathered her now?

"Even decisions I've made were done after learning *beforehand* how the truth's consequences could hurt everyone involved."

Scoffing under her breath, Tierney cast her eyes down. *Sure they were.* She waffled around the issue a bit in her head, really seeing no need to tackle this now. If only the queen could let it be for a time. But of course, she couldn't. It just wasn't her nature. To her mother, she said. "Mother, I can't believe that. Your choice not to tell Haarth and me that he's my father had to do with the protection of *one* person.

You." The accusation volleyed between them. She'd never had reason to accuse her mother of self-interest before.

"Look at me." The queen stroked Tierney's chin. "In truth, I did act in protection of myself. But you, Stah'lief, Haarth, *and* Soonayah all held equal places within my decision too." Her shoulders curved away, but the queen clutched her now and turned her back. "It *is* so, Tierahna. Think on it. I couldn't bring my daughter—the first princess of the land—up in upheaval only because I was in love with someone other than the King. His brother no less. No land deserves such fickleness in their queen when Haarth could just become my consort. A status he just wouldn't lower himself to.

Righteousness behind the words flicked the reflection of the fire in her mother's eyes. "So...you couldn't tell me? And Haarth had to be sacrificed?"

The queen's shoulders bowed. She lowered lids on those same eyes now darkened over past decisions she may never be absolved of.

It was Tierney who then took it upon herself to touch her mother's cheek. She would make this first gesture, wanting to forgive the queen, compelled to forgive her, she urged her mother to lift her head. She needed resolution too. And could only imagine what it must have been like to be in love with one brother and matched to the other. Then have the pressures of the Soonahyin land added to it. The queen reached for her forearm. Hands to elbows, they grasped, Tierney in forgiveness. Leaning forward, the queen rested her forehead on her daughter's and sighed.

A chuckled bubbled up. "You sacrificed Haarth? You will need a strong back for his retribution now that he's back!" Her mother threw her head back in laughter.

Chapter 30

Flight in the notorious Soonahyin weather was an exercise in torture for anyone sensitive to traveling like a rocket. Tierney couldn't possibly be the only one it affected this way. She just couldn't. Though she rocked like a pendulum with propulsion attached—back and forth, back and forth she went—to ride it out, abject terror at watching the ground fly by from the heavens couldn't just be specific to her.

Why must it be necessary, anyway? A nice pilot of a small-capacity flying apparatus was normal for personal use, which was understandable. Not so much for Tierney and for good reason. *Flight was just...unnatural.*

The Kalameshee landscape—in possession of cerulean skies mixed with pinks and lavenders, and fat-fluffy clouds pillowing their arcs—was a foreign revelation compared to *their* cold dutiful haven. Kalamesh lent to notions fanciful enough to have her believe that she may well enjoy piloting someday. At the very least, she could see why her brother Ad'rihl favored flight as a pastime.

But then, *Ad'rihl* tended to leap before he looked on things that tickled his fancy.

Ultimately, they docked into the launch at the tip of Kalamesh. It was perched on the edge of the Rocky Gorge that split Lorgr off from its border. And Tierney lost, yet again, all that self-assurance she'd only recently attained. *Me and flight will never be friends.*

She did dare to remain at the wall of windows overlooking the depths of the bottomless gorge. Her pup was there at her side to support her while she divided her attention.

People to the left below worked, preparing launch after launch on the lip of a dock as if one wrong step wouldn't send them on an endless dark plummet to the gorge's basin. The cool salon their contingent was whisked off to, called attention to itself. Such as it was, you could nearly hear the ping of its shine when you glance around. They awaited their own transport launch in the slick amenities and opulent luxury the Kalameshee royal house provided.

The salon they were in was surrounded by floor-to-ceiling windows. It jutted out as a lip from the launchpad building and the gorge, meant to offer those partaking of its exclusiveness the feel of floating over the gorge. *More of standing over their doom.*

She screwed up her face when she saw who was making his way across golden floors toward her. More lounge seats than had ever been seen in one place dotted his path. Just how many were needed to *rest* for a few moments? You'd think Kalameshees used the things to nest in. The Kalameshee—now in a black shirt clipped to one side of a rounded neck that had a circling in brown and stopped at his forearms and waist, and with black trews shaping his muscular thighs, made of a textured material traditional to Kalamesh—had gone and gotten himself refreshed. *I can see that he might want to feel more comfortable in his home element.*

She pouted, pondering on what they'd been calling him; *The Kalameshee, an appropriate label.* Even though they'd stuck him with it, here in Kalamesh it was moot. They weren't in Soonayah anymore. All the people around them, outside their party, were Kalameshee too. "Torhvald then?" *Hmm. Somewhat different sounding when you said it out loud. Regardless, his actual name it should be going forward.*

Following her interest to the workers on the dock, he eased in next to her and Bak'rah, while she gladly turned away from her morbid fascination with them. "How many have you lost falling to their deaths out there while they defy plain good sense?"

He chuckled. "None. Even when we constructed the launch, our practices were sound. We girdled it with a steep blockade fathoms high, and its gate is only triggered to open as the flying razors release."

They both noticed a man standing frozen facing their window. He was a technician who worked at a terminal and aligned the launch-slings for release. The glass might be distorted from this distance, but they'd caught his eye as if he could see them clearly through it. "I wasn't aware Kalamesh allowed uhm...different people to work here. That Drundel has stopped his work. He watches us even as we watch him."

The Kalamesnee only shrugged. "You have no need to worry about him." As he talked, he started up at her, stroking tingles down her arm and scrutinizing her response to his touch. He had a habit of doing that; watching her for the slightest response to stimuli he was provoking her with. Like he was trying to gauge her every reaction. "There are quite a few Drundel who transplant for seasonal work here. They're simply looking for opportunity as we all are." He scooted ever closer, placing his head near hers too. "And you know they possess exceptional eyesight. It's how they navigate so much of their lives underground." The scent of his breath—fresh, inviting—bathed her lips, turning this public setting personal and putting her in a cocoon of him and her with nobody else to take note of. All the encouragement she needed to scoot closer too.

Really, Tierney? You're that easy? It's like I'm starved for affection. A little attention and I'm at his beck and call? Were his maneuverings designed so intentionally, Kalmeshee-influencer style? She hesitated for a moment. "No doubt he does watch you for your glory from there.

Who wouldn't?" *Such a flatterer. And good at it too.*

Torhvald's eyes caressed the frown pleating the skin between her brows. He eyed her teeth nibbling her rounded lips, and brushed his thumb over her chin, loosening her poor lips from their torment. He leaned in to the now damp plump temptation. "Be at ease. I'm here—"

"Prince Torhvald? Princes Haarth and Ad'rihl advised us of your suggestions about our frostfires. You said the climate here without as much precipitation as Soonayah may make them malfunction? They told us to equip and get familiar with the weapons you offer." They were lucky their party had been given permission to travel with their weapons here in Kalamesh and Lorgr too. Neither land was required to make such concessions. Soonahyins would never have set foot out of Soonahyah without them though after what the small portion of their people had been through in the past.

Still, Tierney groaned. *Ok'nuh! Really? Come on!* His instincts for duty were cardinal even now? She appreciated the Principal guard of Eh'kotah's Sect I volunteering to escort them. She really did. His interruption of what they'd been edging toward in public was probably for the best.

She contorted her face into some facsimile of a smile for him. He and Peetah Pearl had come here for *them.* His presence due to the fact that his climbing abilities were not up to par with the best climbers of the Tempeh Tu. The most elite climbers were in Soonayah, preparing to go back with Eh'kotah to the Dayea mountains. It wasn't his fault, she didn't feel particularly charitable toward him for his interruption. *It was just...horrible timing. I may be easily excited, but will I ever be alone with the Kala...with Torhvald without someone blocking us? Ever able to make a decision as to whether I want to explore more with him or not?*

Torhvald groaned too, but outfitted every guard with scabbards and hilts, anyway. Unlike his customized one, theirs required practice maneuvers until they found those best fitted. He versed guard after guard on the hand movements needed inside the hilts to eject retractable rapiers and fire the lasers, imposing none of his exasperation on the hapless fellows. How were they to know that they conscientiousness was like gnats on an eland beast's behind. All the same, the frustration shared between him and her was a miserable thing.

Tierney chose a small one of the weapons Tohrvald offered too. He told her, "It's called a cutlass." She jousted at Ad'rihl with it, practicing on the feel of the cutlass after he and Haarth outfitted themselves with weapons as well. *I shall take this excess energy out on Ad'rihl, the muskox ass, for what it's worth. That's far better than nothing with all my frustrations still churning inside.*

"Come now." Torhvald gestured to everybody. "We must ask Mlai for proper facilities for me to give you further instructions on firing the cutlasses once we arrive in Lorgr. Notice just came in. Our flying razor is ready for launch."

Perfect! Because, of course, launching was the worst thing on Telluric. Under normal circumstances, no one could ever say they imagined Tierney happy to step down from a flying razor onto a launchpad atop one of the largest inner-peaks of geological structures in the world.

The flying razor slung them from the Kalameshee launch rocket-fast until it pinned them to their seats. With Tierney's cheeks flattened out and jiggling from the force, it then shot them across the Rocky Gorge canyon, over peak upon inhabited peak of Lorgr. The flying razor's planting made Tierney laugh, spontaneously. Actually, she *was* happy to be on solid ground, even though it was a Logren peak hundreds and thousands of fathoms stretched toward the sky.

When they were finally caught and decelerated to touch down, she did good. She didn't vomit right at the feet of her brother, Ad'rihl who was snickering in her ear. The science junkie that he was, he goggled at everything around them, but didn't forget to pound her back where she stooped to catch her breath. It was good his short attention span was taken by the scenes of Lorgr, because with a rough nudge, he went on past her thankfully, though still cackling, and asked, "Do you think you shall be steady enough after you empty your sick belly? Or shall I run and alert Milly to bring their medics to you at speed?"

The muskox ass. Why did Mother insist on sending him here with us, anyway? Ad'rihl's insensitivity deserved nothing but her back. She gave it to him, mustering her breaths and still heaving while Torhvald's palms rubbed her shoulders. The elastic she had for legs would hold her up, even if she had to use Bak'rah as a living brace. The last thing Ad'rihl needed was more fodder to laugh at her about.

Bak'rah and Tohrvald helped her bustle along in hopes a brisk pace would cause a breeze and cool her sweltering skin.

And in addition to dealing with her body's reactions to the conditions here, walking atop the launchpad turned out to be a bit weird too. The turf that their footfalls landed on had a bouncy nature that cushioned their steps. Tierney steadied herself with her hand on Bak'rah. Flying razors big and small, whizzing everywhere were the custom also, it appeared. *I hope these pathways are regulated and secure.* Every now and then one of the razors would cause all of them, except Mlai to duck. Are they so confident in their processes they'd let the razors come close enough to blow a person's hair? *I can't say I trust it much.* They edged to the outside of the razors and sidled in between Haarth and Mlai at a net *simulated by light. It was amazing!* The violet repellent buzzed as they touched it.

With their feet squarely planted at the edge of the launchpad while they pushed and prodded at the net, Peetah Pearl and some Tempeh Tu guards tested if it had weaknesses.

"Oh wow. *They were actually trying to figure out a foreign technology. This is actually happening. I'm here! Experiencing another land. And finally experiencing a portion of my dreams too, my dreams to see a million different things like this.* Tierney's attention stretched a piece beyond *the Tempeh Tu's* doubt of the protection across vast canyons of Lorgren landscape, her first mind being to absorb everything.

As far as sight traveled, spires of geological structures were lit up and connected with bridges and looped walking platforms. Flying apparatuses dashed from one peak's launchpad to another. Arrowed shuttles moved along too. The shuttles crawled connected cables, scuttled inside the peaks, then dropped. Shuttles outside the peaks fell down hills from the spires of the peaks all the way to their bases. Tierney tracked them as deep as her eyes could follow. The Lorgren people went about their eve, as these wonders to Tierney and company were common life for *them.*

Torhvald's ignorance of my land was pathetic. But mine of this land and his is no better.

Their planet, so rich and enhanced by its inhabitants, had done its job well. Telluric was severe in its segregation. Every land afraid of losing something to another. These practices of limiting exposure to one another disadvantaged everybody. No ordinary foreigner was familiar with any other land's everyday life. *It was far past time the newer generations of Telluricians came up with customs for better relations.* "We're all missing out on the best of our planet." *Its people.*

After jogging several paces backward, Mlai took a running leap forward on legs moving so fast she whooshed Tierney's hair like one of the razors as she passed. She sprung herself high onto the simulated net. Its illumination sizzled at the impact and the net bent with Mlai's slight weight and bounced her back to the ground.

A picture of zeal, Mlai exploded into laughter. "I haven't behaved with such antics since my youth with my friend Gymein. The sensory detector net won't falter," she told Peetah Pearl and the guards still testing it. "It gives just enough, captures any object breaking the plain off the edge of the launchpad, then bounces it right back to its hovering state."

Then what was the net conceived of? How could it be there and not be there? Another technology to make note of. Lorgr's desire for more umbereen could possibly be exchanged for some of the technology they had. They had a prowess for advancement, it seemed. Mlai hopped to Ad'rihl, grabbed his arm, and pulled him to walk ahead with her. "You teasing your sister so can only lead to her having a great comeuppance on you one day." She glanced back at everyone else. With Tierney, she shared a sly smile and gestured for the rest of them to follow along. "Come inside the peak, now. The High Council has summoned me."

As they all trailed Mlai and Ad'rihl, Tierney hesitated at the back. When had those two had time to get to know each other so well? "Hmm..." The curious material under their feet created a bouncy little rhythm as she mulled over this new Mlai and Ad'rihl novelty. "It was... quite a bit troubling, really." Mlai lifted one of Ad'rihl's plaits, testing its feel over her hand, and Ad'rihl appeared inclined to appreciate the attention. He also charmed women as sport. Mlai on the other hand was sweet and guileless. A horrible combination for deeper involvement.

Mlai walked them inward, away from the edge of the launchpad and the razors, and Tierney breathed her first breath free of constriction since they'd planted on Lorgr. She may need to talk to her new friend. Ad'rihl was her brother. She loved him. *But I wouldn't recommend him for a relationship with a man-eating veryum.* Though he'd deserve it, he'd probably end up with the veryum pining and crying after him too. The consequence in which she'd seen so many of his conquests end.

Something dangled in her periphery, and her attention was pulled away from Adrihl and Mlai's amusements with each other toward more pressing worries. The place was filled with enough of them everywhere you turned. *Look at all these precarious modes of transport Lorgr uses amongst its peaks.* "Mlai? I hope transport in one of those boxes strung on cable is not where we're heading."

Upright hair bobbing, Mlai shook her head. "For now, we stay on this mainstay inner-peak. It houses Logren patricians. Flying apparatuses are the only transports given security permissions to plant here."

Tierney breathed. *Trailing along flimsy wire negated,* happy now she wouldn't kill her brother. He'd no doubt succumb to an apoplectic fit in laughter at her rocking like a ship in a storm on one of those shuttles.

Also, she was relieved that a mode of travel worse than flight wasn't required of her, so their walk on top of the peak was a cinch. If you didn't think about being high enough to touch the heavens and that a flying razor could flip you off the edge at any moment. Her fears could get the better of her sometimes, it was best to concentrate on where they were going.

They climbed several steps that circled them landing onto a platform. A glass globe whisked up and covered them and then the platform dropped. The more fathoms within the peak they fell, the more Mlai's features sobered, transforming right before them from the amiable Mlai to a calmly resigned imitation of the Mlai they'd come to know. Her vibrancy shut away. And it sent a sense of how this first meeting with the Lorgren High Council might go as a pall throughout their group.

When they got there, more than a hundred Lorgrens had arranged themselves in a widening triangular semi-circle and waited for their arrival into an assembly. The deliberate arrangement portrayed a significance of more than symmetric aesthetics too. The Lorgrens occupying the highest number of the semi-circled seats—at the last level, the furthest up—possessed the least amount of clout. It was obvious who those few in the front were. The true decision-makers.

Tierney's eyes roamed the pinkish beings populating the vast space. *How different they all were, but then how so alike.*

Greyed marble in the stark room paid no resemblance to the warmth exuded by the tapestried halls of the Keep, but the hairs on the back of Tierney's neck stood up. Innumerable empty balconette seats beyond the last of the Lorgren High Council and dark shadows thrown onto the drab grey reminded Tierney of their Hall of Covenance back home. The darkened Hall of Covenance, that is.

When the hall's lights were lowered, with the chornyne stone revealing only moonlight, the room gave off an unnerving strangeness just like this. Tierney shivered, a rush of goose bumps pebbled her arms. No wonder she'd never liked hiding amongst the shadows in the Hall. This room's presence forebode for Tierney a dull kind of peculiarity. An omen that the Lorgren people possessed depths hidden that she hadn't given them credit for.

"Meloy!" The same male Lorgren from their earlier communication spoke first, from a sixth-row seat. Evidently, his High Council clout didn't warrant the first row. "You returned. Your disobedience might just be ignored if you have adequate results from your curative."

Stepping forward to the front of their party, Mlai faced the High Council. "I have chosen my name—Mlai, as is my due." The clang of Mlai's voice, normally quirky, had strength enough now so that those at the highest levels could hear her. "It has only changed a little. I ask if you will please refer to me by it going forth."

"The change of one's name goes along with the change of one's sex. Corsene indulges your self-opinion so much, you forget yourself." The male Lorgren sent a look filled with acid toward Corsene.

Mlai's mother sat center-front, first row.

And her reaction was no reaction. She dignified the male's comment, not at all, which seemed to only make the male Lorgren's face fold further. Her eyes were eating up Mlai's flourishing appearance. Corsene stood from her seat and came down and hugged her daughter. She petted her face and ran her hands all over Mlai, with a check here, testing her muscles there, plumping her back in certain spots, getting a general consensus of her overall well being. An urgency in their second embrace was a testament to their relief at seeing each other. The droll male Lorgren's voice broke into the moment they were having. "Also, we appreciate that the Soonahyins sent a whole contingent as escorts for you. But you're here now. Send them back to their transport. Then you must report to the bay of medics so testing on your recovery can begin."

Mlai spun around to face Tierney, her eyes wide—pleading for something from Tierney that Tierney wasn't sure she knew what it was, let alone, how to deliver it—as Mlai said, "The Soonahyins have never been to Lorgr." The depths of that amethyst stuck on Tierney while she responded to the High Council. Tierney'd never seen them like that before. Panicked. She hadn't *panicked* when she was dying. "Our courtesy must extend a welcome. A true visit as they didn't hesitate in welcoming me." She'd prevaricated only a little. Haarth's hesitancy with her in the beginning had softened the more exposed he'd gotten to her nature. "Their sending members of their royal family warrants an offer of refreshment and accommodations instead of a quick return home."

This stirred the High Council. Corsene went back and stood at her seat. The others of the first row took their cue from her and stood too. They murmured amongst themselves for some moments. "We're remiss in our greeting. Members of the royal family are here?" Haarth, Ad'rihl, and Tierney edged forward. "Please accept our apologies for our poor reception. Accommodations shall be made for all of you," Corsene said.

Mlai turned back to the Lorgren male who had done most of the talking. "I shall escort them to their suites first, then report to the bay of medics. But rest assured, Father, I haven't forgotten myself so thoroughly that I don't remember what's important to Lorgr."

***

"That was your *father*?" At a stand of windows that stretched as high as the level of the peak they were on, Tierney had come and joined Mlai outside the High Council in the corridor, and was glad to escape the oppressive atmosphere of the assembly. From this viewpoint, many of the other peaks could be peered into through their windows. Logrens with busy lives inside them were going hither and yon.

Mlai puffed out her cheeks and grunted. "To match a babe with parents from the lots doesn't require the High Council to have good taste."

It was understandable the subject of her father wasn't a good one for Mlai after the display he'd just put on. Tierney looked to the activity outside the windows for inspiration as to what to talk to her about. "We must be at the base of the peak? I can see people milling about down there at the bottom of the crater. "

"No, we're not that deep. The bottoms of all the peaks are for reinforcement. They only hold machinery and maintenance bays." Mlai raised her arm and consulted some messaging she could see through her skin. "Come. I'll show you your accommodations before they finish their discussions in there. I don't want to be caught up in assembly traffic when they let out."

"Mlai, we didn't intend to stay long." While they traveled back up under the globed platform, Tierney thought it best to give Mlai a heads-up.

Mlai kept her head bent to her arm, but her hair flapped up and down in understanding. Look!" She showed Tierney the light displayed on her skin. "I've been assigned a suite near you in this peak too."

"But didn't you already have your own suite before you left?"

"Yes, but Lorgren patricians change their residences routinely as a security measure. And mine, I'm sure, was assigned to someone else when I left. Besides, they had no idea when I would return."

Or if you'd return. No reason to waste a good room waiting for you. Apparently, the Lorgrens were a ruthless lot in their practice of efficiency.

Mlai showed them their accommodations and announced, "The whole level is yours for your stay."

Before she turned away, Tierney caught hold of her. "Mlai, you've only just arrived. Give yourself time before you're prodded and poked by those medics."

For the first time since Tierney met Mlai, her smile didn't reach her eyes. When she shook her head, even her hair didn't bob with its usual vibrancy. "I must go now, Tierney. Complying may be the only thing staving off further disciplinary actions against me."

Chapter 31

Regardless of Tierney offering no real defense for Mlai from the threat—*they were her own people after all*—they hadn't left Lorgr.

It was just that that look... Mlai's look of desperation had been directed at me in front of the High Council assembly.

Protectiveness over Mlai weighed Tierney's heart and compromised her ability to make a detached decision. *I can't rid myself of it.* So, they remained in Lorgr days and days past what she'd thought they would.

To her credit, Mlai made valiant efforts to keep them occupied while they were there. Duly, the examinations measuring the effects of her curative took their toll. The Lorgrens would deliver her to her suite in the company of her friend Gymein after she underwent rounds of tests, allowing her some time for recovery. Then the next schedule of rounds began. When Mlai awakened, she insisted on showing them features of her land, though she'd fall asleep in the corners when they left her by herself too long.

One of the first ventures she convinced Tierney to partake in? *The worst.* A long trawl of connected cables through the peaks of Lorgr. Tierney subjected herself to the shuttle—*an horrendous mode of travel*—in hopes her going along would lighten some of what Mlai was going through.

A sick belly and flushed skin weren't conditions only consigned to her flight over foreign lands either. The temperate climates of said lands affected all the Soonahyins. Everybody was sick. They took to shedding themselves of layers of clothing, wearing only their underlayer, and procured piles of the lighter Lorgren tunics. Which they changed regularly because they soaked them through.

They set off on one of their first Mlai-sponsored ventures and Tierney was without Bak'rah again. Her sweet pup couldn't go. In Soonayah Tierney held sway. He was tolerated because she insisted. Here, his presence was seen as nothing less than a menace. Her usual object of emotional support denied to her? Sitting right up next to Torhvald, clutching his thigh from the moment they set off hanging by mere *twine* was her support now. He'd squeeze her and rub his hand over hers every once and a while for reassurance.

He and she had been inseparable since they'd gotten to Lorgr. They had such a magnetism for each other that whenever she looked about they would unerringly find one another, their eyes connecting. He studied everyone of course, but his attention to her had her blossoming under his scrutiny. He was always helpful too. It was second nature to him it seemed, and he was always helping out their party. Without the food-tasters there, once he'd tested her food himself and had put shockingly cold slurpie ice on her lips and sucked it off. That was the kind of helpfulness reserved just for *her*.

Now, her skin sweltered at the touch of his. Kalameshee heat emanated off him and through his clothing like he was a furnace. Only she liked it as it settled her some. Of course, she couldn't stop the rocking and the tapping of her foot too. *We're suspended fathoms and fathoms above the ground!* She had to be comforted.

Over-the-way, the indomitable Haarth was as affected by the temperature as much as everybody else as well. Beads of sweat rolled down his temples. At least he stood clear to the other side of the shuttle. She couldn't stand to be near him here in Lorgr. Her inconsistent control of the introspection plaguing her caused her new environment to have a stronger effect on her, she was sure of it.

And Haarth affected with elevated energy levels? Close to me? Excruciating!

Look at him. Correction. Her *father*...Haarth. Tierney had brooded, studying him when his attention was elsewhere since they'd been here. Trying to bore into his psyche, her intent was to figure him out to some degree, and the crux of it was that he was indecipherable. As soon as she'd said she was past communicating over distance and ready to meet; no hesitation, he'd agreed. Excommunicated or not, he'd come. And that was before he'd known he was her father. Before their physical reaction to each other had put questions in both their minds.

She rolled the sound of his title around her mouth. "Father. Fa-ther. Fa...*ther.*" *Still foreign on the tongue like getting used to saying Tohrvald.*

He'd negotiated across the length of Soonayah in a blizzard with reassuring Tierney and supporting her as his only objective. And they'd been just uncle and niece then. She squinted in reflection. How long ago that hapless journey to Outliers seemed, and look at them, well past their borders now. Being committed to a sanctum not hanging over her head. She'd gone from searching for a way to outrun her mother's edicts to needing to remember how to interact with a father in the blink of an eye. In another land, mind you. She hadn't gotten used to the thought of Haarth as her father before they'd needed to come here.

A whole Soonahyin party in Lorgr. *Hanging by mere wires, not so negated as I'd wished. At least I tackled this and didn't come up with a reason to blame Mother like I've done in every other important decision in my life. A first.* That was one accomplishment to tick off as she negotiated this new father thing.

While she ruminated, their shuttle swooped between the current two peaks, making her shudder. "I had no idea these things could move this fast." Her body knew it plenty well. Torhvald was rocking *with* her now.

"No stops for the last few peaks," Mlai's friend Gymein told them. With what they had come to understand as his usual expressive nature, his cheekbones became winged in red every time he spoke. Hands flipping this way and that scored every other word. The Lorgren hairstyle for him started at the crown of his head and shaped to one side. He'd slicked it over in a swoopy fashion that framed his pink features, depicting him as a young man with a quite pretty face, in distinct contrast to the black, utilitarian garments all the Lorgrens wore.

They clanged onto some mechanical device off the cables. It took them into the newly arrived peak, lowering them, much to Tierney's relief. Unfortunately, her relief was short-lived because once it stopped its descent amongst the pedestrians inside the peak, they were pushed onto the outside again. Tierney pincered Torhvald's thigh and screamed as they fell along the peak and leveled out within the very basin of the Lorgren crater.

Of course, Ad'rihl relishes experiencing regular transport as a thrill ride. She rolled her eyes at Mlai's encouragement in his laughter, her pink fingers patting his shoulder. Too tickled by the shuttle's plunge, Ad'rihl was missing the basin.

Their shuttle trundled amid the center of some Lorgren workers. Gymein pointed them out, all styled in yellow jumpsuits and hard-shelled hats with masks attached. Some of the pink faces behind the masks looked at them with their mouths open. Others stopped their work and waved at them. Their party's ethnicities were probably as shocking to them as a trawl through the Lorgren crater was to most inside the shuttle. Tierney asked, "Why do they wear protective gear? Do we risk ourselves down here?"

Gymein, readily acting as an impromptu guide for them, had recall like that of an AI recording. He answered, "We're not at risk because we're only tracking straight through and the shuttles have filtering systems. No one can stay in the basin longer than short installments of time."

"Then why must they wear gear to protect themselves if they don't stay long either?"

The young Lorgren regarded her with eyes that had become as familiar as the day. The exaggerated femininity wasn't there, but Mlai-like they were, nonetheless. Differences between every Lorgren were distinct. Each person's face was their own. The trick was them fostering a projection of uniformity onto the outside world, when in reality—from the styling of the patches of their hair to nuances of the shading in the pink of their skin—they weren't the same. Their bodies varied in size and height, though all slim, like the variances in opinions on the order of their ways. They didn't all believe the same either.

Gymein jested and took joy in just about everything. His sociable nature and Mlai's guilelessness were natural attractants. Traits that made it apparent why he and Mlai were friends. In turn, he attached himself to *them*. Mlai's new protective friends were *his* new friends. He favored them with his knowledge and offered them answers for every question they had. "Unlike the Drundel with their natural filters leading from their nostrils, which lets them spend most of their lives underground, Lorgrens are sensitive to the particles filling the basin. This land created by the Million Starfall Landing is what was allotted to us. This is how we must contend with it," he said.

"But why haven't you reinforced the basin for use instead of the peaks and leveled the peaks, raised your land levels, and given yourself more space?"

Tierney peered up at him. Gymein petted her head like he was rewarding her for winning the day's lesson. Her brother *would* snicker at that. He waved his arm toward the windows of the shuttle. "The workers you see out there are even now engaged in our long-lived pursuit of ground engineering. Lorgr's ceaseless mission since this land became our allotment. Some parts of our land's grounds have been raised, just not all. It's not as easy you may expect."

The subject captured Ad'rihl's attention, and his eyes lit. He opened his mouth to comment just as the shuttle clanged again, signaling a change.

Another one? Great!

They rode the bank of another spire made from craggy rock that had been reinforced with circuited trusses that rigidified it. Gymein informed them that no peak in Lorgr had ever broken apart and collapsed since they'd all been reinforced. There was quite a different kind of beauty down here in the basin of geological structures with the view of the connections and so much activity up top. The vantage point of the crater magnified veins of tinseled striations in the rock on the bottom levels that had no windows in them.

Perusing spire after spire, the veins in the rock winked at them. The spires of the peaks crowded the skies with their crowns of light and movement of people traveling the courses up top. They continued their cycle of dropping from the spires, being *amongst* the movement of light, and climbing up from the rock encrusted with tinseled striations for most of the day. Environs of being enclosed by the peaks wove around them, and sparkled in the periphery as they were covered overtop by cities of light. "My goodness! This is so beautiful." Other shuttles, on less leisurely tours, most likely conveying their riders to needed destinations, whooshed past them. Lorgrens inside stood and sat and watched scenes that flashed over walls used as monitors.

Minding their business, some of them did wave, as both shuttles were covered by the darker atmosphere down here in the basin with light racing past. It was quite the experience.

Once they finished their shuttle trek, they returned to their accommodation peak, starry-eyed and exhausted at the same time if that was possible. They laughed about their stomachs' drops as they'd descended the spires as if they were held up by nothing.

A commotion—shoving, and grunts, kicked up a ruckus in the corridor outside their suites. Just over the way. A few doors beyond their loud rollicking thunder clouds rolled in.

Tierney pulled Torhvald with her and worked her way toward a fray where Gymein tussled with two Lorgrens in official looking green uniforms, who were holding onto Mlai's arms. He clutched at one of the hands holding Mlai, and the uniformed Lorgren jerked Mlai's arm. Then Gymein lost his balance and hit the floor hard.

"What's happening here!" Tierney asked.

"They're taking her for more procedures in the same day." Gymein's eyes, radiating more than physical pain, bored into Tierney's. "She's been weaker this time, I could see it. So we ignored them summoning her throughout the day." He favored his arm and acted as if it had been hurt, but raised himself from the floor using the other one. "She needs a real recovery. They won't be satisfied until they kill her because she refuses to change who she is!"

"Gymein! Be calm. I know what's being asked of me," Mlai said.

Ad'rihl edged forward, eyeing the positions of the hands the uniformed Lorgrens had on Mlai's person. *Oh...kay. This has all the hallmarks of deteriorating into free-for-all if someone doesn't do something.* Tierney thought quickly to skirt in front of her brother and blocked him from moving on the Lorgrens. Haarth's cool stroll to a shoulder-to-shoulder stance with her and Torhvald placed him between the Lorgrens and the rest of their party too. He clearly recognized that they couldn't afford an incident while in a foreign land. So did she.

Ad'rihl's too-high soul-energy seethed off *him* in waves. Peetah Pearl's and the Tempeh Tu's and everybody else's ratcheted up the clouds stuffing the air with opposing forces in the hallway. "Soonahyins can't sit idly by while you're being treated this way, Mlai," Tierney said. Dozens of eyes gauged the situation for any tactical advantage they could take.

"Please be calm. I know what I'm doing. I choose to go. It's for the good of all Lorgr."

"Remove your hands from her," Ad'rihl told the two uniforms. One of them smirked and yanked Mlai's arm with said hand again. *Oh great. What did he do that for?*

A chop whizzed past Tierney and caught the uniform's arm at the elbow. The arm loosed, hanging uselessly at his side. Unfortunately for him, he had another one. He struck out at Ad'rihl with it. Ad'rihl swooped out of the way and twisted the bad arm. "Ahg!" the uniform cried.

He was then removed completely from Mlai, the arm used to flip him, whether he tried to fight back or not. Presumably, he had some kind of training as a guard. It was futile though. Ad'rihl on a tear was nearly undefeatable for anyone outside Soonayah. The guard's struggle with Ad'rihl only made her brother more agile. The flip landed the guard on his head against the wall. Uniform Two shifted, and so did all the Tempeh Tu to fighting stance. His eyes stretched to the point that Tierney nearly laughed.

But this was so not funny.

Again, Haarth walked between the fracas, as cool as ever. Mlai snatched from the Lorgren manacling her when she saw Ad'rihl about to take issue with the other one's hands still on her. She went to Gymein and touched his cheek. "Be calm. My return shall be quick enough. See to our guests for me." She turned from them all then and walked ahead of the manacling Lorgrens in her own stead.

Chapter 32

The exquisite atmosphere—a sack-styled pallet fitted into a hanging bed, they'd brought in trying to suit a Soonahyin's tastes, the cooler in the floor filled with alkaline drink, temperatures turned to icy levels—that the Logrens had afforded them in Tierney's suite likened itself to a balmy pit after that tussle up in the hallway. Haarth cautioned her, "Calm down. You're not fit in this state to make reasonable judgments. Not only is this climate keeping our energy levels too high, but a nasty moment in a corridor doesn't give us authority to intervene in their foreign affairs."

He was right, of course. And just full of good rationale.

Only, he paced non-stop far from her elevated energy on the other side of the room. Still, he affected her and in turn, she set Bak'rah off. Haarth was in no better condition than she. They should both go find some activity to release some energy and put Bak'rah out of his misery.

She hated to admit it, but Ad'rihl was smarter than either of them. He'd taken off to walk the looped trails away from any proximity to possible irreparable damages. He'd realized he'd done enough already. *A bit late with that revelation if you ask me.* And but for the curiosity of something Gymein had said earlier she would have gone with him.

A cackle Tierney held on the verge of a tempest escaped from inside her. Her control was a joke. Her hands shook. Panting riding along with her soul-energy pulsing the cords of her neck was a bad state to be in and be forced to deal with people who didn't know her well. Gymein and Torhvald cut their eyes at her. And who could blame them? The young Lorgren'd had no reason to fear them...up until now. Tierney only hoped she wasn't frightening him too badly. Except, if she didn't get relief soon, she was going to start frightening herself.

On impulse, she approached Gymein and pulled his hand from his mouth gently. It was smeared with pink blood he'd drawn from its fingertips with his gnawing teeth. "She will return as she said, you know." The reassurance was meant for him, and for her too. For it ticked at the grain of trust, the standard a land should warrant in its inhabitants.

Gymein said, "I know she will, but in what condition? A little foreign intervention might just make the High Council less casual with an individual's freedoms."

"What freedoms, Gymein? You spoke earlier of them wanting to change who she is. What did you mean?

"It's not for me to tell Mlai's story. Just know all Lorgrens are born androgyne and they let parents choose girls too often in the lots in past times. They're desperate for more males." He rose to leave the suite, his gait slow, his demeanor changed to the exact opposite of what they'd come to expect of him. The pink in his skin actually dulled. A state that seemed impossible after being around the Lorgrens for a time. Huge holes in his face were supposed to be his eyes and drama oozed from him on his pivot back toward them. "Our physiology can be forced to change our sex, eggs and reproductive cells included until late in our development."

You're jesting, right?

For all things proper, please tell me I heard him wrong. There was no way that could be right. Tierney stared, unseeing at the door after Gymein left that bile of a suggestion fuming the air. Lighting, they'd been informed, calibrated to help a Soonahyin's skin cool washed a patina of luster over pure putridness. This place couldn't tout exceptionalism. Everything here, everything good—their advanced technology, congenial people, wonders of sites and spires had to be weighed against their authoritarianism over their people. And it didn't come close. Their brand of governance tainted everything.

Blinking rapidly at tears crowding her eyes turned to a flinch when a surge of heat came near her side. *Haarth, getting ready to make some point again. I wish he would just go away. You would think I could have a few moments alone.* His advice was beginning to wear on her. For he wouldn't relent on giving it to her. "Reserve your tears for Mlai to tell her own story. We don't know if what he said is her circumstance," he said. The whimpering was starting to irritate her too, Bak'rah slinking over. *The poor pup.* He tried to comfort her with a nuzzle with his snout to no avail. It was Haarth who caught the tear that escaped onto her cheek. Then he left her suite too, his shoulders tight, his fingers worrying his plaits with his own disquiet.

"Let me help you cool your spirits, Tierney."

"Oh." The breach in the silence caused the room to go out of focus, flipped to an alternate place where she wasn't overloaded, wasn't on the verge of doing something that worked against her...again, where people just let her be, then all of a sudden, it flipped back to now. *Torvhald.* She sighed. One day she might flip into that place and not be able to come out of it for a while. Might be for the best. All she wanted now was a few moments alone to settle a mind disturbed and worrying the trauma of forced sex reassignments over and over. She needed quiet. Even Bak'rah's presence was irritating her. Who wouldn't need some solace with the last events that'd taken place? She had almost forgotten Tohrvald was there and was a witness to her distress. Mlai's mistreatment. Her brother's ferocity.

He wasn't just a witness though, was he? A participant as well. He sensed how they felt. Did he feel anything for himself? "Do you—"

He placed a finger over her lips and stopped her question and probably the refusal he expected was coming. "Come. Please. Let me tend you. Your energy levels will give you no peace if you don't do something."

Her eyes skimmed the contours of his back and drifted over the nubby spine extrusions she'd itched to get her hands on again, as she allowed herself to be led to her bedchamber. This could only lead to one thing once they were near a bed. Was she ready for that? Was her mind even stable enough to handle that?

Torhvald closed the door on Bak'rah's nosing his way in. "Some of the Tempeh Tu have been using a cooling solution given to them by the Lorgrens. I scrounged some for you."

The brothers aren't here to block any of your possibilities with Torhvald now, she thought wrapping her arms around her middle and rocking a little. *No one is here to block what's happening like you said you wanted.* For the first time, how far she went with a man was up to her...at last. "Nothing sounds more sublime. You're quite kind, for a spoiled Kalameshee prince." She tittered. Then a scowl came on, another thought occurring, a *change* in her thought processes really that took shape right then. *My brothers are my crutch!* She'd used them as much as she had her mother to avoid making critical decisions for herself. *Looks like I really should consider getting to that sanctum for some counseling when I get back.* "Uhm. Maybe I should put it on myself?"

"No. Please let me do this for you," he said. The green in his eyes like flowering grasses met her soulful browns for several moments, they twined together with the possibilities before them. Here, in Lorgr what they could do with each other was limited only by her inner-waffling. *Her* insecurities.

"I need a few moments," she told him and went and made use of the privy chamber, hands shaking as she cleansed her body. Her heartbeat tripled within the cords of her neck. There was nothing for it. This was decision-making time.

Was she content to hide behind the line of her brothers? Safe. Begrudged from true ownership of her life. Or was times up for that cowardice? Was she ready to be the woman she claimed she wanted to be? Look at Mlai and her people, barely able to make any decisions for themselves. *And I find family members to take cover behind rather than make simple decisions on my own.* She took some breaths from the bottom of her belly, finished her feminine ablutions, then returned to the bedchamber wearing a short dressing wrap. If she delayed any longer, she would lose the nerve to let him see her. Not just her body either. Soonahyins often wore little in front of each other. They were not a shameful people. No. The nerve-loss would manifest in not letting him see her true desires. *Hideaway Tierney is what I should've been calling myself all this time..*

Torhvald's breath caught, echoing in the silence, but he retained some decorum. He averted his eyes and directed her to lay across the bed. Tierney did it with little fuss. Her body hummed with its unleashed soul-energy. The engorged cords on her neck struck her nervous system, paining her with the beat of her own pulse. Her thoughts lessened some from Lorgren abuse. If he could help her calm herself, she would let him. Besides, there wasn't much chance she would hear from Mlai this eve. Her routine was to collapse in her suite after the tests were done pushing her beyond what was good.

This was the best diversion Tierney had. So she watched as Torhvald submerged his hands into a vat of mucky solution, then slathered it on her arm. The gelatinous sludge dripped under her armpit beneath where she lay. "Eek! The Lorgren's use of this sack bedding is odd. But with your slathering that...muck, at least its covering's instant-drying comes to good use." The coverings had a textured smoothness to them. Once he was done maybe they'd still be intact.

"Umpf…" Touching at her thighs garnered bone-numbing compliance from her. He never took his eyes off his task. His removal of her wrap gave him access to all parts of her. Evidently, this required every bit of his concentration. The heat from his Kalameshee hands broke just the surface of the cooling function of the muck, giving Tierney a dual experience as he slathered her near the heart of her womanhood. Arousal pooled in her body like liquid fire.

Scents. Woodsmoke. Evocative. Hazed her nostrils, joining the provocation of hands caressing the swollen cords of her neck, rubbing her thighs, enveloping her senses, taking her away from everything but what he was doing to her. *Good.* Tierney brought his hand, rough-hewn, evidence of his physicality, to her lips and kissed his palm. Kissed his other palm too, muck and all. It had dried some quickly. Then she pulled his head down and their lips meshed as one. *Thank goodness! Finally!*

The foray into no return was instantaneous. He had just explored the surface of her body. His hands now explored her intimately. Any last reticence Tierney had melted away as his thick fingers sank into her already wet core and molded her breasts at the same time. The kissing never stopped. Their familiarity with each other's mouths made kissing a luscious orgy of tongues and lips. Tierney didn't ever want to stop kissing him, but she pulled her mouth from his because the hand at her breasts ignored her stinging nipples. "Please touch me." She attempted to move his hand, but he shook his head.

He still had a little dampness from the cooling liquid on his fingers. He placed his lips on one of her nipples instead. And that was all it took. She bucked furiously against the hand between her thighs within moments of him giving her the attention she craved at her breasts. His mouth tugged at her nipples at the same time as his manipulation of her clitoris with his hot fingers covered in the cool liquid bombarded her every pore. *He's driving me mad!* Tierney made an urgent grab for his wrist and held his hand against her as she grinded her hips, desperate in chasing after the climax her body raced for.

And Torhvald didn't disappoint. He slid several digits of heat inside her, massaging her passage that was slippery from his ministrations. The contractions of her body shot off, legs clenched around his hand and she reached for him, clutching at his muscles. *Why does he still have his clothes on?* Her nails snagged his tunic as he raised himself and kissed lips that were sobbing.

"You taste so good," he said. "I want more of you."

"Don't leave me."

"I wouldn't dare. I must cleanse the liquid from my hands though. I forgot myself. I should never have used it inside you." He moved to his knees, yet Tierney wouldn't let him go. She thrashed her head from side to side. He had too many clothes on. She couldn't think straight after that orgasm. Torhvald eased back in and sank into a sumptuousness of plush lips and plump curves. "I promise I'll be *right* back."

Her voraciousness had him laughing—dragging at him until she pulled the shirt from his body as he moved off the bed. But he returned at speed after he'd taken a cleansing cloth to his hands. He brought one back with him to the bed and settled between her thighs, and cleaned the excess liquid from her womanly folds.

Once he finished exciting her again with the cloth's abrasion on tissues already sensitized to the touch, he replaced the cloth with his tongue. Tierney's hips raised against his mouth. He'd made her so responsive there, an orgasm threatened even though her body was still tremulous and spongy from the last one. His hands, which practically spanned the whole width of her hips held her down against her writhing. The heat from his hot mouth devouring her sent Tierney right back to the edge. Fast. Before her orgasm rendered her senseless,

Torhvald pulled himself up and pushed into her unbelievably tight passage in the long slow joining the two of them ached for.

Tierney hadn't seen him even loosen his trews, but now he was gloriously as naked as she. How long they stared at each other? She couldn't say, but her lids lowered on a whimper as he began to pump inside her.

Full-out movement of his hips had her pulling her knees back high to accommodate his thrusts. All his skill intent on her arousal was lost. His control, gone. She simply held on as he plunged within her over and over again. His hot back now was the one sweltering with wetness. She slid her hands over his spine extrusions, down his shoulders, molding his clenching bottom. Her fingertips scrubbed through the evening growth of his beard as she placed her mouth on his ear and encouraged him. "More. Mo…"

Tierney received an excruciating domination on her body, and loved every drag and pull of it. He lifted her ankle over his shoulder and plunged so deeply into her womb spasms seized all her molecules from her head to her toes and his embedded shaft along with them. "Agh!" He shouted out his release while Tierney tried to control her keening as she continued to spasm

Wow! So that was what it was like. My body feels like its been set ablaze! An orgasm that exhausted her was still not enough to rid the excess soul-energy that had built up. If he didn't move from atop her, she might spontaneously combust. He'd started off cooling her spirit. But everything afterward had sent her soul-energy further and further into spiral. She squirmed because as she lay beneath him, she dragged in more of his heat without wanting to.

It was just too much. Sluggishly, belatedly he rolled to the other side of her—a proclamation that he was depleted. She eyed the sweat pouring from his back, little rivulets of it rolling to bead between his spine extrusions. "Are you well?"

Lids raised to half-mast over gleaming green, leered at her. He cupped her soft belly and pulled her back into contact with him. "I could be no better."

Tierney listened for some time, tucked against him until his snoring told her he slept. She gave him several more moments of rest, then removed his palm from her stomach. Unwrapping herself slowly from his heat, she breathed heavily of the effort it took to control her shudders. The tumult of the day, the heinousness, the uncontrolled dragging in of his hot energy forced her from the bed. With soft footfalls, she dressed and went to the practice range Mlai had assigned them for training with their cutlasses. She brought Bak'rah along as an assurance for him and for her. She would expend some of the soul-energy racking her body before she let loose a pulse that sent Torhvad hurtling across the room again.

Chapter 33

When Korrell showed up a few days later with a reluctance to give more detail about his trip to help Wilowah's Cordalai hamlet, it perturbed Tierney to no end. At a most opportune time, he came and joined them on their stay in Lorgr, only to say, "I have come to facilitate your return home, as mother fears you may take root soon. She sent me in case you need help being dug out."

Tierney chortled. No doubt their mother did believe they'd been transplanted to Lorgr after so long. But there hadn't been a window of opportunity in which to depart, for the High Council left no lag between Mlai's testings.

Haarth pressed on her that they'd served an honorable duty delivering Mlai safely back to her homeland. He insisted that they had no standing in Lorgr's affairs. Time after time his words had the opportunity to resonate too whenever she tried to emphasize to the Lorgrens that their treatment of Mlai was foul. Lorgr was stubborn in its ways. Mlai's mother, Corsene, usually held little sway over this either.

The obscene thing was that Mlai's father was always in the background lobbying the High Council in the other direction. *"She left against our rules and was nearly lost for what we need her for,"* he told them. Gymein professed Mlai's father influenced the High Council by persistently saying, "*We must get all the research we can from her before she runs away again.*"

All the fantasies in the world about traveling hadn't included a need for the influence to stop a people from hurting their own. Tierney searched now for the best moment to tell Mlai it was time for them to go. She just had to find the perfect opportunity to slip it in.

After Mlai's return that day, her recovery was a study in wonder. Within moments of coming from her tests, she led them on a visit to the Lorgren Observatory of the Stars. So this day...at some point she'd tell her.

Tierney was used to the Lorgrens now. They were different, but all in all, they were only people. Except, there was something changed about Mlai when you looked at her. She hated to appear to study her, but she was just shy of figuring out what it was.

Once at the observatory, the outlay of the marvel was so that it took up the whole insides of one of the most rounded peaks in Lorgr. Gymein pointed out its special hollowed design. "The schema allows the upper level of the observatory's ceiling to retract, opening a passage for study of the skies," he said. "Professional astrophysicists work up there."

The black auditorium their party visited lit after a few moments of being inside. Some of them sidled this way and others slid over the black floors deeper into shadows that way. All of them kept close to each other in a formation that would go unnoticed by most attackers. Most everybody. An instinctive and subtle V of penetration. Any group who thought to hide and wait for them in the dark would have been split in two, then flanked and overtaken with Haarth at point. Fortunate for the probable attackers, the place was empty. Soonahyins' protectionism was so inherent to them that no command was needed, no communication. Even the royals fell in line like good little warriors.

Korrell had told Tierney in a very matter-of-fact tone, "I traveled to Wilowah's hamlet, consulted with the clan, and formulated how to rid them of the snowcats with a course of action. I followed it through, then left." Tierney scooted nearer her brother in the darkness after they saw that there was no threat, intent on pulling more information from him than that sorry recollection.

Going amongst the clans of the frozen tundra held the allure of what everyone went there for: the absence of protocols and training and of *being* on guard all the time, the adventures of living close to the land, bracing oneself to receive all manner of sensory. The bleats from animals the Cordalai kept, skids constantly delivering goods between hamlets and from enclaves, smoke from the fireplaces always fired, bonfires, the hammering on the thousands of domed convertible structures called rondavels, snowcrafts cruising through, ice grazing, meals simmering in cooking jets, the smell of ice on the air that only life lived out there could bring you. She missed among so many other things too, her most favored, shedding the formalities of the Keep, skating as a means of transport rather than sport, convoys setting up, lights strung from rondavel to rondavel until permanent energy got charged up, sounds of jack-hammering for ice fishing, sights of the cultivators seeding through the ice row after row and looked forward to experiencing them again when she visited the sanctum there. *"The glory of the frozen tundra."*

Korrell was her one sibling with an affinity for natural things. Her brother took advantage of every opportunity that brought him closer to Tellurician soil. His lack of conversation about his visit was unusual, even for one so solemn as him. "How does Wilowah fare? I haven't had the chance to communicate with her since we last met."

Korrell shot her a look and said, "I can't speak for Wilowah, Tierney when I have no say in how things go for her." Why was he bothered by a question about Wilowah? It shouldn't be personal for *him*. She only asked as an opening into more details about the goings-on in the hamlet.

His eyes registered her surprise, and in turn, the lines around his mouth relaxed. "My travels take me to the frozen tundra so often, I may have let myself become too self-satisfied about it." He tweaked her nose as his response softened. "I think it's you who misses the brace of the winds of the tundra more than I. You should definitely plan a sojourn there soon." He patted her head, tousling her hair, then walked away to examine more features of the auditorium.

Everyone had spread out over the observatory, and Mlai got their attention by lifting her arm with her console erupting. She used the console as an interface with the room. Globes of planets and astrological objects bleeped into view, floated in place, and filled the space. The low lighting's intent became evident. It made their experience exclusive, ensconced within their solar system, light from the stars their guide. They walked among the celestial objects giants of their own world. Then the planets were sent rotating at Mlai's bidding and Ad'rihl asked, "Are they apace according to each planet's revolution around the sun?"

There came her signature, clamped hair bobbing, head nodding. "In a scaled adjustment for this exhibition's duration, yes."

They followed along with the movement of the planets. "How unique!" Tierney said to Mlai.

"I know. There's more though." Mlai grinned.

It was natural for Tierney to return Mlai's infectiousness. As herself again, lively and guileless, she was a delight to behold. It was in that moment that Tierney noticed her cheeks and pinpointed exactly what seemed different about her. "Your skin, Mlai! It's lost some of its pink tint." Her cheeks blushed red in happiness showed in stark relief against the fading pink of her skin. Mlai's hand flew to her face, covering the evidence of the changes. "And your hair! Is that a shadow

I see along the sides?"

The vivacity dimmed from Mlai's eyes, her once spontaneous smile curled down around the edges. Tierney bit her lip and wished the words back that brought attention to Mlai she didn't want. She came to Tierney, took her hand, and placed it against the whisper-soft hair barely there on her scalp. "You have a quick eye. I'm told many blocked apertures of my body have opened from the umbereen curative's effect. The medics say I may experience lots of changes going forth. Some I may not expect."

"And this is worth a celebration, is it not? Not the doldrums, right?"

"It is, but it's what she'll be pushed to do once she's healed far enough to their satisfaction that causes her regret," Gymein spoke into the pause Mlai let linger.

"Gymein! It is I who should speak on my affairs." The Mlai whose will drove her to take a flying apparatus over thousands of parses across foreign lands reared her spirit.

"And only *you* will. Do you understand me, Gymein?" Ad'rihl's glare matched the command he threw at Gymein. "We will respect her privacy." Ad'rihl placed a hand in a familiar way on the small of Mlai's back and ushered her away from their curiosity. "Milly, come. Continue showing us this extraordinary room."

Mlai looked back at them but put her hand in Ad'rihl's to be led away toward Korell and Haarth, who were having a spirited debate on whether the exhibit was true to scale. Korrell appeared to be losing and swiped through the planet Xern right as Mlai waved her hand over her console. They all flinched when he connected with a solid planet. Batted away, Xern bounced back and slapped Korrell on the hip. "What!" He jumped away from the contact.

Ad'rihl crowed at Korrell for getting popped, then went and tested the solidity of one of the asteroids from the asteroid belt near him himself, appraising its texture. They all touched objects, measuring the feel of them until Ad'rihl asked, "How is this possible? This asteroid feels as if it is made of real rock."

"All the celestial objects are virtual simulations designed to mimic their true makeups when transformed solid," Mlai said.

"This is the same technology as the simulated net at the launch-pad?"

"It's similar. Though, the simulated net has a sensory detector and transforms automatically when any stray flyer breaches its zone."

Exploring the many objects consumed them. The ice planet Fel froze their hands when palmed. Ad'rihl sported about, throwing hand-size moons at everyone near him, for the celestial objects to bounce back to their positions as if they were tied to elastic. Heat radiating from the sun stopped anyone from approaching it too closely. They broke down compositions of the objects they could approach with double taps on their solid forms. The configurations for the objects would then appear on them or free-floating in the air out to the side.

An en masse groan grumbled from everybody when Mlai returned the objects to their virtual simulations. She brushed off their objections and waved them to the stands on the outskirts of the room. The virtual representation of the solar system was widened until some of the objects were moved out to the stands where they were. She made Telluric the nucleus still centered down on the floor and enlarged it too.

Then turned Telluric to its other side and zoomed the exhibit in until different lands of their planet came into focus. "Ooh! Wow!" everybody exclaimed as the giant marsh trees of Pigehland burgeoning from its swamp were revealed. The land was covered with trees sought after for their wood certified as one of the hardest substances on Telluric. The weave of the trees' exposed roots was hundreds of times the size of a cruiser snowcraft with trunks twisted and raised above the mucky swampland. They were big enough to hold the largest Soonahyin homestead, even one the size of the Keep with parses and parses to spare. Pigehland—the enormous twisted jungle. The technology panned through millions of structures and buildings tucked in and the transports whisking around the tree trunks. Held aloft of the uninhabitable marshland by its warren of giant marsh tree roots, Pigehland touted its rich metropolis thriving in the harsh environment.

"Are you using the focus-scape technology you just offered Soon-ayah? Lorgr can extend it beyond this side of Telluric?" Torhvald asked. His perusal sharp over the mechanism, like he was contemplating on how to acquire it for Kalamesh too.

Mlai shook her head. "Pigehland is as far as the focus-scape can scope without all lands uploading the technology onto their portions of the alluvial shield. This is Lorgr's goal. As every land once did with the language cone so many eons ago, which enabled us all to adapt to a common language. Telluric benefits—"

Light burst through the swish of the doors, and shattered their seclusion. On a slant through the observatory's displays, two Lorgrens in similar green uniforms to those from the tussle-up in the hallway entered and treated the celestial objects like they were nonexistent. Like they were so used to them that their objective for being there was more fascinating than the objects. They announced for Mlai to accompany them for more tests. Never giving any of them a chance to object, she stood and quickly went with them.

* * *

Under enough pressure, Tierney had confidence in her ability to decimate anyone she deemed an offense. Mercilessly. With her own hands. *Don't really need this aid of a cutlass either.* Despite the fact that she'd mowed down Haarth, Torhvald, and Ad'rihl, jousting them until they were exhausted.

Korrell called, "Foul!" when they jousted endlessly.

Their cutlasses caught hold and Tierney pushed back from him. *Perfect! I wanted to get my hands on someone anyway.* She landed a whip-around kick to his chest. After he hit the floor of the practice range hard enough to rattle it, he just rested there a while.

"Come on. Get up," she taunted him as she menaced around him.

"Woest be to anyone with whom you have real grievance who makes you as angry as this." He rubbed his chest. "I can't remember the last time you put me to the ground. Any real offenders may well get their heads chopped off."

"They may well at that." The first persons' heads she pictured dislodging were the two Lorgrens who'd taken Mlai away from the captivating time they'd been having at the observatory. When you really thought about it though, Mlai's father should have been first. That fiendish Lorgren had probably directed Mlai's tortures to begin again the moment he thought she might enjoy herself too much. But on the other hand, Tierney had no great love for the whole of a Lorgren society which promoted its people to be treated in such ways. Hence her reason for demanding an all-out training session for their entire party.

'Everyone to the practice range, now!' she'd said right after the Lorgrens had taken Mlai away.

They'd become too complacent in this land. On the surface, things were amiable. The people smiled at them and welcomed their exploration from peak to peak the many shops, the administrative levels, people's assigned suites within the residential spires. They were also given tours of the bottom levels of the geological structures used as maintenance bays and reinforced with gigantic load-bearing beams that fortified the peaks' augmentation. All the while, the advantages their ways allowed them to take with their people lurked in the underbelly of the society. Lorgr was not the playgrounds it was filled with nor the uniform consensual society it presented to the outside world. Thus explained Mlai's original escape. *And we brought her back here to this...this...*

Swish. Swish. Swish. Tierney's cutlass whipped through the air. She stood ready at the forefront of the activity awaiting her next victim. Yet, Korrell didn't get up as a volunteer.

They'd used these facilities often during their stay in Lorgr. Torhvald had brought her here regularly alone to help her expend her energy, versing her on the use of the cutlass. His knack for training showed him as patient and adept with the newbies learning to use the intricate weapon. He'd told her this was one of his duties in Kalamesh. He loved working people to exhaustion and getting them up to par on self-defense. He'd often use coming behind her to position her in some way as an excuse to touch her intimately. He and she would lose track of what they were supposed to be doing and end up making love in one of the corners, behind the dividers sometimes.

Tierney's persistence in their training that day had them all proficient with the cutlasses. The memory of she and Torhvald's idyllic times here together were wrenched from her thoughts. They now contended well with Torhvald. And their jousting and smoothly switching to firing their lasers with whip-like movements all while fighting each other feverishly should expel any of their aggravated soul-energy. Notwithstanding, the fever still boiling inside Tierney. Torhvald came to her and said, "Come now, Tierney. We should go see if Mlai has returned. Or haven't you worked out enough of your grievances yet?" He meant to soothe her, she knew.

Only, the doors of the range crashed open and Gymein raced toward them, his face a crumpled mess at that exact same moment. His eyes...*his eyes* were haunted, skittering from one to the other of them. "They attempted to force a conversion on Mlai and caused a severe rejection! Corsene just let me in to see her after she'd been left in that cold medical bay. She laid there in an unconscious state for eons because they thought she had died!"

A red-hazed state-of-mind fogged Tierney's brain and shut down any awareness she had of getting back to their mainstay inner-peak. When they arrived straight at Mlai's suite they found her awake, being comforted by her mother. Corsene fretted when Mlai got up and moved about. Frankly, Tierney thought her active too soon too. "Mlai. There's no shame in showing you're hurt. Especially when your health has been compromised. Rest," Tierney said.

Mlai scurried around and gathered one personal item after another. The configuration of a suite for a Lorgren was quite different from how they'd prepared their rooms. A pedestal bed stood in one corner, tucked tightly within a hair of it's life, in linens with a metallic sheen to them in a serviceable grey color. There was little else in the room. Nothing on the walls. Mlai pushed to the side of a wall's panels that shifted back and revealed the clothing she was collecting all in muted colors, folded on shelves. A push to another side panel and she entered a smaller room that appeared as stark and as grey as this one and came back with toiletries and other personal items.

"Can't you rest and believe no harm will come to you now after they just nearly killed you?" Tierney asked.

"No." Mlai stopped her bustling and caught Tierney's arm. "I know you're preparing to tell me you must leave soon. I endured all these tests for the benefit of Lorgr. But after the liberties they just took with my life while I lay unconscious, I have no trust in my safety here." Mlai's frame trembled uncontrollably, seeming that at any moment she would fall where she stood. "They know they must *ask* the person if she's an adult. They know it! I would never have given my permission! I must leave here too. I beg you to take me with you when you go."

"Mlai!" Corsene raced to Mlai's side. "I pulled sway for your departure last time. I cannot speak on them ever allowing you re-entrance if you leave again." She grabbed Mlai's hand and made her be still. "Your father must have agreed to a conversion without my knowledge. I won't let that happen again, I promise I'll protect you."

"Mother, you should never have had to in the past and now is no different. You can't monitor all five hundred and six days of each span for every possible violation against me. And you're third seat on the High Council. The center of the capstone. I compromise you by not conforming. Lorgr can afford to lose your moderating seat on the council a million times less than it can spare my physical presence here. I promise I'll continue to send information of my recovery to our medics for further research." Mlai looked to Haarth then and said to him too, "Please allow me passage with you. And you don't have to worry that I'll stay in Soonayah. I'll travel on if I must."

"Fa...father." Tierney scrambled to Haarth. "She comes with us. If it causes an incident between our lands, then *we'll* go somewhere else more lenient. And I'm going with her to keep her safe." *Mother will just love that,* she mused, while Haarth nodded his agreement.

After a moment of pondering, his pivot to Mlai held all the authority of Soonayah he needed. "Don't concern yourself with imposing in our land. We welcome your stay in Soonayah." His accompanying hand on Corsene's arm made it apparent he meant his words as a comfort for Mlai's mother too. She'd begun to cry. Directing his next words to her, he said, "She'll be kept close and protected near the royal family."

Gymein pushed through everyone until he reached Mlai. "I'm going with you, Mlai."

"No, Gymein." Mlai shook her head. "I can't let you leave your home. They may never let me come back."

"Then it is no home to me either. They restrict me as well, you know."

"Gymein—"

"I go with you." Mlai's resistance to Gymein faded. An already wilting form, truly frail now, she rested her forehead against his. He acted as if his difficulties in their homeland were as profound as hers. More so even. Like he'd had no success in *his* defiance.

Wherever this new gamble took them, there was probably no one else who deserved more to be by her side than Gymein. He, with just as much knowledge of every nuance of their existence in Lorgr.

No sooner than that muddle was being decided, there was a burst through the doors of Mlai's father storming the room with a line of Lorgren guards trailing behind him. His eyes were stretched and searched the room frantically until he landed on Mlai. He looked spooked to see her up and alert, and gushed his breath out until every person in the room gave pause. Was that relief on his face? Surprising, considering this was his fault.

Haarth aligned the breadth of his body as a barrier between the two, daring him with his bearing to become a threat. His glower bored into Mlai's father's forehead. The Lorgren father couldn't stand face-on with Haarth. All the same, Haarth's posture taunted him to look away. His demeanor was pathetic, his glance slunk from Haarth anyway. When the Lorgren guards fanned out, Torhvald pulled Mlai behind their party, and Ad'rihl curled her close to his side, his arms wrapped around her. Tierney and Korrell led the Tempeh Tu to face off with the guards.

At the frontline, she growled a little. *Was that me?* Bak'rah had been left in her suite earlier, of course...again. The Lorgrens' cruelty had pushed her to take up the disposition he took when he was ready to kill. "Grrr..." This time Tierney snarled at them on purpose. *And I will rip them apart like he would if they come any closer too.*

"Mlai, continue to prepare for our departure," Haarth said, and never broke from his drilling of Mlai's father. "Though Lorgr has brought you near death, I will allow no harm to come to you while you're my responsibility. We leave Lorgr this night," he announced to the room.

Chapter 34

Mlai's father *did* possess some sense of shame. Although, nothing could ever redeem him, he'd crumpled before Haarth.

If you asked me, it was a little too late. Not that anyone would. I would never trust myself with Mlai's father if I got him alone.

After he'd stood by as his daughter traveled thousands of parses on the verge of death before and a confession to being coerced by other High Council members to try conversion while she was unconscious, he still did too little. The scene, them versus the Lorgrens, seethed around the edges so, it had a breath of its own. Like a continuation in pulses of successive events being ticked off by a counter—tick two or four or ten by then—a Lorgren guard lunged at Mlai who stumbled within Ad'rihl's arms.

This could end in no way but bad. Bad as only Ad'rihl can make it this bad, "bad." He'd taken on a curiously fierce protectiveness of Mlai. Her brother could flip the switch on his easy-going personality into terror-inducer in a fight.

And by tick three...or five, nine...or whatever—all the tick offs were bound to happen now—he bashed the guard on his jaw and the guard went reeling. But not before the room inhaled as if in slow motion. Somehow every occurrence that'd happened since Mlai was discovered in those woods had set this course. The guard snatched at

Mlai, causing her to fall and hit her head, rendering her unconscious again. "No!"

And then the room actually arrested.

The only voice to scream an objection surprised them coming from Mlai's father. Even with it, the rebuke didn't stop the all-out frenzy that broke loose. It couldn't have. Being a witness to this was like watching an archive recall what you already reckoned would happen.

Korrell speeded to Ad'rihl, belting blows out with him as other guards struck at Ad'rihl, and they tried to duck the pounding he was giving them. Tierney whirled to Mlai's form motionless on the floor. Like on the outside looking in, objectivity displayed this tableau as the flashpoint of the impasse—Mlai, the unassuming young woman's travel to take refuge in their land (the tick-offs had most definitely started way back then), her discovery...and curative procedure, even Tierney's insistence on accompanying her here, the Lorgrens' imitation of welcoming them and openness—all of it was the precursor for this thing that was happening now.

Tierney's sweep of the guards' legs who were getting too close to Mlai. None too soon. They'd started to pull at Mlai's limp arms while she was unconscious. Gratefully, anticipating Tierney's speeding, Torhvald got there at the same time. He pummeled more guards as she drop-kicked one of them, and eviscerated the ballocks of the one closest to Mlai before she checked on her. Haarth and the Tempeh Tu walloped through guards too. This protection of the innocent would always be worth conflict, even if they *were* in a foreign land.

The Soonahyins whirling and gamboling and springing put the Lorgrens back on their heels. Such was their way in a brawl. Soonahyins tended to act almost gleeful in putting contenders down. Able to let free the reserve finally that they normally wielded in spars and matches, they could speed and use their gifts to their heart's delight. Disappearing and reappearing at will, they caused almost all the Lorgren guards to topple around them. One's crack of his neck slumped him to the floor insensate. Pretty soon, most of them weren't getting back up.

"Stand down!" Mlai's father shouted. A scramble over the Lorgrens littering the path to his daughter got him there, where he pressed an actual *civil* hand to *Corsene's* shoulder. She had moved to Mlai's side too. Up until now since he'd entered the room, he'd looked to be dumbstruck. Was it his guilt eating at him? If it wasn't, it should've been. "Mlai?" he said the name she'd chosen as she'd asked him to in the first place, then caressed her cheek. "Mlai!" It was a little too late for him to be offering concessions *now*, wouldn't you think?

Mlai's eyes cracked open though. A young Lorgren finally receiving some conciliatory behavior would probably wake from death to take part in it. He picked her up from the floor like she was a babe. "I'm so sorry, my daughter. I've been a fool to put you at risk like this." The corners of her lips managed to curve upward. In the state she was in, that she could smile at all outdid any tremors her lips had around their edges. Those standing there parted as he made his way to Haarth, and lifted her from his arms into Haarth's care. "Please...I beg of you to do good by my daughter. All I've done, all I thought was for the good of Lorgr, has done nothing but harm her...almost killing her. And regardless of what you think of me, I never wanted her harmed. She will get no peace here no matter how I try to make things easier for her though."

Easier for her! In his convoluted reasoning, he had thought he made it easier for her? His head fell forward and when he raised his eyes they swam with tears. "I go along with what is asked of us because nothing can change Lorgr's ways. But during the course of things, I'm always there to make sure that they don't go too far...until now. I really flubbed it up this time." He grimaced and caressed Mlai within Haarth's arms, then gestured at them urgently. "You have to get her out of here. I can no longer protect her here. The High Council won't relent just because she nearly died. She will get no more special treatment than what they give to anyone else. Especially, since she ran away before. Take her now! Please!" He stood aside and let them go. Mlai's mother's crying was the background noise to their departure.

Most of the Lorgren guards were down, a mere communication could send an endless number to thwart them that even their Soon-ahyin party would have a hard time contending with. "My pup!"

"The wolf will be brought to you. I still have *some* allies left. Now go, while there's this window I told them about. I led them to believe that I would send you all on a tour to occupy you. Just cover Mlai betwixt your sects, please, Gymein too, and I will be grateful to you forever."

Funny how Mlai's near-death may well have been the only reason they were able to leave Lorgr *with her.* Traveling by way of one of the walkways strung between one peak to another, their whole party rode the edges of stealth and anticipation of a battle. Mlai's father having assigned them a guide that he trusted, said he would waylay anyone curious about their whereabouts until they had gotten well away.

So that they could keep up the appearance of a tour, they took a serpentine route as fast as a whirlwind that left dust in their wake until they were looking out from the *walkway's loop* and felt themselves to have no support around them. The peak they were trying to make it to reared as a mountain in front of them a million paces away. If you stared up at it, you couldn't see its top. The mainstay peak they'd just left was the same behind them. Hung on a string, looming between mountains did wonders for Tierney's fear of heights.

She shouldn't look and... *Ooh, it was such a bad idea.* Just a peek toward the crater's basin made the people appear like insects. And Tierney was sure a flying apparatus would hurtle into their walkway and plunge them to their deaths at any moment. The transports were lit by the windows burning on the sides of the peaks around them flashing here and there and coming right at them.

Whether Mlai's father had truly found some new selflessness or not, she appreciated that they encountered no further confrontations. Even if the walkways were advised to have invisible simulated nets that allowed no one to fall. That was a testament that shouldn't be put to the test. If a battle broke out on the thing she'd surely freeze in action, considering now she jumped every time she thought a bird would jostle it.

But at least taking the walkway that led to a peak that was some kind of transportation center *seemed* the better alternative when they'd first hustled out of Lorgr. Once they entered the peak, every other moment or so, flying razors were released from its launchpad atop its roof. More shuttles than you'd think the peak could handle moved in and out of its spire. There were even moving walkways inside, some going up and down. Their snake between the pedestrians filling the peak, past flying razor after flying razor on the launchpad—none of them theirs—ended at a private access. Inside, the dock was empty and saw them shifting through its isles with Tempeh Tu hugging their front and back. The lights were lowered here and dust was on the dock's surfaces, thick enough that you didn't want to disturb it lest you inhaled it and choked on it.

On they marched, led down some circular stairs to a flying razor prepped and waiting for them. It hummed in a docking station off the side of the peak instead of on top. All the more reason not to hesitate for it to register to those who'd watched their passage before they were off.

Finally!

The circumnavigation of a pathway back to Kalamesh. It wasn't necessarily a reason to celebrate until they were firmly on Soonahyin soil, but it was progress nonetheless.

The question became though, whether they were any safer in this land than in the one they'd just left, because a knot had formed in Tierney's belly again. Without fail, her intuition was becoming more and more on point. She trusted it. Which caused an other-sensory frisson to skitter up her spine with the quandary mystifying her now.

Why is a Drundel worker paying such rapt attention to our party's concerns? It was the same Drundel standing beyond the glass, on the lip of the launchpad from when they were last here. Getting back to the Kalamesh Rocky Gorge launch-station was drama in itself. "Now, we must contend with a Drundel worker who's practically stalking us with his eyes?"

Where was Torhvald? Maybe she did harbor a prejudice against the Drundel people. All the same, she wanted his reading on this one.

The Drundel was so absorbed in watching them that another worker came and tapped his shoulder to remind him to get to work. He should have been preparing a flying razor already in the sling ready for launch. The *Kalameshee worker* frowned as he touched the Drundel and glanced up at the window she was behind too—like his Kalameshee senses detected something from the Drundel worker that had to do with them.

The breath Tierney had been holding finally released when they entered their flying razor. *Good. The perfect time to leave. Now maybe that Drundel can find something else to concentrate so hard on. She* situated herself across from Mlai. *So I can get back to the most pertinent things and keep an eye on her for the duration.* When Tierney thought about it all, she couldn't believe her own current state of mind. Who would have thunk it? Life and it's variables were so funny sometimes. *I'm glad to take flight from both Lorgr and Kalamesh and head back to my homeland. Me. The one who's always seeking adventure, can't wait to get back home.*

Mlai missed her seat on the first try, nearly toppling over. Ad'rihl caught her *just* as he was passing. He took her waist and guided her down. After her near-death situation, the wisdom of her traveling straight through two lands was questionable. She'd slept pretty much whenever she was still, except, she was awake *now*. Questions plagued Tierney. "Mlai? I hope I don't appear forward when I ask you this, but why would your father take such risks with your life?"

"Because." Mlai glanced at everyone else, anywhere else but at Tierney. "He's never understood my dissension, Tierney ." Her eyes with the lids at half mast, alluded to a weight she carried that no one would have guessed burdened her in the beginning when her guilelessness shone so bright in Soonayah. A harness strapped across her chest became uber interesting as she fiddled with its latch. "He has lived his life for the edicts of the High Council. Not excluding me just because I'm his daughter with fickle ideas of independence. Mother insisted on waiting until I was old enough to make my own decision about a conversion when he started pressing for it in my youth. And she hadn't let him choose my sex during gestation and allowed it to happen naturally. To him that was nonsensical. Anything or *anyone* outside the order of our ways threatens chaos. If only we all go along, everything should be okay." Her head fell back and she stayed that way for a long time as if she was drifting to sleep again. Was she? She spoke then without lifting her head, "At least, that's how he always has been. After I nearly *died*...twice, it seems he may be seeing things a little differently now."

"But what of your people's self-expression?"

Gymein's scoff interjected from several seats away. "Self-expression is fine as long as the ways of Lorgr are in no way disturbed."

With just that small pause in the conversation they were having, a cute little gruffle from across the aisle announced that Mlai had slipped into slumber as quick as that, in the time it took for Gymein to speak. Although she was off into dreamland, Tierney still needed distraction. Torhvald's leg bumped against hers and tempted her to clutch at him some more. *I would like not to put a hole in his thigh.* His musculature was something she would prefer to remain intact for stroking when they loved again. It was just that the pulse in the cords in her neck had ticked up.

The flight was rougher than usual. Her rocking mode had gone full-on with a mind of its own from the moment they'd launched. This day's turmoil and the extra bumps mid-flight well set her off. *Bak'rah had better be fine in his compartment in the back or those Kalameshee conductors will have me to answer to.*

Twisting in her seat in hopes that maybe if she spoke to Gymein their conversation would divert her from the dips and wobbles while her stomach roiled, she said, "There's something I don't understand, Gymein. Why are your people's sexes converted even after you've already grown into whole adults? Why not just leave everyone alone? People have a right to be who they are."

"Remember, we are born with both sexes. One is latent. Conversion has a violent, stimulating effect. Triggering the other sex makes it take over in dominance," he answered. "There are some who are relieved to get the conversion. They're thankful because they lean more toward their latent sex, but that's not the one more dominant physically.

"That sounds perfect for those who've never been able to be their true selves. But what about those who *are* who they are? They're already formed as the being they're meant to be. Forcing a change of sex can't change their psyche."

"I agree, but the High Council administers mental conditioning as a part of conversion too."

The policy was abominable! How much degradation of Lorgr's fertilization processes had taken place to cause such practices to be put into play? No wonder dissension whispered among the people they'd come across in Lorgr. Their High Council had better listen to its populace before they had a revolt on their hands. "I can't believe such forced predicaments work."

"As well you shouldn't. I'm proof positive it doesn't work."

Oh, my goodness! So...Gymein decided the stress of their current situation warranted the telling of his own affairs? The revelation slammed a shock into Tierney. In-drawn breaths attested to shock waves hitting others too in the flying razor who heard his confession of conversion already being done on him. It shouldn't have been a shock though after they'd witnessed the Lorgren High Council's heavy use of its authority. It was clear now, Gymein's urgency to come with them wasn't only for Mlai's sake. It'd helped him escape his own persecution. It made sense now that he'd had the vehemence of a thousand men when the Lorgrens were mistreating Mlai.

They traveled high in the skies with nothing but the flying razor's bumble beneath their feet. If anything could take her mind off that, the maltreatment she raged against being done to Mlai, having been carried out to its fullest against Gymein, well did. Gymein's confession had quieted most of the voices that mumbled closely around them too. Most likely, they were discomforted in their wondering about what had been forced upon him. Silence prevailed.

The in-flight atmosphere became downright soothing after a while. A preferable option to thoughts of the injustices Gymein and Mlai had endured.

In fact, the razor's deep drops and rocking didn't register any sense of alarm to anyone.

The constancy of heat no longer assaulted Tierney's senses either. She relaxed...and giggled? Snores came from her side from Torhvald, in such deep slumber, he snorted. And across the way, Ad'rihl flung his head back, mouth open, unconscious to whatever might go crawling right in. Tierney cocked her head to one side, limply. It wasn't like she was in control of the thing. She could barely hold the nubbin up on the noodle that had become her neck.

Something is off-kilter here.

Bak'rah's piteous howls of warning reached her. She imagined his eyes aglow and his coat flashing like it was shorted out, his howls were so frenetic, and she mumbled, "Calm yourself, sweet pup. There's no way I can get to you now. It's only a matter of time before you will relax too."

Next to Ad'rihl, Korrell lifted a hand to help Haarth, who raged against the fixed harness they'd all strapped in before launch. Yet, Korrell's hand fell limp also, his body slumped forward.

Why does Haarth struggle so?

Tierney was experiencing an absolute relief from the guard against her soul-energy overcoming her. Every corpuscle of tension eased from her body. Her eyelids drowsed. A grey mist crowded the edges of her vision and she welcomed the relief it promised. Pulling her toward it, "*Come. Come in,*" it beckoned.

But what of Uncle...Haar...Father? She snorted. She couldn't get his title right with her head so fuzzy.

Haarth's head drifted downward and drool fell from his mouth. Then he popped his head back up and shook it like a crazed animal. Their eyes met. The whites of his steeped with red, and he reached a hand out for her. *Oh, dear Father.* Tierney wished she could convey her feeling of warmth to Haarth. *You need only relax and you will feel comforted too.* But she was made too restful to even move her lips.

Chapter 35

"Tierney!"

"Tierney!"

"Tierahna!" The sting of a slap whipped across Tierney's face. She made an attempt to push the punishing hand away, but her arms were weighed down by anvils. "Tierahna! You must fight! Your strength is your own!" *That voice* with such urgency registered within her fog. Whose will had the presence to force itself into her consciousness?

Haarth. "Fa...father?"

Wailing. Pitiful screaming blanched the fuzziness in her brain too. Her eyes flew open. *Where was Mlai?*

People vomited, falling every other step. Satchels, rubbish, people's outer layers of clothing cluttered the floor and scattered into the air with each bounce of the razor. The people were bouncing into the air too. *Screaming!* Haarth kept tapping her face while utter bedlam careened through the flying razor. *What is going on here!* She lifted her head and shook him off. "There you are. Keep moving. Get her loose. The Kalameshee next," Haarth said to Korrell. "I'll help free Ad'rihl. We must get him to the conductor's cab and get the controls back."

"Torhvald?" He lay at her side at an angle awkward enough, he must be putting a crook in every part of his body. *Why does he slumber that way?* "Torhvald!" His screamed name bolted him awake as if she'd lit fire to him. He bucked at a harness that had locked across him instead of automatically retracting after their launch. Korrell took a wicked-looking dagger to the cushion of her harness and sabotaged the hinge and loosened her. Then did the same for Torhvald's. Haarth and Ok'nuh worked at Ad'rihl's which was proving more stubborn than everyone else's.

Where was Mlai? Everywhere people stumbled about as the flying razor veered and pitched. Everyone went around helping wake others, freeing them from their harnesses.

Tierney listed however the flying razor swung. Her head swam. She pitched forward and ejected everything from her stomach. Torhvald held her, helping her brace her body. Haarth and Ok'nuh half dragged, half carried Ad'rihl lurching to the conductor's cab so he could override the erratic auto-conductor and pilot the razor.

Waking the Kalameshee conductors proved too hard. Their Kalameshee constitutions found it harder to metabolize foreign substances. They held on to them just as they did their energy. How Torhvald woke at her scream of his name was a mystery. He must have somehow been attuned to her even in his unconscious state. The pitiful keening sobs continued to blare over the din in the razor, but Tierney couldn't see who they came from.

Nowhere in the sea of people could Mlai's bright face be found either. Tierney fell forward to the floor as the flying razor took a terrible deep dip. When she tried to stand, her legs collapsed beneath her and so she crawled through the crush of feet and legs, on instinct following the sounds of weeping. Wailing.

And there she found Mlai, lying slumped over Gymein...who wasn't moving.

The contents of Tierney's stomach belched to her throat, threatening an eruption of nothing but bile this time. Bitter...nastiness, "Ugh."

She disgorged it to the side, between people's feet into a grate. *For all that is good! This has to be a nightmare...please be a nightmare.* In an act of pure selfishness, she pulled Mlai away from Gymein into her own embrace. Together they cried for a time, rocking each other. Mlai's sobbing and sobbing racked her body, trembling against Tierney's, frenetic in its pulsing. "We gave him poison reverser up his nose, Tierney. And we shocked him and shocked him...his heart wouldn't beat. He *can't* wake up!"

"Someone get the breather now! We must press fresh air into him!" Tierney hollered.

"We tried that! No one can wake him up!"

Tierney's eyes moved over Gymein's face unmarred by injury, but pale and lifeless, and a sickening rush of fear struck inside her. *What possible alignment of the stars could make this poor boy's death okay?* Mlai's face was awash in tears when she pulled back, and stark red because of the new changes to her skin, and she said, "I woke first. I think because of the recent recovery of my body. Then Prince Haarth woke next. And we could see he wasn't breathing. We tried...we tried to bring him back, but he still has the regular Lorgren chemistry. We're extremely vulnerable to poisons. He couldn't withstand whatever they put in this air. He has died, Tierney! Tierney he's—!"

"Everyone to your seats and strap in!" Haarth rushed toward them. "The flying razor isn't on auto-conductor. Someone is controlling it from outside. Ad'rihl must wrestle the controls back!" Still too weak to stand, Tierney's heart thudded inside her breast. She hadn't noticed that Torhvald had followed her. He lifted her by her waist and got her to their seats where they fumbled to put their arms through their harnesses. A glance back showed Haarth hastening with Mlai's languishing form and strapping her in too.

The flying razor shifted hard left, then right, dropping several fathoms. "Ahh!" They screamed before Ad'rihl controlled its momentum. Still, steady it was not. Racked with revulsion, Tierney nearly threw up again and had to turn her head away from Gymein. The additional abuse his poor lifeless body, shifting untethered all over the flying razor took, was a ghoulish thing to witness. But it was too late, they'd forgotten that though he was gone, his body would need to be secured too. His cold palm brushed her ankle as he passed. The horror of it stuck behind her eyelids. Something like that, you just couldn't unsee. *For the love of life, what is happening here?*

Mlai's reaction was crazed, bucking and writhing against her tethering, and had to be causing harm to her body that she definitely couldn't afford. Haarth had trapped her in her harness on purpose.

Something also gave him the presence of mind to grasp at Gymein's arm and catch him as he toppled past him. The once intractable Lorgren deserved the dignity of not being thrown around the razor. Haarth hugged his motionless body pinned against his own harness. He straightened Gymein's neck, and lay his head on his shoulder, and just held him there. With those actions, Mlai's screeches turned to groans, her gaze trapped on Haarth, and Gymein lifeless in his embrace.

Then Ad'rihl shouted out to them, "Brace yourselves! They won't give up control! I must crash to keep us from heading straight to their abduction spot!"

Ad'rihl banked the flying razor so fast to the right, they all screamed. Their legs flew right with the movement. They veered right again in a deep swerve forcing them to hold onto each other to stay upright, nearly turning them upside down. Then they were descending started faster and faster than could possibly be safe.

"Ahh! Ugh! Oh!" the cries were deafening.

The descent was pulled up short, but the speed didn't stop. "Hold on!" Ad'rihl yelled. "The speed gives me more control! I must try something! Everybody, hold on!"

The flying razor bumped and juggled. Piercing sounds filled its insides with an unworldly *screeeeech!* Everyone continued to scream along with the racket as the razor skimmed some surface creating friction on its speed. At last, after the ear-bending skimming slowed the razor to Ad'rihl's satisfaction, he skidded to a rumble and stopped in a bank of some kind.

As the door flew up, people stormed from their seats trying to get to it. Havoc reigned as they exited. Ad'rihl jumped from the cab and went straight to Mlai and grabbed her. He carried her out among all the ruckus as she protested. "Move! Everyone out!" Haarth ordered. "We must see how this land lays before us now."

Tierney still couldn't support herself. "The heat!" Her body became overwrought with melting, boiling inside, and this time it felt undefeatable. "*No good serves our people from close proximity to the heat of the flames.*" Her mother's words were irritatingly right. Only too much heat from the sun undermined them too.

A whimper mewled on the air and pierced their ears *My poor pup is in that compartment.* "Bak'rah! I must get to him!"

Haarth nodded to Torhvald. He then gently laid Gymein across the seats and Tierney fell over him, any strength in her legs was gone at the sight of his body. She kissed his cheeks. They were marble cold now, and caressed his sinews, which had already stiffened into the throes of death. "My dear boy, I'm so sorry. You were owed...so much more than this. I'd thought you'd finally get to be the you—you deserve." She began to weep again. If only he'd made it to Soonayah, nobody there would've cared about the sex he'd chosen as long as it was *his* choice.

"Get her out of this wreckage! I'll get the wolf," Haarth said.

Tohrvald bent also and touched the Lorgren's head. He ruffled his little patch of hair, and when he lifted his head his eyes were glistening too. That the boy was gone was abominable to anybody with a conscious. In her weakened state, it was easy for Torhvald to lift her gently from her feet and haul her from Gymein's body and they exited out onto a sand-covered landscape.

"The desert. No wonder." *Its heat. It was excruciating!* Tierney shifted within the strength of Torhvald's arms. The flying razor banked within a sand dune, wobbled, the dune's height spilling over and covering the whole front of the razor and she wouldn't turn away until Haarth came out of the wreckage with Bak'rah following behind. They headed straight for them, then Haarth told Tohrvald, "Release her. She will stand on her own."

Torhvald lowered her down his body, and despite him easing her, when her feet touched the ground her legs collapsed again. She hit the ground hard and latched onto her trusty pup. He whimpered, but Bak'rah with his sturdy body, was so attuned to her, he came closer as if he understood she needed help to steady herself.

Clearly with a sense of urgency for their current state of affairs pressing his actions, Haarth swept her to her feet. He made her focus her attention on him, hands on either side of her face. Tierney tried to overcome her impaired state, but Haarth was not only too close, he touched her, which agitated her soul-energy. A Soonahyin's first instinct was to buck against anything that agitated the soul-energy. How *much longer can I stand this heat overwhelming me?* His fingers sank ever harder into her face.

"You're feeling the connection between us, as do I?" he said to her. "This is *natural* interaction. *Don't* fight it. Use me to spring from, and you will only be enhanced. All the Soonahyins here feel an effect from so much energy from the sun." He removed the support from her face and she wilted again. Haarth swung to everyone still recovering from the wreckage, only now they dealt with the effects of the sun, and he bellowed, "Soonahyins! We are different from everyone else!"

He gestured to the three Kalameshee conductors just rousing and exiting the flying razor. "We're not used to the high temperatures here constantly feeding our bodies. Our constitutions' normal state is to fight to attain energy! We-must-not-be-overwhelmed! We must become fired. Use this heat as endless energy to fight what is outside of us now!"

Voices, people shaking themselves out, murmurs of agreement rippled across the Soonahyins now galvanized with Haarth from the debilitation of the sun. Tierney rallied at his words too. Torhvald touching her back, fed her even more energy and she rose of her own will. A wee seed inside unfurled, set aflame. She caught onto it, realizing it'd been there all along. This was that insistence within her soul that had always been there, always pushed her along.

Again, Haarth turned back to her and put his hand to her face. "You're the first Soonahyin princess! Your power doesn't deplete you; it's your strength. Will it as your own!"

Every atom inside Tierney now ignited at his words. Her soul-energy screamed. Haarth's unshakeable will at her front and Torhvald's hand at her back—his face near her ear—sent her introspection exploding, flying further than she had ever experienced before. From outside the heated funnel her mind blazed, a whisper from Torhvald against her ear pierced through. "Remember. Embrace those signatures you feel. Make their energies a part of you."

Tierney could sense everyone's focus on her. Mlai came to her and placed her hand on Tierney's shoulder, adding her light body energy as well.

I should be reassuring her.

Yet, her intro-spection held her in its sway. In her periphery, she sensed her brothers moving close about her too. Ultimately, the reality was the situation's urgency pressing her, pressuring her. *Control. I must control it now. Come on. Come on. You can do it. It's yours to...* And then through sheer will, her own gumption hijacked her introspection, taking control like she needed. *I did it! I did it! Mine to control. Now direct it* to a distance beyond them on beings further away in the desert. "People pour from an opening in the sand. They're racing toward us. I think we crashed far beyond their expectations," she said.

Korrell and Haarth patted Ad'rihl's back for his forethought in diverting the flying razor from where the scourge planned.

"Opening in the sand?" Peetah Pearl's intuitiveness picked up one other issue. "Where are we?" she asked.

Consoles alighted from trew-slits and Mlai's ejected from her arm. Haarth answered before anyone could consult them. "You will get no readings from those here. I'm sure they jammed our connections to the alluvial shield. The flying razor had no communication either."

On a thought, he flung a look at Mlai and she shook her head *"No."*

So, they had blocking technology that affected Mlai's inner mechanics too.

"We're thousands of parses off course. They've diverted us to the Olum desert as they did with me before." Haarth said.

"Who are they?" Peetah Pearl asked.

"The Drundel," Haarth answered.

"Oh! No! How can that be!" Grumblings surged throughout their party? All Soonahyins had knowledge of Haarth's kidnapping and escape, and his sect's demise.

Tohrvald nodded in agreement with Haarth's estimation, he said, "Tierney noticed a Drundel worker at the Rocky Gorge launchpad whose interest in us was too intent. They surely just laid in wait for us until we returned from Lorgr."

Another wave of energy ripped through Tierney from the Drundel. Urgency fizzed from them to her, up her spine into her brain. They affected her to the point that she stumbled onto Bak'rah even as the hands around her supported her. His occlusion fed into her, triggered by her and the circumstances probably, meshing with her introspection. "Bak'rah...my pup."

His whimpers escalated to howls, snarls really that intensified as their situation did. Already close to her, he pressed closer, accompanied by the extraordinary glow of yellow eyes and his flashing coat. Their party saw him as an eerie shadow, ghostly white, a specter of an animal against the backdrop of sand. But to Tierney, the connection between them mounted, drawing whimpering sounds from her too. "Bak'rah detects nothing grave, no deadly intent. Their silhouettes aren't yellow, not red either. They're like some weird ochre color. So they're charging at us for what then!"

"They mean kidnapping as their goal as they did me and my party before!" Haarth looked to Torhvald.

"Kidnapping? They know we will kill them in their slug-holes if they attempt that."

"You're too fast with your belief in our capabilities. We may fight well, but the Drundel are fiendish with their skills out here in this dessert," Haarth intoned with gravity underlying his voice. "Kalameshee, you're an empath. Gauge what they mean to do with us." Then to the entire crowd, he said, "Everyone get your frostfires ready—"

"Remember, the frostfires may not work in the desert. And I can't get a feel for them this far away," Torhvald told them.

"Then everyone, ready your cutlasses too and set them all on paralyze," Haarth commanded. "We can't litter the desert with Drundel dead if they don't mean to kill *us*. We must try and avoid an all-out war here. We can head them off and surround them, immobilize them, before they overcome us and take us into their catacombs. If they get us in there we may never get out."

With tremors racking her frame, Mlai lurched away from those who were congregated around Tierney, and cried, "They've already started a war! Or do we forget Gymein's body still lays in that razor even now being buried in sand? I will fight for blood."

"You will not fight at all! Your welfare rests in my hands and I won't have harm come to you under my guard. Besides, you haven't once practiced with the cutlasses—"

"I don't need *your* weapons. I'm built with my own, which I intend to use, and no man who tries to hold me here will stop me."

"Mlai—" Haarth started.

"I will be her Principal since I have no ward assigned to me here." Peetah Pearl stepping forward as Principal for Mlai was not surprising. She was forever Tempeh Tu. "I pledge my life in her protection."

"I stand in second," Ok'nuh said, shifting from amongst the ranks of the Tempeh Tu as well.

Haarth shook his head. "No," he replied, even though he could never stay behind and guard Mlai himself.

"My contingent will enfold her in its formation when we deploy, and I will make sure she only immobilizes them as you've charged, Haarth." Ad'rihl shot Mlai a pointed look daring her to disagree, or else Haarth would see to it she sat out the confrontation, even if it *did* mean staying with her.

Mlai gave a short nod in accordance with Ad'rihl's words. This time the bobbing of her hair didn't allude to her spirited nature but was an omen to them all. What they were undertaking was somber indeed. Disastrous consequences could prevail if they weren't precise. Haarth pointed to Korrell. "Korrell your speeding is the fastest here. Who of the Tempeh Tu can keep up with you?"

"My garrison's training breeds their compatibility with me," Korrell said.

"Then you deploy first to the other side of the teeming Drundel. Go now!" Korrell and his contingent took off across the sand disappearing and appearing at will as they speeded.

"Who's next fastest?" Haarth asked.

"I am!" Ad'rihl answered, ferocity bouncing off him. His glare stalked after the figures of his brother's contingent that had now reached a great distance from them.

"I knew this wouldn't work. Mlai will have trouble—"

"I have never been outrun by any man." Haarth, interrupted again by a Mlai who was unrecognizable. Her brow scowling, breath hissing and face contorted by such a torrent of fever, its sweetness may never see the light of day again. "This day makes no difference," She retorted and turned her back on Haarth. She insinuated herself among Ad'rihl's Tempeh Tu, snaking in within their ranks.

"Then go! And pull up to Korrell's flank." Off they leaped at Haarth's command. Mlai's biomechanical legs moved at an unnaturally breakneck pace. Not only did she keep up with Ad'rihl and his contingent, but she passed them at some points as they traversed the desert.

"Tierney, your contingent must come after mine and close the circle and hopefully bottleneck the opening in the sand. But I need you here with the conductors. Stay and continue to attempt communication on your consoles—"

"You insult me. No Soonahyin royal sits by while their warriors fight. If mother were here, she would be first to battle. You should expect no less from me...Father." Tierney's sneer on the title afforded him all the resentment in her soul at being treated as a cosseted princess even now. This was battle. Her family couldn't buffer her from that too. "You must go now, or you will be out of sync with Korrell and Ad'rihl. And I'm coming after you and fighting by your side as I should!"

Haarth waited one last moment, exchanging a frown with Torhvald. "I expect you to protect my daughter with your life, Kalameshee. Let no harm come to her." Torhvald nodded...decisive, immediate. And Haarth and his contingent bolted like lightning toward the action too.

A trail of Soonahyin royals speeding toward battle.

Inconceivable!

But there they were, racing beneath an unforgivable sun toward ends unknown. A strumming started up inside her body at the thought of it. The possibility of a battle, it's costs, it's ramifications—oh indeed, such contretemps had a pulse of their own. A rhythm more potent than the poison they'd ingested. She sneered. *The innocence of the Starfall rhyme can't comfort me to this beat.* A babe's rhyme just wouldn't do. Headiness laced her blood with her soul-energy pumping, lighting up her veins. The propellant in the Soonahyin bloodline that had sustained their fighter creed for millennia. *This has maintained my people against the greatest adversities. It will be a sustenance for me too, not something that overbears me. I will it so.*

The strumming with her soul-energy innervated manifested outward in a rocking and slapping of her foot against the sand. She called out the start of war, "Impi!" to her contingent. Who responded with the fight chant, "Ngomumo!" The anticipation of Haarth's lead reaching a certain point nearly lifted Tierney off the desert floor. One last guttural cry and they vaulted, speeding to the fray in time to join in as all the action began. *I hope Torhvald can keep up. For I cannot help him along with this.*

Chapter 36

"The Room of Sovereignty." *Pretentiousness personified,* Ana'kerah chortled to herself. *Utterly stuffy.*

In spite of the stuffiness, she did cherish walking floors covered by the opulent Dynasty Rug. In her youth she'd spent days wallowing in the history of the plush rug that traced the dynastic branches of the twelve Soonahyin clans depicted trailing from the rug's center over fields of royal purple. Unfortunately, her efforts to connect the current generation to the beginning of their lines had been in vain, when the weaving scribes invariably came and weaved into the lines the connection of newly birthed babes from all across the land while she was still tracing.

If only the innocence of youth still claimed such absorption of her attention. Now, her presence in the Room of Sovereignty demanded awareness of the ceiling made of panes of etched optiglass which opened to, *"Sunrays alighting truth upon all Soonayah's leaders taking audience within."*

Alighting truth alright.

She shifted crosswise. *Alighting my face.* She chuckled. The concentration of the sun scorched the side of her neck from that angle. A decadence of hundreds of candelabras hanging from the frames of the ceiling, bedecked with thousands of diamonds and gems of Soonayah blinded you if you looked at them too long. And the voluminous tapestries and marble walls iridescent in their sheen, never relented in reminding her of her responsibility as queen.

So reflective of my nature. Ana'kerah smirked and tipped her head to acknowledge the few leaders who graced the Room of Sovereignty so far. *If it were left up to me, we would have our first meeting in the sparring arena. A vy would be perfect for loosening these first airs right off. Stuffiness begone.* She grinned.

This day, Ana'kerah presided over Reception of leaders arriving from every part of Soonayah for their off-docket assembly. This room, this Keep, and all its overstated luxury were theirs too. Most times Ana'kerah saw herself on a much simpler level.

How ironic the leaders' footfalls were. They glided over branches inscribed with their own names in the dynastic lines of their clans. As she made her way through the chancellors and chieftains, she picked up on a Cordalai clan chieftain speaking to a woman she called Wilowah. She noted the members of the clan, then slipped into a slitted-incline, and ascended its crest. This was the entrance to the Room of Sovereignty's brilliant center mount. The bird's eye view of the Room of Sovereignty.

A short circle upward that raised her above everyone else, and her eyes roamed those early-arriving as they mingled amongst each other. They shared in the pleasure of reunion because their time apart enmeshed them in the trivialities of their own dominions and hamlets. This was probably the first time they'd been together in a while.

At the ledge, Ana'kerah caressed a hand down the arm of jewels encrusted on a helm. The circular, path upward and the two helms crowning the center mount symbolized the rest needed at the end of the ancient Soonahyin migration. Their people's settlement into the frozen oasis they had been allotted. Their claiming of Soohayah.

Apart from my Accession Day, I can't remember ever sitting in these helms. Even when Stah'lief ascended we hadn't sat in them, being such

Soonahyins.

She took stance from a perch beside them and glanced again over smooth skin stretched over the high cheekbones of a yet-aged Ahn'Trunkh Cordalai chieftain.

The direct daughter of her line, Wilowah's bone structure carried the same characteristics of their genes. Ana'kerah admired Wilowah's proud carriage and what she took action upon herself. "She requires special seating," Willowah told the members of her clan and the Keep's assembly aides. She gained assistance for her foreparent by reminding others of the chieftain's malady of the bones. Ana'kerah observed nothing but graciousness in Wilowah's demeanor and thought the beauty in her resemblance to her chieftain astounding and her clan members responsive to her instruction.

Then why did Korrell display a mysterious reserve about his undertakings with them?

Only one way to find out. "Wilowah Tordum Litem Ahn'Trunkh." Her dutiful manner, despite Korrell not offering a well-spoken word of their clan, afforded Wilowah first respect. She'd be greeted by all her names. "I commend your care for your chieftain," Ana'kerah said.

Wilowah jerked her arm crosswise from her body, palm out, the gesture of regard in quick salute. The queen's address had obviously caught her off guard. "Our chieftain's presence in our lives has graced us to no end. Us honoring her is a pittance in exchange."

The edges of Ana'kerah's lips lifted. A diplomatic answer, inclusive of her whole clan, when it was she directing all their movements. After she had appealed to the elders of her clan without success, no doubt her use of this same wit was how her hamlet's snowcat problem had ended up before the queen herself. If Korrell encountered this woman's shrewd handling of her clan and his plans ran in any way awry from hers, Ana'kerah was unsure which of the two of them prevailed. "I hope Korrell coming and helping your clan settled well with ridding the hamlet of its snowcat pests."

Wilowah's amber eyes peeled wide. For several moments, she hesitated. She returned the queen's gaze, then shied away from their probing and shuttered what looked like vulnerability shining from the depths of hers. "He did...uhm...we were able...uhh, so yes."

The clan chieftain stood with care, spurred after Wilowah tripped all over her answer to the queen. "He serviced us with his time as the faithful steward all Soonayah's people can take as an example. And the concern he took for our hamlet while he used his training in the preservation of the snowcats and their removal embodied him as a naturalist and his capabilities as a true leader." The Ahn'Trunkh chieftain spared Wilowah a frown with one brow lifted—as if to ask, "*Are you recovered enough from your clumsy response, and now can join in on the pleasantries afforded us by the queen?*" He—"

A barrage of marching feet cut through the swish of the room's doors at the same time that Ana'kerah's armset started buzzing like it was trying to vibrate off her arm. The fracas, with Eh'kotah at its charge, peeled a path through the Soonahyin leaders straight toward Ana'kerah. With them coming so headset on reaching her as they seemed, she didn't get a chance to check her armset, and muted it until later. "Eh'kotah. The custom of receiving the leaders of Soonayah shouldn't be interrup—"

"We've received a warning from the High Council of Lorgr. The Ministry of Communication may still be buzzing you now. But I told them this required me to deliver the news to you in person."

Ana'kerah pulled herself up short of the reprimand she intended for Eh'kotah. She was *glad* he was *here*. She'd persuaded him not to go to the Dayea mountains until after assembly. But no progeny of hers interrupted her speaking in formal settings. Her heart's thudding within her chest froze at the look on Eh'kotah's face. Whatever had caused his jaws to clench and that steely look in his eyes had to be dire. *Oh boy.*

"Our people's flying razor has crashed into the Olum desert. The Lorgren High Council traced its passage from Lorgr with the new focus-scape technology like they gave us. The razor was taken over and diverted by the Drundel."

Ana'kerah leaped from the room's center mount, speeding without hesitation, she landed within paces of Eh'kotah. "Impossible! Those dreadful Drundel aren't that foolish! What could've possibly made them do this?" Outcries from those who heard the shocking news resounded around the room.

"Those murderous outlaws! We must destroy them this time, Eh'kotah," she said. "Call up a full brigade of Tempeh Tu. We'll kill them all if we have to—"

"Mother, every Soonahyin leader from every part of the land arrives here, in-Keep as we speak because you called an impromptu assembly. Under no circumstance should we skirt the tradition of Reception and allow them to be greeted by a Keep abandoned of most of the royals, especially you. Unless of course, the intent is to set off a call to war of every battalion across Soonayah. The Security Council will see to that."

Ana'kerah tripped over the questions bombarding her brain, Eh'kotah's logic hobbling her thoughts. She was ever the queen of deliberation, methodical about every consideration and happening in her land...only this concerned her whole family. "A call to war is what it is! How many Drundel lay in wait in that treacherous desert?"

"Hundreds," Eh'kotah admitted. "But we think they were thwarted from their original plan. The razor crashed far from them. They scurry in search of the crash site now."

"Contact our people and guide them to another course."

"We can't communicate with them and there is no other course they can take and outrun Drundel. They will eat up any distances between them. We all know they have animal-like speed, but they're skimming sandsurfers too." Eh'kotah had an unnatural stillness about him as he detailed the tactics taken by both the Drundel and their people. Known for being deliberate in his diplomatic ways, the tic along his temple told the truth of the control his calm air was costing him. Ana'kerah grabbed his hand.

"I can't stay here if my entire family is in danger," she said. "And we have no way of warning them!"

"The Drundel carry no weapons and we're sure our party knows what is happening. They race as we speak toward the Drundel with weapons set to paralyze."

"The filthy, dirt-scuffling animals! They mean to kidnap them as they did before! Our people must turn away from them or they will be dragged into some forsaken underground trap never to be seen again!"

"Mother, no amount of racing can outrun hovers skimmed and designed for just the types of elements there are down there. Besides, Ad'rihl, Korrell, and Haarth won't turn and run when the safety of everyone around them is threatened. Not to mention, Tierney."

A cackle choked out of her throat. Ana'kerah lifted her hand, flitting it around her neck, the tissues inside tightening on the ball that stuck there. "You're right. She probably leads the charge." Her head dropped and she sucked her belly in against the angst riding right at her core. Shudders filled her with the thought of what was happening to her people, her family. She clenched her jaw, fighting against showing her terror in front of everyone. The patronage expected her to be strong. When times were dire was exactly when fortitude was needed at the fore, but she didn't know if she had enough in her to keep from loosing it over her family. *This is what I feared all along.*

Eh'kotah lifted his mother's hand clasped within his and kissed it. "I go now mother, to aid them."

"Take a squadron of javelin flyers. They should get you there in enough time," she said.

Eh'kotah balked. "We shall set off a planetary incident with Kalamesh instead of Drundel." A drastic proportion of flyers could trigger dissension with other lands. "We can't deploy a full squadron over Kalamesh without stopping at their border."

"Then take at least ten filled beyond capacity with Tempeh Tu and don't stop at the Kalamesh border. I will ease King Ocierus of any fears the javelins are for Kalamesh." Ana'kerah squeezed Eh'kotah's hand, her energy riding hot, convulsing from her to him. "Go and get my family back to this Keep!" she said with all the righteousness her voice could carry.

A hand brushed Eh'kotah's arm, and he turned and found Wilowah hovering there, her face pinched inexplicably, vying for his attention. "Uhh...your broth...Prince Korrell? Uhm...he's not hurt from the crash is he?"

"No. He was the first to battle." The gathering chancellors and chieftains around him began to shout questions at him and Eh'kotah ignored the fracas and surged through them to make strides for the door. He called commands over his shoulder to the Principal Sect I of his Tempeh Tu. He then engaged his armset and said into it, "Ready ten javelin flyers filled with as many garrisons of Tempeh Tu that can fit in them. We hunt Drundel this day."

Chapter 37

So, this was war.

Pandemonium reigned everywhere one's eyes could see. Here, a Drundel swerved past them on his sandsurfer and lobbed his long arms like sledgehammers with some people toppled by them too. There, Drundel worked in teams and split off when they had their eyes on a particular Soonahyin to put down for good.

Bottlenecking the flow of Drundel exiting some strange kind of escape door hidden in the sand proved impossible. Why their party had figured surrounding them as planned would work was ironic anyway. The Drundel surged in hordes from the door and a bottleneck became moot. And *oh boy, had Mother been right about this.* Witnessing Soonahyins fighting in battle really, really put her outside of herself. Being there and not there was ever triggered by trauma and remained to be seen whether it was a help or a hindrance. Something Tierney could have avoided if she hadn't come here.

Throughout legions of Drundel their party members remained dispersed in a makeshift circle. At the furthest point through the sea of clashing people, Korrell fought a spirited bout with four Drundel at one time. He whipped his cutlass laser at one and the Drundel fell spasming and didn't move again. Korrell twisted back and paralyzed the next one approaching at his back too. The next two had the presence of mind to try to tackle the juggernaut from either side at the same time. He chopped one with his frostfire and the other one he shot with his cutlass. The last one possessed some kind of resistance against the paralytic and shook it off after a few spasms. Korrell had no choice but to run him through with the cutlass' rapier. The angle the blade went through nearly detached one whole leg from side to groin. After he handily dispensed with them all, he moved on to more comers.

Although Peetah Pearl and Ok'nuh gashed valiant swathes through any Drundel closing in on Mlai, Ad'rihl contended with unbroken waves of Drundel driving at *them*. Yet, he kept Mlai's electrifying form at a right angle to himself. Her spry-agility was an *utter* sight. No wonder she'd had such confidence in her fighting capabilities. She did have a weapon of her own. The ultimate weapon.

"Her cords. They seem alive!" Tierney exclaimed.

The cords Mlai had ejected from atop her arms when she'd helped rescue them from their plummet from the cliff, didn't only *save* lives. Little had they known, she controlled the bizarre pink appendages like any limb of her body and could switch their usage to weapons. She shot a pink plasma substance with flowing whips of the cords, onto the Drundel and paralyzed them. If the Drundel tried to latch onto the whipping cords, they jerked back hands sliced from fine bristles running along the cords which she stiffened when they touched them. And like Mlai, Tierney put up a fierce fight for herself as a wall of cover was being defended around her too.

Torhvald's savagery revealed itself wholly on the desert planes. She shifted catercorner to him, impressed that he used his empathic gift to anticipate the Drundel and thrashed or paralyzed them before they got good shots at them. In his match with her brothers, he'd stood strong in the face of their opposition. Here, along with Bak'rah and her Tempeh Tu garrison he fought in a furor. The Drundel were trounced from the ends of his laser and fists leveled, and blood spurted at some points.

I can't afford to lose sight of my own combat despite Torhvald's help keeping the teaming Drundel off me. Have to keep a presence of mind right here in the present, Tierney. Stay focused! She took advantage of the cover they afforded her, allowing herself mere snatches to mark everyone else's clashes throughout the battle. If she followed her party members' skirmishes too long, she risked Drundel getting too close to her. It was fine, though. The pain whenever they connected with her body was dulled inside her little world.

So, it might have been a benefit after all, allowing her to pinpoint Haarth wielding both his frostfire intermittently after giving it long pauses to gather the little to no precipitation the desert offered. He parried most often with his cutlass laser. *Uncanny! Identical movements to my own. We even fight like each other.*

Him, it seemed with the power of a cannon. Drundel toppled around him like pins, less an arm sometimes. After detaching a few limbs, he would then run them through with his cutlass' rapier when they wouldn't stay down. Tierney witnessed him actually lift one Drundel off his feet with the tip of his rapier exiting the Drundel's back. The gore of the Drundel's intestines fell from his gut when Haarth pulled back, disemboweling him. *Ugh!* She turned her head.

A fierce, unforgiving desert sun fueled the Soonahyins' soul-energy with an unceasing heat that they fed on in continuance of a battle that seemed unending.

At every angle a person could swing, thumps and grunts from participants carried on the humidity of the air. Most often, the Drundel let loose with animal-like screams and pained bellows as they fought with their bare hands and met up against a Soonahyin force who used weapons in return.

But the weapons were to no avail.

The Drundel made up for their lack of weapons in sheer numbers.

They concentrated their efforts on attempts to trap them with lassoes which stiffened into hard brackets once hooked onto the body.

We still have one salvation. The Drundel have no idea who we royals are.

They tried the ingenuous lasso maneuver on everyone they assaulted. However, Mlai stood out as the one Lorgren being protected within the company of Soonahyin royals. And the Drundel sent tides of their ranks after her and Ad'rihl's garrison. They managed to get her snarled into one of their lassoes, her arms, and cords pinned up inside the lasso too, useless. Peetah Pearl beat the Drundel holding Mlai in the contraption back, but couldn't hold them at bay until Ok'nuh forced them back using the brute force of his size like a battering ram.

A sign if ever there was one spread across the whole Olum desert. Or maybe just within the dunes that surrounded them. Or maybe not all. Her razed brain could have been playing tricks on her, but everything went silent. A warning as if in anticipation of some devastation. Then every fighter on the sweltering desert froze, sharing one infinitesimal moment...of horror.

Ear-splitting, ominous-wretched-creaking roared.

"The sand is shifting!" some unfortunate soul screamed.

Underneath all the progress Ok'nuh made against the Drundel, the sand beneath those facing him fell away. Into a ragged crack revealed under the collapsed sand, they plummeted.

With the opponents who had just been before him gone, Ok'nuh swiped at thin air. He balanced on his toes but lost his battle with the nothingness his arms swiped right through. He followed the Drundel he had been fighting into the crack.

"Ok'nuh!" A lasso whipped the full length of Tierney's face. Punishment for her inattention to her own predicament. But she had the indestructible Tohrvald defending her back. She maintained the front onslaught handier than she would have been able to without him.

She clocked the Drundel who whipped her with her frostfire across his throat and flipped him hind-end over head off his sandsurfer, then paralyzed him with her cutlass. Not having learned her lesson well enough clearly, her eyes returned to where Ok'nuh last stood.

There now hung Peetah Pearl with her muscles stretched appearing to nearly rupture from the strain. Tierney would have called out to her too, but the puckered whip now on her face still stung from her last negligence, reminding her to mind her defenses. Nevertheless, the scene left at the crack in the sand hollowed out her belly. With one hand, Peetah Pearl held Mlai's trussed-up form and her grip on the edge of the morphed sandstone crack with the other. Her name bubbled up Tierney's throat anyhow, as the stress on Peetah Pearl's face professed the battle she was losing.

Mlai slipped from the hold Peetah Pearl had on her wrist and she scrabbled to keep her *fingers* held in her grip. Somehow, Mlai had managed to slip a cord through the lasso's clutches and joined it in Peetah Pearl's grip too. Then Ad'rihl speed-dove straight to the edge of the crack after carving through an impossible ten opponents. He reappeared at the exact moment Peetah Pearl's clawing lost its grip on the sandstone because slippery blood saturated her fingertips. He caught her wrist and she swung Mlai to him. Ad'rihl grabbed Mlai with his other hand and in one motion threw Peetah Pearl to the safety of the ledge with the other.

The implosion of the sand into the sandstone crack had set the other side of the sand at a ridge. It revealed people atop it. Actual other people. Beings just standing there. They were Drundel too, but their skin held brown undertones instead of the standard bleached-pale shade normal for the Drundel. They made no move other than witnessing the atrocities the opponents were delivering on each other. Astride lopers—the dependable animals of the desert used in distant past periods for expeditions—they heeded the cause of neither side of the battle.

Across the dunes, despite the heat causing the air to distort, the largest male Drundel on the ridge zeroed in on Tierney. His soul-energy slammed into her, traveling the distance stretched between them, and she doubled over. Chaos, bodies falling around her, thrashing sounds of the cutlasses being whipped ensued and time stood still for the two of them. She rose again fast, lest she became lassoed by one of the Drundel fighting her. *Come on. Stay in this, Tierahna! Unless you want to end up trussed up like a dressed bird like Mlai.* The male's eyes shadowed from this distance, bored into hers. Neither of them broke contact until a bellow from Haarth echoed above all the other bedlam.

The tanned Drundel finally had a reaction to their warring. He flinched at Haarth's outcry and shifted as if readying to go to his rescue. But Haarth needed no rescue. His outrage was over *Korrell's* troubles. Drundel dragged Korrell by a trapped foot, his leg snagged at an angle. Even the rampage that was Korrell, struggled against the bonds and couldn't sit up and free himself.

The Drundel weren't so ignorant that they couldn't detect the concentrations of Soonahyin fighters centered, with at least one particular Soonahyin in the middle.

They have found us out. We royals being protected in the middle of our garrisons are their focus now.

The Drundel pressed inward with their numbers on the perimeters formed around each member of the royal house and now had Korrell captured.

Haarth would never let up. And those holding Korrell outnumbered him aplenty. No matter. They struggled to keep Korrell contained. Haarth speeded right to the stiffened contraption between Korrell and his captors in the blink of an eye. He lanced the ties so fast, the straining Drundel couldn't react. Then he pulled Korrell to his feet.

Korrell's leg bent at an angle no normal leg should, unless of course, you counted the Drundel with the hocks on the backs of theirs like the fastest of animals, as normal. *They were animals! What other creature could be this savage?* Korrell's normal leg crumpled him back to the ground. Haarth stood protection over him and heaved him up again. Korrell held onto Haarth, and they both battled the foes encroaching to abduct them, but they missed the Drundel on a sandsurfer charging for Korrell again, like he'd sniffed out his weakness.

The crack of the sandsurfer's crash with Haarth's skull reverberated across the desert sands. Time stood still, and for sure, everyone on the desert had to have heard the fracture. The sound was so deafening in Tierney's ears it must have resonated parses and parses until the desert gave away and only the trees and the mountains it rolled into could block its echo. No, it's true. When you had this thing like she did, sometimes you could block every other thing out and follow something like sound. Formlessly. Wherever it might go. You didn't need a body or a...present state of mind for that.

Grunts and screams and shouts frittered away. A wash of white noise rushed Tierney's hearing. She shook her head, nearly slipping so far away she'd be nearly catatonic and no use to anyone around her. *Come on. Come on, girl. Stay with it!* Blood gushed, spurting as a fountain from Haarth's head. Before his heavy weight hit the ground, the deadliness of the impact seized her throat in its grip.

"No! Father...?" Horror projected outward from every cell in her being and she fought like a crazed thing, paralyzing and chopping arms and throats with her saber. No longer taking care with what she did. Stabbing through the gut when she had to, she plied her way to Haarth's unmoving form and Korrell's savaging even with his lame leg stunting his movements. Her efforts cut at their knees, the Drundel between her and the unbelievable desolation of Haarth lying deathly still on the desert sand.

We should have aimed to kill every wretched Drundel in this forsaken desert.

They couldn't be held off with paralyzing. It was ineffectual when they replenished their ranks interminably. Fresher bodies slithered from the cracks as the Drundel in the fray fell. Whatever good the sun did forcing its energy into the Soonahyins' bodies was lost. Desperation rode the cords on the sides of Tierney's neck as tightly as her soul-energy did.

Torhvald and Bak'rah didn't yield, but a Kalameshee wasn't re-energized from the sun, and Tohrvald stumbled when more and more Drundel pushed his doggedness to its limits. Bak'rah, her faithful comrade, true to his heart, didn't comprehend the intricacies of immobilizing the Drundel instead of killing them. What her sweet pup understood was that Tierney was in danger. He savaged the throat of every offender he attacked.

And in turn, they hunted him.

With deliberate aim, the Drundel shot for him with the pointed ends of their sandsurfers. Tierney couldn't speed away to Haarth and defend Bak'rah and keep the Drundel from herself too.

Then there was Torhvald. *Her man at arms. Can't lose sight of him either.*

His being a Kalamesh royal might give him value in capture. None of them could afford to be taken into the Drundel land where no known foreigner ever traveled. But their efforts were futile. Their whole party was being overtaken by Drundel.

A howl pierced the haze of the horizon as the sun set. In the desert, scorching heat bled fast with the sky's wane from pink to purple to night. And all that energy artificially forced into Tierney by the sun withered with its waning. She was crashing. She fell to her knees over her sweep pup, his white coat seeping with blood. And the Drundel swarmed.

Chapter 38

Javelin flyers. One of Telluric's fastest transports, could not fly fast enough for Eh'kotah. "Come on. Come on," he beseeched. As they drew upon the flashing hotspot in the desert, Eh'kotah's normal cool-headedness altered into intense command at the scene he witnessed. He called out directives for the ten javelin flyers' placement over the battle and the strategic release of fighters by grappling hooks at certain points. Eh'kotah and some others needed no assistance dropping.

He jumped from the flyer's hatchway and disappeared into a speed dive in the sky. A seismic clash on the already unstable sand heralded Eh'kotah landing amongst the battle and the Drundel who overpowered his people.

Ruptures cracked open, swallowing people by the dozens. The tanned Drundel sitting frozen on the ridge then slammed into action. They first rescued Ok'nuh, then went after the rest of the Soonahyins trapped in the sand craigs. They brought Drundel back up only after all the Soonahyins were above ground. Some of the Drundel fighters had been smothered in the first sand crack, some crushed against the sandstone beneath the sand.

The more bodies that volunteered to enter this bloodshed, the more of them that were crushed when the sand collapsed. Tierney looked away from the dead, shuddering, her conscience pricked, her spirit doing a nosedive to the bottom of her gut. *An abominable waste of life, even if they are Drundel.*

Eh'kotah's tremor had benefited the Soonahyins to one great effect. He'd knocked *everyone* off their feet, ensuring the Drundel lost a little of their advantage. Also, the addition of Eh'kotah and his fighters weighed on the Drundel who had to be exhausted in the battle that had stretched on and on. In any event, the ground dwellers still had them beat in numbers.

Tierney's fighting spirit renewed in a vengeance with the addition of Eh'kotah's garrison. She rose from the bloody mess made of Bak'rah's hunch and this time clawed the rest of the way toward Haarth and Korrell's position, with Torhvald battling unfaltered at her side.

A few paces involving more combat, and a sleek-angled transport descended above them. *What is that?* At first, upon glancing toward the horizon it was congruent with the landscape. Angled like a curved scimitar, the flying apparatus flew from the edge of Telluric and swooped down over the battle. Wind rushes and an ear-splitting whine sent them bracing. Once it was separated from the land, the wings of the transport appeared as a flying black specimen in the sky. Lorgrens dropped into the battle from the transport whipping their cords. Those who never warred had come to fight.

And just beyond the furthest sand dunes, Tierney was startled to see a flood of Kalameshee warriors too. Over the last swell from a rise of sand, they called battle cries out to the Drundel.

To the Drundel's credit or cowardice—however generous an observer would judge them—they ran. The tunnel dwellers scurried to hidden doors on swivels that revealed even more cracks in the sand when they flipped them open. Left to fight, amassed groups of Soonahyins, Lorgrens, and Kalameshees clobbered those Drundel who stayed behind.

The shamelessness of one stubborn Drundel stooped over Haarth's body was unbelievably depraved. "Get off of him!" Tierney wrenched at his attempts to still shackle Haarth's body into a lasso. Beside herself with fury, she scrapped with the Drundel.

Her heart pounded, near beating out her chest as she threw her frostfire to the ground, its uselessness a hindrance to her now. Any means she had to subdue the Drundel, he cut off, restraining her other hand that held the cutlass.

As they scuffled, everything coalesced in her mind on sight of the sand around Haarth's head saturating with his blood. The very essence of his life seeped from him while this Drundel stole precious moments with this obscene scuffle. *He's dying!* "My...father!" Tierney's soul-energy shot like lightning to her sternum. Blinded to everything around her but Haarth, she loosed the energy through her free hand.

A hole greyed and withered the Drundel's torso the same way her pulse had done the wolf outside Outliers. Except the wolf had been intact enough to run away. The Drundel now possessed a hole where his heart should be beating, seen clean through to the other side. Had the wolf run into the woods and died as the Drundel before her now did? It was very likely. But she couldn't be bothered by it.

They have made me into a killer. Something gave a little inside Tierney as the Drundel dropped from her like the empty shell he'd now become.

A brokenness on default helped her crawl over his corpse with no more remorse than she'd have had for killing an insect. *Finally!* With Haarth now, even out cold his body was made of sturdy stock. She couldn't lift him. So she prostrated herself close to his ear and begged him to hear her. "Unc... Father...pleeease!" So unlike his fierce self. "His face!" Utterly unnatural this serene. Tierney ran her hands over him as she lay draped over Haarth's still form, pressing a hand filled with her tunic to his head. So vital before. How could his will allow him to leave from this world like this? "I have only just found you…please…please stay with me. Do like you told me. You must fight! Get up from this ground!"

She clawed at Torhvald's calf. "Help me! Help me get him up! He needs the Frozen Folly." If it wasn't for Torhvald shaking her hard and making her focus on his blurred features, Tierney might have tipped right over the edge yawning up at her. She'd been half in, half out of it, anyhow. Someone pulled her shoulder and she lashed out, scraping and hitting the offender. Tohrvald said, "Calm yourself! Its Korrell's face you mark and he's trying to help Haarth."

Korrell shifted her over and placed his hands over Haarth's heart, one on top of the other. That was not any indicator of help as far as Tierney was concerned. This was how they positioned their hands when they pulsed right up against someone. "You stay back! Get off him. You'll only hurt him more!" She scrabbled at Korrell's wrists, ripping skin from his arms, but he proved immovable.

His stillness, the gravity in his eyes captured hers, and she paused. They hobbled her distress. *All* the fight went out of her. His eyes were as saturated as hers, tears spilling from them, pleading for her understanding. Depthless pools they were, mirrors to her own sorrow. The last times she could remember her brother's face stricken like this was at the death of their father and their foreparents' crash into the ferber trees.

Okay, Korrell. I've stopped it. What is it now? What do you want me to do?

In the end, it was the abiding conviction Korrell conveyed with no words that quelled her. Tierney had ceased her desperation, her hands now softened over his. She rocked and sobbed at the unfairness of it all. She was sapped to her core, and still she willed Korrell with all the strength she had in her.

A residue of heat began emitting from his palms into hers.

And with Haarth too hurt to exhibit throes from his injuries, Korrell moaned seemed to channel *Haarth's* pain, then he looked away to some far-off place only he could see. His eyes blurred. Sweat poured down his face and tremors racked his body, but he didn't let go of Haarth and neither did Tierney him. Awareness of those clearing broken bodies from the battlefield, lingering Drundel roundup, Eh'kotah and Ad'rihl rushing their people to the javelin flyers faded as the build of energy soared between the three of them on the sand—locked in death's grip.

When Tierney detected the energy emanating from Korrell diminishing, a scream screeched inside her head. For fear his connection with Haarth would be lost, she squeezed the turmoil to a brick within. Korrell's energy diminishment continued all the same until Tierney no longer felt it reach her and her emotions, overwrought from the battle on them that day shattered. She did scream. "Korrell! What're you doing? You *can't* let him go!"

And the world around her tilted into that void....completely.

Her brain clicked into a sort of static mode, fizzing. More likely it was seething in anguish, but somehow her mind pitched itself on its own, into a vacuum like it was sectioning her off from too much trauma. She only had the capacity for her father right then. Her brothers' movements and their interactions with the foreign commanders hovering around them, Torhvald rubbing her shoulders, even Korrell's determined presence beside her ceased their existence over the plight of her father dying right there. For he was her father. She thought of him in no other way now. Haarth with his stubborn authority, always pushing at her role of comfort as princess of the land. How much of his critical guidance would she lose? She'd come to envision his presence in all aspects of her life without thinking about it. His manner was so strong she'd taken his availability for granted as if he'd always be here. For her. When he had been about to embark on a love affair with her mother that she was sure would be like none they'd ever known. He had dreams and desires too. And he deserved to live them out. And of of course, he'd be looking forward to exploring *their* new relationship. He'd already shown that.

He can't die before I have time to truly learn him as a father. It was only right that she have more time with him. Who would fight with her mother over which parent was right? That part where she'd needed his will and he pushed her to rely on her own would have happened for what, if she couldn't commiserate with him about it once they escaped this depravity? Looking her mother in the face...*no, no, no, no Lu'nil...*

To look Lu'nil in the face without her father would descend her soul into an abyss, never to return. *Please...no.* A groan wrenched from her bellows. For any grief to crush Lu'nil would deservedly destroy her. She would gladly fritter into nothingness. No moon, no stars, just blackness devoid of warmth...

Something tickled her fingers, somehow registering in spite of the static in her brain. A flutter of energy so pure it left her breathless, niggled at the fingers still wrapped around Korrell's wrists. The heat whispered across her skin, yet bathed her mind in a searing healing so fine, it wrenched her from her crippling thoughts. Her heartbeat tripled in joy. Her soul-energy re-ignited in her body. Cells traumatized in battle bloomed like a marigold turning toward the sun.

She smiled down at Haarth, yet on the brink of death. The flutter exploded from Korrell's hands, forcing itself into the semblance of Haarth left in his body. It knocked her away from them both, skidding her across the sand as if she where a flying razor needing catching. Tierney lay where she landed. Finished. Warmth oozed into her from the sand, providing a perfect rest for her bruised back. *I'll just stay here forever. No sense in moving. This is so restful.*

Only not with a monumental colossus bigger than the whole world popping above her! Ad'rihl's noggin. It blocked the view of the purpling sky and wasn't restful at all. She sighed and still took the hand he offered, they would need to get out of here now. He lifted her up to her feet, clearing her toes clean off the ground, laughing and he said, "Haarth breathes. Somehow Korrell healed him and brought him back from death."

"I know." Bone-weary, she tried to grin in return. Having felt the power of that healing as it was doing its job, she had a good idea of the end result it would grant Haarth.

"Eh'kotah cracks open the ground. Korrell heals. And you gun pulses away from your body!" Ad'rihl rubbed his hands together. "I look forward to any new gifts I have coming too!"

"I did no such thing."

"You did. I speeded toward you just as you released that pulse. Your hand wasn't in contact with that Drundel. The pulse traveled through the air to reach him."

Tierney didn't argue the point. If Ad'rihl said he saw the teal flash travel through space, then she may *have* pulsed the Drundel while she wasn't in contact. She had been so desperate to remove him from Haarth, she couldn't rightly refute the possibility.

Eh'kotah walked up to them and said, "We must hurry and leave this place before the Drundel recoup and send more fighters after us."

Tierney looked about. "Bak'rah needs a medi—"

"He's already loaded. He and Ok'nuh receive curatives as we speak as they are two of those the worst injured."

"Can Korrell not heal them too?"

"He has depleted himself on Haarth. He truly was at death's door."

They came even with Korrell sitting with Haarth who was still in an unconscious state. Eh'kotah bent for Haarth, and Korrell swatted his hands away. He stood favoring his leg, yet lifted Haarth over his shoulders anyway. Eh'kotah and Ad'rihl formed as braces on either side of Korrell. They managed to carry Haarth to the javelin flyer in a slow perambulation with Tierney in the rear, and of course, Torhvald followed behind.

Chapter 39

Javelin flyers flown at Mach speeds over thousands of parses to the arid desert inevitably ran out of the power fueling them on the trip back.

Great! There was no choice. They would be delayed again. The javelin flyers and their over-filled capacities of Soonahyins stopped in Kalamesh at the province right at its border called Urainpeda and onto its launchpad for power.

They docked and King Ocierus of Kalamesh met them in person. "Your entire party is invited to one of our land's most opulent retreats." He was magnanimous in an offer of restoration, access to royal medics, and simple respite after their ghastly ordeal.

But I just want to go home.

Tierney appreciated the offer. And allowed, of course, their injured party members administering of the Kalameshee curatives and to partake in a much-deserved rest. However, she said, "Once we have powered up we won't delay getting back on Soonahyin soil." Eh'kotah, Korrell, and Ad'rihl agreed.

Under no circumstance would their injured be moved to a retreat unescorted. A large contingent of the Tempeh Tu went in guard of the other injured Tempeh Tu. Mlai, Tierney's brothers, and their garrisons stayed close to Korrell and Haarth. Tierney was to join them after she had reassurances from the medics of Bak'rah's mending hunch diagnosis.

Subsistence on adrenaline alone wasn't good for anyone, even I know that. Her anticipation of seeing Haarth awake and recovering was the only thing keeping her going since she'd picked her bruised and battered body up from the desert floor.

The desire since her youth for exploration and an adventurous life had more than been fulfilled in her journey to Lorgr and the tour of the land there. Haarth's previous catastrophe notwithstanding, it had never occurred to her that the queen's obstinance about border crossings was well-founded. She'd reconciled Haarth's kidnapping as a disastrous misfortune. *I never thought it could happen again. Oh but, not for lack of the Drundel giving it one nightmare of a try.*

A full-out battle committed against them by the Drundel was a fantasy far removed from any imaginings Tierney had the capacity to come up with.

And lo an behold, my need for self-fulfillment nearly got us all killed.

Whenever her mind tripped in the queen's direction, it blanked on what she would say to her. Instead, she hurried to Haarth's curative suite. A few scrapes and gashes dotting her own body had been tended to, a displaced shoulder having been wrenched back into place bringing tears to her eyes, the other hurts mended together with healing bandages and healing glue. Her wrist was diagnosed as sprained and now sported compression wrap, courtesy of that Drundel she'd last tussled with. It was probably crass to think, "*You should see the other guy,*" considering he was dead. But she did. Her mind was spinning in all sorts of directions.

Her injuries' throbbing barely registered. If Haarth's prognosis was improved, Tierney would do backflips, sprained wrist and compromised shoulder and all, and gladly brave her mother's rebuke just for the security of soon stepping over the Keep's threshold.

When she entered Haarth's suite what she met there threw her off, stunning her senses almost to catatonic. The sight was of none other than the queen of Soonayah herself, chiding an *alert* Haarth. He chafed at the medics picking at him, whose intent must be to send him back to the brink of death.

On the edge of a pedestal he sat, his hair unplaited falling forward from his shoulders while medics poked at the wound on his head and Haarth sucked in a breath. The queen's fingers tangled with his near his wound, caught in his frizz as she slapped at the hands he used to impede the medics' work. Korrell and Ad'rihl, and Mlai stood to the side smirking as the queen admonished Haarth like he was one of her offspring. "Stop! And let them tend to you," she chided him.

Everyone had been right about Tierney taking her hair after her father's legacy. *They had just gotten it wrong about which father.* As an unbound frizz, Haarth's hair looked identical to hers. And she was struck motionless by it's silhouette around his hearty build. *Goodness!* He was a robust and conscious being again. *Thank the stars above!*

Her giving a good impression of a statue near the door frame caught the queen's attention. Their eyes met. Mutual expressions in the depths of them roiled together until Tierney's were swimming. Grief was the most prominent holder, for the death of so many and the war they'd come through. Horror for the atrocities they'd had to commit against other beings, even doling out some of the death themselves. She blinked rapidly to stave her eyes from flooding over. Regret... *Should I ever have tried to come to Lor...* Then duly, the queen reached a hand out to her daughter.

To Tierney, the welcome was the berth of all maternity. A respite. An offer of comfort only a mother could bestow.

"Matah!" She rushed into her mother's arms and lay her face snug in the heat of the queen's neck. That scent. *Oh goodness! That everlasting scent of my life,* so becoming of a mother tickled her nostrils. And the queen rocked Tierney, fostering the rhythmic reliance that had concerned her before, determined to soothe her daughter with it. For she must have understood the need of it now. She calmed her daughter's shudders with a palm down her back.

Haarth's hand stroked hers, save that was not enough for Tierney. Still wrapped within her mother's arms, she dragged Haarth into their embrace too. He chuckled and his fingers brushed a tear from her face. "Shh...my daughter. I'm here. We're all here. We survived."

What if he had died though? And Ok'nuh. Ok'nuh's back... Her eyes filled again. If Korrell had possessed no gift to heal, Haarth would have died out there on that sand. *Because of me.*

"Aw, how beautiful. Korrell, hand me a linen. I think I shall cry too." Ad'rihl mocked them, while wiping fake tears from his eyes. Tierney was so relieved, she didn't mind Korrell's bark of laughter. Nothing could dim the feeling that seeing Haarth animated and bickering with her mother evoked. His blanched face as tranquil as an iced sea while his life force seeped from his body could never be scrubbed from her brain. Laughter was the best tonic in the world after experiencing something like that. She even laughed at Ad'rihl when Korrell clacked up to him with a brace on his leg and slapped him on the back of his head.

"They fitted you a skeletal brace?" she cringed as she asked him, yet couldn't look away from metal pins extended from the brace clasping Korrell's legs through muscle and bone.

He nodded. "It doesn't pain me. The brace and the numbing prove quite effective. I'm well pleased the brace was available. I almost pushed my leg beyond repair by lifting and walking with Haarth and continuing to fight, I'm told. But I would rid myself of my own leg for a man who sacrifices himself without hesitation as Uncle Haarth did." The two regarded one another as respect passed between them.

"There was no sacrifi—"

"There was. I was a part of it, remember. I watched as you jumped in front of that sandsurfer even as you saw it heading for me," Korrell said.

"Perhaps we should pass linens all around. I think we're working up to an all-out crying fest here." Tierney took her turn slapping Ad'rihl's head.

Then the door opened to Torhvald, and Eh'kotah too came in at his side. With them brought a damper that dimmed the light-hearted banter in the room. Torhvald's expression sobered them right back to the reasons they were there. "Queen Ana'kerah, my father...King Oceirus asks if you will grant him an audience before you leave."

***

Hearth and Ana'kerah...in the aftermath.

Ana'kerah's duty as monarch of her land compelled her to the meeting with the king of Kalamesh. Then rightfully, all the members of the royal family insisted on accompanying her. Their whole party, including every mobile Tempeh Tu, was escorted to a space a touch too small to hold their procession. Half the Tempeh Tu who came ended up guarding their presence from outside.

Inside though, every Soonahyin sprang forward into instant combat posture. The Drundel Preeminence, Gnord, and his devotees revealed themselves from a shadowed corner, with too, too much gall in his step for one who had been involved in ambushing them. He laughed and looked to the king of Kalamesh, "Ocierus, they are ready to battle. And we come here for peaceful redress on your sovereign land."

Ana'kerah looked to the king of Kalamesh too. The king held his hands up at eyes burning accusation at him. "You set this up as an ambush!" She proclaimed.

"I didn't. I would never condone such a thing on my land. He was en route when he communicated that he needed our urgent arbitration between your land and his," Ocierus said.

Ana'kerah blistered them both as she said, "Do you exert no precautions over who enters your territory? And you've already condoned it on your land. Isn't it enough they have made death mazes of slug holes in that treacherous desert you make no effort in exercising any control over?"

"Harrumph." Gnord's face pinched.

Ana'kerah likening his people to the large worming ground animals was a debasement to the Drundel. Many lands used the slur against them.

"Kalamesh's claim on the Olum desert has been challenged since time unknown," he said. "As the Tellurician Land Commission's bias was proven to us all eons ago, by them granting Kalamesh the biggest stretch of land uncrippled by devastating environmental woes. The Olum desert is a critical one of our accesses to land not suffocated by the blight of sandstorms covering Drundel, and we keep our claim in it."

Ana'kerah threw up her hand at Gnord's tired refrain. "I should kill you where you stand. Your cry for sympathy is lost with this age-old argument of Kalamesh's preferential treatment. Soonahyins were given the choice of a frozen wasteland which we turned into a bounteous harvest...from the ice mind you! Yet you take possession of one of the few pieces of land you claim free of blight and use it for murderous traps for other people!"

"Those tunnels underneath the sand are our means of sustaining ourselves! My people travel there for relief sabbaticals when they can.

But we suck the air through those catacombs for our everyday use of clear air."

King Ocierus interjected himself between the two rulers in a moment escalating beyond the bounds the small retreat room was designed for. "Queen Ana'kerah, they've used the desert for air since both our lands were founded. Kalamesh isn't so cruel we would keep fighting a claim which would cut them off from their easiest connection to clear breathing."

"So you absolve yourself of the warring atrocities they carry out down there as if you have no responsibility?"

"Those tunnels were not built as traps and we have never once murdered one Soonahyin soul." Gnord's voice rose above Ocierus' in response to Ana'kerah's accusation. "It was you *foreigners* out there who were *slaughtering our* people."

Ana'kerah moved so fast she couldn't be stopped. She disappeared in a speed, then landed on the Preeminence of Drundel's neck. Alongside the Drundel—whose people possessed reed-tall statures—Ana'kerah's slight build seemed insignificant. Except his windpipe constricted with ease under her clawed hand, and he struggled for breath.

Despite the pressure on his throat, Gnord's face contrived an appearance of calm, and so none of his people reacted. It saved them from ending up annihilated at the hands of the Soonahyins. "You say you haven't murdered a Soonahyin when it's a miracle Haarth even breathes. One of the most elite Tempeh Tu guards ever may never walk again. And what of all the people you cut down the last time you made such transgressions against us? Should we think of them as nothing!"

Haarth forced himself between the two and backed away from Gnord with Ana'kerah at his back.

Gnord tracked every nuance of Haarth's movements, his face

carrying contradictory expressions. His grimace was one of contempt, but not so his eyes. His eyes' trace of Haarth's bearing were near slavish in their jealousy. "Ah, the invincible Prince Haarth. So precious to his land they never stopped searching for him even after a span of us feeding them false proof."

"False proof?" Haarth stilled. A generous person would now have pity for the object of his quiet question. "That desert was littered with parts of my traveling team's bodies. A portion of my principal's leg had been cut off and left to rot in the broiling sun."

Gnord smirked, except he failed to realize massaging the neck crushed by Ana'kerah's hands didn't convey the condescension he aimed for. "The operative word there is rot. We removed the leg from the guard so the rot wouldn't spread to the rest of his body. Having it to leave and be found was a bonus."

"Do you jest about his life? About all their lives? If you do, you show yourselves for the dirt-scuffling animals you are." Haarth's stillness should have telegraphed to Gnord to shut up. The tension choking the air communicated quite effectively that he was on the verge of taking up the offense against Gnord where Ana'kerah left off. The patch of plaster covering the wound in his head did nothing to detract from that. He had the intensity behind his eyes of a serpent ready to strike. "You *have* killed Soonahyins. I heard all you did to Irdulon myself, from my vault next to hers. The heinous sounds of your removal of her fingers remain a burden that haunts me to this day!"

Gnord swatted away Haarth's emotions as if they were gnats at a picnic and shrugged. "Have you never wondered about the ease with which we marked your position?" And his arrogance would be his undoing. "Irdulon's regular communications with our man-at-arms. Her true love. They are to this day matched with offspring abundant. She was so intent not to match with Stah'lief...*the charmer,* the volunteer of her fingers for our purposes was a relief to her—as long as afterward, she could abide in Drundel with our man-at-arms as far away from Stah'lief as she could get."

A pulse rocketed Gnord to the other side of the room, pitching him into the foolish devotees standing behind him.

So that's where Tierney got it from. Haarth hadn't touched Gnord with his hands.

Chapter 40

Only the brown Drundel from the desert remained standing. He of all of them had had sense enough to take note of Haarth's mounting anger. He'd removed himself from the proximity of Gnord's ill-conceived instigation, and shook his head at the debacle his people portrayed falling over each other as they picked themselves up off the floor. Gnord, finally on his feet, his features folded said, "One would think you would appreciate learning your people aren't dead."

Ana'kerah started for his neck again and Haarth held her back. "We show no appreciation to you for not killing our people who never should have been taken. Taken and kept! Never knowing their homes again. Their families having no relief of their grief, *believing* them dead. They *were* dead to us! And for what end?" she asked. You gained nothing but our wrath for these violations against us! Where are they? Bring them to us now!"

Gnord's nostrils thinned, his mouth simpered, his tone turned to wheedling. He seemed to have forgotten his pretense of confidence. He started forward toward the Soonahyins. The brown Drundel, the only one exhibiting any prudence, pressed a hand to his shoulder and stopped him before he got too close. "Irdulon told us we could gain knowledge of the formula you use to allow asteroids through your portion of the alluvial shield if we could get it out of one of your royals. Or have those back in your land cede it to us. We are looking for enhancements for our land just as you have. The Drundel people deserve the prosperity and health and clean air any land can afford its people. We're no different than you."

"You are nothing like us! We shaped our land through back-breaking industry, not by listening to some traitorous woman who has no knowledge on official affairs. And you follow this strategy again spans later, when you know she has no contact with us?" Ana'kerah's lips curled back from her teeth as she said, "What of that teeming Sea of Ore between our lands you put no efforts in taming? It's flourishing with benefits begging for use, yet you stage battles and kidnap our royals setting our lands as enemies forever." She cackled. "You're so foolish, you don't realize no royal has knowledge of any formula! Our Ministers of Science couldn't even tell you, as our methodology changes for every Starfall iteration!" Ana'kerah swung around to Haarth. "Did you know this is why these fools violated every inter-territory accord?"

Haarth shook his head in thought. "I remember interrogations at the beginning of my capture, but I was so drugged the details are foggy. And then, after so much time passed, they came sparingly and only with concerns about how Soonayah would reckon against their actions. Which is how I escaped between them. The inquisitions were so few by then."

"He tells the truth. After we gained no information from him, and your land never even answering when we used leverage, and killing all my men at that meet-up—we just needed information on Soonayah's capability to track us underground and through the sandstorms. No one accounted for your licenses against us having crippling effects on us even until this day. We need some relief, Queen Ana'kerah. We persist for our own survival."

"By encroaching into our lands, warring against us, and attempting to kidnap our royals again?"

The light of the retreat room shone quite bright. The sun slanted in through the windows as well, to mingle with the retreat's lighting and reflect off the moisture beading on Gnord's temple. He raked fingers that shook through hair as pale *as the* light, running in a strip down the middle of his head. "There should have been no war. With the dosage of tincture we put through the razor's vents, your people should have been unconscious and conducted to our portal with no incidents. We have archives of Haarth's features. With them, we still couldn't find him amongst so many with skin and hair and stature as your people have in the midst of all that chaos. We were sure if we just had so many of your royals in our custody, we could convince you, Queen Ana'kerah. Parting with the formula is no great loss. Once we'd released them, you would have no reason to strike back against us. And never, not once have we entered into Soonahyin land. You would slaughter us if we did."

Every Soonahyin in the room laughed. The Drundel clearly had no idea who they were or how they operated. The perversity in Gnord's thinking was actually asinine. Haarth edged closer to the Drundel and again the one tanned Drundel shifted positions. This time he angled himself between the two lines of antagonist. Haarth gave him his full attention for the first time, gauging his stance, noting his bearing. He kept the brown Drundel in his periphery, but said to Gnord, "If you engage in warring tactics, then you should expect war as the outcome. There's no correct dosage of *poison* for people whose metabolisms are quickened by the sun's heat. Not to mention the two other peoples from foreign lands whose vitals were being sustained by the air on that razor. And even had we all slumbered like babes as you stole us away, your history with me should have warned you that we don't give in to the pressure of extortion." Haarth shook his head.

A glare up and down Gnord spawned a curl to Haarth's lips. Gnord's decision-making was stupid and destructive. "Not once during your torture, in all the time you kept me there did I answer one of your questions. Not even my name. I risked an escape and death in the desert rather than let you think you would ever get what you wanted from me. And my people would have let me die too. As they should. No one holds leverage over Soonayah." Haarth turned his back to the Drundel, contempt riding the rigidity of his shoulders. "We must leave. My control wanes. This...man even denies the attack on you in the Okehfey Wilds." he said to Ana'kerah.

"You didn't escape so cleanly as you thought...Prince Haarth. Your arrogance is so like your brother Stah'lief's, it astounds me." Gnord reached to turn Haarth back and the brown Drundel blocked him. He pushed at the brown Drundel but when he didn't yield, Gnord slapped his face. "You should recognize the inheritance of that arrogance in your offspring, Prince Haarth!" He barked at Haarth's back. "If you thought this Drundel belonged to Irdulon or one of your guards who remain in Drundel, you're quite wrong. He's yours."

Haarth swung back round, his eyes seared to the shoulder of the Drundel blocking Gnord from overstepping his bounds. The Drundel slowly faced him. A thickness in the air ran rampant with speculation. Only Gnord's cackles resounded. But even the insult of them couldn't penetrate the fog of disbelief permeating the retreat room's air. The Drundel having tanned skin was obvious. The hair half-shaven from his head was brown and blonde too, though the light did hit ash highlights attesting to his Drundel heritage. His cranium carried ridges extended from his nostrils like all Drundel, ensuring every breath taken filtered the air of the dust common to their homeland. However, his brow and jawline, even his build were replicas of Haarth.

"Have you never told of how you tricked your way out of my dungeon from your gullible vault attendant with seduction? Then killed seven of my men? And of course, you never looked back for any consequences, did you, *Prince Haarth*? It's amazing that you didn't recognize your family traits in him right away. You saw he and his ilk took no part in our attempts to take you. They hold themselves above us, living separately out there in the desert." Gnord reached for the other Drundel again but drew back fast at Haarth's glare.

"Touch him again and I separate your hand from your body ."

"We've never touched them. Never curtailed how they choose to live. You can see he's strong and robust."

Haarth ignored Gnord from then on, not willing to dignify his tyranny and allow him any other words in his own defense. His eyes ate up the one who he claimed was his son. "You mute your energy. Is that intentional?"

The brown Drundel nodded. "I didn't intend to reveal myself. I'm only here as a balance. Though his reasonings are asinine, the Preeminence is still the leader of our people."

"So you claim yourself as Drundel?" Haarth asked.

"I'm both Drundel and Soonahyin. Drundel is the most of what I know."

"And your name?"

"Kahfey Haarth Soonayah Lupin."

He'd been given Soonayah's family name as a connection. Haarth's name just like Tierahna. Someone had *understood* the importance of who he was. His mother, no doubt. His look to Tierahna then, their eyes meeting, alluded to him understanding it too.

"You must come back with me," Haarth said.

Kahfey shook his head. "I wish for a life in which I can learn my father's land. We all do. But Mother has done well by me, and she deserves a life of her choice in her own home. Which I can't assure if I leave."

"Will you keep communication with me?"

"I will," Kahfey said.

"We'll allow any who wish for their lives back in Soonayah open passage. But we must have some relief, Queen Ana'kerah. My people have suffered long enough!" Gnord called out as the Soonahyins ignored him and proceeded out the room. The last guards didn't leave until after the royals began to file out.

Ana'kerah gave one last response to Gnord before she walked through the door. "Your people should rebel for a leader with better far-sight. You say you haven't killed Soonahyins but haven't once acknowledged the death of that Lorgren boy whose body even now is being taken back to his home. I can't speak for the Lorgrens response to this savagery, but I'm sure it'll be punishing when it comes."

She looked at King Ocierus and said to him in a matter-of-fact tone, "Our borders are closed to all Kalamesh for now, except the one with true character who risked his life for my daughter. As our lands have a common border and interests in kind, under no circumstance should this meeting have been arranged as a surprise to me. Expect all your people in Soonayah returned in no more than three days."

Gnord's cry after the queen and her assembled's retreat echoed outside the room. "We had no way of knowing your people would bring the Lorgrens back with them! The start of our plans couldn't be stopped, we—"

The door closed on the Soonahyins' exit.

* * *

Torhvald

"All is not well in the house of Gnord. He should have much to answer for if his people will ever hold him accountable," King Ocierus said to his son.

The reception room of the retreat echoed now that the Soonahyins were gone and with King Ocierus finally convincing Gnord his best course of action was withdrawal back to his homeland to regroup for new strategies. Torhvald agreed with his father's opinion, but knew his father's role in the situation wasn't clean of fault either. King Ocierus was forever sly in his maneuverings. He'd studied his father enough to know he had some motive for what he'd done. "Why let him come, Father? Queen Ana'kerah was right. Gnord doesn't have the freedom to travel here as he wills. You would've shot him out the sky if you hadn't wanted him here."

Ocierus shrugged in that negligible way of his. "He needed a neutral party for an intervention on this disaster he created. And I thought for the good of all, diplomacy was called for before we end up in the middle of two lands in a full-fledged war."

Torhvald shrugged as well. He couldn't fault his father's logic on that account. "I couldn't predict all that drama happening in having the two lands in here though," Ocierus said. "Did you see how Queen Ana'kerah flew across the room at Gnord? Heard of it, but never seen speeding in real life before. I thought she would rip his throat out at any moment if it weren't for that Prince Haarth of hers holding her back. She's a spitfire of a woman to be reckoned with."

Torhvald recognized the gleam in his father's eyes and was glad to disabuse him of it. The way the Soonahyins ran their land had him calling into question quite a few machinations he'd been a party to in his own. How the *Kalmeshees* used their gift to read others like it was a gauge, always measuring and adjusting what they said, and how they reacted according to whom they were dealing with and the particular situation. Deceptive almost, never truly being themselves.

His approach to meeting the Soonahyin royals in the first place was the perfect example. Especially when compared to how in-your-face the Soonahyins we're most of the time. He preferred how he interacted with Tierney. The two of them speaking their minds and keeping each other honest. "You *should've* anticipated *ruination* to reign in here. We have only just gotten out of a battle with them! And the queen of Soonayah is most definitely a force of reckoning and much more. Although, I'm sure if you noticed Prince Haarth's protection of her, you could read in their profiles as easily as I did what they mean to each other. So, I hope you have no designs to charm her. I would think four matches, my mother included, and thirteen sons and daughters would be more than fulfilling for you."

The king of Kalamesh threw his head back in laughter. He favored his son with an appraisal after he was finally over his humor, assessing his demeanor. Torhvald walked back and forth and settled at a window that displayed the scenery of the sanctuary surrounding the retreat.

The burbling brook. Birds feeding and bathing in a pool. A profusion of flowers scenting the air. The trees around the retreat, secluding it from prying eyes. Then off he went to pace again, unmoved by the tranquility. His gaze had caught the last of the Soonahyin Tempeh Tu who had guarded the retreat from outside, to the point of invading and posting up in the sanctuary. They were leaving now that the Soonahyin royals were boarding their transports. It made him itch to hurry and get this conversation over with his father. "You couldn't be more right, my son. Having the matches of your mother and her peers and all the offspring they have given me grants me an overabundance of favor. But with a woman like Queen Ana'kerah at my side, I might feel settled for life. And just imagine the power of her land and ours combined. It makes me all a quiver."

Torhvald stood solemn at his father's jesting. Ocierus' suggestion of an opportunistic joining of Kalamesh and the allegiance-driven

Soonahyins all for more power wasn't funny to him. His mind was occupied elsewhere on changes crucial to his own life. He knew how he wanted to be now (his gift a part of him, but not ruling his every action)...and who he wanted to be that way with.

"It seems you impressed the queen with your ferociousness on behalf of that daughter of hers. Her gratitude will be of great use in future negotiations." Torhvald snorted, deciding right then that he wouldn't help his father with anything that would take advantage of Soonayah. "That princess I sent you for is just as much of a stunner as her mother. It's good they have no idea you were charged with cajoling her back here whether her mother wished it or not. Seducing her must not have been a problem *at all*."

"I didn't seduce her. And I never would have brought her here against her will, Father. No matter how much leverage over them means to Kalamesh."

King Ocierus patted his son's shoulder. "I know you wouldn't have. It's just good they know nothing of it, now that I see getting back to her makes you bide your time with *me* with impatience. Should I expect I'll see you back in Kalamesh soon?" He had informed his father while still in Soonayah that he would stand by Tierney even as she journeyed beyond Soonayah. That admission had been met with his father's cackling at his dutiful son following behind the princess' whims.

Torhvald shook his head. He didn't know how often he would come back to Kalamesh. What he *was* sure of was his love for Tierney, and that he would live with her wherever she was happiest. *If* she would have him.

Chapter 41

Several days later, a mid-size snowcraft cut through snowy terrain with it's optiglass top slid open. On such a moderate day for Soonayah, the outing brushed soft as powder snow and cold wind over Tierney and Torhvald's hair and tingled their cheeks. Bak'rah's tongue hang long as he lapped at the snow. His mouth gaped open appeared to smile his delight in the experience.

This is perfect. Just how I remember it.

They reached an area in a wooded surround, quiet and still. Trees stripped of their leaves stretched over every pace of forest, yet didn't obstruct the view with their prickly branches. And they waited. The thick pallet of snow through the woods was pristine. No footfalls marked it of any living thing stirring. "Are you sure this is a good place for him? It seems so isolated. No creatures abound at all," Torhvald asked after they had waited for some time.

"It is. On my last sojourn, I saw packs of wolves here. Several packs. My snowcat craft couldn't get me through this passage fast enough. But Bak'rah got so roused, he nearly toppled us over." Tierney lowered herself to her sweet pup and ran her hands through his coat. With delicate fingers, she was mindful of his shoulder hunch. She felt a bit of a ridge there through his fur, a bit of scarring on the mend. Even though the medics proclaimed him well on the way to recovery after his last bout with water from the Frozen Folly, Tierney detected a slight stutter in his gait still. "I calmed him by opening the optiglass just as we did and he and the wolf packs exchanged howls like they were speaking to each other. I think they may be his family. In a craig near abouts here is where I found him stuck against a wall."

"How you found him still baffles me. Were you exploring nearby when you came across him?"

"No. On a convoy with my family's Cordalai clan. We stopped and regrouped, and I heard him crying a pitiful sound. He was near death in that craig. I just about killed *myself* getting to him."

They walked into an empty wood as they talked. Snow continued to fall. The soundlessness of nothing but their voices and crunching feet created the surrounds of an eerie world their presence didn't disturb. If anything, they complimented the place as witnesses to its unmarred serenity. "He couldn't harm me. He was too weak. So, he let me hold him and climb down, lest he fell by himself and broke his neck. Except I slipped too, and we started to tumble. That was the first time I ever speeded with another being." She graced her beloved Bak'rah with another gaze. "He was really but a pup then. A big abandoned pup. And we have been in synergy and he has never left me since."

Bak'rah stopped his sniffing motions suddenly and looked off. A ways beyond them, a pack of wolves roamed a ragged hill. "But now you send him away?"

Bak'rah looked back at Tierney, then again to the wolves. "Bak'rah go!" He whimpered and lowered his head, shuffling back to Tierney. "No, sweet pup. You must go."

Again, he looked at the wolves searching hills partially free of snow for their prey of the day. Tierney swore she witnessed longing in his eyes. "Go, my boy! Look, they wait for you." If she cried Bak'rah would never go, but he had to.

She would never risk his life again just for her own selfishness of companionship in him. He deserved better. Every rambunctious, freewheeling, hunt-filled hound dream, she wanted for him, and he would never have as long as he was her constant shadow. Her sacrificing guardian. Tierney turned from him and walked away. She thought of her happiness in her youth, trouping with her siblings and father through woods like these. They reminded her of the woods her brothers described camping in.

She herself had never gotten beyond the requirement of warding off heat-seeking lemmings and crawling scarps to enjoy camping. Her brothers captured both as boys—mostly the ten-legged scarps—because as all the animals of Telluric did, the lemmings possessed enhancements from the soil. When cornered their adrenalin hyped and made them fiercely fighting little foes, who aimed unerringly for soft flesh with their bucked teeth. The hard-shelled scarps, though their pincers hurt just the same, sought burrows beneath the snow. They had enhanced adaptability for survival even if the snow froze over. Which made their flesh a succulent treat, after capturing them and cracking their shells, and roasting them over an open fire. Tierney never found the delicacy of scarp flesh, though savory, worth the necessity of setting up airborne soundwave diffusing devices in just the right spot to repel all the possible little camp invading creatures at least fifty paces away. Just to be allowed to sleep on the covered, but still cold ground? *No no. I'm smart enough to pass on that.* She was happy to partake of any scarps her brothers brought back from their lauded camping adventures in the warm, dry comfort of the Keep.

She didn't look back, but Bak'rah didn't move onward to the wolves either. She concentrated on those happy times with a singular mindset, hoping Bak'rah felt no inkling of how torturous this decision was for her. Once they had walked some distance and were near the snowcraft again, Tierney dared ask Torhvald, "What does he do?"

"He watches you."

"I feel his whimpers as if he is standing here next to me." Her voice broke. "Please, we must go now. I fear I can't hold out much longer." Not up to it herself, Tierney handed the conducting over to Torhvald.

Inside, they watched Bak'rah's slow lope forward. The closer he got to the waiting wolf pack, the more he sprinted uninhibitedly. Tierney lay her head against Torhvald, rocking them both, tilting the snowcraft too with the rhythm. Her tears drenched his back the further they got from Bak'rah.

"My pup. My sweet boy."

She wept as if grieving his death until her stomach cramped. Her body actually palpitated with anguish. Regardless of the depth of her loss, he would have a family of his own now to traipse this perfect sweep of land with. Which Tierney couldn't have designed better for him herself. Thick snow here preserved abundant frozen scarps beneath its rushes and infestations of lemmings and various other vermin plenteous in offer as prey for the wolf packs. And hidden beneath the icy cover, buried in some of the granite caves, wolf dens flourished in protection from the veryum who would menace them.

My sweet pup living the wild wolf's life he is destined for is all that matters. She tried to let that thought console her the distances the snowcraft traveled.

Back at the Keep, Ad'rihl was inciting a ruckus for some unknown reason. Boys and girls trooped behind him chanting, "Starfall time! Starfall time!" adding more excitement into an already heady atmosphere. The Soonahyin chancellors and chieftains and every member of their juntas, which included some family members too, remained in Dameerh.

Groups of them resided in the Keep's guest residences. They stayed close to the Hall of Covenance to hash out involved plans concerning more accessibility at the border. The response to the recent events between Lorgr, Drundel, and Kalamesh, and future cross-border travel for Soonahyins.

It was happening. What I've always dreamed of. Soonayah strategizing how to open its borders more.

Ironic really, now that Tierney didn't believe in it anymore. The issues her land took up were those that had driven her to defy the queen and meet Haarth in the first place. And she wanted no parts of them. After the horrendous events of the past recent days, Tierney no longer believed going to foreign lands offered the education she once thought vital for Telluricians. *Not if while visiting said lands, one witnessed atrocities being carried out against their own people. And if one couldn't hope for the security of existence in the places without being hunted down, assaulted and tortured, or even worse.*

Gymein's requiem pyre—set ablaze, floating out to sea the day they observed his life—had reinforced this new mindset for Tierney. The Lorgren requiem had been so final. He was dead, she knew that. His body had turned to ashes as they'd watched it drift away. Altogether different from Soonayah's replenishment of the soil with their reduced remains. The ceremony which *celebrated* the cycle of life. How ever someone's soul leaving their body forever was reconciled, death up close brooded in the psyche.

I need a talk with Mother. She was already picking up the habit of talking things over with her mother as she'd done in her youth. The prospect offered a relief to have someone always there with the wisdom and care she would need going forth.

She found her mother in her and her sisters' most favored salon instructing her regent to handle an incident concerning one of the Cordalai chieftains and several members of his junta, who were staying in the guest residences. The queen greeted her and Torhvald after her regent left. "You let the beast go?"

She'd just left him in the woods. *Still too raw for picking over.* To her mother, she said, "He's with his family now," and nothing more.

The queen's hawk-like stare scoured eyes that glistened and a head that had been downcast too often in recent days. She raised Tierney's chin with her hand. "Do you believe you did the right thing?"

Tierney recoiled at her mother poking at the rawness of it all but went ahead nodded. "I know I did."

"Then I am happy for him and for you. You put his needs before your desire to have him with you," she said, then grinned in Torhvald's direction. "Besides, with your new companion here always at your side, Bak'rah may have started to feel neglected."

Tierney pulled a face, grateful for how easy her mother made Torhvald's presence acceptable. Regardless of whether or not her spirits were high as of late, she would rally in Torhvald's defense if need be. He'd proved himself over and over again for her when she hadn't asked him to. Her trust in him was implicit enough that they planned a move to Haarth's Oxhild territory—and soon. He would be close to Kalamesh and she could start living as she wished in a new place. This issue needed to be broached with her mother too. "Mother, Torhvald is one of the reasons I sought you out. We intend to move to Oxhild. Your approval...if you approve, we will broach Haar...Father about the move next."

The queen's expression sobered instantly. She scored Tohrvald's stance and he returned her regard. "I'm told I shouldn't call you the Kalamashee anymore as you have earned the right to be addressed in first respect."

"I appreciate—"

The queen waved away his gratitude. "Are you intending a match with my daughter, Torhvald?" she demanded.

"Mother! We haven't decided—"

"Yes," he said. If she'll have me, I do." Tierney sucked in her breath. A thrill shivered inside her because she already knew she would have him. Waiting for more time to pass would be more prudent, only her mother's question pushed the subject in their faces.

"Then I approve your move." Tierney and Torhvald broke into laughter. They hadn't expected to persuade the queen this easily. "And Haarth and I were already thinking to ask if you would be interested in a move to Oxhild as an apprentice to the new Viceroy there. Your interests seem to lie in areas of politics. Haarth is coming back to the Keep on a permanent basis, so this all follows our plans." The queen grimaced. "You'll just need to win the people over for *their* approval of you if the position is to your liking." The queen looked to be heartened by the interplay between the two: a kiss and sighed breaths they'd apparently been holding. "You two must be planning many forays into Kalamesh once we have done our work here in assembly?" she asked the next most logical question.

Here it goes. Tierney's joy skittered to a halt. Time to relay her complete turn-about. "We may not take many forays together. Even still, Torhvald will be right there on the border. Travel to Kalamesh should prove effortless for him."

The queen sniffed and arched her eyebrows at them. "Believe me when I say, having a man who leaves you on your own more often than he's home isn't real living for matched people. Especially for young people just striking out in new relations."

"Our intentions are different, Mother." *It's not my situation to be coerced into a match with someone who is more like a brother than a lover to me as you were,* she thought. "Besides, I've come to the realization that you were right after all. If in every new land we journey, someone will see us as an opportunity ripe for exploitation, then it's safer to stay within *our* borders."

"But what challenges lie within the margins of what's most comfortable for you?" The queen smiled at Tierney's bucked eyes. "I'm not as inflexible as you think. I've shifted my stance from fear of what I can't control. And besides, we'll never be cowed by any other land on Telluric. Rather, they shall learn what being a Soonahyin means if they make transgressions against us. Drundel is getting another critical dose of that right now." The queen came close to Tierney and took her by her shoulders. She squeezed them tight. "Your limitations are what you set for yourself. Do you agree?"

Tierney nodded. "I agree, Mother. But..."She chopped her hand through the air. "I had no choice but to hurt people...maim them...to take someone's life! People outside of me can affect what I do. They can force reactions from me I never would have taken on my own!"

"Such is life. The difference is of no more account here in Soonayah or there, exploring a foreign land. Exerting control outside ourselves will always have ramifications, no matter the culture of those we contend with. For they have free will too." The queen rubbed the back of her fingers over Tierney's cheek and kissed her. "Now come and find Os'carah. She just left before you came, she was searching for you. The dance theater is in play this eve and she means to see to it that you're there."

"I...no. I can't—"

"Come, Tierahna. You must rally your spirits. Don't forego the opportunity of the theater in play with so many Soonahyin leaders taking part. It's something you won't be offered often. You must come." The queen gave Torhvald a hefty push on his back toward Tierney. "If you don't come, you deny Torhvald here one of the most unforgettable experiences of his life."

Rarely is Mother this amiable. However, no fault could be found in a mother's joy whose progeny came home alive and whole from a hard-won battle. With the queen and Haarth pursuing their renewed relationship, she now had someone who was more than capable of relieving her of some of the weight of her mantle. The assembly process was long and intricate, but progressing on issues a majority of Soonahyins wanted changed. The queen was in good form.

Tierney found herself obliged to take a cue from her mother. At some point, she'd have to reconcile with everything that'd happened. With what she'd had to do. Come to a place of dealing with it. She'd see if Torhvald was up to a trip to a sanctum on the frozen tundra for a while. She had looked into the resort's therapies they offered, the intensities of the voluntary sessions. And couldn't wait to take part in them, having even more—*like war and death and having to kill someone with my own hands*—to add to what she needed help with now.

The dance theater could actually be a balm to the psyche. I just need to give it a chance. She sighed and sent Torhvald to her brothers for instruction, and she went as she was told and prepared herself to partake in the dance come eve.

Chapter 42

Tohrvald

Festivities involving a majority of the Soonahyin leaders and their juntas and the upcoming Starfall and dance theater events in Dameerh amplified a place known for its resplendent air. Residents of Soonayah—used to the dominion's goings-on—joined in on the buildup permeating with laughter, with an openness to each other, and an anticipation of what's promised. The Soonahyins hobnobbed with the Kalameshee, Torhvald Coleman Beard, the princess' new companion who walked the streets among them too.

Torhvald explored by himself while confounded why everyone in Dameerh prepared for a simple dance with such intensity. As instructed by Tierney, he'd sought her brothers' help with his preparation. Ad'rihl had jested with him. "Your solid build's stretch of that thin fabric might just burst it."

He wore a short-fitted sleeve like every man wore for the dance. His, showing too much of his gonads as far as he was concerned.

Torhvald's laughter at his own expense along with Tierney's brothers had echoed through the changing room. His frame *had* hulked through *one* sleeve. Attendants swapped one after another for him and still, they found none contoured rightly for his body. Eh'kotah could commiserate because he was a similar build. He chose the least revealing for him. "You must contact my outfitter for future garments if you intend to stay in Soonayah."

He was attired as he was told appropriate. The brothers had stayed and continued even more preparations. He left out of the Keep seeking inclusion in the streets bustling with Soonahyin excitement. The brothers were still having their hair loosened and washed and re-plaited and were washing themselves using special ablutions designed for male enhancement within the dance. They informed him all their outer garments except their sleeves were removed for the dance. Only, the outer garments held special significance too. Torhvald was clean, his hair glistening a burnished gold. *Enough was enough.*

He'd donned his cloak, tunic and trews, and boots, appreciative of Tierney's advice on acquiring the new garments. The shukka insulation lining them kept him nice and toasty and quite dapper. A Kalameshee dressed in Soonahyin wear. *Not the laughable hulking giant anymore.*

He proceeded without all the layers he'd brought from his homeland for warmth, and wandered around to the eatery they had visited before and had fare containing lommel blubber prepared in the scrumptious way Soonahyins had with their food.

"How do you make that giant fish so delicate like this?" he asked the proprietor.

She chuckled, "Trade secret," and winked at him and bustled to her other patrons.

He indulged in a sweet course from the Rising Bun, then followed along behind some clans of Cordalai Soonahyins into a public entrance to the Frozen Folly. *How do the regular Soonahyins do it?*

Not keen on spoiling the hard work the Keep attendants and Eh'kotah spent on his preparations, Torhvald didn't partake in a deep-dive into the Folly, even though he could use it after that battle had left scrapes and little hurts everywhere. Rather, his observations of clans of Soonahyins practicing their Ritual of Ume opened his eyes to a significant revelation.

Even though he believed the Drundel Preeminence Gnord, right about very little, one thing he had been right about. *The fool.*

Throughout Telluric, it was said amongst all the other lands—some of them still holding resentment—that Kalamesh had been shown favor by the Tellurician Land Commission and was allotted the only landmass on Telluric free of environmental blight. Yet, history told that the Soonahyin people had walked away from inclusion in such a farce on fair play. The choice left to them afterward was never-ending migration until they'd met the end of any land left in a frozen presentation. The land now known as Soonayah. They'd claimed it as their own.

Given what most considered desolation and through the sheer force of who they were they'd progressed beyond what was imaginable. How significant a discovery the Soonahyin's reaction to the umbereen and the combination of its effects along with the other minerals and additives in the soil must have proven to a people forging an existence in the unforgiving landscape.

So many commodities just in this one place. No wonder the people here embody such profound essences. And hopefully they will be willing to share some of the commodities now that he was here and could help the diplomacy along.

The Soonahyin's disposition, their very will, surely shaped their acclimation to all things Soonahyin, conforming them against the land itself.

Therefore, he found questionable the Soonahyin's relentlessly feeding on the heat from the sun when they were in the desert, although it had kept them hyped in battle. Never coming down to allow restoration could have devastating effects. Torhvald wondered if it were even possible for the Soonahyins to spend long periods of time away from their land when their makeups were conformed to only what their land had on offer.

To stay in another land, they would have to augment their soul-energy somehow. For most Soonahyins, could they even thrive away from home? How did those who'd stayed in Drundel do it? He watched an elderly Soonahyin man bent with ailments, emerge from the Folly river spry and rejuvenated. "Astonishing!"

He left the Frozen Folly after witnessing that perfect example of his thoughts. Eve had long passed over the short Soonahyin day once he headed back to the Keep. His Tempeh Tu with him advised him to meet Tierney and the rest of the royals already at the dance theater. He was escorted to a door different from the one they'd used when they'd first visited. It was opposite the front. They walked through a guard patrol. Some of the patrol wheeled missile lasers around the theater.

"Those are wicked looking. Are they powerful?" His Tempeh Tu guard nodded...noncommittal. "More Soonahyins secrets, huh?" The guard shrugged.

* * *

Tierney

Most of the royals gathered in an anteroom off the main floor.

They stripped themselves of everything except their sleeves. Mlai's excitement at the prospect of the dance manifested per her usual bounce, clamped hair bobbing in between the order of royal brothers. Everyone was grateful that she still had some bounce in her.

"I'm so excited for the dance," she said, clapping her hands.

Her exuberance was a bit...muted. *Gymein.* His death changing her forever was the nature of things at this turn in life. Pure guilelessness lost its shine with an encroachment of time's travails and tribulations.

They came up into the dance theater from underneath the dial, into the center of the dance floor, and exited from the dial stage down onto the floor. Soonahyins filled the theater to the hilt. They crowded the upper landing surrounding the dance floor too. Everyone made room for everyone else as they were willing to dance in unusual spaces in order to take part in this special occurrence. Leaders from all across the land and the royal party and their full retinue of Tempeh Tu were among them. The hum of excitement surfing the room magnified to a clamor no one could hear themselves over.

Nyoma swept onto the stage of the dial and flourished herself around. She flaunted her flawless dancer's body in her feminine version of the sleeve which left one shoulder revealed. "What a glorious night it is for the dance!" she shouted above all the noise.

A roar rushed from everyone when the roof of the theater flew open and the flames in the walls whooshed to life around them. The theater, balanced on rockers for ebbs and flows, took a deep pitch with a streak of heightening energy from the crowd.

Tierney noticed Ad'rihl steadying Mlai's stutter-step, one hand on her waist. Torhvald's skimmed and steadied hers too. Then his hand edged around and palmed her belly.

"Mmmm..." Through the sleeve she wore, the roughness of Tohrvad's fingers created friction against the thin gauze, titillating her before she danced one step. His gaze wandered over her bared shoulders as appreciative as when he'd dunked himself when she'd first appeared before him in her water costume. She hoped what he saw was similar to what she admired about him. Her wrist still in the compression wrap, a few nicks and bruises but overall a quite pleasing view. His biceps were as chiseled as a sculpture and Tierney caressed her hands over them. He shook his head, eyes awed, and Tierney pulled him close. In his ear, she said, "You have seen all of me. My look should be no surprise to you."

This night her look was even more breathtaking, her hair cleansed and puffed to its full glory. Her sleeve contoured to a fullness of curves the norm for Soonayah but put a dumbfounded look on Tohrvald's face. Her skin shone its specialness as if aglow.

He grinned at her. "My amazement comes in knowing I shall gorge myself on the perfect specimen you are come leaving this theater this night."

Nyoma's voice broke into the moment, raised by an amplifying device worn on her throat, she announced, "Soonahyins!" She looked down toward Mlai and Torhvald, "And our rarefied guests!" She then dragged a shaker attached to the wooden dial through its crevices. The column fell open like a bloomed flower and revealed the plush red insides. Nyoma, as a master performer, made a show of maneuvering the dial and its golden medal inner-workings.

First, loud whirring screeched out, then the sound morphed into an intoxication. A rhythm that beat into the soul, interluded melody in slow-fashion. The crowd swayed with it. The queen's regent caught first fervor. He came up from behind the dial as they had, but hopped from the stage, forgoing the steps, and ran as if chased.

His flat-out sprint turned, stripping a path through everyone circling the dance floor around the dial. Lorneam, Bernehvelle's man, grabbed him. Their arms touched skin to skin, from hands to elbows. Lorneam shuddered from the contact and Bernehvelle came behind him in support. A string of people touched hands to elbows from Lorneam and the regent's beginning link. The theater pitched again. This time everyone inside ebbed with it. "Ehh…"

"Soonahyins!" Nyoma called to the crowd, inciting their intensity even further.

They responded back, "Soonahyin souls do not lie!"

Bobbing up and down, Nyoma raised her fists hammering them to the sky with the beat. "What do we do!"

Every Soonahyin in the theater shouted, "Share in touch! Soonahyins heighten in dance!"

All Soonahyins could dance. It was a part of who they were. With Torhvald up close on her, Tierney rubbed her hips against his and encouraged sensuality into his movements. If he let go, his first experience could well rival the exhilaration Soonahyins underwent while in the dance.

Young and old moved alike. Os'carah and Lu'nil danced in their sleeves similar to water costumes, attracting all the males in their vicinity. The rhythm rode every brown shoulder, animating hundreds of bronzed legs of their own accords. No being's staunchest reserve could withstand the ferocity of one's soul-energy inflaming from its core.

Even the old Cordalai chieftain's body, whose bones no longer obeyed directives from her mind, quickened as it was innervated to do. No longer feebled and ailing, she moved in step as everyone did. Korrell swiveled just near her, his wide shoulders' movement blocked the figure right next to the chieftain. An intricate sway accommodating his brace revealed it was Wilowah he moved against… intimately. *Wow! No wonder Korrell was so reticent about his interaction with her hamlet.*

Flames flared within the wall next to them to the beat of the Soonahyins rocking the theater. Her mother's words sounded within

Tierney's brain, "*No good serves our people with long proximity to the heat of the flames.*" She made sure to mark that the flame-screen's protective capabilities still did its job.

When Soonahyins originally engaged in the dance out of the necessity of girding their soul-energy, and their need for innervation, no mechanism existed to guard against the flames. In her youth, as she practiced in the theater with her siblings and the other young ones of the Keep, Tierney would stare at the wall of flames anxious of them leaping beyond their screens, concern overtaking her after the many tales told of those whose euphoria caused them to lose themselves to the fire.

A frown similar to hers of her youth marred Mlai's features. She shifted her and Ad'rihl's position away from the wall, more toward the dial. Tierney didn't blame her for her caution. Especially considering how easily *she'd* toyed with her connection in the heat in recent days. She caught Mlai's arm to reassure her. The Logren's eyes were dull. Tierney hated that for her. The amethyst so bright with wonder before, had now aged, world weariness would be a permanent accessory for her now.

"No worries, okay?" Hands to elbows, she shared her own warmth with Mlai as if she were Soonahyin.

A kick of energy surprised her coming from Mlai. But it shouldn't have surprised her at all. Foreign or Soonahyin constitution, everyone connected during the dance fed off of each other. Hopefully, it would rally Mlai.

Soul-energy levels ascended and the excess was trapped within the ferber wood walls which attracted and harnessed it for later use. As the Soonahyin were ones to do, they wasted nothing.

The most noticeable contrast of the young Tellurician women was their skin. The color of Mlai's arm blushed with pink, held against Tierney's lustrous sienna gleamed starkly in the firelight. Yet, Tierney was certain she detected more darkening to Mlai's skin, likening it to a deep mauve now. Tierney basked in their differences. Delighted she shared this tradition with her friend *and* Torhvald, whose heat which undulated behind her gave off a different kind of contrast, altogether.

She could still believe in the ideal of fostering relations with others of different lands. People who recognized and appreciated each other's differences *may well cease* carrying out atrocities against each other. *It could start with us. Our friendship, my and Torhvald's relationship could be the catalyst to better relations for everybody.*

Laughter barked from her when the crowd ducked. Nyoma gyrated and lunged toward them from the stage. Never having known she possessed the gift of speeding, the crowd reacted as Nyoma must have expected they would. They "Oohed" and "ahhed." She disappeared from sight and landed within Eh'kotah's arms. He played into her dramatics and gripped her toned thighs. She swooped her body and wrapped her legs round his neck and fell backward, whipping herself around him.

The spectacle of Nyoma contorting herself on Eh'kotah, her feet never touching the ground, wasn't liable to be topped by anything Soonahyins could ask for in a dance theater in play. The atmosphere took its toll on Tierney. The beat's heaviness strummed inside her gut. The pulse in the room throbbed in her heartbeat. Her natural attraction to rhythm was pushed even beyond what was normal for her. She closed her eyes and every person's energy became hers. She lost herself to the dance. *Off to your own little world again there, Tierney?*

She wasn't close to the heat from the flames in the wall and still her introspection engaged. Good. Better that than losing herself for moments at a time. All those around her became a part of her. Their energies set her aflame. With their passions so high, she latched onto Torhvald, as a mooring in the storm. This time she could control the intensity. Even though her lids were lowered—shutting off visual connection to them all, protection against overloading—in her mind, the people appeared a perfect depiction.

The sienna of their skin burnished in the light of the flames. The silver from the moons and gleams from the stars of Telluric glanced off the near-naked bodies, writhing in sleeves designed for maximum exposure, revealing the exquisiteness in the browns of their skin.

Tierney lost track of her feet touching the ground because they circled the dial with so many leaders and gifted people. Who knew whose speeding triggered another's. Those with the gift to speed swept everyone along until one moving person couldn't be divined from another...and the crowd burst into rapture.

Tierney opened her eyes and saw a scene not witnessed since the days she'd spent wide-eyed in youth: Queen Ana'kerah, on stage starting the time-honored sikkya tradition, dancing better than the best of dancers. Peetah Pearl and Tempeh Tu surrounded her.

The queen of Soonayah was distinguishable through the cover of Tempeh Tu and Haarth's rugged profile, moving as Soonayah bred in him too.

The raucousness exploded out of the theater in reaction to the queen joining in on a theater in play.

***

The Tempeh Tu

A few of the battalions of the Tempeh Tu guarding the theater outside smiled in anticipation of their turn to come after the spectacle of the royals in the dance theater was put to bed.

Chapter 43

Tierney and Torhvald...loving

"I can only take this for so much longer."

If she didn't leave soon, Tierney feared the exhibition she would make of herself. A royal coming to a spasming peak in the middle of a dance theater. She wrapped herself around Torhvald while they devoured each other as they danced without a clue how such public theatrics came about. Untangling from him slowly, reluctantly, she led him out.

Something different charges the ice in the air now. A tang of newness billowed, fostering a sense of anticipation in Tierney. As she'd ridden through the gates of the Keep with Torhvald in their company for the first time, she'd known things would never be the same again. She couldn't have been more right. Now, she didn't fear her destiny but looked forward to it.

Tierney assured Torhvald his presence within her quarters in the Keep was fine. "Better this than a display of Tempeh Tu holding up the corridors, guarding the terrace and outsides of *your* lodgings while we love inside."

Her guards peeled away one by one once they entered the Keep until she was left alone with him in her quarters. "I wonder about your guards. Do they never have regret? Those on patrol around the theater missed out on an explosive time inside."

Tierney shrugged. "They get their turns in shifts. It takes a special kind to take on the honor and responsibility of becoming a Tempeh Tu. Not all who attempt trials for the post are confirmed. They're considered elite, their caliber a prestige in Soonayah, even if they choose to leave after a time. Besides, I heard tell the Tempeh Tu are high-strung and blow the doors off the theater once they have put the royals to bed." She patted a place next to her. "Why don't you come over here, my prince? I want you next to me."

Torhvald had first found Soonayah's use of suspension methodology odd. But since sleeping in the bed that hung in his lodgings, he awakened to bones and muscles reinvigorated and had no argument with the practice now.

The sheer-draped sumptuousness Tierney invited him into looked almost as decadent as she did. *Almost. Nothing could outshine her.* His feet moved of their own accord to be with her. His hands went to connect immediately with her skin. After the effects in the dance theater had sensitized him, he was left bereft of her touch just on the short trip to her quarters.

Tierney's skin was gossamer in its softness and he would never get used to her sharing herself with him. He pledged he would never take for granted this privilege she gave him. He was more than glad to pledge himself before her and her parents at any time too.

The sleeve she wore left her shoulders bare. He toyed with the tie between her breasts. "Why do your people wear anything at all in the dance if you must wear clothes so insubstantial as this?"

Tierney chuckled. "What do you think we do separated up here in the Soonahyin cold? Why must all foreigners believe we're some sybaritic tribe of pleasure-seekers who can't control themselves? We wear sleeves during the dance because as much exposure as possible is needed to take advantage of the exchange of soul-energy. Yes, passions are raised when energies are high, and incidents of people becoming too engrossed and crossing boundaries of decorum do happen." She sucked in a breath. Torhvald had pulled the tie covering her breasts. He exposed her body all the way to her waist for his gaze. Satisfaction flourished inside her at the unmistakable heat in his eyes." The dance's purpose is an avowal of our existence. Any surge of natural response to such elevated passions should be taken to private places meant for intimacy between partners."

"Like we've done."

"Yes, like us."

Torhvald slid his hands around her waist and lifted her to her knees before him. He devoured her small waist, putting his hands on her thighs beneath her sleeve. Before he followed through on the promise in his eyes and latched onto her breasts never kissing her, Tierney bent and caught his lips to hers.

His groan into her mouth affirmed that that was the right decision. He skated his hands from her thighs, over her buttocks, and molded her flesh. "Luscious." Tierney took a turn groaning when thick fingers slipped underneath her buttocks, between her intimate folds. She was riding the residual crest from the dance too, and his fingers teasing her appetite this soon pushed her passions exponentially higher, and they were only just starting.

Even though he kissed her as she wanted, he didn't ignore the breasts he'd laid open for himself. He pulled her over his lap and filled one hand with her breast. The sleeve she wore was shed, and she helped him extract himself from his. They went back to her straddling his lap with nothing between them but their hot, lust-filled scents. She wrapped her hand around his neck beneath his hair and soothed his extruding spine. Her fingers followed along it, rubbing over its knuckles and nuances. "Does it hurt when I touch your spine?"

"No. Your touch only excites me more."

Tierney needed him inside her now and eased herself over him. When her body was slicked and filled to the capacity of her womb, stretched to accommodate him, they both groaned into each other's mouths.

From the onset of their loving, her movements weren't gentle. Torhvald's support during the recent dilemmas intensified Tierney's connection to him. Which she now admitted started way back at his break-in into her suite at Outliers.

Something no one other than her family ever did, was show arrogance in the face of trespassing against the First Princess of Soonayah. He'd galled her haughtiness all out of proportion. Her reaction to him should have warned her then how responsive to him she was.

His skin on hers, his heat feeding hers, caused Tierney's energy to reach explosive levels. She rocked uncontrollably against him with his hands around her waist spurring her on. He pulled her forward and feasted on her nipples.

The soul-energy within Tierney flashed inside her core and caught the apex where she and Tohrvald's bodies joined in scorching sensation. It shot up her sternum and she fell on top of him, no longer capable of holding herself up. The cords on the sides of her neck burned with engorgement and Torhvald nipping at them didn't help the fever inside her.

A climax seized her, erupting from every pore of her being. Her hair whirled. Her bed's furious rocking suggested that they'd speeded some distance beyond it and had come back.

Tierney wouldn't know. Her eyes were closed against the frenzy driving her insensate. And she was only glad the bed's suspension kept it from knocking a hole in the wall.

Torhvald was having none of that though. He flipped her witless form to her back. He was after even more satiation, and he continued to thrust within her with hard deep strokes into the night. Tierney's groaning, though tortured, encouraged him.

* * *

"Days of Soonayah are too short, Tierahna. You shouldn't spend them sleeping the sun away." *Kind of sweet*, the breath of the deliverer of those words that warmed Tierney's face...*and was totally out of place.* She cracked one eye open and sighed at her sister's features invading her space. Though she thought Os'carah quite captivating, she was blocking the effects of *that aforementioned sun.*

The best part of waking. I need the sun.

Tierney's most favored part of the day in the season of long nights in Soonayah was waking and taking advantage of as much of the weak morn's sunlight as possible. Her sister's presence curtailed that routine. Spurred by Os'carah's examination of Torhvald's nakedness beneath her lashes, Tierney jerked the coverings over his lap . "It is altogether well, Tierney. You *should* cover your man. I've seen enough of him though for comparisons with what the men of Soonayah have on offer. I'm relieved to know, my dearest sister, that you won't miss out."

Tierney caught Os'carah as she moved off the bed. "What do you know of Soonahyin men's bodies, Os'carah? Should Mother and I have a talk with you about your excursions to the hamlets of the frozen tundra? Should we trace what you do out there, dear sister?"

Os'carah continued off her sister's bed. Her usual cheery flounces now tempered by a stiffened spine as she pranced in front of the sun-rays glimpsing in through Tierney's terrace. "I'm no girl if you didn't know, Tierney."

It seemed her brothers' over-occupation of making sure her suitors held a standard worthy of her, had left room for the fledgling Os'carah's maturity to flourish—for experimentation with free reign. "So, you admit to dealings with men?"

"I admit nothing," Torhvald grumbled and jerked in his sleep, stirred by Os'carah's pitch that rose right there at the end when she was quite aggravated. "And to think of the effort I put forth to get into your quarters with good news for you. How little you deserve it."

"A transgression I take issue with too. If you've compromised that young analyst in the transmission center to get in here again, Os'kie, I'll have no choice but to tell Mother. And what type of persuasion do you use to coerce the hapless fellow, anyway?"

"Tierney! You well know threatening in Mother's name is beyond all rules set between us siblings! I use nothing more shameful than *your promise* when you bargained with me any access I needed of you if I allowed you your sojourns with little fuss. Now you renege!" Torhvald chuckled underneath his coverings. "Isn't it enough you sleep the little time we have left away in bed with your consort? I hear the Keep's rumors as well as anyone else. I know you're to move to Oxhild away from me!" Os'carah huffed toward the door. And Tierney speeded naked from the bed to stop her.

She gave a tug to her sister's arms that were crossed over her body. Tierney held her, hands to elbows, and pulled her in for a little heat. "Os'kie, don't be an over-sensitive babe. We talk of little else than seeking the futures we dream of. Now, Mother can offer no excuse for allowing you travel to Oxhild to visit me whenever you see fit."

Os'carah turned her nose pointedly away from Tierney's nakedness. But Tierney squeezed her cheeks and gave her a juicy kiss. "Ugh...!" Os'carah smirked, yet kept with her pretense and scrunched her nose as she gave Tierney a once over. "You had best dress and rescue your comrade. He's been isolated on the outer gates of the Keep, save his aim is to get to you if by sheerly howling down the Keep's walls alone."

Tierney leaped from her sister to cover herself in a tunic while she searched her quarters frantically for the rest of her clothes. "Bak'rah! He's come back? Who dares leave him out in the cold?"

Os'carah grinned at Tierney's reaction as if she'd expected it and tossed her a pair of her leggings. "Yes, he has journeyed his way back home and he isn't alone. The guards wouldn't risk his strange companion inside the Keep, even if she came with Bak'rah. And he wouldn't enter without her."

"She?"

"We think it's a she. He's as protective of her as he is of you."

When Tierney went for her wolvien shukka boots, Os'carah drifted to the door. She glanced back at Tierney, frowned, and readied a scowl if needed. "You mustn't forget Starfall is this eve! A caravan for snowsurfing has been arranged. Ad'rihl—"

"Snowsurfing? I fall more often than I stay on them."

Their eyes met and Tierney recognized the longing in her sister's. "You promised, Tierney."

"And I shall not disappoint, Os'carah. Just know my falling will be half of everyone else's entertainment." Os'carah shrugged and left, a skip in her step after that.

"The youngest of your lot seems quite indulged." Torhvald rose and began to dress too.

Tierney laughed. "Oh, she is at that and more." Then she shrugged too. "But this tends to be the case when your father, the king, has died before you could ever know him."

Chapter 44

"Bak'rah! You mated a beauty." Of course, she was a much smaller version than the male wolf, but her coat shone as bright a white as his. Hers marked with smatterings of greyish-blue across her back, leading from the tip of her nose, and threw the most brilliant eyes in relief against the white fur surrounding them. Eyes bluer than an icy sky over the frozen tundra. Unlike any Tierney'd ever seen on a wolf. They had an uncanny sentience to them too, very like Bak'rah's.

The female wolf watched Tierney's every move near her mate. She snarled when Tierney braved closer to them both as she laughed and kiss all over Bak'rah. Tierney rasped her hands through his fur and combed it back, examining his shoulder hunch. *Healing nicely.* He hadn't reopened the tear traversing this far back to the Keep.

Or neither showed the slightest limp, prancing around as he was and jumping her when she stood, lapping at her face. She stopped just short of rolling around in the snow with him. "My boy! My good boy! I'm so happy to see you! They exalted in one another like they had been lost from each other forever.

The new mate gave up her growls after some time of Tierney and Bak'rah romping together like two pups of the same pack. All the growling and territory claiming hadn't done her any good so far. She prowled forward herself, and sniffed at Tierney's hand, eventually joining in on the frisking too. She may as well give in. The two of them would never let a proprietorial mate dampen their adore for one another.

Torhvald rubbed Bak'rah's head, he rubbed through his fur and checked his shoulder hunch too, marveling at the circumstances. "He came all the way back to the Keep for you." The female wolf's unease toward people prolonged Tierney and Torhvald's approach with her.

And so, they spent some time steadying her, circuiting her throughout the Keep, and familiarizing her with people. Oh woest be to anyone with the temerity to act on how they thought the Keep should be run. Lastly, they came across Bernehvelle. She was in the middle of admonishing two chancellors whose daughters didn't attend lessons given on the observation deck the last eve. Her eyes widened at their presence not just in the company of Bak'rah, but with another wolf too. "Two wolves! How can any homestead be asked to contend with wild beasts roaming its corridors?"

"That's okay. We'll leave." Tierney preferred not to run afoul of Bernehvelle's command over the Keep. She knew better than to take on an unwinnable fight, and volunteered to walk with the wolves on the outskirts. Instead, Bernehvelle waylaid them and asked for some moments to cover some fundamentals for young people such as them starting out in a life together.

Turned out these fundamentals Bernehvelle thought necessary were wide-ranging and....uhm a bit tedious. Like all things needed to start a household, organizing said household, appropriate behavior matched people should have toward each other, decision-making processes, the birthing of babes, the raising of said babes, traditional versus modernized roles, *so-called beasts within the home*, travel etiquette...

Once she neared the end of the "*Day-long all knowledgeable Bernehvelle*" session—as Tierney and Tohrvald had taken to calling it behind her back when allowed a few moments to themselves—Tierney took notes on her armset as Bernehvelle instructed her to. It was Bernehvelle who reminded them of Ad'rihl's caravan that was leaving at that very moment, and hustled them to join in with it at the outer gates.

To travel along in a convoy with so many different families and different people in all the transports was a practice in nostalgia for a Soonahyin who hadn't sojourned with a Cordalai hamlet in recent times. The tradition in their culture started in the very founding of their land when the first Soonahyins searched for their home eons ago. Large caravans were practical for journeying across the land, especially for the Cordalai. They gave *Tierney* a sense of belonging—not just as a royal, not even just as a Soonahyin—but as an affirmation of her connection to the long-dead Soonahyins who'd carved out life in a place that must have seemed unconquerable.

Masses of them had died in the passage alone. The living persevered faced with nothing more than frozen whiteness. Tierney channeled the audacity of such bravery whenever she was in a convoy, affirming her inheritance and challenging her role in the longevity of the Soonahyin saga. "Oh wow, Tierney! Self-important much?" After a few too much reverie on softness like that, she laughed out loud at herself. *Relax for a change and just be present.*

"Look, Tierney. Another caravan. Enclave-crafts tracking behind the professionals for the season's hunting." Lu'nil had asked if she could ride along with Tierney and Torhvald and the two wolves, slotted into the craft surrounded in toasty comfort. Ad'rihl, at the head of the caravan he'd organized, had preened like a cock when they'd started the trek out of Dameerh to the Alayufs slopes. He brought Mlai along in his snowcraft. Instead of towing collapsed homesteads, the rondavels, like the migrating Cordalai hamlets did, every transport carried snowsurfers attached to their sides. But still the feeling of a moving family convoy was the same.

Lu'nil bumped her shoulder, a familiarity they used with each other all the time, and pointed to the white stampede. The drove was thundering the ground from some distance away. "Do you remember us trailing the hunters with our hamlet in our youth?"

Tierney laughed. "I remember quite well sneaking off in a speed and spooking two eland beasts until they nearly killed me. Of course, only you could get me out of the way and still capture an eland for the stockpiles."

Lu'nil grinned and shrugged. She'd never been arrogant about her physicality. Never rubbed it in Tierney's face that Tierney could be a bit clumsy and imprecise in her movements sometimes. "We both have our strengths. That's why I've always been behind you, pumping you up to challenge our constraints. I've never been good at all that debating. But I guess it will be my part now to speak up for myself, as you're going and living as you have fought so hard to do."

Torhvald interrupted, "We're here, at the crest of the Alayufs slopes. Ad'rihl is motioning for everybody to get out of their snowcrafts." The two women remained where they were. Ad'rihl, the muskox ass, didn't dictate to them when they moved.

They sat there staring at each other, Tierney-and-Lu'nil-speak, that codex file for language prevailing without words as ever it would. A thousand parses between them and they'd probably be able to make known to one another their feelings, what was going on, if one of them were in distress. Somehow they'd find a way. Then Lu'nil finally said, "I shall find it a challenge without my ferocious sister championing my decisions from now on."

They touched hands to elbows on instinct and rested their foreheads against each other. "I shall only be in Oxhild...and never will I stop championing you. Even if I were separated to the opposite end of Telluric, would I find you and fight for you."

Lu'nil drew away from Tierney, turning her face away as well. To think about it, Tierney could never recall seeing Lu'nil cry. Even in their youth when Stah'lief had died and after their foreparents had died too, Lu'nil had stood off to the side on her own, but no tears had fallen. It was Tierney always filled with passion who was quick to emotion.

Lu'nil looked at her now with her eyes swimming, nearly overflowing, and it was humbling when you considered how rarely Lu'nil let her passions spill over. She ducked her head before the tears could fall and murmured, "I know that you would. It's just that times are no longer the same. We'll all be forging our own paths now it seems." She swiped at the tears quickly. "It's just a little sad to me, that's all."

She finally got out, pulled her snowsurfer off the side of their transport and threw it flat. It hovered, waiting for her. She jumped on it all in one motion, and rubbed her face into her sleeve as she swooped the surfer down the hill to join Mlai, who waved excitedly at them.

What could Tierney say? Them growing and changing was inevitable. They had to. Maturity caused for a person to seek out something for themselves. Make goals, have dreams and desires and to try to reach them. And possibly part from girlish ways, and drift *some* distance from people too. It wasn't intentional. The snowsurfing was a wonderful way to at least have some time together. *I do hope Mlai really enjoys this too.*

Later, after several tumbles, and Tierney's latest feat—head over heels, face smushed into a heap of snow—she threw her hands up. "I surrender," she told her landing spot and limped away. "That's the last fall you'll have to save me from. I know when *I'm* beat." *Lamenting to the snow now, Tierney?* She snickered at herself.

Better I get back to my snowcraft. She sat inside its open hatch and caught her breath. Then laughed at Torhvald too, snowsurfing too close to another surfer at a tricky bend near the bottom of a slope. This was one of the more medium-sized hills of the Alayufs slopes and he got his feet knocked from under him on it. Luckily, he stood unharmed and covered in snow, having landed in a nice bank of powder. He belted out with laughter.

She loved that about him. How he could laugh at himself and gave him credit for being a quick study as well. Snowsurfers weren't quite the same as their sand-surfing counterparts and it took some time to learn the differences between the two. Torhvald had a knack for it. His last fall was only his fourth. Far less than the number of topples she'd taken. Expressly the reason she now sat and watched. He came and joined her in the glorious heat wafting from her snowcraft's hatch, which cocooned her quite nicely. "How do you fare? I think I may have left a bone or two back there in the snowbank."

"Snowsurfing is no friend of mine either." She gestured to Ad'rihl, Lu'nil, and Os'carah racing with other surfers while they performed speeding tricks and never lost track of their surfers. Korrell sat off to the side, on a ridge the same as she did, his brace limiting him to stay nestled in his back hatch too. They'd waved and laughed with each other in awe of the other's antics a few times. "My siblings can have it all to themselves. Besides," she scooted over so that he could have seat, "look over there. The Starfall has started." She pointed to the sky. "You can make out the asteroids just as they come in."

The regrettably short Soonahyin day waned. If you looked carefully, you could make out eve covering the sun and crystallizing the aster-oids that entered the atmosphere. *This* eve, the sky would served as a wash of purples and lavenders in a backdrop for the Starfall. The asteroids' reduction morphed into bursts of hot orange and sparkling amber. The last one's fantastic flare of blue garnered the reaction of breaths whooshing out at the spectacle. Torhvald's regard of the sky was with his eyes and jaw stretched open. Bursts of color trailing to the land were a sight for anybody. Resting her head on his shoulder,

Tierney pushed her arm beneath his and pulled back a little further within the snowcraft's heat. Though the day's sun shone weakly over Soonayah, with its absence came a brusquer cold. "Have you never stopped and watched a Starfall before?"

"You forget, Tierney," grimacing at her ignorance of her privilege, he answered, "no other land has Soonayah's mode to reduce the asteroids. We can't dare allow them this close to see them clearly before we destroy all those we can. I doubt any other land on Telluric witnesses Starfalls as Soonayah does."

"Oh. Didn't think about that."

Some stirring about inside wobbled the snowcraft, and the two of them shifted to let Bak'rah and his mate out. "We must name her," Tierney proclaimed. "As Bak'rah's mate, she's entitled to a name."

"Uhh...what about Beauty?"

Tierney shook her head. "Too obvious. Something more befitting her temperament."

"Grey?"

Tierney chuckled. "She *is* quite solemn, isn't she? But with those eyes... Blue!"

Tohrvald nodded. "Blue suits her."

"Then Blue it is."

The wolves sniffed about the snowcraft, then Bak'rah looked at Tierney, and when she reached for him he didn't come to her hands.

"He's brought his mate to meet you. Looks like they're ready to head back now."

"Bak'rah?" The tremor in her voice must've provoked him to trot up to her and lick her all over her face. Tierney hugged herself against his heat. "Are you leaving me, boy?" In spite of her heart's ache, her spirit admitted that Torhvald was probably right. And as she suspected he would, Bak'rah drew away...she let him go.

"Oh...my sweet boy." Her gaze longed after him and his mate's figures loping away for a long time. Winks against the snow, they faded until the white of their fur could no longer be made out against the horizon.

"Come on, now. You're missing the best of the Starfall." Torhvald kissed the dampness from her eyes. And kept kissing, more little kisses stemmed from the innocence of the first ones. Or maybe not that innocent—he was still a Kalameshee, after all—what had seemed comforting became something else. Too inviting, they delved into the fullness of taste and tongue and sweetness. He suckled her plump lips. Soon, he'd laid back and she lay on top of him. They explored each other as far as they could within the confines of the snowcraft's hatch.

This is so perfect, I could stay here with him forever, Terney thought. Then they were toppled to one side against one another. Hoverers always hovered, so a force had to come into contact with the snowcraft to make it loose balance. They hurried to the hatch's opening and caught echoes of someone's cackles as they loafed down the hill.

"Tierney and Torhvald. The two T's! Lovey lovey. Loving it up. I can't believe I'm just thinking of that. That's your moniker from now on, the two T's. Get out and surf!" Ad'rihl ordered, swerving back toward them. Ad'rihl forgot that they hadn't called Torhvald by his name in the beginning. He'd had to earn that right. *That's* why he hadn't thought of it before now.

"Your brothers." Torhvald followed the figures sweeping the slopes. "Do they still believe me unworthy of you?"

Tierney grabbed his palm and nudged her fingers between his. "Not at all. They look on you with respect after all you've gone through with us. Ad'rihl is just a muskox ass. Even Haarth...my father says he approves, and his word is unshakable."

He enveloped her hand with both his and pulled her into his arms. "Just noticing, but I didn't recall seeing Eh'kotah once among the surfers."

"He stayed behind. He prepares himself and his Tempeh Tu for another sojourn up the Dayea mountains. He's finally going, determined he'll uncover the source where the woman he claims he saw in the mountains came from." Her eldest brother's will was inexhaustible and his protectiveness of Soonayah ferocious. Her father died pitting his strength against the changeable tempest that was Dayea. But Tierney believed if *anyone* could conquer the wretched mountains, it would be Eh'kotah.

Lu'nil was right. Things were changing from their youthful existence. Their generation's discovery of their own selves, their own aspirations were right in front of them now.

A thrill shimmered through Tierney for her new life to come. She resolved that she would travel with her man to Kalamesh as she wished. No man held sway over her will as her mother said. *I am the director of my life.*

The snowcraft rocked again, this time from vibrations beneath the snow. *Good omens.* One of the asteroids had been landed nearby and fed its riches into the soil. The ground beneath them rumbled back and forth and Tierney laughed as Torhvald frowned. The rumbling caught up inside her still and she laughed again at a rhythm so inherent in her, it tied her to the soil. She'd run away to Haarth at Outliers when she'd thought her mother's words to Bernehvelle meant to rid her of this. Now, she rocked in sync with the rumble of Soonayah and sang her most favored rhyme.

" Star up high, oh so grand,

open the sky, and implant the land

Blazing to ground seeds Soo-nah-yin,

All in kind—plant, animal and man,"

Her father...her first father, Stah'lief's smooth baritone rang inside her head. In remembrance of him taking his time with her to imprint the Soonahyin mantra on her heart, she rocked with the thought of him. As she always had since the night of his death, the first time the rocking had taken over. Her reliance on rhythm had started with that very trigger. His death. Her despair over-burdening her, she'd ended up rocking herself to sleep that night and singing their special rhyme they'd shared together. She'd tempered grief for her father the way *her father* had taught her to...with rhythm. *And I've never forgotten, Father. In my comforting, I've had you with me always.*

"Star so rich, empowers everything

Wasted Soonahyins desolate in journey unwaned

Open your soul and take ice land in

Souls don't lie, stars feed all men

Share in touch, Soonahyins heighten in dance."

She lay back in the snowcraft with Torhvald molded to her side and coached him on the last line of the Starfall rhyme.

"Share in touch, Soonahyins heighten in dance."

He had a nice voice. Tierney smiled at his earnest effort to repeat the line. She realized he would always try for her and she him too. The optiglass top was clear, a frame of the sky just for them while they lay there. But still, they missed the better part of the Starfall wrapped in each other's arms.

Epilogue

ernehvelle flitted through the receiving room closest to the skyview which circled the Dome of Clarity at the top of the Keep. She swept a wolvien shukka throw up while she fussed to herself. "Those two numbskulls should know better." Bracing winds hit her in the face at the top of the spiral stairs up to the skyview. Out on the deck, she skirted around the clarion dome and couldn't get to her targets fast enough. Bernehvelle whipped the fur covering around Ana'kerah's shoulders with none of the deference she should have shown a queen. "One would think a person who has been queen as long as she has, would know to come prepared for these winds up here," she grumbled and stalked away.

Haarth chuckled. "You allow Bernehvelle the upper hand too much."

Ana'kerah turned and smiled after her friend moving as fast as her old bones could carry her back into the staircase. "She has been a bit sensitive as of late. With you coming back, it makes her departure more real. And Tierahna leaving just adds to it. I've given her a little leeway, she has no appetite for change."

"As of late? My memory serves me well, woman. The Bernehvelle of our youth was no less crotchety than she is now." They both laughed. How right he was. Any form of Berneh was testy by nature.

"Maybe my need for her as my crutch as I managed this queenship forged her most assertive traits to the front. It has been no easy reign."

Ana'kerah meant her words as a mere explanation, but Haarth took them to heart. He wrapped her fur-covered form in his arms. "You must know the greatest remorse I shall ever have is the disaster I caused, choosing my own selfish wants and going to Kalamesh rather than listening to you. I would never abandon you, Anah. But for my choices, we wouldn't have spent the better part of our lives apart from each other." He shook his head and Ana'kerah squeezed his biceps.

"Have no more regret. We're here together now, and I wouldn't have it any other way. Or we wouldn't have a reason to come up here and spy on our offspring as they surf the Alayufs slopes."

He smiled, but looked away toward the middle distance. When he spoke again, he revealed how far off his thoughts had wandered. "I can only continue to ask for your forgiveness. I didn't know the consequences of my escape—"

Ana'kerah stopped him mid-speech with a kiss and rearranged the wolvien covering so he stayed warm beneath it too, and she snuggled back within his arms. "You have no fault in your own kidnapping. You escaped that torment however you could."

Haarth squeezed her in return. "I don't know what I ever did to deserve you." He lowered his head and drank in her scent from her hair. "You know, there in the desert when my captors chased me, I could never allow them too close. There were too many of them. It was then that I sent my pulses away from my body for the first time."

She turned and looked up at him from within his arms. "Just as Tierney did? In nearly the same place!"

"And both against the Drundel. I would think it's our people's destiny to meet up against the Drundel in that desert if it weren't for them attacking you in the Okehfey wilds. But honestly, I'm starting to doubt that too. Really, it's too unlike them to hold up in our land. They would freeze to death before they got ten parses. He breathed deeply, his breath growling a bit. "And then Tierahna killed one of them with one pulse as you're able to do."

Ana'kerah needed no reminder of that....*gift*. She grimaced. The sight of someone falling at her feet in death...by her own hands haunted her. And Gnord was still denying he'd sent insurgents into their land. Which *was* odd as Haarth said when you thought about it. Drundel possessed a physical intolerance to cold. How *would* they have survived? That Drundel body had felt wrong too. It had slithered as if his skin slipped unattached to bones. She hated to associate Soonahyins in any way to the Drundel. Only, they were still people, with the same physical makeup. Even the Logrens with metal enhancements in their bodies had Tellurician physicality. When that person had fallen from her in the woods, his body hadn't been right somehow. Hadn't felt Telurician at all. They would have to investigate the anomaly further.

Still, he was dead. Killed by her hands. She wished the experience on no one. Yet, her daughter would now have gone through the same horror. "That's a combination no one would ask for. Death by hand in an instant and at a distance. Do you think it was the high heat from the sun that gave you two the ability?"

"I can't say if only that. Both the situations caused our passions to be so high, rampant energy release was inevitable."

"What do you think accounts for Korrell's ability to heal you, then?"

"I know only that I will be grateful for it for the rest of my days." It was Haarth who then turned her chin up to peer into her eyes. "You know him having such a gift means you have it too. You must learn to harness it."

Ana'kerah pursed her lips. "Our progeny surpasses us. Isn't that the way of life? You told me your gift like Tierahna's introspection made *you* near catatonic in the desert. She's learning to use hers."

They both glanced up as an asteroid was reduced. The brilliant flash brightened the enclave's landmarks like it was day for an instant. "Them surpassing us *is* the way of life." Haarth said, "But I believe you can heal just as Korrell did if given the right circumstance. Their gifts are not so far from ours. Theirs are extensions of ours. My brother in our youth could rumble the ground like Eh'kotah does too. It surfaced when he was angry, even indoors."

Ana'kerah shook her head. "It *would* be Eh'kotah with a gift like his father's. So like him in so many ways, he frustrates me sometimes. He prepares to climb that wretched mountain as if he doesn't remember it surely killed his father as much as the fall that cracked his head did."

"The mountain is inanimate, Anah. Stah'lief was reckless and we both can attest to enough anguish he caused to know that's true. Eh'kotah takes meticulous care with everything. Whatever there is to discover in those mountains, he's the one who will do it."

Ana'kerah released her breath on a long sigh. She trusted in Haarth's judgment. Really, Eh'kotah's too. He was a timetable of dependability. Faithful, like every coming day. It was just that finding assurance within Haarth's arms came as a wonderment to her. If *he* believed Eh'kotah sure and capable enough also, then she wouldn't worry.

She snuggled deeper against him under their covering. The vantage point of the skyview was spectacular. The Frozen Folly beamed its familiar blue charge of reassurance over the bustle of the high seat dominion. People's excitement from recent events in Dameerh hadn't quieted yet into the night. Beyond the lights of the sloped roofs of the dominion, movement lit the roads too guiding Soonahyins hither and yon. If she left the heat of Haarth's body, she could spy through the ocular device attached near the Dome of Clarity on Tierney and her siblings snowsurfing beneath an overcast of Starfall.

Out of sight of Dameerh, the solare corona danced color across the sky for all those Soonahyins privileged to witness it and a Starfall at the same time.

A white-hot burst of Starfall cracked across the sky making eve into day again. *That one is being landed somewhere to seed the land aplenty,* she thought.

"Of course, it's only right."

"What is?" Haarth asked. He turned her face up to his and delved within her sweet lips.

"That I should take this night and watch a Starfall anew with you as our life together begins again."

About The Author

For more info from Yolanda join her mailing list here: yolandafayedaniel.com

Yolanda Faye Daniel is the author of fantasies, romance, sci-fi, and non-fiction, including her upcoming New Adult Fantasy/Romance debut Starfall (Telluric: The Queen's Children). She was born in Atlanta and currently resides right outside the city she loves. A Federal Analyst by day, her nights and free time are spent haunting thrift stores for old books, debating her kids, and bingeing on movies.

www.ingramcontent.com/pod-product-compliance
Lightning Source LLC
Chambersburg PA
CBHW060941190726
48286CB00005B/1379